Praise for
Worlds Collide

"Enter the glamorous world of Hollywood heartthrob Jack Harrington as he battles for a faith more fulfilling than anything fame or fortune could hope to provide. Alison Strobel creates a compelling hero in *Worlds Collide*."

—LISA SAMSON, author of *Women's Intuition, Tiger Lillie,* and Christy Award–winning *Songbird*

"I love this book! Alison Strobel has a voice that is relevant to today's reader. *Worlds Collide* is funny, heartbreaking, and far too close to reality. If you're looking for a fast-paced read filled with Truth, look no further!"

—KRISTIN BILLERBECK, author of *What a Girl Wants*

"Interesting and entertaining, real and relevant. A captivating read from the get-go."

—PLUMB, Curb Records recording artist

WORLDS COLLIDE

ALISON STROBEL

WATERBROOK
PRESS

WORLDS COLLIDE
PUBLISHED BY WATERBROOK PRESS
2375 Telstar Drive, Suite 160
Colorado Springs, Colorado 80920
A division of Random House, Inc.

All Scripture quotations are taken from the *Holy Bible, New International Version*®. NIV. Copyright © 1973, 1978, 1984 by International Bible Society. Used by permission of Zondervan Publishing House. All rights reserved.

The characters and events in this book are fictional, and any resemblance to actual persons or events is coincidental.

ISBN 1-57856-793-9

Library of Congress Cataloging-in-Publication Data
Strobel, Alison.
    Worlds collide / Alison Strobel.— 1st ed.
        p. cm.
    ISBN 1-57856-793-9
    1. Motion picture actors and actresses—Fiction. 2. Hollywood (Los Angeles, Calif.)—Fiction. 3. Biography as a literary form—Fiction. 4. Married people—Fiction. 5. Biographers—Fiction. I. Title.
    PS3619.T754W67 2005
    813'.6—dc22

                                                                    2004023545

Printed in the United States of America
2005—First Edition

10 9 8 7 6 5 4 3 2 1

This book is dedicated to my parents, Lee and Leslie.
Thank you for feeding my literary addiction
and for giving me permission,
through your endless encouragement and enthusiasm,
to pursue my dreams.

☆

So many people, so little space. Oceans of thanks to:

God, the Ultimate Author, for the beauty of language, the power of story, and for giving me the gift to create.

Dad, for the genes, my first typewriter, and all the encouragement when I was a kid.

Mom, for giving me my first feedback on this manuscript, being my proofreader extraordinaire, and loving this book as much as I do.

Doug Scott and the Axis Writing Team, for getting me back to the page and helping me grow as an artist.

Dee Tsiakals, for giving me a reason to drive through Hollywood and celebrity-watch on the I-5 for the first time. This story was born on that drive.

Jennifer Stephens, Maggie Dix, Nicole Griebe, and Amy Hilliker, my first real audience, for being so kind. You made me believe others would actually want to read this thing.

The Stoneybrooke Staff—that phone call couldn't have been more fun. Thanks also for your prayers, support, and enthusiasm.

Dudley, for convincing me this was a good book, for being so easy to work with, for all the ideas that made this thing even stronger, and for being such a gifted editor.

Daniel, the most supportive and encouraging husband a woman could ever dream of. You astound me with your enthusiasm for, and pride in, my work. I'm so glad we're in this together, come what may…

PROLOGUE

I'VE ALWAYS BEEN a firm believer that celebrities are just like the rest of us. I've had my fair share of star encounters, and for the most part I was never that impressed. But even I have my weaknesses, and Jack Harrington has always been one of them.

He first became popular when I was in high school. When I practiced my interviewing skills in the mirror as I dressed for school, Jack Harrington was always my subject. "Mr. Harrington," I would say in my best no-nonsense reporter voice, which I'd been cultivating through my position on our school's newspaper, "your new project is quite a departure from your previous work. Tell us what seduced you into taking such a controversial role." I always imagined myself pinning him with my penetrating stare, silently daring him to bare his soul. I admit there was some melodrama in my imaginings; I had always been a love-story junky and hopeless romantic. Of course my fantasy would always end with Jack falling for me, Jada Eastman, the astute and charming reporter who had finally enticed him to explore his deeper, emotional side. Such excitement was hard to find on assignments for the *Central High Herald*.

I found myself in California after college, working as a fact checker for the entertainment department of the *LA Times*. I kept my writing skills honed by joining a writer's guild downtown, where I met a biographer who took me under her wing. She hired me to help her on her current project: the biography of a prominent director. This experience was invaluable, and it started my interest in writing life histories. She mentored me for the next three years before I finally got my big break: the opportunity to write an "instant book" on a Hollywood scandal.

It seemed like a smarmy thing to do at the time—two actors' lives were already ruined forever by the revelation of their secret affair and manipulation of various high-up producers and directors—but I'd learned over the past couple years that, to eventually get what you want, you had to temporarily take what you could get. I earned brownie points with the publishing company, though, when I broadened the book's coverage through a creative use of my old fact-finding contacts, and not long after the project was completed, I received a call for another book.

Sheer luck seemed to catapult me into the paths of some pretty famous people, and by the time I was thirty, I had written three biographies and assisted two celebrities in writing their memoirs. But these experiences shed light on sides of human nature I didn't really want to see. It was my job to get them to dump their stories, and I soon discovered the path to fame is paved with a lot of pain, both suffered and inflicted, and a lot of decadent and twisted living. Secrets kept hidden for decades would surface unexpectedly in the middle of an interview, as if the teller could no longer contain them. It was often obvious the story wasn't being told to be part of the biography, but just to ease the weight of the person's conscience. It was my job to sort the tellable from what was best kept hidden, to know what to reveal and what to return to the vault of memory. But all the information remained in my head, and I could never look at those people, or others like them, in the same way again. Disappointment in discovering the tarnish on the stars of Hollywood left me with a marked disdain for celebrity and fame, and though I continued to accept work from them, I developed a resentment toward them that slowly ate away at me and left me jaded.

It was in the depths of this cynicism that I received the call from Jack Harrington's assistant asking me if I would consider helping him and his wife tell their story.

Now, you have to understand that even though I had come to pretty much despise celebrities, Jack still held a special place in my heart. The tragedy of his girlfriend's death, the storybook quality of his marriage—

they saved him from the disapproval I harbored toward his colleagues. Plus there were rumors floating around about an illness, as well as some spiritual fanaticism, which made me all the more curious about him. Not that rumors carried much weight with me. I'd heard too many and seen how few were true. But still, they fueled my interest. And of course, some schoolgirl crushes just refuse to go away. I accepted the invitation to meet with the Harringtons and discuss the project.

I didn't know much, just the same stuff everyone else did: his start in television, his girlfriend's death, his social activism, the truly Hollywood-like events that led to his marriage, and his absence from the public eye for nearly five years. But I'd also heard stories recently that linked him and his wife with what sounded to me like some religious cult. I hoped my childhood crush wouldn't turn out to be a wild-eyed groupie of some self-proclaimed prophet of the God of who-knows-what. I was tired of interviewing people who gave me even more reason to hope Hollywood would someday meet a catastrophic end.

When I first met Jack and Grace at their home in Pasadena, Jack had only just begun to show signs of the illness I'd heard rumors about. His wife, Grace, whom I'd tried not to loathe before even meeting her (how was he going to fall for me if she was there?), exuded a warmth and authenticity that, I had to admit, drew me in at once; I understood immediately how one of Hollywood's brightest stars could have so easily turned his back on the pretense and shallowness of so many industry women to marry a "commoner."

Their daughter, Bree, just a few weeks past her seventh birthday, had her father's extroverted charm and intense blue eyes, along with her mother's kindness and even-keeled personality. Her kindergarten art hung everywhere in the house, having been given the treatment usually reserved for original Picassos. Within a few minutes of my arrival I was pulled along on a tour of her work by the young artist herself.

I'd been there over an hour before Jack, Grace, and I finally sat down to talk about the book. I steeled myself for in-your-face zealousness, tel-evangelist fervor and sheen, but instead I found myself drawn to this down-to-earth couple who neither took lightly nor exploited the influence they had. So far they were what I'd hoped they would be, yet I had a hard time believing they wouldn't eventually turn out to be die-hard religious nuts. I wondered how long they could keep up their facade of normality during our conversation. Despite my hopes, I was convinced this type of kindness and guilelessness would never last; they would probably try to lull me into a false sense of security so they could suck me into their cult. I found myself warming to the thought of exposing them through my hard-nosed research and reporting. The schoolgirl crush was finally fading. My interest was piqued.

I'm the kind of person who can't resist a challenge, and to me their charm and easy conversation were the throwing down of the gauntlet. I accepted the job then and there, signing on to write the story of a couple whose romance and lifestyle were already the stuff of legend in their cor-ner of the world. I broke out the minirecorder and, over the next six months, became like a fourth member of the Harrington family. We'd sit together in the living room, on the deck, or in the kitchen—wherever they felt like being at that moment—and I would listen to their stories.

More fascinating, though, was the way they listened to each other's side of the story, as if they'd never heard it before. Watching them together became an education in intimacy: their undivided attention to each other, their respect for each other's version of events, her unobtru-sive actions to make him more comfortable as the illness wore him down over the following months, and his tender gestures of unabashed love for her and Bree. I worked hard to keep myself from falling in love with these people, but it didn't take long to realize it was impossible.

I didn't know it at the time, and I don't always like to admit it now, but this job eventually changed me—my views, my beliefs, my life.

GRACE

THERE IS ONE particular morning that seems like a good place to start my side of the story. I was awakened by keys being fumbled into the lock on the front door of my apartment. Still half asleep, I rolled to face the nightstand, where the clock glowed some way-too-early time. The front door creaked as it was finally opened, and I jumped when it slammed a second later. The drunken shuffle of Dylan's feet through the living room was all the warning I needed; in a heartbeat I had the shower running and the bathroom door locked safely behind me. I watched the second hand on my Seiko make its rotational trip—once, twice, three times, four times, five—before I finally opened the door to find Dylan sprawled on the bed—shoes, clothes, and all—passed out cold.

Dylan was my boyfriend at the time. We'd been friends in college and settled in the same area after graduation, which is when we really hooked up. After a few months of serious dating he moved in with me, not because our relationship was so deep, but because rent was killing me and I was lonely without a roommate. Our relationship progressed down a weird road where we were comfortable together but not really in love: a relationship of convenience. There were occasional times of mushy affection, and they were nice while they lasted, but even so they seemed a bit contrived, like we needed to indulge in them now and then to make it seem as though our relationship was really going somewhere.

But lately things had been off-kilter with him. He was distant, preoccupied. Where we had once shared the responsibility of keeping our place presentable, now he was shirking his roommate duties and leaving me with all the grunt work. The biggest change, though, was in his sudden attraction to alcohol. He had never been a big drinker, but he went from having one or two beers a week to having enough to render him disgustingly drunk on a frequent basis, and then coming home sometime around dawn. I didn't appreciate sharing a bed with someone who smelled as though he'd gone swimming in Guinness, and I appreciated even less his drunken advances; thankfully, I was usually awake in time to hide out in the bathroom until he had passed out on the bed.

On this particular morning, I arrived at work about an hour after awaking to Dylan's stumbling entrance, bearing my usual breakfast from the café down the street. On my desk was a small stack of invoices left from the day before—data entry was one of the many dull facets of my job—but I ignored them as I ate, polishing off my donuts and tea with ritualistic devotion.

Dana, my cubicle-mate, showed up around nine with more donuts. She was younger than me, only twenty-two, and just out of college with an oh-so-marketable degree in Italian Renaissance Music. She was working here while she figured out what to do with her life— like the rest of us. "Happy Monday, my friend!" she sang. "And how was your weekend with Dylan, the king of charm?"

I laughed around a mouthful of donut. "Oh, just *grand.* Cleaned the castle—by myself, you know, since these days the king himself barely stoops to tie his own shoe, much less pick up his own trash." Dana laughed. "Leftovers for dinner—twice—and the big, comfy bed all to myself since he didn't come home until past five a.m. both nights."

Dana's face fell as the fun left the conversation. I hated to bring it down, but I didn't want to lie, either. The whole thing was really ticking me off, and Dana was the only one to talk to. "Oh, Grace. Where was he?"

I shrugged and rolled my eyes as I polished off the dregs of my tea. "Beats me. I didn't ask. I'm getting sick of his excuses. He was drunk as a sailor this morning, and I couldn't bear the thought of him breathing beer down my throat, so I got in the shower before he even made it to the bedroom." I didn't bother mentioning how rough he had been Saturday morning; I didn't want Dana to think it was worse than it was. I knew perfectly well this relationship was heading downhill; I didn't need anyone quoting battered-women statistics to talk me into ending it. I just needed some time to figure out what to do with myself.

The day passed as it usually did: work interspersed with the occasional game of Free Cell, vending-machine lunch, idle chat with Dana, and switching off my computer at four. "I wish I had the energy to get here as early as you do," Dana pouted. "I was ready to go home an hour ago, and I still have an hour left."

"Aw, poor baby, you have my sympathy," I cooed. Dana swatted at me and chuckled as I stepped out of the cube. "See you bright and early tomorrow."

I walked out to my car, realizing the last thing I wanted to do was to go home. I didn't particularly want to see Dylan, because he had been unpredictable the last few weeks, and I did not deal well with unpredictability. So I drove instead to the Barnes & Noble down the street.

I bought a mint hot chocolate and settled at a table in the café with a *Newsweek*. As a rule, I never watched the news on TV or read the newspaper; it always depressed me, and I knew anything really important would make its way to me eventually through conversation or rioting mobs. But every now and then I would check in on the world, and the safe, cozy environment of the bookstore café seemed a good place to do it.

I sipped my cocoa, reading every article except the ones on politics, which never interested me under any circumstances. Toward the back was an article on national housing trends. I scanned statistics on population flux and other dull subjects until reaching one which stated that more people moved to California last year than to any other state in the union. I had never been to California, but the article made me wish I had. It was in the seventies in Southern California right now, and here I was drinking hot chocolate and scraping frost off of my windshield in the mornings before work. Unfortunately, it sounded like the cost of living was way more expensive than I would have ever guessed; I wondered briefly what a job like mine was worth out there.

After finishing the magazine, I returned it to the rack and wandered the aisles of the store. I loved reading, but I hadn't been doing much of it lately. A display in the center of the main aisle held a number of books that looked good, and I made a note of some of the titles for later.

My stomach rumbled audibly; apparently it was time for dinner. I made my way back to my car, pulling my coat tighter against the bitter wind. I hated winter. I'd grown up here in Chicago and endured nearly twenty-five bitterly cold seasons, and every year I wondered how much longer I could put up with window scraping and ginger walks over icy sidewalks.

On the way home I swung by the library and ran in to check out a couple of the books I'd seen at the bookstore. As I drove home I mentally planned the evening: make a quick dinner, then change into my pajamas and curl up on the couch with a book and another hot chocolate. Then I pulled into my space in the parking lot and saw Dylan's truck. It was the first time in weeks he'd been home early. It made my stomach drop.

This knee-jerk reaction angered me. How dare he cause me to feel like this? He was supposed to love me, or at least act like he liked me. Even if we knew things weren't really going anywhere, that wasn't an excuse to act like a jerk. If he wanted to break up with me, then fine, do it, but don't put me through this emotional turmoil. This was my place, it was my furniture inside—I was letting him live there because we were committed to each other, but if he wasn't going to act committed, then he could just pack up and get out. In a sudden and uncharacteristic fit of assertiveness, I decided to tell him as much.

Having worked myself up into a strong and righteous indignation, I gathered my books and marched up to the apartment. As I ascended the stairs I went over the various ways he might respond: ignore me or pretend nothing had happened, yell at me for something he had no business yelling at me about, plead for me to forgive him, and so on. For each of them I came up with a response that would show him I was not one to be kicked around. In fact, I marveled that I even had to do this; we were a good couple. Granted, he did some things that drove me mad, but I was sure there were things about me that irritated him too. But there wasn't anything we couldn't work out. We just needed to spend some time together, to sit down and talk about how weird things had been lately and why, and figure out what we could do to fix them.

I reached the apartment and, with a final deep breath and squaring of the shoulders, opened the door and went in.

Three plain brown boxes sat in the middle of the living room. What had he bought? I closed the door behind me and set the books on the entry table before shrugging off my jacket. "Dylan?"

I heard him curse softly from the bedroom. "Back here," he barked. I had started toward the bedroom when he appeared with a fourth box in his arms. He set it atop one of the others, deliberately avoiding my eyes, and then grabbed his jacket from the back of one of the kitchen chairs.

"Finally getting rid of some stuff?" I asked. It was the only explanation I could think of, that he'd gotten around to going through his side of the closet and his boxes in the storage closet on the balcony, something he'd promised to do for months.

He zipped up the leather bomber he'd been wearing since we'd met and hefted one of the boxes, still not meeting my gaze. "No. I'm moving out."

I blinked. I blinked again. Then I remembered to breathe, and eventually I remembered how to speak, but by that time he was out the door with the first of the four boxes. I stood in place, not knowing where to move to, and watched silently as a few minutes later he returned and took down the second box, then the third, then the fourth. Then he didn't come back up. I finally stumbled to the balcony and walked out to the railing, staring over to the parking lot. I saw my car, its windshield already frosted, and the empty space next to it, a rectangle of blacktop stark against the snow where his car had sheltered it since that morning.

I stood with the door open behind me, staring down at his vacated parking space for ten minutes before noticing how cold it was. I went back inside, sliding the balcony door closed and locking it behind me, a habit Dylan had always mocked since no one could get up there from the parking lot anyway.

I walked to the bedroom and changed out of my khakis and blouse, dropping them onto the floor, and pulled on my pajamas. My stomach was grumbling even more loudly, but I didn't want to eat. I didn't really want to do anything. Even so, I walked back to the living room, locked the front door and turned off the lights, then picked up one of the library books from the entry table and walked back to the bedroom. I lay down in bed, pulled the comforter up to my chin, and opened the book, but after staring at the page and not comprehending a single word, I dropped it to the floor. Out of habit I set the alarm and turned out the light, and only then, enveloped in darkness, with the scent of Dylan's cologne emanating from his side of the bed, did I cry. My shoulders shook, and my throat constricted and ached; I felt like I was choking. He had left his pillow, because it was mine, really, and not his, and I curled myself around it, squeezing the life out of it, demanding that it tell me why he left. I realized then how much I'd grown to love him.

"What a jerk!" I exclaim with more force than necessary. Her experience echoes one of my own just a little too close for comfort. "Did you ever hear from him again?"

Grace laughs and shakes her head. "No, and good riddance, frankly. But it was just what I needed, and God knew that even though I didn't. If he hadn't left I never would have moved, and coming to California was one of the best things I ever did. It never would have happened if Dylan had stuck around."

I try to contain my sarcasm, but some leaks out despite my efforts. "What—God made your boyfriend wig out and get abusive?"

She shrugs. "I can't speak for what God will and won't claim responsibility for. But I know that He had a plan for me, and it required me to be here. Maybe something else would have brought me out, but how can we know what might have been?"

I cringe inside. There it is, that religious chalk-it-up-to-Providence crap I'd hoped so much not to encounter. So far she sounds more level-headed than most religious people I've talked to, but that probably just means she's good at playing this game. I try not to let this count against her and ask her to continue.

It was hardly a restful night; sleep came in bouts. My alarm beeped me awake, and for three blissful seconds I was without the memory of the evening before. But then I rolled over and saw the empty space beside me, and everything came back in a wave so strong it nearly washed me off the bed. I felt as though I'd been hit by a truck; the last time I'd looked at the clock it had been 4:36. I didn't have any tears left, and there was a vacuum in the center of my body sucking at my insides.

I stayed in bed for a full ten minutes, trying to decide whether to go to work. What I really wanted to do was call someone and spill my guts, go through a box of tissues, and eat an entire box of Godiva chocolates. But then I realized I didn't have anyone to call, because Dylan had been the person I had spilled everything to.

Dana was the closest thing I had to a friend those days, and she'd be at work. And since I'd need as much money as I could get now that Dylan wasn't paying part of the rent, I knew I should probably go to work, too. Not the conclusion I'd been hoping to reach, but I was too responsible to do anything else. I pulled on my khakis—still on the floor from the night before—and a sweater lying crumpled on the floor of my closet. I threw on some makeup, but not enough to fix any of the damage that a sleepless night of crying had caused, and left.

I still beat everyone to the building, but instead of putting work off until after breakfast, I grabbed a bagel and dove into my in box. The last thing I wanted was downtime that would force me to think. I'd finished all the leftover invoices by the time Dana came in, but once she was there I let myself fall apart, and neither of us got anything done for an hour.

"He just left without saying anything?"

I shook my head, dabbing my eyes with a crumpled tissue. How much crying could one person do? "Nothing. He just moved all the boxes down, and I stood there staring at him like an idiot. I kept expecting him to say something, but he didn't."

Dana sat back in her chair, shaking her head. "Where is he now? Did he tell you where he was going?"

"No, and I have no idea where to even look. Not that I would bother. I certainly don't want him around if he's going to be like that."

"Absolutely; he's not worth the time it would take to even start thinking about where to look. It's his loss, honey; he doesn't deserve you."

Both of us were silent awhile, and after a few minutes I straightened in my chair and tossed away the tissue. "I've wasted way too much time on him already. Enough of this. I have work to do, you have work to do, so let's just work. Okay?"

Dana nodded, her face mirroring the resolve I had mustered. We turned to our computers, and until lunch neither of us spoke or played a single game of Free Cell. At lunch Dana invited me to join her and Carrie, another office girl, but I declined, saying I wasn't hungry (which was true, despite the fact that the hot chocolate at the bookstore had been the last thing I'd consumed) and that I wanted to get some more work done (which was a lie). The truth was I didn't want to stop focusing on something, because I knew the minute I did I would crumble again. So I worked like a woman possessed until quitting time, then got in the car and drove to the bookstore. I couldn't bear the thought of going back to the empty apartment.

I bought a hot chocolate and a sandwich, my hunger having finally caught up with me, and flipped idly through another magazine. I had chosen one on interior decorating because I'd decided on a whim to redo the apartment; I wanted nothing to stay the same and remind me of Dylan. The focus of that particular issue was on California homes. They looked so airy and open and bright and colorful—a sharp contrast to the gloominess outside the bookstore window. I loved the bright, warm colors and mountain views. I tried to imagine my apartment painted in Spanish yellow and sunset red, but it just didn't seem like it would fit.

I finished scouring the magazine for ideas and returned it to the rack after polishing off my drink. My mind felt unsettled, and as I drove home, I mulled over some half-thoughts that were starting to coalesce into a full-fledged idea. When I got home I was so preoccupied with what was running through my head that I wasn't disturbed at all by Dylan's absence. I made a quick dinner and planted myself at my laptop, scouring the Internet for the information I wanted until I hit a wall. I crawled into my pajamas and was asleep within seconds of getting into bed. I slept like a rock until my alarm went off the next morning.

For the first time in months I didn't beat everyone to the office. By the time I stumbled in I was actually looking forward to the day, thanks to the research I'd done the night before and the decision I'd made.

"California?" Dana was staring at me as though I'd grown another head. "You've got to be kidding! Why California? You'd have no job, no home—what would you do when you got off the plane?"

I leaned back in my chair and began to count off the reasons. "Look, I spent all night thinking about it. Number one: I *hate* this weather. I stopped enjoying snow once I outgrew sledding. It's nothing but a hassle, and it's depressing. Two: nothing is tying me down here. Three: no man to worry about, no family to be with. And four: this job isn't what I plan on doing with the rest of my life. I mean, come on, you'd leave too in a heartbeat if you had a better offer, right?"

Dana sighed and nodded, but she was far from convinced. Not that I blamed her. I was probably one of the most unadventurous, unexciting people ever born; packing up and moving across the country wasn't very *me*. "I'm just worried about you, that's all," she finally confided. "You've had the week from hell, and anyone would tell you that making important decisions in the midst of an emotional crisis isn't the wisest course of action. I mean, shouldn't you wait till spring or something? Give yourself time to get over Dylan and look for a job and a place to live."

"My lease is up in December; I'd never find a place to live for just three months! And I've got *some* contacts in Southern California that can help me with the details; it's not like I'd be totally on my own." I was exaggerating this last bit just slightly; I had *a* contact, but I hadn't talked to him in years, and I had no guarantee he'd even be willing to help me. But at this point I was working just as hard at convincing myself as I was at convincing Dana, and I wasn't about to examine every little statement I made. I was building a good case so far; I didn't want to ruin it with reality.

"So what are you going to do, then? Hop off the plane, find this guy, and beg him to find you a job and a house?"

"Um…something like that." Dana groaned, and I laughed. "I'm kidding! I'm going to write him, tell him I'm moving out there, and would he happen to have any advice as to where I ought to look for a place to live? And California is desperate for teachers, so I'd actually be able to use my college degree. Novel idea, eh?" I smirked wickedly at Dana; I took every chance I could to rub in the fact that I was at least marketable. I hadn't been in a classroom since my student teaching days, but I knew I could find a job if the market was as wide open as California's seemed to be. The Chicago suburbs were saturated with teachers; my only option had been Chicago public schools, and those kids would have eaten me alive.

Dana was silent for a minute before speaking again. "I'm not going to be able to talk you out of this, am I?" She knew the answer as well as I. "Well…you'd better let me sleep on your couch when I come to visit, then."

"Of course!" I laughed. "We'll hang out on the beach, drive into LA and Beverly Hills, and go celebrity hunting." We snickered until one of the other administrators walked by and plopped two massive stacks of invoices on our desks, at which point we decided it would be best to earn our paychecks and get back to work.

My body may have been working, but my mind was sorting out details for my move. I had five weeks before I'd be homeless, which meant I had five weeks to get myself out to and successfully settled in California. I'd never made a major move like this before, and I didn't have the foggiest notion where to start planning, although getting the California end of things figured out seemed pretty crucial.

Over my lunch break I composed a letter to my "California contact," Gary Rosebaum. He was supposedly my godfather, although our interactions over the years had had nothing to do with God. When my parents had divorced at the end of my high school years, he'd made me promise to come to him if I ever needed anything. I had a feeling he was just trying to make up for the fact that my father had pretty much abandoned us, but throughout college he sent birthday and Christmas cards, so I felt like I could at least ask him to help me find a roof to live under.

After posting the letter I jotted down the list swimming in my head: find a moving company, cancel next year's lease, polish up my résumé, let Mom know I was moving. I mentally winced at this last item; I hadn't talked to her in six months, because we'd argued over my "dead-end job and dead-end boyfriend" after I'd turned down a job in her firm. She'd never forgiven me for not going into law like her, and when I'd flat-out refused to work in her office, she'd exploded. I decided to tell her I had broken up with Dylan and not the other way around; I didn't want to endure the "I told you so" speech I was sure I'd get if I admitted he'd left me, which she said he'd do from the beginning. I hated it when she was right.

Dana returned from lunch and we chatted a bit as we worked. Having moved from Boston to Chicago, she had a bit more experience in the whole relocation thing, so she gave me some ideas of where to start. At the end of the day I went back to the bookstore, a habit I was beginning to enjoy, and browsed through the travel section looking at books on California. Gary lived in a small town in Southern California called Rancho Los Lagos; it seemed as good a place as any to start my search for employment, so I took down some notes of nearby town names, and then went home to spend the evening in front of my computer.

It didn't take long for my bubble to get close to bursting. California was way more expensive than Illinois. Moving in and of itself was more costly than I'd anticipated. But it was the thought of leaving the state I'd grown up in for a place I'd never even visited that was really starting to scare me.

Now, I am usually a smart girl. I tend to lean toward logic and reason when dealing with problems, and for the most part I have a lot of common sense. But there are times when, for no apparent reason, I make decisions that don't seem to make any sense at all. One might look at all the evidence I am faced with, and then look at my response, and think that I must not have studied the evidence to begin with. For instance, downing six mixed drinks in an hour on my twenty-first birthday after a full seven-course meal. Or staying with Dylan. I know what the logical choice is, but the fact is, I just don't care.

This proved to be one of those times. I threw caution to the frostbitten Chicago wind and dared fate to take me on. By the end of the night I had called my landlord, canceled my lease, and purchased my plane ticket to California. I was throwing myself into this decision and not looking back. California or bust.

Jack grins at his wife and snickers. "California or bust, eh? That's so Hollywood of you."

Grace thwaps him on the arm as she rises from the sofa to pour more iced tea for Jack and me. "I have my fair share of melodramatic moments."

"So you just left?" I am impressed with her moxie and tell her so.

She waves it off, and I fear more God talk. "Just one of those instances in life where—well, haven't you ever done something out of character and amazed yourself, only to find later it was one of the most life-changing decisions you'd ever made?"

I have to admit I had. My whole career is based on such a decision. "From Bedford, Virginia, to Los Angeles, California," I confessed. "I'd never been out of the county before that move."

"Aha! Then you know what I mean," she says with a triumphant gleam in her eye. "And now look where you are."

Look where I am, indeed. "And you, Jack?" I ask, trying to shift the focus from myself. I'm not used to having the interviewer-interviewee roles reversed. "Any out-of-character decisions that changed your life?"

He laughs. "One or two here or there," he grins. "Although my journey out here was just a matter of time, and everyone knew it. Reily, Vermont, is hardly the home of theatre and film."

JACK

HOPPING A PLANE and landing in a city I'd never seen was nothing compared to what happened a year later. I don't think I'd ever been so nervous.

I'd never been to a real audition before. I'd auditioned in the past, sure, but that was small stuff, school plays or community theatre. Not *real* acting. *This* was a real audition. With a real casting agent. For a real television show. And I had absolutely no idea what to expect.

I knew others who had gone through auditions before, and what they described didn't sound too awful, and I'd been accepted for every part I'd auditioned for in the past year (granted none of it was professional), so I was going in with a lot of confidence. But once I got to that fourteenth-floor office and saw how many other people there were, and how much more, I don't know, handsome? professional? experienced? they looked, every shred of confidence I had went out the plate-glass window.

The assistant called me in and introduced me to the agent in charge of casting for *Every Other Night.* He looked me over, asked me to read, shook my hand, and out I went. That was it. The whole thing was over in less than five minutes, and I was left to wait in agony for The Phone Call.

It arrived the next morning: callbacks at nine on Friday. Went back, read again, thank you very much, we'll call you if we want you, and another agonizing wait.

The call I'd always dreamed about arrived the following week. I was in. My first professional acting job!

Unfortunately, it was a short-lived program that was doomed

from day one by bad writing and worse casting. I would try to preserve my dignity by telling you that I was the only one there who had any idea what he was doing, but the truth is I was as clueless as everyone else.

Now, the whole point of all this is that *Every Other Night* happened to air on the night Dale Montgomery from Montgomery Casting was home with the flu and channel surfing to kill time before bed. Had he not been sick, he would have been out at a benefit dinner with his wife and might never have seen me on the show. And had he not seen it, he never would have put a name with a face when I read for a part that had opened up on the award-winning police drama, *Deep Cover.* The twelve minutes he saw me on television were just enough to give me an edge over the other thirty-six men auditioning for the part of Gabe Morrison, and as a result, I got the part.

So that's how I got the job that really launched my career. By "launch" I mean that I actually had a steady job, my own place, and a gorgeous girlfriend, a fellow actress from *DC.* See, in Hollywood, it's not just the job that defines you; it's the life you live along with it. Once I had all the trappings of success, I *was* a success. Twisted.

My schedule was pretty structured once shooting began that December. Get up early, rehearse or tape all day, come home, rehearse some more on my own, work out, get together with Madeline, the girlfriend, go home, go to bed. Rinse and repeat. Throw in the occasional interview or publicity deal, and that was my life for about two years.

Madeline and I dated for nine months, but then Debra Sills came on the show, and we really clicked. She and I dated on and off for a year before calling it quits; we were both loose cannons when it came to relationships, so really it's impressive that we lasted as long as we did. She broke up with me to date some guy she'd met during an off-season gig, and I took a break from women for a while.

I started getting bit parts in movies, and my character was written into some action that really stretched me as an actor, but I found I was spreading myself too thin. On the one hand, I wanted as much exposure as possible—that was how I'd get known in this town. But on the other hand I'd worked hard to get where I finally was, and I didn't want to ruin it by going down that road so many green actors go down: working yourself into the ground and getting burned out and pushing yourself onto bigger and bigger projects. That kind of lifestyle had never paid off for anyone; they always ended up drinking themselves into their graves—or at least into forced retirement when no one was willing to take the chance of hiring them—or else they had mental breakdowns and ended up on the After-School Special circuit. But I also didn't want to be in the same place doing the same thing five years down the road. I learned quickly that the life of a serious actor is one big balancing act.

Those first three years on *DC* were heaven for me. I finally felt like I had come into my own, like I wasn't fudging in the slightest if I wrote "actor" on the occupation line of surveys or credit applications. When you're stuck doing community theatre you never feel like a real actor; it's just a hobby, something you do in your free time, and you have to squeeze it in around whatever it is you do to pay the bills. But once I got on *DC,* all that changed. I was getting paid to do this. I even got some fan mail, which was both flattering and a little frightening. It is incredible what people think you're like just from watching you act and reading a few interviews.

But it can get messy too, because you start seeing a pattern of what people are thinking about you, and you start feeling this pressure to push yourself into that role until you're acting 24/7: during the day at your job, and the rest of the time for the rest of the world to make them think you are who they want you to be. Suddenly you discover you don't really know who you are. The true you is obliterated, and this persona that's been pieced together from opinions and

interviews and assumptions and rumors starts to take over. The industry is like the Bermuda Triangle of reality: once you get in it, reality
sort of turns inside out and backward—not just for you, but for
everyone who observes you. They get sucked into the madness just by
watching *Entertainment Tonight*.

In an attempt to preserve my own sanity and prolong my career
I decided not to take any work during the off-season after the third
year of *DC*. I stayed away from interviews and media appearances,
and instead I lay around my apartment a lot, reading and thinking
about what was next now that I had accomplished my goal of breaking into acting. I'd already come to the realization that television
wasn't the be-all, end-all that I thought it would be, so my next goal
was to figure out what *was*.

Those three years had given me a lot of Hollywood-life experience, which tends to pack more into a year than most people experience in a lifetime. I went to a lot of parties, met a lot of people, kissed
a lot of women, slept with a few of them, made contacts, schmoozed
and brown-nosed, sampled a mind-boggling array of mixed drinks
and street drugs, and listened in on a lot of conversations about
enlightenment and transcendental experiences, all in an attempt to fill
that hole that I thought my job would fill.

This last bit—the spiritual stuff—seemed to be a pretty serious
fad among most people I met. Acting wasn't enough, living life wasn't
enough, sex and money and relationships weren't enough—we all
seemed to come to that conclusion eventually. Yoga, meditation, kabbalah, spirit quests…everyone was into something that was supposed
to satisfy the void, and I never heard about the same thing twice. Half
the people I knew not only had personal trainers and therapists, but
they had spiritual advisors as well, and spent nearly as much money
on experiencing religion and seeking enlightenment as they did on
their gym memberships.

I was considering dabbling in the spiritual when a new actress was introduced into the cast that next season, a beautiful brunette named Dianne, and she was bigger into the enlightenment stuff than most people I'd met. We hit it off and started getting together outside of work. I was thrilled with the prospect of having found someone who might lead me through the maze of religions and philosophies I'd been reading about, and she was equally excited at the opportunity to lead me. Not long after we started seeing each other, she invited me to attend her weekly séance. Intrigued but slightly dubious, I accepted.

She was in the process of working through mother issues in therapy, and the fact that her mother had died five years before and was no longer around to talk to was making it difficult. So Dianne's plan was to summon her and ask her a few things straight out. She'd been to three séances already, but Mrs. Wallington's spirit was being uncooperative and had yet to show up when requested. I was with her on the fourth try, when Mrs. Wallington's spirit was again a no-show— although the spirit of another customer's great-grandfather blew out the candle on the center of the table and slammed shut a window, which put an end to my forays into the spiritual realm. It pretty much ended Dianne's interest in it too; she only went once more before giving up entirely and going to primal scream therapy instead.

Dianne and I began dating seriously toward the middle of my fifth season on *DC.* She was everything I had ever hoped to find in a woman: beautiful, talented, intelligent but not intellectually threatening, driven, and *amazing* in bed. In my opinion, sleeping with her in and of itself was a transcendental experience. Forget all that spiritual crap the rest of Hollywood was throwing itself into; if you asked me they just hadn't found the right person to sleep with.

Once sex was part of the relationship, we pretty much relocated to the bedroom. We didn't go out very often; we'd put in a few minutes at the parties that were good for us to be seen at, and then we'd make excuses and leave for home, usually whoever's home happened to be closest. She lived on the other side of the city, and it didn't take long for us to get sick of the your-place-or-my-place question, so after six months we decided to move in together. My place was closer to the studio and slightly larger than hers, so in she came.

Living with someone—sharing a bedroom and bathroom and personal space—was a new experience for me. The friends I'd lived with before had all been other wannabe actors with weird schedules, which meant we usually didn't see much of each other. I didn't know the protocol. How much rent do I charge? Does all of her stuff get equal room? Do I take down some of my art so she can put up some of hers? What if she doesn't like my dog?

We had already agreed not to talk about marriage until we'd lived together for at least a year, to see if we were even compatible, so I didn't know how enmeshed we should allow ourselves to get. Dianne laughed off all my fears and said I should relax and not worry so much, that fate and destiny would sort themselves out without my help. I was afraid I'd drive her away, so I shut up. This was the first relationship I'd had that had a shot at marriage, and I didn't want to do anything that would jeopardize it. Plus, Dianne was the first woman I'd ever loved, and once I realized that, I decided that love was what I had been missing all along, that if the rest of Hollywood was really in love (in which case, by my logic, they'd also be having amazing sex), they wouldn't need all those spiritual distractions. The Beatles were right. All you need is love.

Things with Dianne and I as roommates started out great. We'd run lines together over dinner, watch movies, work out together—she had incredible strength, she'd put me to shame—and of course spend as much time as possible in bed. The first five months were bliss. Everyone on *DC* thought we were a great couple. And we were!

But there were some definite problems. For one thing, we weren't very good at the whole confrontation thing. She'd turn tail and run at the first sign of conflict, and to be honest, I was a bit pushy at times. For example, there was a new guy on the set of *DC* who was in a few episodes, and he and Dianne were in some really intense scenes. Dianne hadn't had much acting experience before making it onto *DC,* so to her credit, she probably didn't understand that intense acting can bring on intense feelings between the actors involved. It was *totally* obvious that the two of them were experiencing this, and this upset me, but I'll admit I didn't handle it very well.

"You were *all over him,* Dianne!"

"I don't know what you're talking about, Jack. What should we do for dinner?"

"You couldn't keep your hands off him; it was so obvious! Everyone saw it."

"I don't want to cook; do you want to cook? Let's go out somewhere."

"Dianne, knock it off! What's going on with you and Ty?"

"*Nothing* is going on, Jack; I don't know why you're so upset!"

"Look, I know how it works, okay? I know getting involved with someone in a scene can carry over to reality. But you have to be careful…"

Dianne grabbed her purse and keys. "I need to eat. See you later." And then she was gone.

I sat in my favorite recliner and stewed for a while, rather than go after her and apologize for overreacting. I mean, if it really was just a matter of her getting carried away in the scene, then it meant she didn't really feel anything for him, right? So what was my problem?

Hindsight being 20/20 shows me that I was the king of envy and didn't even know it. That scene with Ty and Dianne was just the start of it; it seemed like nearly every week there was someone or something threatening to take her from me—at least that's how I saw it. Anything could set me off—even our director:

"Why did Carl want to talk to you?"

"Just some directional stuff, character stuff. Nothing big."

"He couldn't have talked about it on the set?"

"It wasn't a two-minute discussion, Jack, it was some big-picture stuff; it took a while. Let's do something tonight; want to rent a movie?" (It didn't take me long to figure out Dianne was big into distracting people when they were angry.)

"Well if it wasn't personal, then he wouldn't have had to meet with you privately."

"Let's get something funny. That new Brice Thornton movie looks good." (Dianne grabs her purse and keys and heads for the door; I continue to smolder.)

Or her career:

"You took the part?"

"It's a great opportunity, Jack; it's great exposure."

"For what, your acting or your body?"

"Both. So?"

"You'll have to move to New York, won't you?"

"For a couple months, yeah. No big deal."

"We'll never see each other. How can you say you love me and then be okay with leaving for two months?"

"Get over it, Jack; people do it all the time."

"Yeah, and how many of them do you know that stay faithful?" (Dianne busies herself with the mail; I try in vain to get her to answer.)

Even her friends:

"We're just going to a movie and some club. I'll be home by two, I promise."

"LA isn't safe at two in the morning."

"LA isn't safe ever, and you don't seem to have a problem letting me go during the day."

"You and Crystal and Julie have been going out all the time lately; do you like their company more than mine?"

"They're women, Jack, it's a different kind of company. You and the boys drink your beer and watch football, me and Crystal and Julie go to movies and hang out at the club. Same thing."

"If they're so much fun, maybe you should move in with them."

"Maybe I will." (Dianne storms into the bedroom; I panic in the living room.)

When she came home at two, as promised, I hadn't moved from the living room, having thrown myself on the couch after she left and having spent the next six hours mulling over our relationship while channel surfing. What if she did leave me? I loved her. I didn't want her to leave, ever, even for five minutes. I couldn't bear it if she left me for good. I became obsessed with making sure she stayed with me. I began buying her flowers, taking her out, buying her jewelry and clothes, taking her on little vacations. I thought if I could show her how much she meant to me, she wouldn't need to hang out with anyone else, and wouldn't even *want* to.

But instead of drawing closer like I thought she would, she started edging further away. She started going out with her friends even more often than before, and even going out alone. I'd stay home and watch TV or eat or work out, but regardless of what I was doing my mind was always thinking about her or, more accurately, thinking about the men she might meet while she was out and whether or not she would go home with them. We stopped having sex, although it was not because of any lessening of desire on my part. She almost never left without us having fought about it for ten minutes or more, and when she got home I'd either give her the cold shoulder or else fawn all over her. Neither response was appropriate, I realize now, but then I was in such mental and emotional turmoil that I didn't know what else to do. Dianne was my religion, my stuffing for the hole that gaped in my soul. Even with my career I knew I wouldn't have anything worth having if she were gone.

One relatively calm and enjoyable night we were eating dinner at our place when we got on the topic of college. I had never gone, she had gone but never graduated, and I asked what it was like. Dianne told me about her two years at NYU—frat parties, early morning classes, football games, and finals—and I asked how she'd managed to get there when her parents had so little money. Her parents' lack of financial stability had been a topic of conversation more than once, and it surprised me that they'd managed to find a way to get her through two years of it when they couldn't afford to own a car. "I worked my tail off when I wasn't in class," she finally admitted.

"Wow." I was impressed. I'd always known she was ambitious; it shouldn't have surprised me. "Where did you work? *When* did you work?"

"Night shift," she said. "Class during the day, worked at night."

"Full time?" I laughed in amazement. "How did you have the energy to go to class?"

"Well…I didn't work a full forty-hour week… I just got paid a lot." She suddenly stopped eating and carried her plate to the kitchen. "I'm full. Do you want to rent a movie tonight or something? I don't want to just sit around."

I was wracking my brain trying to think of a job that paid that well and had a night shift. I couldn't think of one. "Um, yeah, that's fine, let's do that. But where did you work—"

"Just drop it, okay?" she snapped. "It paid, I got through school as long as I wanted to, it doesn't matter what I did, just that I was able to do it, okay?"

Whoa. That hit a nerve. Waitressing doesn't cause that much secrecy. Factory work? Bartending? What night job pays enough to get someone through college but is too embarrassing to admit to?

That night, while Dianne slept, my mind idly wandered the list of possible night jobs a college student might have. Usually Dianne was more than willing to divulge her history to me; nothing had ever been off-limits before. This flat-out refusal to talk was highly uncharacteristic.

A new possibility popped into my head, not that I could believe it. Would it be plausible? I thought over what she had said, looking for an incompatibility, hoping I was wrong. For fifteen minutes I turned it over in my head, getting all the more irate and astonished and curious as I did. Finally I shook her awake, unable to stand the suspense and, in a half-snicker, half-whisper, half expecting her to say no, I asked, "Hey Dianne—you weren't a hooker, were you?"

Her body language said it all. She froze for just a second too long, her eyes wide in surprise; I could practically see the wheels turning in her head. Before she even opened her mouth I knew it was true. "You *were!*" I was laughing with astonishment, but anger was slowly seeping into my system. "I can't believe it, you—"

"*Stop it!*" I'd never heard her scream like that before. She was crying, the covers pulled up around her shaking shoulders. "Stop it, just forget it," she choked out between sobs. "I *told* you to drop it, why did you keep—I had *no money,* Jack, *none.* It was fast money and easy work on a big state campus in a huge city. Me and a couple other girls made a business out of it. *That's* why I left, that's why I didn't graduate; I'd end up in classes with them, they'd whisper things when I walked by, it was a nightmare. It worked for a while, but I couldn't do it anymore…"

I was dumbstruck, sitting up against the wall and staring at her. Part of me wanted to rage at her, part of me wanted to gather her up in my arms and comfort her. Tenderness won out, and I pulled her to me and held her while she shook. "It's okay, Dianne, it's okay, I still love you, it's okay…" I wished I had a script; I had absolutely no idea what to say to her.

After a while she rolled off my lap and leaned against the wall next to me, staring down at her hands. When she started speaking, her voice was so quiet I could barely hear her. "I got tested last month, Jack. I do it every three months, just in case, you know? I went last month, and…" She bit her lip and closed her eyes. "I'm sorry, Jack."

My mind froze, rejecting the possibility behind her apology. "For what, Dianne?" I tried to hold her hand, but she pulled it away from me.

Finally she looked at me, her eyes still swimming in tears. "I got HIV."

I shake my head. "So that's the story." I've heard about her death, of course, and the HIV, but I've never heard anything specific. "What a shocker."

Jack lets out a laugh. "That's the understatement of the year."

I notice Grace has slipped out at some point during Jack's narrative; odd, since usually neither one leaves the other during their side of the story, unless Bree requires some attention, but even then they come back quickly. Jack seems to read my thoughts. "Grace still has a hard time with it all." He chews his lip for a second, staring out the window beyond me. "She doesn't like to talk about Dianne. Not jealousy, I don't think," he adds quickly, as if wanting to defend Grace's character. He shrugs. "The reality of it is still hard to bear."

I nod. "Understandable, certainly."

I watch him as he stares out the window behind me, his face blank. I sit silently, waiting for him to continue, but he doesn't say anything until Grace reappears holding a tray of snacks that she sets on the coffee table between us. Jack watches her as she moves about the room, and I study them both for signs of strain or discomfort now that the root of so many of their problems had finally been broached. But Grace refills drinks, arranges food and plates, and then bends to kiss Jack gently on the cheek before taking her seat in the chair next to his. She seems fine, and I see a look of relief flicker across Jack's face as she jumps back into the conversation.

GRACE

THERE'S NOTHING QUITE as daunting or exciting as an apartment full of cardboard boxes waiting to be emptied. The first step is always hooking up the stereo, since unpacking can't be done without decent unpacking music. My preference has always been Aerosmith. After that, I usually employ the whatever-is-closest method: whatever box is at your feet is the one you empty next. It didn't take long that early December morning before I was completely wrapped up in the job, singing along with Steven and the boys and dancing my way around the mess.

I unpacked for six solid hours, fueled only by adrenaline and the continental breakfast I'd had at the hotel, before realizing, one, I was starving, and two, I was in my own place in Cali-freaking-fornia! I forced the second thought out of my head long enough to order delivery and find my plates and silverware, but it came back as soon as the pizza guy was gone.

"What am I doing here?" I said aloud to myself through a mouthful of mushroom pizza; panic was beginning to set in. Fear and apprehension had been hovering at the edge of my consciousness for the past week as I'd packed my belongings and boarded the plane in Chicago. From the moment I made the decision to throw myself into this move, I'd forced myself into a state of confidence that all the details would be sorted out with a minimum amount of trouble, and by the grace of God (and I mean that literally), they had. But now reality was setting in, and I wasn't sure if I'd done the right thing.

Gary called me a week after I sent him my letter. He said he had an acquaintance who worked at a nearby church, and that he'd call him and ask if the church knew of anyone with a room to rent or who needed a roommate. Turns out there was a couple going on a four-year mission trip who wanted to rent out their condominium. They were scheduled to leave the week I had planned to arrive but were still without a subrenter. Their furniture had already been loaned out, and the rest of their stuff was already in storage. The church contact called them on my behalf, and within two days they had checked my references and sent me a lease.

A week later Gary called back because another friend of his had just lost his administrative assistant, and would I like to interview for the position when I got to California? I'd looked into the process for acquiring a teaching credential in California and knew it was going to take me a while to complete, so teaching for this year was out of the question. My second day in town, armed with my admittedly unimpressive résumé, I went to the offices of Williams & Williams Consulting, which were conveniently located fifteen minutes down the freeway from my new home, and an hour later emerged with a job that would start after the weekend I moved in. It was one amazing God thing after another.

"God thing," I break in. "Is that when—?"

Grace grins sheepishly. "Oops, sorry; shame on me for reverting to lingo." She sets her lips for a second, seeming to think. "A 'God thing' is when something happens just the way you needed it to, and there was no way you could have orchestrated it yourself. You could call it a miracle, although I tend to think of miracles as being…I don't know…more like the defying of natural law, you know? Like cancer disappearing, fatal injuries not being fatal, that kind of thing. But a God thing is…well, just like what happened to me: jobs materializing and a roof being placed over my head with practically no effort on my part whatsoever. You look at the odds and think, How did that happen?" She shrugs and smiles. "And I reply, 'It was a God thing.'"

"Like a coincidence."

"You could call it that, yeah. But we believe that there are very few things in life that are just coincidences. There's a master plan, and we only see glimpses of it, and when we don't see the whole thing, we say, 'Oh, what a coincidence.' But in reality it is God setting us up for exactly what we needed. More like a divine coincidence."

Apparently my doubt is written like text all over my face. Jack laughs. "Mull it over," he says. "We can talk more about it later."

I'm hoping we won't talk about it at all—their God talk makes me uncomfortable. Not because of them; they aren't pushy the way so many other religious people are. They're just so matter-of-fact about it. This is what bothers me, I think—that they see it as fact. I work hard to shelve my personal feelings about this and urge Grace to continue her story.

Even though things had gone incredibly well up until now, the anxiety I had warded off for so long began to break down my resolve. What had I been thinking? Why, of all places, California? Sure, the winters were a lot more tolerable than the often-arctic conditions I'd weathered my whole life, but I'd never minded the snow and subzero windchill that much, had I? And I knew no one in this state, except for Gary. But he wasn't really my friend; he was my godfather, my parents' age, and not exactly someone I'd want to spend my time hanging out with.

So I was back to square one, which was Alone in a New Place, and for no good reason other than I apparently wanted a change of scenery. As I finished off my pizza I tried to reassure myself with the fact that, so far, things had gone great. I had a home, I had a job; what else did I really need? I'd make friends eventually…somewhere. Not that I knew where I'd find them. The office staff at the firm had all looked much older than I. Maybe I could take a class at the community college or join…something. What did people join these days? Book clubs? Political campaigns?

I practically felt my brain short-circuit and realized I needed sleep. I mentally berated myself for not having set up my bed—one of the shortcomings of the whatever-is-closest unpacking method—and halfheartedly packed up the rest of the pizza before shuffling through boxes to find the bed linens. After throwing the bed together I threw myself atop the sheets without changing clothes, yanked the comforter over my head, and was asleep before I could even consider setting an alarm.

I slept like the dead, but when I awoke nearly twelve hours later, I found I had no energy to face the day. At first I wasn't sure why—was it all the unpacking still to be done? The mental exhaustion from the last few weeks? It was unclear until I found myself jumping at the slightest noises and fearing the unfamiliar surroundings, and then I knew what my problem was.

I didn't want to be alone.

In all my daydreams of California, I'd pictured myself with people: living with a roommate, working in an office full of other young people, hanging out in the evening with some friends at a nearby restaurant and, most important, meeting a blond, tanned surfer boy and starting another relationship. Instead, I'd moved into a one-bedroom apartment by myself and taken a job in an office where I was at least fifteen years everyone's junior, and I had no idea how to meet new people. I was terrified that, six months into this ill-planned venture, I'd still be alone.

I let myself cry, knowing it would happen eventually anyway, then forced myself to get up and shower. I had no food in the house other than my leftover pizza, and since that never appealed to me for breakfast, I decided to walk to the shopping center at the bottom of the hill and get some groceries. The walk would allow me some time to think about what I was going to do to find some friends, and it would give me the chance to really examine my neighborhood for signs of other twenty-somethings.

It was an incredible day. I couldn't believe the first week of December could be this warm! People were outside in shorts and T-shirts, walking dogs and washing cars; it felt more like Easter than the Christmas holiday. My condo community was full of children and pets, all running around the parking lot and the narrow street that meandered through the development. I walked out to the main road and down the hill where two huge shopping centers faced each other across a busy street. Fast-food franchises rimmed the edges of the parking lots, and as I surveyed what stores filled the strip malls, I realized I had basically everything I'd ever need within a ten-minute walk: grocery store, pharmacy, gas station, restaurants, office supply store, numerous clothing stores, and, my favorite, a giant Target. Next to the Target was a pet supply store, and I decided on a whim (which was apparently how I made all my decisions these days) that what I needed was a little unconditional animal love. My parents' allergies had stopped us from having pets when I was a kid, and I'd been wanting a cat for a while. That would be my next course of action: to find an animal shelter and get myself a four-legged roommate.

I grabbed some basic food necessities and lugged them back up the hill. Once home, I unpacked some more, promising myself that once I had things more or less organized and cleaned up, I would let myself get a cat and explore the area a little more. Once I had the place sufficiently set up, I changed clothes, called the nearest animal shelter for directions, and took off.

Before going to the shelter, I drove up and down the major streets near my condo, trying to fix locations and street names in my head. My first few days had been spent running from one specific place to another, and I hadn't had the chance to really explore. As I drove farther out, I passed another Target and stopped in to get some cat stuff so I'd have it as soon as I brought one home. I didn't want to leave the poor thing stranded without food or a litter box; the last thing I wanted was to be cleaning up cat pee from the carpet of an apartment that didn't even belong to me.

I grabbed a small box of litter and a bag of food, then wandered into the housewares department to find dishes for food and water. There I found exactly what I was looking for: a pair of psychedelically painted ceramic bowls, much more interesting than the plain plastic dishes in the pet section. I hoped my new cat would appreciate my artistic taste.

From there I consulted the map purchased on my first day in town to figure out how to get to the shelter. I'd never been to one before, and I didn't know what exactly to do once I got there, but then I remembered that *everything* I'd done in the past week had been a new experience, and so far I hadn't made any fatal mistakes. How hard could it be to pick up a cat?

I entered the shelter and my ears and nose were assaulted with the sounds and smells of many, many animals. The receptionist led me to the cat section, where I decided I'd rather take all of them home than have to choose between them. I looked up and down the row of cages, and each was cuter than the last. Drat. This wasn't going to be easy. I was going to have to come up with a new strategy.

I asked the nearest volunteer which cat had been around the longest. She'd seen me perusing the cages and smiled. "Can't decide?"

"It's a lot harder than I expected."

She pointed down three cages. "The black American shorthair in cage five has been here three weeks. She's really skittish; a lot of people come here with their kids, and she's not real good with kids. Too loud and energetic. The kids, I mean." She grinned.

I peered into the cage. The cat was curled up in the corner, looking traumatized. Her gold eyes stared out unblinkingly from her solid black face.

"Want to check her out?" I nodded, and she unlocked the cage. I set my hand on the floor of the cage and tapped my finger lightly.

"Come here, cutie," I coaxed. She leaned forward and sniffed in the direction of my finger for a moment, then stood and inched closer. I slowly moved my hand up to her face and scratched underneath her chin. She began to purr and rubbed her head against my hand. I picked her up and held her against me, and she stared up at me and pawed lightly at my shoulder.

The volunteer chuckled. "I think we have a winner."

The minute I opened the cardboard carrying case the shelter had given me, the cat leapt out and took off down the hall. I followed her into my room, where I saw her tail disappear under the bed. I didn't blame her for being terrified, and while she was hiding I set up her food and water in the kitchen against the wall, and her litter box in the small utility room. I hoped she was smart enough to go looking for the box instead of doing her business under my bed.

I crossed three of the items off my list and considered my next move. I definitely wanted to find the library and get some books; evenings were going to be really boring around here until I found some people to hang out with. I finally decided the cat would be able to fend for herself, and might prefer to explore the apartment without some crazy human trying to pet her all the time, so I went back out to the car and consulted the map for the location of the library. It wasn't too far away, and the listing in the Yellow Pages had said they'd be open for another hour.

When I got home the cat was out of her hiding place and munching on the little fish-shaped morsels that made up her meal. I knelt down and held out my hand, and after a few moments she walked cautiously toward me and sniffed my fingers before burrowing her head in my palm and purring like a fine-tuned engine. I sat on the floor and stroked her sleek, black head, trying to think of a fitting name. I didn't want to name her something prosaic or cliché, like Midnight or Ebony. As I pet her, she rolled over, nearly doing a somersault, and flopped on her back in apparent ecstasy. A name came to me as I laughed.

"Hey, Joker, whatcha think about that as a name, huh?" She continued to purr and didn't really seem to care one way or the other what I called her, so I figured that was as good as anything.

It was getting dark out, and I decided to curl up with one of my books and spend the rest of the evening chilling out in anticipation of tomorrow: my first day at Williams & Williams. The cat evidently liked this idea as well; she settled beside me on the couch, snuggled between my side and the back cushion, and purred contentedly before falling asleep with her head on my stomach. Getting a cat had definitely been a good idea.

A little before ten I went through my closet to decide what to wear the next morning, then set the alarm and climbed into bed. Joker, who hadn't seemed too pleased about being awakened from her nap on the couch, made herself at home beside my pillow and, after getting situated, stretched out a paw and rested it on my elbow. I melted.

I glance around the room. "I've seen the dog, but I don't remember seeing a cat," I say, thinking back over the days I've been here so far.

Grace sighs. "Yeah, she turned out to be great with just one person in the house, but not real thrilled with the prospect of two. After we got married she sort of flipped out, and we gave her away."

"Aw, how sad!"

She shrugs. "*C'est la vie.* We think Bree is allergic, anyway, so we probably would have given her away eventually."

As if summoned by the mention of her name, Bree sprints into the living room and throws herself onto her mother's lap. She seems to oscillate in her opinion of me; some days she is friendly and outgoing, other days shy and quiet. Today is a shy day. She leans up and whispers in Grace's ear. With a smile, Grace nods and gathers the girl into her arms before standing. "Someone needs a story before bedtime."

She bends Bree down to Jack's level, and he plants a kiss on his daughter's forehead. "Sleep well, babygirl. Give Oliver a hug for me."

"Who's Oliver?" I ask.

"He's my owl," Bree answers. "He's not real."

I stifle a laugh. "A pretend owl?"

Bree's little eyes roll. "A stuffed owl."

"Ah, I see," I concede. "Maybe I can meet him."

"We'll think about it," Bree mumbles as Grace carries her out. We all laugh at that as they disappear around the corner.

I glance at Jack. "So...want to pick up where you left off?"

His eyes dart to the stairs that Grace has ascended with Bree. "Probably should while Grace is preoccupied," he says quietly. I can tell he still worries about her reaction to this part of his story. He takes a deep breath and closes his eyes for a moment. I know where this is going, and that it must be difficult to talk about. Usually I am oblivious to my subjects' inner turmoil over their stories, unless it shows itself in tears or tone of voice, and even then I still probe and push, ever so gently, for the whole story, telling myself it is the only way to get a true narrative. But for once I want to provide an out.

"You know," I say quietly, "if you want to skip it—"

"No, no," he says quickly, his eyes opening as he straightens in his chair. "It's what happened, and as much as we might hate the things we do or the things that are done to us, they're our history, you know? If you deny them you're just lying to yourself, and that never does anyone any good."

JACK

Needless to say, Dianne's and my relationship took quite a turn that night.

Dianne was convinced I'd leave her, but I was determined not to, even though every inch of me was screaming for me to run like hell. A few phone calls got me the address of an LA clinic that used the rapid test. I made an appointment as soon as possible and endured the longest hour of my life before getting back the results I'd hoped for: I was clear. So far, anyway. We tried to make light of it, scheduling my next testing in three months and dressing it up like a date: give up a little blood, then dinner and a movie.

Dianne's half of the medicine cabinet began to look like a small pharmacy: four different medications of varying colors and sizes, lined up like round, stout soldiers at the ready, eagerly awaiting their chance to pummel the virus coursing through her body. We both read up on all the new research and theories of HIV treatment, and she stepped up her workouts (as did I, in a show of solidarity). She decided not to tell the rest of the cast or crew of *DC,* and we became almost fanatical about watching for cuts that might leak poisoned blood onto an unsuspecting costar and about assaulting all sneezes and coughs with an army of homeopathic drugs and remedies.

The biggest difference, however, was that the linchpin that had held our whole relationship together without us even realizing it—sex—had been pulled right out of the machine. So far I didn't appear to be infected, but we certainly weren't taking any risks; even with a condom, intercourse was out of the question. Obviously there were other options, and I was more than willing to take (and give, of course)

whatever I could, but Dianne would have none of it. She lost all interest in being physical in any way. Six months of this began to take its
toll, and the machine began to fall apart.

On top of everything, Dianne began to shelter herself from everyone. She didn't want to tell her girlfriends, and since they'd wonder
why she wasn't drinking when they went dancing, or why she wanted
to go home early, she just stopped seeing them altogether. She became
as much of a recluse as a working actor can be: go to rehearsals and
tapings, go work out, go home. The worst part was the effect the pre-
scriptions had on her. They made her sick, but not in any predictable
way. Some days she'd be fine; other days she'd be a mess. She managed
to push through it and continue working, and I was continually
amazed at how people readily believed the stories she made up about
her intermittent dizziness, nausea, and lethargy.

At first I stayed home with her every night, keeping her company
or just being around when she didn't want to talk or do anything. We
soon discovered that our mutual interests were close to nil, and we
quickly ran out of things to talk about. One particular evening made
it obvious to me that our relationship really had no grounding, no
foundation. We'd halfheartedly discussed the idea of dressing up and
going out on a real date, something we hadn't done in months, and
when the night rolled around we both went through the motions of
dressing and preparing as though we were going to a funeral. Suddenly Dianne stopped and looked at me as I wrestled with a necktie.
Feeling her stare, I looked at her and saw in her eyes what she was
going to say.

"Pointless, huh?" I said. She nodded. I stood in front of the mirror, feeling awkward. "Don't feel like even attempting it? 'Fake it till
you make it' and all that? We might get into it once we get going." I
brightened my face and smiled. "Dinner, theatre, painting the town
red…" I gave it all I could, but I wasn't even convincing myself.

She tilted her head to one side and smiled sadly. "Points for effort."

"Dianne, look," I began, putting my arms around her. It had been a long time since I'd done even this simple gesture, and it felt forced. I realized, sadly, that it *was* forced. "Things might not be going the way we want them to, but every couple has their hard times, right? It doesn't mean we can't get through it."

She laughed. It sounded almost genuine. "You're kidding, right?" she said, pulling out of my half-embrace and crossing the room to the closet. She pulled off the dress as though she hated it. "If we *had* a future as a couple, then maybe you'd be right. But we don't. We've never even *been* a couple. We've been…masquerading as one. *That's* what we've been faking—a relationship. Admit it: we've never been serious. We've been exclusive, but that's not the same thing."

I watched her undress, stick the dress back on the hanger, and pull on the pajamas she'd been spending so much time in. I was angry, but not at her. It wasn't her fault, and she hadn't said anything that wasn't true. That's what I was angry about. I had been lying to myself, had allowed myself to believe the lies. She was right, and had I been honest with myself I would have known it long before. How could I have let myself—both of us—get into such deep denial?

It was downhill from there. I did all I could to draw her out, to get her interested in things—any things—but she wouldn't have it. I finally gave up and left her to wither. I wasn't about to hole up with her every night and let her suck the life out of me, so I started going out.

At first it was out for a beer with some of the other guys from *DC*. Then it was dinners, and then parties, and then staying out until four in the morning smoking pot and getting tanked. There was a part of me that would say in this rational voice, "Now why exactly are you doing this? You don't enjoy it, you're hung over nearly every night, and you said this was exactly the kind of thing you weren't going to ruin your career with." It was true; I was heading down that path I'd sworn never to tread, and here I was, map in hand, traipsing down it with no intention of turning back. The only thing I wasn't doing was sleeping around, but I knew it was only a matter of time, even knowing Dianne was at home.

Eight months after Dianne's confession, I woke up in bed with Penelope Jones, a fellow *DC* member. At first I stared at her sleeping form in utter confusion. *What happened?* We'd always flirted off and on, but only casually, the way friends flirt when they know nothing will come of it. After my head had cleared slightly, I groped back through the shadows of my hangover to the night before and finally remembered all that had occurred. I felt sick, and not just from the countless beers and shots I'd consumed.

I woke her and fumbled apologies; her indifferent response was, "Hey, no strings. We agreed on that last night. No need to apologize. You leavin'? See you later." She smiled and kissed me on the cheek and went back to sleep. I didn't remember this agreement at all, but I was glad we'd made it nonetheless. I wondered vaguely what excuse I'd given her about Dianne, hoping I hadn't said anything telltale about her illness, but I didn't want to think about it anymore, and I raced home to find Dianne asleep on the couch where she'd waited for me all night. I begged her forgiveness, kissed her, and listened meekly while she ranted, and it wasn't until after she'd fallen asleep in my arms that I realized I reeked of Penelope's perfume.

Either Dianne didn't notice or didn't care, but whatever the reason, it was never discussed. I took this as my wake-up call and vowed never to do that again. And while I never did indulge in any other woman while I was with Dianne, my heart was definitely not faithful to her. We drifted so far apart emotionally that it was almost painful being home together. I forced myself not to stay out until all hours anymore, but I spent as much time away as possible, be it at the gym, someone else's place, or a bar. It didn't matter where it was, as long as it wasn't my place. We lasted like this for another three months, and then came the explosion, the night when it all hit the fan, and months of resentment and fear and anger erupted like a long-sleeping volcano.

It all started one Friday night. I'd been out at a coworker's condo slamming down shots of on-the-spot concoctions when, around 11:30, I finally decided to go home. I staggered in past midnight, assuming Dianne would be asleep; instead I found her sprawled on the couch, my dog Bailey nudging her flung-out hand and whimpering. An empty bottle of Scotch sat on the coffee table, along with a half-finished bottle of soda—which she apparently stopped mixing with the liquor early in the evening, given how much of it was left—and an empty bottle of vodka. A large aspirin bottle, empty, peeked out from beneath the sofa. My first thought was of the alcohol's interaction with her meds. I panicked when she wouldn't respond to my shouts and called 911; within minutes paramedics were tangling her in IVs and loading her onto a cart.

I rode in the back of the rig, shaking with fear, wondering aloud what she'd been thinking. One of the paramedics had taken down the complicated names of all her drugs, and when I'd asked what they did when mixed with alcohol, his response chilled me: "Anything from pancreatitis to liver damage to neuropathy. Depends on her blood levels."

I was left in the waiting room for what seemed like forever. I paced and agonized and downed copious amounts of water to try to dilute the alcohol in my own system and clear my foggy head. Why hadn't I stayed home; why had I stayed out so late; why had I drunk so much? I berated myself for not being there and stopping her, and I prayed to no one in particular that she not die.

Finally a doctor came out to give me the details of her condition. She was better than expected—most likely because there was no trace of her HIV meds in her system. "That's not possible," I countered, "she takes them three times a day! How could they *not* be in her system?" He looked at me like I was an idiot, which I was, because had I been sober I would have realized what he was saying: she'd stopped taking them. I tried to think back to the last time I'd seen her take them: always first thing in the morning, right before brushing her teeth; always during lunch on the set, when she'd disappear into the bathroom to take them so no one would see; always before bed, which I hadn't been around for in a while. It dawned on me that I hadn't actually *seen* her take them in ages. There was no way for me to tell when she'd stopped.

I sat in the plastic waiting-room chair as emergencies came and went, bursting through the ambulance bay doors or coming in from the parking lot. I kept my head down, buried behind a three-month-old issue of *Newsweek,* hoping no one would recognize me, but everyone was too preoccupied with their own personal traumas to notice me.

I took Dianne home nearly two days later, after convincing a social worker I'd be there to take care of her and that she didn't need psychiatric attention. It wasn't often that I tried to flex my celebrity muscle, but I did it with all the charm and charisma I had, and it worked.

We'd hardly spoken at the hospital. There was complete, stifling silence the entire way home. Dianne dropped heavily onto the couch and leaned her head back, eyes closed. I set my keys on the table and stood by the door, my stomach churning like molten lava. Finally, in as even a voice as I could manage, I asked, "When did you stop them, Dianne?"

For a moment she didn't move. Then, wavering on unsteady legs, she stood and stalked into the bedroom and slammed the door. I barreled in after her, shouting loud enough to disturb the neighbors. "You stopped taking them! When? *Why?* And a whole bottle of Scotch...*and* vodka...*and* the aspirin on top of it! You could have *died,* Dianne—"

"*That was the point!*" she screamed. It stopped me in my tracks.

We stared at each other from opposite sides of the room, the stillness and silence quivering with tension. "That was the *whole point*. But you came home too early. Since when do you come home before midnight?" She said it with such venom that for a second I felt guilty for not having stayed out later and allowing her the time she needed to do herself in.

But the anger I'd been holding in for so many months wasn't about to be squelched by her animosity. "My apologies, Dianne; you should have just told me that's what you wanted; I could have helped! You're not living anyway, you might as well stop taking up space. You sit around here doing absolutely nothing, just waiting for *it* to finally take you over." Her face was a mask of shock; this was obviously not what she'd been expecting. I reveled in that look, drawing energy from it, and continued my rant. "God forbid I should have my own life, though, right? Did you really expect me to sit around here and get sucked into your pity party? Sit around here and watch you disintegrate? I have a life, and so do you, and if you don't want to live yours, that's fine, but don't expect me to forfeit mine!"

Tears were streaming down her face by this time, and I was shaking with the intensity of my own words. Our eyes were locked, boring into each other with palpable force. After the silence seemed to have swallowed us up, she spoke in a voice so low I could barely hear it, and with sarcasm so thick I could taste it. "Forgive me, Jack, for making your life so miserable. I don't know what I was thinking, imagining you cared enough to try to help me. Give me a couple hours and I'll be out of your way so you can get on with your life."

I hadn't expected this, although I don't know what else I thought would happen. The thought of her not being around jarred me back to my senses, and my selfishness was suddenly clear. "Dianne, the doctor said you shouldn't—"

"Shut up and get out and leave me alone," she hissed with such strength and anger that for a minute I was scared of her. She looked like she was about to fly apart into a thousand pieces. I backed out of the room, and once I was past the threshold she stormed forward and slammed the door in my face. I grabbed my keys and ran down the stairs to the garage, then jumped into my car and sped out onto the street without even looking. I headed for the highway and drove for an hour before finally taking an exit toward the foothills. I was north of the city now, near the base of the surrounding mountains. I parked at the edge of an old gas station lot and bought a soda before returning to my car and sitting in the shadow of the station's rusted sign.

I knew Dianne would be gone when I returned. It saddened me that I didn't really care. I knew that I should. I wanted to. But I didn't. I wondered if she was right. If I had cared more, could I have helped her? Did I not love her enough? Did I love her at all?

This question disturbed me, because I thought I did. But if I really did, then would I have allowed us to drift so far apart? Would I have stayed with her, stuck in that apartment, while she hid from society and waited for something to happen to her to either make her better or worse? I did try to drag her out of it, I reminded myself. I did try to get her interested in other things and not fixate on what she had no control over. But she refused it. So it wasn't my fault. At least, not that part.

And then I remembered that she could be dead now. I could be tracking down her parents somewhere in Iowa, calling her friend Julie, and calling Carl, telling them all she'd drunk herself to death. But I had come home in time; I had done at least one thing right. At least I thought it was right; she apparently had a different opinion. But I figured most people would have sided with me.

I wanted to go home and apologize, but I didn't know where to start, and I didn't know how sincere it would be anyway. I mean, I *was* sorry, but did that mean I wanted her to stay? Honestly, I didn't want her around anymore, not with the attitude she was sporting. Like I'd told her, it was her life, and if she wanted to end it, that was her business. I wanted no part of it.

I let my mind wander over and around all these obstacles in my head until the sun started to slip behind the hills. Then I climbed back into my car and steered it back toward the apartment, which by now would be vacated of her few belongings and strangely open and empty. I considered pointing the car toward Todd's, where I'd been before coming home to an unconscious Dianne, but that would only be prolonging the inevitable, as well as pitting myself against the temptation of drinking myself into oblivion—Todd's favorite way of socializing. When I got home, Bailey greeted me with loyal devotion, the afternoon's screaming match apparently forgotten or stuffed down into his doggy psyche. I changed clothes and clipped on his leash, then took him out to the park for a long jog, which I spent thinking about just how horrible things would be on the set the next week. We'd been off this week courtesy of Carl's daughter's wedding in Italy, and I was grateful for the downtime while I tried to sort through the emotions stirred up by all that had happened. Over the next few days, I psyched myself up for reclaiming my life, my independence, and most important, my single status. I also tried to imagine every possible scenario I might be met with upon returning to the set and encountering Dianne, and figured out what I'd do and say for each so I'd be prepared.

There had been one scenario I had not anticipated, however, and of course that was the one I found when I arrived. I walked into the rehearsal room Monday morning and was met with curious stares. I noticed quickly that Dianne wasn't there, which was surprising since she was usually so punctual. Within minutes Carl was beside me, asking in his usual businesslike tone if I could meet with him for a few minutes. I followed him into an office where he picked up a supermarket tabloid and laid it on the desk in front of me: "Dianne Wallington Suicide Attempt—Will Midnight Visit to ER with Beau Jack Harrington End Their Relationship?" I stared at the headline and a picture of us taken at a party months ago, before this whole mess started, made to look like it had been ripped in half. I couldn't believe how fast that had made it to the papers. And how had it in the first place? Who had seen us there? I mentally thanked no one in particular for the fact that the HIV thing hadn't made it out yet.

I looked at Carl and shrugged. "What do you want me to say?" I asked.

"Is it true?"

"What, that she OD'd on purpose?"

"Yeah."

I paused to think for a second, then shrugged with an apologetic look. "You'll have to ask her."

"You guys break up?"

"She moved out, so I think so, yeah."

"She came in this morning, and someone had this. She saw it and took off. Debra went off after her, talked to her for a bit, and brought her back. They're still in the john."

For a moment I was bemused: both my exes together, probably bad-mouthing my selfish ways. But mostly I felt uncomfortable. "Well, what do you want me to do, Carl?" I didn't ask it spitefully; I just didn't know what he was expecting of me. I wasn't her keeper.

"You gonna be able to work with her, stay professional?"

I rolled my eyes. "Carl, come on, I've gone through breakups with people on the show before and it hasn't affected the way I work. If there are problems, they won't be from my side of the fence."

Carl chewed on that for a minute, then nodded. "All right, well, that's what she said too, and we've lost enough time, so let's go." I stood and followed him out to where the rest of the cast milled around talking and reading scripts. I saw Debra and Dianne standing together near the door to the rehearsal room. Dianne's arms were folded protectively across her chest, and she looked like death warmed over. I did my best to shove aside all the crap from the past week and get into a work mind-set.

We put in a full day, but it felt like two by the time it was over. All I wanted was to get out of there and go home. I was exhausted from forcing myself to focus on the script and not allow my mind to wander to Dianne's predicament. I kept reminding myself that it was her decision, but eventually I realized that wasn't exactly true: it hadn't been her decision to overdose and then face the world over it. She'd been hoping to escape the whole thing altogether and leave the rest of us to deal with it. But I figured I'd rather have found her and stopped her than to have her death on my hands.

I cringe. "That's a lot to go through."

He shrugs and flashes a half-smile. "Well, yeah, no getting around that. But you do what you have to do. I might not have tried as hard as I could to help her, but I don't think it would have mattered in the end. She just didn't see her life as ever amounting to anything. She didn't think she'd make it through the illness, so she didn't want to bother trying. Once someone has their head set that way, there's not a lot you can do but pray for them." He pauses; his eyes get sadder while I wait for him to finish. "I wish I'd been praying back then. It might have changed things. I don't know."

"You really think you could have fixed her?"

"Me? No, I couldn't have. God could have."

God again. I hope my disdain isn't clear on my face. I wait for him to continue his narrative.

Dianne and I managed to "keep things professional" as Carl had requested, and in fact managed to act like amiable coworkers, even friends at times. It was a bizarre dance that amazed many of the others on the set. Todd confided to me later that the cast and crew were betting on who would crack first. I really didn't think either of us would crack, but even so, the end of the season couldn't come fast enough.

When the end finally came, Carl hosted his traditional Happy Summer Hiatus party at his place in Beverly Hills on the night the season finale aired. It was a classic cliff-hanger, and we mocked ourselves while we watched the show and feasted on the decadent catered food. The final scene, a spectacular helicopter chase and crash that leaves Todd's character's life in the balance, sent us all into hysterics when we remembered the bloopers that had occurred during the taping. We rarely could watch the show and enjoy it the way the rest of the world did; all we'd remember were flubbed lines and stunt mistakes that made even the most intense scene seem comical.

After the show was over Carl handed out champagne, and we toasted to the success of another fine season. As everyone was draining their glasses, Dianne cleared her throat and said quietly, "I have an announcement to make." All the glasses came down, drained or not, and all eyes turned to her. She avoided looking at me as she glanced around and said, "I've decided to make this my last season. I won't be back in the fall."

Jaws dropped, mine included. As I stared at her I saw for the first time how worn she looked. It was hard to pinpoint exactly what gave her that appearance, but in fact there was no one specific thing; she just looked exhausted. We were all tired—it had been a long and stressful year thanks to wavering ratings—but she looked like she'd been through the wringer. I wondered if she was off the drugs again, or if she'd ever gone back on them at all. Was this the virus running its course?

Carl spoke into the shocked silence. "Dianne and I have already discussed it; we'll be writing her out through a transfer to a new precinct. I've said it to you already, Dianne, but this time I think I speak for everyone when I tell you that you'll be missed." Murmurs of agreement rose in a soft cloud, and those standing near her wrapped an arm around her shoulder or kissed her cheek. As the group began to disperse, Dianne spoke for a moment with Carl before they embraced, and when they parted she headed for the door.

I watched her leave and saw the door close behind her, and before I knew what I was doing, I was on the walkway outside the house, running after her. "Dianne, hold up a sec."

She paused for a moment before resuming an unsteady walk toward her car and saying over her shoulder, "I don't want to talk, Jack. Good night."

I continued to run anyway and caught her arm before she unlocked her car. "Dianne, please, give me just a minute."

She sighed and turned around to face me, leaning on the car and running her hand through her hair. "What?"

Good question. What did I want to say? Why had I come out here in the first place? "Um…I just wanted to tell you good luck," I finally stammered. "What are you moving on to?"

She mustered the energy to look irritated. "I'm not 'moving on' to anything, Jack. I'm leaving. I'm moving home."

I blinked and accidentally laughed. "To *Iowa?* You hated it there! You couldn't wait to leave! Why are you going back now? You've got talent, Dianne, you shouldn't—"

"I have AIDS, Jack!" She spat the words at me like they were bullets. The alcohol on her breath wafted toward me and watered my eyes. "It's not getting better, it's running me down, and I can't deal with the pressure of this place on top of it. Not anymore."

I was astounded. "It's already progressed that far?"

She folded her arms and avoided my eyes. "Not yet. But it will, you know that."

"But what about the meds?"

"They make me so sick—I feel better when I'm off them and dying than when I'm on them and putting off the inevitable."

I didn't know what else to say, and it was obvious that she didn't want to talk. I backed away a step, and she turned, opened the car door, and practically fell into the seat.

"Are you sure you're all right driving home, Dianne? I can drive you, or get you a cab or something."

She avoided my eyes as she started the engine. "I'm *fine*, Jack. Good night." She slammed the door and threw the Mustang into gear. She worked it out of its spot between two other cars on Carl's giant circle drive, and I watched as she sped around to the street where she turned left without stopping or seeing the Land Rover speeding straight toward her.

The only car crash I'd ever seen had been on a sound stage during the shooting of *DC,* and it had been entirely choreographed. This was so fast and loud and unexpected that for a second I was rooted to the ground by the sheer power and noise of the thing. But then my adrenaline kicked in, and I screamed for someone to call 911 as I ran to the cars, now smashed together like some mutated machine. The Mustang had been pushed up onto the parkway and against a tree planted at the edge of the curb. I heard shouts behind me as people poured out of Carl's house, then his neighbors', and I nearly went sprawling as my body tried to move faster than my feet toward the mess. Glass crunched under my shoes as I approached the wreck, and I shouted hoarsely for Dianne.

The Land Rover's front end was crushed accordion-fashion to half its length and melded to her door. I climbed over the Land Rover's hood and knelt beside her—I didn't feel the bits of glass embedding themselves into my knees through my jeans—and gently touched her cheek, slick with blood pouring from a gash in her head.

I pulled at my shirt, popping buttons, and yanked it from my back, then wadded it up and gingerly laid it against the wound with one hand and applied pressure from the other side to keep her head from moving. Blood soaked through the shirt, and before someone could give me something else to use like I was yelling for them to, the sound of sirens was heard and growing louder down the street. Their lights came into view before the rigs themselves; it looked like a carnival reflecting off the drooping fronds of the palm trees that lined the street. Suddenly someone was pulling me off the Land Rover, and I heard myself say to the medics, "She's got HIV." In my head I begged her to forgive me for spilling her secret.

Someone dragged me back to the curb and gently pushed me down to the grass. I stared at the firefighters and paramedics working as someone inspected my knees. It took me a minute to realize he was talking to me. "We should take you in and have someone check you out. Got a lot of glass in there, looks like." I nodded mutely and turned my attention back to the wreck. The uninjured driver of the other car stood on the opposite side of the street staring wide-eyed at the mash of cars. The paramedics around Dianne's car were talking rapidly to each other in the foreign language of medispeak; I stared in fascination as bags of liquid were passed from one to the other and tubes snaked through the window. The medic that had inspected my knees stood and faced the crowd gathered behind me and asked them to disperse.

I remained where I was, fully intending to watch everything until she was safely in the rig. Instead, Carl came up and knelt beside me. "Why don't I take you to the hospital so they can check out your knees, okay, Jack?"

"No, I need to stay and—"

"You don't want to see her like that, Jack. Let's go now; we can be there when they bring her in."

There was a hint of that tone of voice you use when reasoning with a child, but I knew he was just trying to help. And I knew he was right. Someone handed me a towel to wipe Dianne's blood from my hands. When I tried to stand, pain shot through my knees, and I could barely straighten them to walk. Carl and Todd half carried me to the nearest car in the circle drive, which happened to be mine. I fished the keys from my pocket and handed them to Carl, who helped me inside. A five-point turn rotated the car in the direction of the unblocked side of the driveway, and we were off.

Being in the emergency room was like a twisted form of déjà vu; everything was vaguely familiar from the last time I'd been here with Dianne. Carl did most of the talking for me, since I'd settled into a mild state of shock. They picked glass out of my knees for quite a while, and I sat in a daze, not feeling the doctor's tweezers, and stared out across the nurses' station to the ambulance bay doors, which were barely visible from where I sat. Time seemed to drag, and yet when I looked at my watch, I found that more time had passed than I realized. The ball of adrenaline was replaced with a ball of fear, because I realized the longer Dianne was out there and not in here, the smaller her chances were of surviving.

Finally a gurney burst through the doors, surrounded by three familiar paramedics who were joined by doctors and nurses. They wheeled the gurney into a trauma room—the same room, ironically, she'd been wheeled into before—but the medics, having given all the information they could, stood in the hall and watched the doors close. They stood talking for a moment, and then one of them spotted me. He went to the nurses' station and leaned across the counter, talking to one of the nurses and pointing in my direction. She nodded and looked back at me, then resumed her work.

I wondered how long we'd have to wait for news of her condition. The medics milled around for a few minutes, then disappeared when I wasn't looking. Not much time had passed when people began to appear from the trauma room. One of the doctors spoke to the nurse at the station who had talked with the medic, and she pointed me out to him. Just as he started toward me, a loud group of people poured into the ER—the rest of the cast. They quickly saw Carl and me in the small curtained room and ran over. The doctor walked past the group, his eyes focused on me, and before he even reached me, I knew what he was going to say.

"You are the gentleman that—"

"Just tell me." I cut him off with a voice that sounded nothing like mine.

He took a breath and looked me in the eyes. "We did all we could to revive her, but it didn't work. I'm sorry."

The doctor's face dissolved as tears spilled down my cheeks. I leaned my head back onto the stiff hospital pillow and listened to the muffled cries and gasps from the rest of the group. The doctor who had been extracting glass from my knees slowly disappeared behind the curtain that shielded us from the rest of the waiting room. The cast crowded around my bed, all of us sobbing and hugging in disbelief that Dianne was in that room over there and no longer alive.

I've never cried at anyone else's story, but as Jack speaks, I look away, blinking and trying to distract myself so as not to break down. We sit awkwardly, and I hope Grace won't show up again and see us in this state. When Jack finishes, I hear him take a deep breath and stand. "Want anything else to drink?" he asks.

I shake my head. "Thanks, no, I'm fine." I dab at my eyes with the napkin in my hand, feeling foolish. "Want to break for a bit?"

He looks at his watch. "It's been a long week."

I smile. "Yeah, these projects can be really draining."

"Maybe we should start up again Monday. Grace can start her end of things again for you."

I nod, catching the hint. "Sounds good. Tell Grace I said good-bye." He smiles in a faint, distracted way. "I'll see myself out. Have a good weekend." He nods and returns the sentiment, then disappears up the stairs.

GRACE

IT DIDN'T TAKE me long to discover that a cat is a far cry from a real friend. Regardless of the fact that most of the staff was my parents' ages, I was looking forward to starting my new job and meeting them. Maybe they had cute surfer sons they could introduce me to. That was about the extent of my expectations for how this job would help me—little did I know what it would really mean for my future.

Aida, the previous administrative assistant, met me at 8:30 to show me the ropes. For the first four hours of the day she led me around the office and introduced me to the rest of the office staff, and then explained every facet of the job, from filing and client databases to billing procedures and the computer system. By lunch my mind was swimming with terms and instructions and a ton of little details that I was positive I'd never remember. At this point I was completely convinced Mr. Williams had made a grave mistake in hiring me, and made a mental note to start looking for "Help Wanted" signs on the way home.

Salvation was met at lunch in the form of Jane Upton. A warm and jovial woman, she was the assistant for Mr. Williams Sr. and promised to help me keep my head above water. Better still was her offer to have her daughter, Missy, call me for coffee. Missy was a year older than I and had just finished getting her master's degree out of state. I was so excited at the prospect of getting to meet someone younger than forty that it didn't occur to me how bizarre it might be for this poor girl to be told by her mother that she had to go out with a complete stranger.

This didn't dawn on me until later that evening. Suddenly I felt terribly embarrassed, like I was back in elementary school, the new girl in town, being asked to come over to play by girls whose mothers had forced them to ask. I hoped Jane would forget, then hoped she wouldn't, and then the phone rang and Missy was asking if I'd like to meet her for coffee after work tomorrow. She sounded friendly, not at all like a woman being coerced, so I accepted.

We met at a coffeehouse down the street from the firm. A tall blonde with a deep tan (a description that fit most of the women I'd seen in California) sat waiting on a couch inside the café, whom I guessed correctly to be Missy. She treated me to a mocha, and all fears of uneasy conversation were put to rest when, after only a few minutes, our similarities bridged the gap of unfamiliarity. Before either of us knew it, nearly two hours had passed.

"Oh Missy, I'm so sorry; I had no idea how late it was!" I said when I realized the time. "I hope you're not missing dinner or anything."

She laughed. "Our family meals are usually of the fend-for-yourself variety. You're not missing anything important, I hope."

I rolled my eyes. "I have no plans, ever. That's why you're here, remember?"

She looked sympathetic. "I thought Mom was just exaggerating when she said you didn't know anyone."

I shook my head and shrugged. "Well, yeah, I guess that was a bit of an exaggeration. After all, I know your mom, and Aida, and both Mr. Williamses. Think any of them would be up for dancing Saturday night?"

Missy giggled. "Oh my, the thought of my mom dancing is a bit much for me." She sobered quickly as she poked the straw around her plastic mocha cup. "It's weird, though. I hadn't really thought of it, but it's not that easy to meet people, is it? It's one thing to be in college and join student groups, but it's not like there's a big 'join up' festival every fall in the real world, laying out all your options." She finished off her second mocha and tossed the empty plastic cup in the trash bin behind her. "Do you go to church ever? That might be a good place to meet people."

I nearly laughed, except I figured that perhaps she thought that was a good idea because *she* went to church, and I didn't want to offend her. "No, actually, I don't. My parents weren't into that when I was growing up, and I never really saw the need."

"I go to one in Laguna Viejo; there's a Sunday night service with lots of people our age. They organize social stuff. Might be a good place to meet people, if nothing else."

I nodded, trying to look like I was considering her offer. "That sounds pretty cool. Maybe if I get desperate I'll check it out." The words were out of my mouth before I could filter them, and I was instantly embarrassed.

Missy didn't seem to have noticed, though. "Well, I guess I ought to go home and get some dinner; two mochas on an empty stomach probably wasn't a real smart idea. But thanks for meeting me for coffee; it was great hanging out with you."

I laughed. "Are you kidding? I'm the one who ought to be kissing your feet in appreciation. Being alone in a new state has been almost more than I can take."

We headed out in the evening chill toward our cars. The palm trees in the parking lot were strung with Christmas lights, and I laughed out loud when I saw them.

Missy looked around, unaware of what I found so amusing. "What?"

"The trees! Christmas lights on palm trees—that's hysterical. It looks so...not right."

"Really?" Missy studied them with a critical eye. "I think they look cool."

I chuckled as I unlocked my car. "It just looks weird without any snow to go with it. Well, and the fact that it's *palm trees.*"

She grinned. "Will you be going back home for Christmas to visit your parents or anything? Maybe see some snow-covered trees?"

I blinked. It dawned on me that Christmas was only two weeks away. My face must have betrayed my shock, because Missy was instantly apologetic. "Ooh, was that a touchy subject or something? I'm sorry if I—"

"No, no, it's not that at all, it's just that—wow, Christmas is really, really soon, isn't it? I'd totally forgotten. I'm used to snow and cold telling me to start my Christmas shopping, and that never happened, so I just… Um, no, to answer your original question, I have no plans at all for Christmas. I don't really see my family anymore, and I've always just spent it with my other displaced friends. Do people even get Christmas trees out here, or do they just decorate their cacti and oleander bushes?"

Missy laughed. "No, people buy real Christmas trees. They sell them in parking lots and stuff."

"Oh…you know, now that you mention it, I guess I have seen them around. I don't know why that didn't remind me. I think I've just been so absorbed with the move and getting settled and everything."

Missy nodded as she opened the door to her car. "Yeah, moving can do that to you. Well, hey, you have my number, and I have yours; let's get together again soon, okay?"

I felt a buzz at the thought of finally having a friend—either that, or else the caffeine was finally kicking in. "I'd love to, Missy. And thanks again for the mocha."

We waved and got into our cars. I maneuvered out of the parking lot and onto the main street, and managed to find my way home without getting lost, noticing for the first time all the Christmas tree lots. But as soon as I entered the apartment tears welled up in my eyes. *Christmas.* I'd forgotten Christmas. But even worse, I had no one to spend it with.

I flopped on the couch and disregarded the grumbling in my stomach. I was suddenly depressed. I'd been doing pretty well for a while, but this was a reminder that I was alone and unconnected, and while that was never fun, it was a million times worse at Christmas.

Joker jumped onto my lap and mewed before sidling off to settle on the couch. At least I had a warm body with me for the holidays, even if it couldn't help decorate a tree or go Christmas caroling. Maybe she'd enjoy a bit of eggnog.

"Missy had a great time with you, Grace," Jane gushed the next day at work. "I hope you had fun too."

"I did!" I assured her. "We have a lot in common. And it was nice to hang out with someone my own age—no offense."

Jane laughed. "None taken. I think I'd worry if you preferred the company of people your parents' age." She sat down on the edge of my desk and gave me a weird look. "She said you didn't have any plans for Christmas. Is that true?"

I nodded. "Yeah. I wasn't planning on going back to Chicago— need to soak up more sun before I throw myself back into the deep freeze." I tried to sound light and unbothered by the fact that I was spending the most family-centered holiday without any family.

Jane let out a sigh I would later come to recognize as a preamble to an offer one would be stupid to refuse. "Well, I can't bear the thought of you by yourself on Christmas. All our family—my siblings and Simon's—live out of town, so it's usually just the four of us. We would love for you to join us, if you don't want to spend it by yourself."

My heart danced. Christmas with a family! "Oh, Jane, I would love to. But are you sure it's not a big deal? I don't want to disrupt any traditions or anything."

She laughed and waved her hand dismissively. "No, not at all! We usually have a big lunch around one, and then go down to the beach in the evening and build a bonfire to roast marshmallows. In between we just watch movies and snack and down gallons of eggnog. Hardly sacred traditions, believe me. We'd love to have you."

I leaned back in my chair and marveled at her generosity. "Thank you so much for the invitation, Jane. What can I bring?"

"Oh, just yourself, there's no need to bring anything."

"Are you sure?"

"Absolutely."

I sighed. "Sounds great. Thanks again, Jane. I really appreciate it."

"No problem. I'm glad you'll be joining us."

Jane wasn't the only one looking out for the new girl. The other women in the office had taken to me as well. They saw me as a little lost lamb, a motherless child who needed someone to keep an eye on her and make sure she was all right. They weren't pushy or overbearing; in fact, they were quite subtle in their surrogate parenting. Casual questions about how I was settling in were always followed up with, "Well, if there's anything I can do…"

There were, of course, the offers of blind dates and invitations to Christmas parties and weekend barbecues where single nephews or sons would also happen to attend. It seemed as though they all knew someone I'd just love to meet, and suddenly my social calendar really was full—not that any of these eligible bachelors ever ended up being someone I was interested in or who was interested in me.

All these social engagements ate up the days before Christmas, and before I had time to even consider shelling out thirty dollars for a tree, it was Christmas Eve. I spent the afternoon at the mall, strolling peacefully among the throngs of harried shoppers and looking for a nice gift to bring to Jane's family as a thank-you. I found the perfect thing in a candle store: a silver pillar with a red ornament-shaped candle. Half off, too, so I splurged for gift wrapping.

When I got home my answering machine beeped at me. At first

I didn't know what the noise was. I had never missed a call before, because so few people knew my number, much less had a reason to call me. Jane's bubbly voice greeted me when I hit the button.

"Hi, Grace! It's Jane Upton here. Listen, I completely forgot to invite you to the Christmas Eve service at our church tonight. It's at 8:00, we'll all be going, and we'd love to have you join us. It's not fancy or anything, you don't have to dress up, and it's only an hour, so it won't drag on forever." She chuckled, as if to indicate that she was completely aware that most people expected a Christmas service to drag on forever. "Anyway, if you'd like to come, we could pick you up, or you can meet us there. Give me a call and let me know if you're interested, and I can give you directions to the church, or you can give me directions to your place and—whatever, I'm babbling, I always do that on machines. Sorry. We'll be leaving here around 7:40 or so. Talk to you later. Bye!"

I groaned and flopped onto the couch. I'd never gone to a Christmas Eve church thing before. I was inclined to forget it, but on the other hand I felt like I ought to humor Jane and her family as a way of showing my appreciation for their hospitality. Then again, it might actually be enjoyable to sing some Christmas carols and be around people who really love the holiday.

But I had to admit, the whole idea of church made me nervous. I didn't have anything against religious people, no matter what they believed—except for the pushy ones; I didn't care for them much. But all the gods, all the rules, all the heavens and hells and in-between places, all the ideas—they all conflicted, they never made sense. How could you know if you were right or not? It seemed like one big gamble, and regardless of where you put your money, chances are you were going to lose. If it helped you be a better person, then I figured it was okay; I just didn't think I needed it to be good. I had enough self-discipline.

I waffled, weighing the pros and cons, and then decided, finally, to go—but only because I didn't want to ruin my chances of becoming friends with Missy. I called Jane and got directions, and she described a place for us to meet. I had a pretty good idea where the church was, but I wanted to leave myself plenty of time to get lost. I arrived ten minutes early, and after finding a parking spot and wandering a bit, I found the place where Jane had told me to meet them. I stood and watched people coming in, humming along with the Christmas music that was floating out of the building. Not long after, I spotted Jane and Missy, along with Mr. Upton and Missy's younger brother.

"Merry Christmas, Grace!" Jane said, throwing her arm around my shoulder in a friendly hug. "This is my husband, Simon, and our son, David." We all shook hands and exchanged hellos before Mr. Upton ushered us into the building. Missy and I walked down together behind the rest of the family and followed them into a row of chairs.

Once we sat down, I allowed myself a good look at the room. It was packed with people: old, young, children, families—there must have been six or seven hundred people there. There were tons of Christmas lights, strung along the walls and hanging from the ceiling. The stage at the front was cluttered with risers for the choir, music stands and chairs for a band, and a large wooden podium in the center with a microphone sticking up from its top. I had only been in a couple of churches in my lifetime, but I'd never been in one with a stage like that. Nor had I been in one without pews; we were sitting in upscale folding chairs with seats upholstered in a dark cranberry.

"So what do you think?" Missy asked with a grin.

"Definitely not what I envisioned, that's for sure. I didn't know churches had stages."

She chuckled. "Well, this church tries not to be super-churchy. It's not very traditional. Not that tradition is bad or anything; it's just not for everyone."

I nodded. "Well, for someone who doesn't know anything about the traditions, it's a relief."

She nodded to the program in my hand. "See anything you like?"

Upon entering the sanctuary we had been given a program listing the order of the service on the front. The rest of the pages—five of them—were filled with ads for ministries and events coming up at the church. I began to read them all with some interest. "I didn't know churches did anything outside of Sunday services and weddings and things."

"Oh yeah; this one does, anyway." She pointed to a notice in the corner. "That's the service I usually go to, the one with all the people our age I was telling you about."

I nodded and read it, then moved on to the rest of the ads. I was only able to read the first couple of pages before the lights dimmed and the stage began to fill with singers and musicians.

We sang five Christmas carols along with the choir, and when we sat down after the last song I decided that those fifteen minutes had been worth my coming here. It had felt wonderful to sing those familiar songs and revel in the Christmas spirit.

A middle-aged man walked from the back of the stage to the podium and began speaking; the program indicated he was the senior pastor and that he was delivering a message titled, "All I Want for Christmas." I wasn't that interested in listening to his sermon, but I didn't think it would be polite of me to go back to reading the program, so I forced myself to pay attention—or at least make it look like I was. I spent a lot of time scanning the crowd as far as I could see to the left and right of us without making it too obvious that I was looking around.

I saw some handsome men in the crowd, and the women next to some looked far too old to be their girlfriends. Maybe I'd meet a nice religious boy. I tried not to giggle at the thought. I'd never dated anyone religious before; that would be a heck of a change after Dylan.

I'd started a mental tally of all the ways a relationship with a religious person would be different when the pastor said something that caught my attention. "Christmas is a celebration of the beginning of the end." I perked up. I'd never heard it described that way before. It sounded a lot more sinister than "Christmas is love"—or peace, or goodwill, or any of the other ways I'd heard it described. "It is a celebration of the beginning of a life that would be cut down in its prime, silenced at its most glorious point—at what we now call Good Friday. Christmas is the beginning of Jesus's life here on earth, of thirty-three years of living among His creation, and teaching them what it meant to really live. But there was always a shadow over that life. Jesus always knew that the other half of the story would catch up with Him."

Whoa there! What was he talking about? This was going a bit beyond the feel-good Christmas story I'd been expecting: Mary and the baby and no room at the inn—I'd gathered that much over the past twenty years of caroling and watching *A Charlie Brown Christmas* on TV. I wasn't sure what all this talk about the other half of the story was, but it didn't sound very joyful to me, which was what I'd been expecting. I tried not to listen to the rest of his sermon, and instead cast my eyes as low as they would go to try to read more of the program in my lap, but the pastor's words still got into my head.

"So as you celebrate this year, and you think about what Christmas means, ask yourself this question: which part of Jesus's life do you live for? Do you live for its beginning: the perfect baby, the gifts from kings and the Wise Men? Or do you live for its end: the grown man, hung on a wooden cross like a criminal, so that His gift might be given to you? That gift is being held out to you now; it's held out to you every day of your life. The question is, Will you accept it? You'll get gifts tomorrow that will someday break, be lost, shrink, whatever—but God is handing you a gift right now that will always be perfect: it's the gift of a life with Him. All you have to do is accept it."

He stepped away, a soloist came forward, and the band began to play a song. I was totally oblivious to the words being sung, because the words of the pastor were ringing in my head. I was confused by what he'd said, and I was kicking myself for not having paid attention from the beginning. What was this business about what part of the story you lived for? And what was the deal with Good Friday? I'd seen it on calendars before, but I didn't know what it was. Was this preacher guy saying it had to do with death? Didn't sound very good to me. And this gift thing totally boggled me. I didn't know what to think.

The woman finished her song, and the pastor returned to the podium. He asked the congregation to stand and bow their heads for prayer. I bowed along with everyone else and listened to the prayer he prayed. He said that if anyone wanted to accept the gift God was offering, all they had to do was pray along with him, and then he began to speak about sinning and reconciliation and forgiveness. I was still confused. This was a weird Christmas service. I decided I'd have to ask Missy about it sometime.

The prayer ended, and the pastor bade everyone a merry Christmas. The lights came up, and people began milling around, visiting, and talking.

"So what did you think? Was it strange to you or anything?" asked Missy.

"Not weird, no," I lied. I couldn't help hesitating. "Well…all right, a little weird, but I'm just not used to church at all. I don't really have much to compare it to. But it was okay." I smiled.

"I'm glad it didn't scare you away for life." She grinned and was about to say something when two other women our age rushed up the aisle toward Missy.

"Hey, you guys!" She hugged them both, and then made the introductions. "This is Grace, she works with my mom at the firm. Grace, this is Joy and Taylor."

Joy smiled. "It's great to meet you, Grace. Is this the first time you've ever been to the church?"

"Yes it is; I just moved here at the beginning of the month."

"You've got to come with Missy to Sunday night sometime," Taylor said. "It's so fun. Much more"—she wrinkled her nose as she thought—"engaging than this. But tonight wasn't bad."

Missy snickered and said to me, "We're all a bit biased toward Sunday night; don't mind us."

"I've gotta get back to the family; just wanted to say hi," Taylor said. "It was good meeting you, Grace. I hope we see you again sometime."

"Same here," Joy said. "Have a great Christmas, you guys!"

"You, too!" Missy said, giving them both another hug. Both girls leaned over the chairs and gave me a quick hug as well before heading back to their families. "They're so much fun," Missy said after they'd gone. "The three of us hang out a lot. We do a Bible study together once a week and sit together at the Sunday night service. There are some other girls in the study too, but Joy and Taylor and I are pretty tight. You ought to come out with us sometime; I think we'd all have a blast."

"That would be great; they seemed really nice." I refrained from throwing my arms around her and begging her to make plans right now for the four of us to get together. The idea of having girlfriends again was almost too wonderful to imagine.

Jane leaned in between us. "Dessert, ladies? Dad and David have a hankering for pie."

"Absolutely," Missy agreed.

"How about it, Grace?"

"Are you sure? I don't want to impose."

"No, no, nonsense; we'd love for you to come."

I grinned. "I'd love to then, thanks."

"Great! Why don't you just hop in the car with us, and afterward we'll drop you back here at your car." I agreed, and we headed out to their SUV near the back of the lot. On the way we listened to Christmas carols on the radio; a local station was playing them nonstop until New Year's. David had us in stitches until we got to the restaurant; he kept changing the lyrics on the spot. Once at the restaurant, we each indulged in two half-slices and the conversation never stopped. I never felt out of place with them; they were the very definition of welcoming.

That night, with Joker curled up on the pillow above my head, my thoughts wandered from the Uptons to the pastor and his sermon. Part of me was curious. But the rest of me was ambivalent, and not entirely sure why it was a big deal. I fell asleep wondering what the rest of the story was.

I arrived at the Uptons' house at one the next day, bearing my candle gift and nothing else. I'd contemplated bringing a bottle of wine, but I didn't have the money to buy something really good, and I didn't want to give them something lousy. Plus I knew drinking was a touchy thing with religious people, and I didn't want to offend them.

Jane greeted me with another hug and directed me into the family room at the back of the house. There was a huge tree there, decorated with multicolored lights and tons of ornaments, with gifts piled beneath it. I added mine to the pile and moved to the couch where Missy was sitting. I could see Mr. Upton—Simon—and David in the backyard, fussing over the barbecue grill.

"Well, I'm sorry," I said, "but it definitely does *not* feel like Christmas to me. No snow, no windchill factor, no need for a fire in the fireplace…"

"Ah yes, but after dinner we can go to the beach, or go for a walk, or open our presents out on the patio if we want to."

I made a face, mentally weighing the two options. "I don't know…

I guess it's up to you all to convince me that this is acceptable Christmas activity."

Jane brought over a glass of eggnog for me. "Dinner should be ready in a few minutes; the grill wasn't cooperating."

I gaped. "You *barbecue* at Christmas? This is insane!"

Jane laughed. "Not quite as popular back home?"

"Well, seeing as you'd have to dig your grill out of a snowdrift…"

"Ah, good point." She chuckled. "It's a different world out here, that's for sure."

Missy took me on the grand tour of their gorgeous home, and we ended outside on the spacious patio. "It's so warm out here that I keep thinking we're celebrating Memorial Day and not Christmas. We could eat out here; it's so nice."

Missy snickered. "I think we will, actually."

Jane, as if on cue, burst through the door carrying a tray of food. "Missy, can you help me bring things out?" she asked as she laid the tray on the side bar next to the grill. "Oh nuts, I forgot to set the table out here."

"Oh, let me, Jane. I have to do something to earn my meal."

She grinned. "Oh, all right—but only because neither of the boys would have any clue what goes where." I followed her inside to collect the goods, and then set the table as Missy and Jane went back and forth from yard to kitchen, bringing more and more food every time. I didn't know how we'd eat it all.

We all fended for ourselves at the buffet on the side bar, then settled at the table. Simon prayed, including me among the things to be thankful for that day, which made me blush. After "Amen," everyone began eating at once, exclaiming through mouthfuls of food how delicious it all was. And it was! I hated to admit it, but our family had never had a meal this good at any holiday. I felt a twinge of disloyalty to my mother, who had never been much of a cook or hostess.

When we finally stuffed ourselves to the point of bursting, everyone waddled back into the family room to flop onto the couch, recliner, or floor, and moan about never eating again. I was again grateful that I hadn't been stuck home alone for the day.

After a while we managed to right ourselves, and the gift-giving began. I sat back against the couch watching everyone scramble to and from the tree. Mixed among the gifts were two marked "To Grace, From Santa." Missy handed me one after everyone else had opened something.

"Oh, you really, *really* shouldn't have given me anything," I insisted. "Just having me here was enough of a gift, really."

"Well, Santa didn't seem to think so," Jane explained, eyes twinkling with false innocence.

The first gift was practical, and I appreciated it: a spiral-bound *Thomas Guide* map for both Orange and Los Angeles Counties. Simon grinned. "You'll never have to wrestle with a folding map again!"

The second was a coupon book for different restaurants and attractions in the area, another useful gift. I was touched by their thoughtfulness.

"Thank you, you guys; that was so sweet of you. I love them!" I reached over to the tree and picked up my gift to them, then handed it to Jane. "Not nearly as useful as your gifts to me, but just something to show my appreciation."

Jane opened the box and withdrew the candle pillar and ornament candle. "Oh, it's beautiful! And it matches the family room too!" She set it up on the mantel, where it did indeed match her decor. I gave myself a pat on the back for a gift well chosen.

"Time for movies!" David chimed in a singsong voice. "Grace gets first choice, since she's the guest."

"Enough with the guest stuff, already!" I looked at the titles stacked in a small tower: *It's a Wonderful Life, A Muppet's Christmas*

Carol, The Matrix, and *Miracle on 34th Street.* I looked to Missy, confused. "*The Matrix* is in with the Christmas movies?"

She smirked. "That one's David's fault. He claims it's a different take on the Christmas story." I looked to him and he shrugged, flashing a wicked smile.

"Well, while I do love *The Matrix,* I think *It's a Wonderful Life* is a bit more my speed for the holidays." Everyone agreed, even David, and we all settled down with glasses of eggnog and a plate of Christmas cookies to watch the movie.

After it was over Simon suggested a ride to the beach to roast marshmallows around a bonfire. Jane grabbed a bag of marshmallows and five skewers, and David and Simon lugged some firewood and kindling into the trunk of the car. Missy gathered everyone's coats on her arm and found an extra for me, since the sun was down and the wind was picking up. We all piled in and took off for the beach, singing along with the Christmas carols on the radio.

The beach was dotted with families, but the crash of the surf breaking onto the sand drowned out all other noise. We found a fire pit, and the boys set up camp as I wandered to the edge of the water. I'd never been to the Pacific Ocean before, and I told Missy as much as we stood staring out into the rolling blackness.

"You're kidding! Never?"

"Nope. Been to the Atlantic once, but never here. I'd never been to California before I moved out, and I didn't really know where the beaches were, so I didn't bother to come down."

"Wow. Well, welcome to the Pacific." We chuckled, pulling our coats tighter around us as the wind whipped off the water and into our faces. Jane called out that the fire was ready, and we ran back to its warmth, huddling around it and warming our hands, then roasting marshmallows to varying shades of brown. David provided the flaming marshmallow Olympic torch and jogged in slow motion around the beach. None of us ate much, having gorged ourselves on a huge lunch and far too many Christmas cookies, but the experience of being on the beach on Christmas was enough for me.

After a while the wind started to really bite, and we decided to go home. Simon and David doused the fire, then we all ran back to the SUV. Once we reached the house I gathered my gifts and made for home.

"Thanks again, Jane."

"It was fun having you, Grace, I'm glad you came."

Missy gave me a hug and asked if I wanted to get together sometime during the week, to which I of course agreed.

"Merry Christmas, you guys!" I called as I headed out to my car.

"Merry Christmas, Grace!" they chorused back.

I drove home listening to the same radio station and singing at the top of my lungs. In a way I was glad the day was over; I'd been stressing about it the past two weeks, and I was glad I didn't have to think about it anymore. But on the other hand, I'd had a great time, and I didn't want the day to end.

I brought my gifts into the house and was greeted by a mewing Joker, who shut up as soon as I fed her. Suddenly exhausted, I pulled on my pajamas and crawled into bed. Once there, my mind went back to the questions I'd pondered the night before, and for the second night in a row I fell asleep wondering what the whole deal was, and kicking myself for not asking Missy when I'd had the obvious chance.

JACK

MOVIES AND TELEVISION shows are great, because they almost always spare you the awkward and fumbling times after crises occur and people are left to pick up the pieces. "Six months later" fades in and out on a black screen, and we're dropped back into the lives of the characters *after* they've spent morning after morning lying in bed, trying to find the energy to get up, and day after day unsuccessfully trying to avoid anything that will throw them back into their grief. I wanted desperately for reality to fade to black for just a minute, for crisp white words to appear and disappear, and for reality to come back into focus a couple months down the line, or even better, a whole year later.

Honestly, I would have settled for a week, just seven days of pain and grief and depression and guilt I could skip and not have to deal with. But even this Bermuda Triangle has its limitations, and one of them is that time insists on marching along and carrying you with it every excruciating step of the way.

Dianne's death marked a turning point in both my life and my career. I became an advocate of AIDS research and safe sex, doing commercials, giving money, and attending charity dinners and other events. Truth be told, I only dove into this stuff in an attempt to assuage my guilt. Everyone told me over and over I wasn't to blame, and I wanted to believe them. But I couldn't.

I worked harder and longer hours than I ever had before, because going back to my apartment meant going back to Dianne's ghost, hovering around the edges of the place like a premigraine aura. I took guest appearances on other television shows, accepted nearly every movie bit part I was offered, and lifted my ban on interviews to bring more attention to the causes I was supporting.

When there was nothing else for me to do, I worked out at the gym, channeling all my frustration and anger and depression into free weights and running and rowing machines, or hung out at Todd's place with whoever else happened to be there. Todd was a confirmed bachelor whose loft was always Party Central. He could drink for an entire evening and still perform on the set the next day. "Practice, my friend," he once told me when I'd asked how he did it. "It took a lot of practice to get to the point where I could work through my hangover. But it's worth it!" Odd logic, but I wasn't about to argue since it gave me an escape when nothing else would. I started down the accursed road for the second time, but this time I didn't bother talking myself out of it or pulling myself back. I'd gone through hell, and I felt I deserved a bit of a distraction.

It worked for a while. We were halfway through the next season of *DC,* and things were going well: ratings were up, Emmys and Golden Globes were won by various cast and crew, including myself, and the tabloids and magazines were finally leaving me alone. But then my well-oiled machine began to break down. It started with what would have been Dianne's and my anniversary. I woke up that morning, and it slapped me in the face, but I managed to push it to the edge of my subconscious until the end of the day. I went to the gym and worked out for a while, nearly busting the rowing machine with my ferocity, and then headed straight for Todd's. That was one of the great things about Todd: he was always home. He didn't have to go anywhere; all the fun came right to his door and asked to come in.

"Jack, my man!" Hearty handshake, slap on the back, big grin. Todd was in a perpetually good mood, fueled by alcohol and the occasional hit of pot and, of course, the absence of any serious relationships to bring him down. "No woman, no cry," was his anthem.

"Whatcha up to today?" I followed him to the bar, where he hopped the counter and fixed my usual.

I donned my acting hat and mirrored his joviality. "Not much, that's why I'm here, looking for something to do. You?"

He shrugged and poured himself a drink. "Reading scripts and watching the game." He nodded to the pool table. "Play a game?"

"You mean whip your sorry butt? Sure thing, bring it on." We laughed as he racked up the balls, talking trash and chalking up the cues. I felt the strain of my buried emotions threatening to push themselves past the facade I had constructed, so before they had the chance, I downed my drink and slipped behind the bar to get another.

"Your shot," Todd called as he hopped onto a barstool and waited. I chugged on a bottle of beer on my way back to the table, talking myself into enjoying the evening and out of cracking at the seams.

I managed to last for about half a game before I started hitting the cue ball so hard it was bouncing off the table, and after a while Todd finally asked what was going on. I covered it up with some macho comments about trying to distract him so he'd lose his lead, but then a ball bounced straight off the felt and into his drink which sat on the table. Todd cursed. "What's wrong with you, Jack?" He swiped a towel off the bar and carefully mopped up vodka and glass.

I leaned against the wall. My hands were trembling. "Our anniversary would have been today. Two years." I finished off my beer, nearly spilling it with my shaking hand. I stared at the ceiling but could feel Todd's eyes. I heard him swear softly under his breath as he stood and carried the towel back to the bar. He pulled two more bottles out of the fridge, brought them back to the pool table, and thrust one into my hand—his cure for everything—then motioned for me to follow him back to the television. He loaded a Playstation game and handed me a controller before falling into one of the two leather recliners positioned in front of the huge flat screen.

We played in silence for a while, the roar of the cars and music in the game filling the room. Loosened up by the alcohol, I started to ramble about what I'd been going through. He listened and kept the beers coming, and at some point after midnight, I passed out on his couch. He woke me in time for us to get to rehearsal, which I stumbled through under the disapproving gaze of Carl and the cast. Carl took me aside at the end of the day and asked what was going on, and I apologized, explaining what had happened and asking for his patience and forgiveness, which he gave with one condition: that I get myself pulled back together, and that I never show up to rehearsal like that again. I promised.

My promise held for a few months, but then things began to fall apart. I began drinking heavily again, this time at home, wallowing in my depression and allowing memories of Dianne to haunt me. I started smoking pot on a regular basis, craving an escape from the ache that enveloped me, or at least something that would dull it. I managed to put on a sober face for Carl and get through rehearsals, but then I developed a crazy phobia that Carl would see through it and I'd lose my job. This triggered panic attacks, and after my third one on the set, Carl ordered me to see a doctor, who supplied me with little pink pills that would calm me down. The warning on the bottle clearly stated No Alcohol, but rather than letting that deter me from drinking, I merely waited the allotted time for them to get out of my system before drinking my six-pack at night.

This arrangement worked for a while, until we reached the anniversary of Dianne's death. Our annual end of the year party was a week earlier than the actual date, but still it loomed before me like the Grim Reaper himself, daring me to pass him without paying an emotional toll. I decided to pay ahead of time. The night of the party I prepped myself at home with a couple of my chill-out pills before taking off for Carl's. Once there, I drank surreptitiously so no one would see how much I was downing.

When I woke up the next morning I was still at Carl's, fully dressed and sprawled atop one of the guest beds with a sharp pain in my side. My head swam and I lay on the bed for an hour after waking up, trying to think past the layer of clouds enveloping my brain to what had happened the night before, trying to figure out what I was going to say to Carl when I saw him. When I finally gathered the strength to get up, I shuffled to the bathroom, where my reflection shocked me.

My face was bruised and a nasty abrasion reddened my right cheek. My lip was swollen and bloody, and I found bruises on my arms and chest. I sat in the bathroom for a long time, feeling terrified and wishing I knew where my meds were. Finally I gathered the courage to find Carl and ask what had happened.

He was in the kitchen reading the paper when I walked in. He cast one glance at me, silently stood to pull out a chair for me, and got me a glass of water and a couple painkillers. I took the pills and drank the entire glass of water, realizing how parched I was. Carl filled it again, and again I drained it. He sat down next to me, then leaned back and waited for me to make the first move.

"I don't remember anything," I admitted. I couldn't look him in the eyes. "All I remember is watching the show and…laughing about something…" I thought for another minute, then shrugged. "That's it."

Carl nodded and thought for a minute. "We watched the show. We did the toast. Debra and Todd presented the gag awards, people sat around, played pool, talked. You and Todd were playing pool with Derrick and Debra, during which you reportedly drank about four Long Islands, and then Derrick mentioned Dianne, and you blew a gasket." He paused a moment, letting the words sink in. "You ranted at Derrick, jumped him; he pushed you off, and you hit the edge of the pool table. You tried to fight him, he refused to comply, so you took off and fell down the front steps. We were going to take you to the ER, but you woke up a bit, so we decided to spare you and the show the bad publicity and let you sleep it off here."

As Carl recounted all this, bits and pieces broke into my memory and surfaced as fragments like a dream. Somebody yelling, my side smashing into the edge of the pool table, a plastic jug of pancake syrup—my gag award for "Sweetest Love Scene." I closed my eyes and hung my head, not knowing what to say to apologize.

Carl spoke instead. "This has been a rough year for you, Jack, I'm aware of that. I know you've been drinking, doing pot. You've done a pretty good job hiding it, but I've been in this business for thirty years; I can read my actors like a picture book. You've been pulling it off at work, so I didn't say anything; you cleaned yourself up after the first time and I thought maybe you'd be able to do it again. But this is obviously a lot more insidious than I realized—than maybe even you realized." I slowly nodded, eyes still closed, letting Carl's clear, smooth voice wash over me. "I think you need to take a break, Jack. From *DC*."

It took a second for his words to sink in, but when they finally did, I knew he was right. I didn't want to admit it; I wanted to fight back, but I didn't have the energy, and I knew deep down that I couldn't take another season. I nodded.

Carl leaned across the table and tried to make eye contact. "Listen to me, Jack. You're a good guy with a lot of talent. You don't have to let this ruin you. Get yourself some therapy, check into a clinic if you need to—do whatever you have to do to get through this, because you could go far in this business. But at the rate you're going, you're heading for the same end as a lot of other talented people we don't remember, because they ruined themselves early in the game. See what I'm saying?" I nodded silently. "And if you need money for this stuff, you just let me know. We'll work it out, all right?"

I forced myself to look him in the eye. Carl was a good man, I'd always known that. He was also the closest thing I had to family out here in California, and I didn't want to let him down. "Thank you," was all I could muster, and I hoped he could see in my eyes everything else I wanted to say but couldn't find the words for.

He nodded and stood. "Breakfast?"

My stomach lurched at the thought of food. "Uh, no, but thanks." He grinned slightly, and I grinned back—a lopsided, exhausted, defeated grin. "I'm going home."

"Let me drive you back," he said, reaching for his keys on the counter.

"No, I'll be all right—"

"Look." He stared at me hard and spoke with a firm voice that told me there was no point in arguing. "I'm driving you home, because you're in no shape to drive, and I don't want to lose another actor to another bad decision." I dropped my gaze, nodded, and followed him out to his car.

"So that's why your character was killed off."

Jack nodded. "You watched *Deep Cover*?"

I wasn't about to admit I'd planned my evenings around it. "Yeah, enough to know when people came and went. That was a great episode too. Really touching."

"I don't think I've seen that one," Grace admitted. "I was never a big fan. *ER* was more my speed." She winked at Jack, and he laughed.

I was grateful for her remark, which diffused a bit of the gravity in Jack's storytelling. It was hard to imagine someone as talented and personable as Jack falling into such a destructive trap.

"So then what?" I asked.

I left *DC*, which was painful, but definitely the right thing to do, and started seeing a therapist. As for detox, I counted myself as lucky for having only a few months of bad habits to get over instead of years; as it was, it took more willpower and discipline than I thought I had to kick them, and it was only thanks to Carl's and, surprisingly, Todd's accountability and help that I got clean.

I continued to campaign for AIDS research and safe-sex education, but I cut down on a lot of the publicity work. I didn't exactly become a recluse; I was just tired of being with people and dealing with people and talking to people. I wanted to be alone for a while.

I spent a year like this, seeing my therapist three times a week, reading and working out and doing the occasional Hollywood shindig. I steered clear of all-out parties, because I was afraid the temptation of alcohol and marijuana (or any other drug, for that matter) would either wear me down or throw me into a self-righteous fit about the evils of mixing chemicals with the dysfunctional life of the average actor.

That summer I received a script from Franklin Young, a director I'd worked with before. He offered me my first-ever lead role. I read the script twice in a weekend and loved it. It was a drama, which I didn't usually go for; I fancied myself more an action/thriller kind of guy. But this part was intense, and the writing was incredible. My character, a young, homeless, ex-military guy in New Mexico, saves a kidnapped Navajo woman from her abductors and offers to accompany her back to her reservation in Arizona. In hindsight, the chance to play a hero is most likely what drew me to the part, to make up for not being one in real life.

My confidence was pretty low at the time, so I waited a couple weeks to respond while psyching myself up for the job, and read the script over and over during those weeks to the point where I was already starting to learn my lines. Finally I called Franklin and accepted, and then found out the best part: shooting would be out in the desert, far from Hollywood and Los Angeles and the constant reminders of Dianne.

I was grateful we were shooting in the winter; the desert wasn't much fun in the middle of July. My costar, B. J., was a beautiful Navajo woman who had never done a movie before but was a natural. She was in awe of the whole process, and we spent a lot of time together when we weren't filming, talking about what life was like for a full-time actor. She drew me in with her innocence and simple views of life, and while I wasn't attracted to her in a dating kind of way, I enjoyed being with her and seeing filmmaking through her eyes.

Rehearsals started on the set in December, and we worked until two days before Christmas. B. J. was sitting in my trailer keeping me company while I was packing to leave for the week we had off. "What will you be doing for the holidays?" she asked.

I shrugged. "Don't know, actually. Probably just hang out at my place, relax a bit."

"You won't go home to your family?"

I paused in my packing. I hadn't even thought of that as a possibility. "I hadn't considered it," I finally answered.

"You aren't close with them, then?"

"We're not, like, feuding or anything," I stalled by hunting for the book I'd been reading. "I haven't been home in a long time. Mom always extends the invitation, but the past few years I've stuck around home. My home in LA, I mean. Always just hung out with friends."

"Go home and see your family." She spoke it like a command.

"Why?"

"Because you have a family to go home to. Someday you might not, and you might regret it. Blood is thicker than fame and fortune in Hollywood—or, at least, it should be."

I let her words rattle around in my head as I continued to pack. By this time I had enough clothing to last me three weeks, but I needed an excuse not to look B. J. in the eyes. *Why not go home?*

Because they had no idea what I'd been through, other than what the tabloids and celebrity-watching television shows had reported. I'd stopped going home once I'd gotten onto *DC,* and while I still talked to my parents now and then on the phone, I'd never given them the unabridged version of what had happened with Dianne and me. Plus, I had changed so much, lived such a different life from them—I didn't know if I'd even be able to relate to their small-town lives anymore. But B. J. had a point: I was lucky I had them at all.

I finally stopped packing and looked her in the eyes. "All right then, I'll go home." She laughed. "What's so funny?"

"Maybe you ought to just ship your whole trailer." I looked down; my suitcase was never going to close. Embarrassed, I began removing items and placing them on the bed as B. J. watched on with smug satisfaction.

Reily, Vermont: population 16,264. I hadn't been back here in nine years, but nothing important had changed. The only big difference I could see was that the water tower that loomed at the edge of downtown had been repainted to say Reily, Vermont: Childhood Home of Jack Harrington." Mom sent a picture of it after they'd finished, right after my first nomination for a Golden Globe award. It was embarrassing, but flattering.

I drove my rental car through town, taking in all the long-forgotten sights. It hadn't been a bad place to grow up. I wondered how many of my classmates still lived here, having taken over the family business or started a family of their own. My younger sister, Abby, was one of those who'd married her high school boyfriend after college. He managed his dad's paper mill finances, and she stayed home with the twins.

I'd called Mom from the airport so she wouldn't have a fit when I showed up on the porch. As it was she'd screamed me nearly deaf when I told her where I was. Her sisters and their families were in town too; she could hardly believe her luck that everyone would be together.

Now here I was, thrown back in time, wandering the streets I had once ridden through on my bike. The houses all looked the same: beautiful colonials with picket fences and holiday wreaths on the front doors. Twinkling Christmas trees, probably harvested from the forest just north of here, glowed in each front window. I parked on the street in front of my parents' place and smiled. Looked exactly the same, of course. Nothing here ever changed.

My mother threw the door open before I'd even gotten out of my car. Dad watched, beaming, as she threw herself at me on the walkway, and when we reached the porch he hugged me briefly—very uncharacteristic of him; I'd been expecting a handshake—and ushered me into the house.

It was like every Christmas I could remember. The tree was up in the bay window, with all our childhood ornaments hanging around the winking lights. Stockings hung from the mantel, carols murmured from the stereo in the basement, and a fire crackled in the fireplace. Mom's sisters were there with their families, my cousins all adults now. Abby's two girls were the only out-of-place elements that reminded me this was not a Christmas from twenty years ago. Well, that and the fact that I had a place at the adult table now for dinner.

Christmas Eve dinner was usually ultracasual since the next day's meal would be a feast. We ordered Hank's Pizza—unmatched by anything in LA—and sat around the dining room table talking mostly about me, much to my embarrassment. It was an odd mix of celebrity awe and familiarity; my own mother got stars in her eyes when I talked about the people I worked with.

Later in the evening as we talked and reminisced, Abby tapped on her glass and cleared her throat. "Doug and I were going to wait until tomorrow for this, but I just can't keep a secret when everyone is here right now." A smile split her face as she announced, "We're pregnant!"

Mom let out a squeal and threw her arms around Abby, the twins bounced with excitement, and everyone shouted congratulations. "When are you due?" I asked when things had died down a bit.

"June 7," she said with a grin as Doug planted another kiss on her forehead.

Dianne's birthday. The glass in my hand shook suddenly. "That's great," I choked out. No one noticed my reaction; they were all focused on Abby and Doug. I leaned back into the couch and closed my eyes against the emotions that were called up by that date. I suddenly wanted a drink.

I stood and excused myself, then headed for the front porch. Snow was falling, and the air was still. I felt like I'd been running; my heart was pounding and my breath hard to catch. The sharpness of the air slowed me down, though, and I breathed deeply and stuffed my hands into my pockets, watching the snow fall silently onto the streets where it melted on the cement.

I heard the door open behind me; I didn't have to look to know it was Mom. She slipped her arm around my waist. "Dianne?"

I nodded. "June seventh is her birthday."

She nodded silently, both of us watching the Galverstons decorate their tree in the bay window across the street. "You didn't talk about her much when you two were together. I didn't know how serious it was until after she died; the magazines said more about your relationship than you had." There was only the slightest hint of hurt in her voice; I was instantly guilty.

"Yeah, we were sort of serious, but I knew you wouldn't have approved, us living together and everything. And when she got sick, I didn't know what to do with it, and we couldn't really tell anyone, so secrecy just became the norm."

She shrugged under my arm, which I'd draped over her shoulder. "I know Los Angeles isn't Reily, but don't underestimate us, honey. It's your life to live; you never seemed that worried about my approval before you dashed west to do your thing, so why start now?" We both chuckled, and she gave me a squeeze. "But I understand the secrecy thing. May not like it, but I do understand."

I could feel the bubble of anger and guilt and sorrow making its way out of its hiding place and into my throat. "It was so hard, Mom. Watching her die like that—even before the accident. Watching her just waste away. And then the crash…" I still shuddered at the memory; therapy can only do so much. "I may not have loved her enough to marry her, but I loved her enough to have been better for her, and I wasn't."

"You won't get very far beating yourself up, Son. And it's not forward motion. You're just spinning your wheels."

"I know, but…" I didn't know what else to say. I'd said it all to my therapist, to Todd, to myself, and I was tired of voicing my thousands of fears and worries about being able to take care of anyone, ever. "Now the new baby will have her birthday, and that's one more thing about her I'll never be able to forget."

She chuckled. "Honey, due dates are hardly set in concrete. The twins were a week early; who knows when this one will come. They're not that dependable, trust me. Could be June ninth, could be the fourth, who knows?" She gave me a motherly squeeze. "But even if it is the seventh, you can see it as a new chance to take care of someone. You can be the cool uncle that he or she can always talk to and who always sends the best presents, and after a while the memories of that child's birthdays will replace the memories of Dianne's. Just give it time."

I squeezed her back and took a deep breath, trying to repack all the emotion into the box I stored it in.

She patted my back. "I'm freezing, let's go in."

I nodded and followed her into the warmth of the house. I was relieved that she understood about Dianne, and that she wasn't angry. It was strange to be this old and still worried about how my parents would react to what I did. I wondered how much more of the Hollywood gossip she'd gotten wind of. If she, or anyone else for that matter, knew about my breakdown, no one was saying anything, and I was glad.

Inside the house people were starting to drift and disperse. The kids were downstairs, the women in the kitchen, the men in the living room. Uncle Paul held out a cigar and invited me to join their conversation. I sat down on the arm of the couch and puffed cautiously, listening as they discussed business. They were all in business of one stripe or another, and listening to them talk about financial worries, board troubles, and the need to soothe the company president was like listening to a foreign language. I let myself blend into the background, observing this alien activity, until the conversation veered around to hobbies and pastimes and finally movies, when I felt a part of things again.

After a while the women started reappearing and dropping hints that they were ready to turn in. The kids were summoned from the basement and coats were retrieved from the guest bedroom.

"Will you be here tomorrow?" one of the twins asked. I'd already forgotten which was who.

"Absolutely. Will you be here?" I tickled her and she squirmed and laughed. I couldn't believe these two gorgeous girls came from my little sister. It was trippy.

Mom, Dad, and I stood out on the porch waving our good-byes until we couldn't take the cold anymore. I helped Mom clean up the dishes in the living room and basement, and then grabbed my duffel and froze. "Hey, Mom?"

"Yes?"

"Um…do I still have a room?"

She laughed and hugged me. "Of course! We barely even changed it; all I did was clean."

"Well, that in and of itself would render it completely unrecognizable." I winked.

"Tell me about it!"

It was spooky, like stepping into a time warp. Movie posters for *Terminator* and *Star Wars* were still on the wall; my desk still stood in the corner by the window and sported framed photos of my family and myself with friends from high school. My dresser, my bed— everything waited for me right where I had left it.

Mom came in as I was crawling under the covers. "Man, just like high school. Checking to see if I have my alarm set?"

She chuckled. "No, just coming to say good night." She smiled. "I miss having you around, Jack. It's good having you home." She sat on the bed and tousled my hair. "Seeing you on TV isn't nearly as good. Exciting, but not as fun." She waggled her eyebrows, and we laughed. She leaned over and kissed my forehead. "'Night, kiddo. See you in the morning."

She left and closed the door quietly behind her, and I basked in the warmth of home.

Christmas Day was joyful chaos. We opened gifts late in the morning, and everyone was tremendously gracious toward me considering that I'd brought no gifts whatsoever. In the early afternoon we sat down to a massive dinner. I wore out the phrase, "This is so good," about two minutes into the meal; I couldn't remember the last time I'd had a homecooked dinner. I ate till I thought I'd be ill, but for the first time that feeling wasn't so bad. And when I realized there would be leftovers for later, I was thrilled all over again.

After dinner everyone split up like they had the night before, but this time I headed into the kitchen to help with the dishes. Mom could barely believe it. "Never once did you do the dishes without me issuing threats!" she laughed. I couldn't explain it to her, but I wanted to be with her and my aunts, and especially Abby, whose motherhood and stable life simply awed me. I missed the company of guileless, uncomplicated women; I needed the reminder that they existed.

As I supplied the elbow grease to remove what was baked onto one of the pots, I listened to a conversation that sounded just as foreign as last night's. This was about family, marriage, kids and their grades, discipline issues…things I'd never thought about. I realized I'd never heard women talk to one another about anything besides dating, acting, and sex, and the contrast was astounding. It took me a second to figure out how to classify these unfamiliar topics of conversation: they were normal. Noncompetitive. They were free of the fear of rejection or breech of confidentiality.

I thought back to the conversations between the men the night before: same thing, with a dash of friendly male competition. So this was what it was like to be a regular, nonfamous adult. I couldn't decide if I envied them or pitied them, if I wanted to stay and be absorbed back into the life I'd grown up in, or run far and fast to escape it again. I lost myself in my thoughts, comparing my life against theirs—until laughter called me back.

"What?" I demanded, and then saw the puddle of filmy water on the floor at my feet. "Aw, man."

"When was the last time you did dishes, Son?" The gleam in Mom's eye was unavoidable.

"Each of my meals comes in its own dish, which is conveniently disposable," I hotly retorted. This drew the laughs I had meant it to, and I withstood their jests and teasing as I mopped up the water from the floor. Mom wrapped her arms around me and grinned. "You're not domestic, but I still love you."

"Thanks, Mom; you're swell."

"Just make sure you marry a nice girl who knows how to cook and keep the kitchen clean, and you'll be fine."

I laughed. "I'm surrounded by actresses, Mom, not Donna Reed wannabes."

"Can't actresses cook?"

"Well, yeah, I guess…but why would they if they can afford to hire someone else to do it?"

"Or eat out," my Aunt Claire added.

"Well, yeah," I conceded, "but then you're dealing with the paparazzi, people wanting your autograph, fans auctioning off your uneaten leftovers… Why bother?"

They were wide-eyed. "Wow, is it really like that?" Aunt Maureen asked.

I laughed and winked. "Only sometimes."

"Jack—do they really not cook?" Mother looked concerned. Leave it to her to worry about the domestic skills of the women I kept company with.

"Of course they can cook!" I laughed. "As well as anyone else can who doesn't spend a lot of time doing it. I was kidding, Mom." I kissed the top of her head. "Yes, they cook—not nearly as well as you, but they manage." I winked at her, and she swiped at me with a hand towel.

"So when are you gonna settle down with some nice girl and start a family, eh?" Mom asked. The topic I'd avoided so well was finally here.

"Oh, Mom, I don't know. Family means all sorts of juggling, and I don't think I'm coordinated enough."

"Oh, nonsense; if you love someone enough, you'll get coordinated."

"Yeah, but I'm not looking to leave acting. Actor-actress marriages are nearly impossible to maintain long term, and what normal person wants to be married to an actor and deal with all the crap we have to deal with?"

"Hey, don't underestimate us normal people," Abby quipped. "All it takes is a sense of adventure, don't you think?"

"It's an adventure for a while, but after that it's a burden. Imagine photographers snapping pictures of you and the twins when you pick them up from school, or when you're trying to have a romantic dinner out with Doug. Raising kids in LA isn't easy in the first place; doing it when your face is plastered on billboards and bus stops complicates it even more. And marriage itself—I don't know, I don't think I'm cut out for it. I'm too selfish."

Mom frowned and thwacked me again with the dish towel. "Well, get unselfish. Even if you're not married, it's not healthy to think of yourself as the center of the universe."

"I don't; I just like my life the way it is. I don't want to change it for anyone."

The twins chose that moment to burst in and demand more cookies, and I was grateful for the distraction. I was selfish, but I really didn't want to change anything. Diaper duty and school carpools weren't for me. What Dianne and I had before things went downhill had been perfect: the understanding that we weren't committed for life, that we were in it for the sex and companionship, and that our careers came first. When we'd started falling into the Real Relationship Trap, things had gone haywire.

But there was no denying that Abby and Doug and the twins had something very attractive. Maybe Mom was right; all it would take was the right woman to change my mind.

My brain was still working on this when the night came to an end, and when I boarded the plane on New Year's Eve to go back to LA before returning to the desert to resume shooting on January second. The twins had given me finger paintings as a going-away present, and when I got back to my trailer, I taped them to the wall above my bed. When B. J. asked who they were from, she got a smug look on her face.

"What's that look for?" I demanded.

"Home did you good," she said simply. "I knew it would."

GRACE

AFTER CHRISTMAS, Missy and I started hanging out a lot more. We'd meet once or twice during the week, usually for coffee or dinner at my place. A church friend of hers threw a New Year's Eve party and invited me as well, and it was great fun, albeit nonalcoholic and therefore a much more sober event for me than previous years. But it was still enjoyable, and definitely preferable to sitting at home alone.

The new year saw a gradual expansion of my social circle. Missy and I started hosting a biweekly girls' night at my place; we'd order in pizza and rent movies and sit around talking till the wee hours. I really liked her friends; they were all-around nice people. They all knew each other from church, so that or God in general would occasionally find its way into our conversations, but it wasn't really that bad. Part of me had been curious about the whole thing ever since that Christmas Eve sermon, but I wasn't as interested in it as they seemed to be. Even so, we always had a great time.

My New Year's resolution was to get my California teaching credential, which proved to be no small task and made me wish I'd gone with something easier, like ending world hunger or bringing peace to the Middle East. I did some research and found vague descriptions of the hoops through which I needed to jump, but nothing was clear-cut. For a state that was desperate for teachers, they sure didn't make it easy. But I knew that my time at Williams & Williams was limited, not because of my performance but because of my interest—or lack thereof. Office work was fine for a while, but hardly my dream job. It seemed a pity to have wasted four years of college on a degree I'd never used, and I really did like teaching. I hoped hard I'd be credentialed in time for the spring hiring fairs.

One Friday in late January the girls arrived as usual. Missy brought the pizza, Joy the drinks, and Taylor the movies, one of which was *Evita*.

"Oh!" I squealed. "I've always wanted to see this! The score is fantastic."

"You know the *Evita* stuff?" Missy asked.

"Oh yeah, I saw it in Chicago. I'm a huge musical fan. *Les Miz, Phantom, Chess*...I did musical theatre in high school too, and I always wanted to do *Evita*."

Taylor's eyes glinted. "I think you need to showcase your talents, Miss Winslowe."

"Oh no—"

"Oh, come on, sing something, please?" Joy begged.

I hadn't performed for an audience since senior year, but I grabbed a taper candle and struck a pose before launching into the first verse of a *Les Misérables* tune. It didn't take long to remember how much I'd loved doing this. I finished the verse and chorus and then bowed and replaced the taper amid their hoots and applause.

"You know," Taylor mused, "we're looking for someone to sing with the college band at church." Taylor volunteered with the college ministry and always invited us to come hang out with her little group of freshman girls. "It's a really fun group of people too. They do all worship songs, but those are really easy to learn. You would be great!"

I squirmed in my seat. "I don't go to your church, though."

"That's all right. We'll vouch for your character. Seriously, you should think about it."

"Who else is in it?"

"Let's see...Kate sings lead a lot, Mike leads the band and plays guitar, Dale's on drums, Tom's on bass..."

"Wow, you mean it's a real band?"

They all laughed. "As opposed to a fake band?" Joy asked.

I rolled my eyes. "No, as opposed to a...okay, don't be offended: as opposed to a church band. You know, piano, organ, hymnals."

"Ahhh. Gotcha," said Taylor. "No, no hymnals, no organ. I don't think we even own an organ!" They laughed. "They're a great band, really. Not quite as good as the band that plays Sunday night but still good."

"A regular band plays at the service too?"

"Yep."

Hmm. Curiouser and curiouser. I'd just assumed Christmas had been an exception, a special event with volunteers from the congregation or something. It didn't seem very churchy to have a band. Their church was sounding less and less like a church every time we talked about it. I conceded in my mind that maybe I *should* check the place out, just once, just to see what all the fuss was about. I'd met so many people from it through Missy already anyway, and Joy and Taylor were quickly becoming good friends as well, so maybe it wouldn't be that bad. "What time is the Sunday night service again?"

"Seven."

"Maybe I'll come this week."

"Wow, really? That would be awesome!" Missy said. "Want to meet us there, or want me to pick you up?"

"Um…I'll meet you there." I wanted my car for a fast getaway if I decided it was lame, or worse. There are some weird religions out there these days; a girl can't be too careful.

Sunday night rolled around, and I was standing in front of my closet, trying to figure out what to wear. I'd forgotten to ask Missy what the dress code was. Dress up? Business casual? Jeans and a sweater? It was cold out these days, colder than I thought California knew how to get, but it was still better than dealing with snow. I finally decided on black jeans and a sweater. Comfortable, with the appearance of being more cleaned up. And besides, I could always plead ignorance.

I met the girls at the front entrance where I'd met Missy's family for Christmas Eve. The place was packed, and it was close to starting by the time I arrived, so we went in quickly to find seats together before it got too full.

It was the same room where the Christmas Eve service had been held, but it didn't look anything like it had that night. Obviously all the Christmas stuff was down, but even that wasn't the biggest difference. Art hung on the walls—original pieces, I discovered as we walked past—and the stage was filled with band equipment and a living room setup. The lights were low, and clublike music was playing just loud enough to make you raise your voice when you talked to people. We found seats off the center aisle toward the back and sat down with just enough time to glance through the program before the lights dropped and the band started.

This was definitely not church like I'd expected. The band was incredible; they did a song that had been on the radio for months, and everyone was singing along like it was a concert. A young surfer-looking guy gave the sermon and held my attention far longer than I would have expected when discussing religion. But he didn't just discuss religion, so maybe that's why; he discussed life.

The service ended after an hour. The lights came back up, music came back on, and people started milling around like they had done before the service, this time making plans for the rest of the evening.

"So what did you think?" Missy asked after Joy and Taylor took off to track down a friend of theirs.

I grinned. "To be honest, I was expecting to hate it. But I really enjoyed it. It's…fun. I didn't expect church to be fun."

She laughed and nodded. "Yeah. God shouldn't be boring; I think that's just wrong. 'Course, everyone's idea of boring is different."

"Heh, true. Well, by my standards, this was not boring."

Joy and Taylor returned with some other girls and suggested a trip down the street for dessert. Missy and I carpooled together to the restaurant, talking about the service the whole way there.

This became a weekly tradition, just like our girls' nights. We'd meet at the service, all sit together, and then go out afterward and hang out. Every week I'd meet someone new, the service would be great, and I'd leave wondering why I hadn't heard more of this stuff before. The things Paul (the speaker guy) talked about made sense, which I'd always thought was impossible; religion wasn't about reason, it was about superstition. Or so I thought. At dinner afterward, I'd ask the other girls questions and we'd debate and talk, and usually by the end of the evening I felt a little clearer about another aspect of this God thing.

Joy, Taylor, and Missy were fast becoming the closest friends I'd ever had. Their camaraderie was unlike any I'd experienced with girl-friends in the past. There was a solidness in their commitment to each other, the way they looked out for each other and cared for each other. I felt privileged to have been allowed into their little minicommu-nity—not only *allowed* in, but *invited* in, my presence actually requested. Even my resistance to their beliefs didn't seem to deter them from being with me. I felt safe with them, like anything I told them would be heard with an open mind, and that they wouldn't judge me. I felt *loved*. It was a new experience, one that I found myself clinging to in near-desperation because having it showed me just how much I'd longed for it, and I was almost afraid I'd wake up one day to discover I'd been ousted. I prayed that wouldn't happen.

February and March passed like a high-speed train, and my California credential slowly took shape. A good thing, too; my job with Williams & Williams was far from fulfilling and was starting to get on my nerves. Overall it was a decent job, and I tried to remember that. I still had the energy at the end of the day to wade through school district applications or to try to figure out what exactly I was going to do with this God thing. And as time wore on, that became my biggest question: what *was* I going to do?

I'd been meeting the girls at the Sunday night service for nine weeks when one night all the tumblers seemed to fall into place and a huge door opened up in me. Paul said at the end of his message, "So what it comes down to is this: meaning or no meaning, purpose or pointlessness. Do you want to recognize the fact that there is a reason for being here, for getting up every morning and breathing and working and hanging out with people, or do you want to just shrug your shoulders and say, 'Whatever. Life just happens; you're born, you live, you die, that's it'? But before you answer, realize that there *is* meaning, there *is* purpose. If you don't want to admit it, that's your choice, but choosing that doesn't make it true."

That got to me. I was almost angry at Paul for being so challenging, but as his words sank in I felt the logic of them. There was a truth that I wasn't facing. I was just skirting it, poking at it now and then with some intellectual jousts, but not really engaging myself in grappling with it. I'd heard it every Sunday night, in one form or another, for nine weeks. I'd seen Missy and Taylor and Joy live it in their actions and words, in the way they treated me and each other, and in the indescribable kind of life they seemed to have. The only thing standing between me and what they had was my acceptance of it and my willingness to give myself to it. No, not *it*. *Him*. God.

At the end of the service Paul prayed and invited anyone who wanted to accept this truth to echo his prayer in their own heart and mind. I did a mental inventory of myself to see if there was anything holding me back, and a part of me *really* wanted to find something. But there wasn't. I prayed with him, the first time I'd prayed with a specific recipient of my prayer in mind, and was filled with a heat and wild energy that felt as though it threatened to levitate me above my chair. The service ended, the lights came up, and I looked with amazement to Missy, not knowing what I was going to say. My face must have given me away because she suddenly had tears in her eyes.

"Grace," she laughed, "you're practically glowing!" I nodded and found I couldn't speak, my throat was so tight with tears. She threw her arms around me, and we laughed and cried and grabbed at Taylor and Joy to tell them I finally understood, I finally got it. I believed.

"Uh...believed what?"

Grace smiles. "Believed that Jesus is who He claimed to be. That God exists and loves us and wants us to love Him back. That we need someone else to pay for the wrongs we've done if we want to connect to God. That's what Christianity is."

I laugh. "Along with a whole lotta other crap."

"Like what?"

I roll my eyes. "Oh, please. You know. Like church and proselytizing and being pushy and telling people they're going to hell. That kind of thing."

Jack chuckles, jarring a slumbering Bree who has curled up in his lap. "Two things counts as a whole lot?"

"That's more than two!"

"Well, not really. Proselytizing and being pushy and telling people they're going to hell all pretty much happen at the same time, don't they?"

I am surprised he'll admit they happen at all. "Well, I suppose," I concede. "You're not denying it then?"

"Just clarifying first. Are those the only items that make up that 'whole lotta crap' you mentioned?"

I sigh impatiently. "Does it matter?"

"Not to me, no, but they're your objections. You should just make sure you know what they are for sure, that's all."

How could I have had a crush on this guy? Talk about nosy! "I'm sure there are others, trust me; I just can't think of them under pressure." I smirk. "So what's your defense?"

Jack shifts Bree in his arms. "Why don't you come up with all of them and we'll tackle them all in one blow?"

"Oh come on—"

"No, no, think about it awhile first. We'll devote a whole evening to your objections."

I throw my hands up and slump back in my chair. "Look, we're not here for my conversion. Whatever. Grace, you want to keep going?" I have to work to keep the annoyance out of my tone. The nerve, honestly!

Grace smiles at Jack, a smile I can't decipher, and continues her story.

That night we went out for dessert with all the girls I'd met over the past weeks and hung out with after the services. There was a foreign exhilaration that kept swirling around in me in a way that should have been distracting and out of control, but instead seemed only to focus me more on this belief that seemed to sit in my soul, a core around which my whole being revolved.

From there on out the spring seemed to fly by. I started attending Missy's small group every Monday evening. They were studying the book of James, which I instantly loved, and they were amused by my insatiable appetite for information about God and the Bible, which I'd never read before this. Every other Friday Missy and I still hosted our girls' night, which was expanding to the almost unmanageable size of fourteen but was such fun we couldn't bear to limit it or stop. And on top of it all, I joined the college band, and we rehearsed Sunday afternoons, and the college group met on Wednesday nights; soon nearly every evening was chock-full. I was in heaven.

JACK

SHOOTING WRAPPED at the end of January, and then I was home. It felt weird to be back in my apartment: I still hadn't managed to rid the place of Dianne's memory, and I was beginning to doubt I ever would. After talking to some friends and getting their advice, I finally hired a Realtor, and she set me up with a great flat on the other side of the city. It was huge and beautiful; even my unsophisticated eye could tell this was an impressive place. I moved at the end of March.

Working with Franklin confirmed that film was the direction I wanted to head with my career. Television was fun and steady work, but film was a different kind of fun—and where all the real money was anyway. I was getting a lot of scripts now too, so after moving into my new place I started reading them and talking with directors. I was finally moving up the ranks of Hollywood society. I was one of the lucky few whose dream of a fruitful acting career was actually coming true.

And yet something had been eating at me since Christmas. B.J. said going home had been good for me, and I believed her, but as time wore on, something in my life was feeling more and more wrong. I kept thinking about Abby, the twins, my parents, Reily, my time there with them and how fulfilling it had been. They had a lot of things I didn't have: stability in their lives, true love, family—*normality.* Of course, I had a lot of things they didn't have: over two million sitting in the bank, established directors sending me scripts, an exciting life. There was nothing exciting about living in Reily with 2.5 kids and a minivan.

But there *was* something attractive about being content. And that's what they all were: content. Happy with their jobs, their families, their spouses, their *lives*. Honest about the fact that nothing was perfect, but also perfectly okay with that.

I was not content.

It took me a while to figure this out, but over the course of a few weeks it came to me. I would read scripts, filter out the ones I liked, weigh the salary against the time commitment, and choose what movies to accept. I'd go out with friends for drinks sometimes, do a little pot, then come home and sleep it off. I'd go out to parties, give speeches at benefits, talk to the press. But something was wrong inside.

Once I allowed myself to be honest and stop filtering the ideas and emotions I was experiencing, it became clear: I hated my life. Well, save for the acting; that was the best part. But being an actor isn't like being a janitor or a lawyer or a secretary or a salesperson; you don't get to just do your job for a while and then stop. You're doing your job 24/7. You're famous all the time. Out at lunch, on the way home, at three in the morning; if someone sees me out, they don't see a guy crossing the street; they see Jack Harrington, the Movie Star— "Quick, go see if he'll sign your T-shirt!"

I wondered what my life would be like thirty years from now. What would it have all amounted to? So I'd made a bunch of movies and some TV shows—so what? Was that an acceptable use of a life?

I didn't know if it was or not. On one hand, it was a heck of a lot better than being a drain on society and not doing anything. But on the other hand, I wasn't saving lives or fighting for justice. I was making millions of dollars to pretend to be someone else so people could go to ridiculously overpriced theatres and spend ten bucks to laugh or cry or get scared or whatever. That was the point of my life: to be someone else. I couldn't even be *me*.

This started to bother me. I started looking for ways I could make my life more worthwhile, something to justify taking another breath and using up precious oxygen. I started working with more volunteer programs, squeezing them in between projects and parties. I started giving away more money to the causes I supported and to others that I didn't really understand but sounded good. I started going to protests with other Hollywood do-gooders to save trees and things. I wanted to ensure that, when I died, people would remember me for something else besides being an actor who amassed millions for being good at playing pretend.

But it wasn't working. I started comparing myself to my family again. They weren't running themselves ragged trying to support every humanitarian cause in existence, and they weren't giving away their money to charities left and right. (Well, Mom did drop coins into *every* Salvation Army bucket she passed at Christmas, but that wasn't the same.) They weren't standing out in forests linking arms with hippies and singing old folk songs around an ancient redwood. But they were still happier than I. What was the deal?

Love. There it was again, that pesky reality. They were married, they had kids, they had someone to kiss and make love to and hold hands with on walks around the neighborhood. I thought back to when Dianne and I had first started dating and how I'd been convinced that all anyone needed was love. I'd been pretty happy then. But I'd just told Mom I didn't want to get married and have kids, hadn't I? Truth be told, that was only partially true. I didn't want kids, but only because I was sure I'd screw them up. And I was selfish, but wasn't everyone? And hadn't I stopped being selfish for a little while when Dianne and I had started dating? I'd gladly given up my plans in order to go out with her or go where she felt like going for dinner. It hadn't lasted, but then maybe that was a symptom of how incompatible we really were, that we really weren't meant to last for very long. And there were a lot of couples who *did* make it in Hollywood; they just didn't get as much press as the ones who married after dating three months and then got divorced a year later.

So maybe I was just scared of screwing up another relationship. I'd messed up in a *major* way, and I couldn't guarantee I wouldn't do it again. But everyone was screwed up; no one was capable of having a perfect relationship, so maybe I should just get over it and start dating again.

That was my plan. I started sizing up the women I encountered: were they pretty, did they seem intelligent, were they fun? I went on a few dates. A couple people even tried to set me up with women they knew. But I always managed to find something wrong that would disqualify these women I met: weird laugh, bizarre taste in clothes, too flighty, too focused… I became the king of flaw-finding.

Trish Gardner: great woman, really nice, very smart, but she did this thing with her hair. Twist twist twist around her finger, untwist untwist untwist and toss over her shoulder, even though it was barely long enough to stay back there. Then it would fall back in front and she'd do it again. And again.

Hayli St. John: great conversationalist, very intelligent, and after three dates I thought perhaps this might have some potential. Then on date four she started singing with the radio. Voice like fingernails on a chalkboard. I didn't return her calls after that.

"You're just looking for excuses," Todd told me one night over Guinnesses. "You don't want to get involved with anyone, so you pinpoint these relatively minor quirks and call them major character flaws that you couldn't possibly put up with."

I mulled that over for a while, then admitted he was right—odd for a guy whose most serious relationship had lasted six weeks. "So what do I do?" The fact that I was asking *him* was a sign of my desperation.

"Stop being afraid of whatever it is you're afraid of: commitment, intimacy, relationships, whatever. I mean, you don't have to marry the next woman you find; if it doesn't work, you break up and find someone else. Happens every day; that's the way it goes."

I had to admit, I was impressed. It seemed like sound advice. I'd just stop being afraid of whatever it was I was afraid of. But what exactly *was* that?

Alannah Moore and I met at one of Todd's parties. She was beautiful, with Latin roots that gave her a deep tan and sultry brown eyes and great curves. The only thing I found mildly annoying was this weird thing she did with her mouth when she swallowed. But I was determined not to let that deter me. I asked her out. We did dinner at a small bistro downtown. We had a great time. I asked her out again. We rented a movie and carried out Chinese. I ignored the gulping and we had fun. By the third date I barely noticed the gulping, and I realized that we got along. I'd done it! I'd pushed past the fear and was in a relationship!

Then after three months, a diamond bracelet, a weekend in the Bahamas, and a shopping spree in New York, she told me she didn't think we were "clicking," and would it be okay if we were just friends? *Friends, sure thing, no problem. Oh, before you go—does this knife in my heart belong to you?*

I was back to square one, except this time I knew what I was afraid of: getting hurt. I knew the crap people were capable of pulling on each other because I'd pulled it on Dianne, and I was terrified of someone pulling it on me. Alannah had done it, albeit not as badly as I had on Dianne, but that was just luck, a close call. She could have completely screwed me over. So where did that leave me? I wanted a relationship but was afraid of what might happen if I got into one. Catch-22.

So it was either no relationship or relationship with ever-present fear. Or flings. I decided flings had a lot of merit; very simple, no juggling involved, no strings attached. Like that one night with Penelope; it had been fun, and the watchword had been "no commitment." Just acting on mutual attraction. Maybe that would tide me over—till what, I didn't know.

But as it turned out, even that was difficult. I discovered there weren't nearly as many women out there looking for noncommittal trysts as I'd expected there to be. And it didn't take me long to figure out that piling up a number of these encounters might come back to haunt me in the form of tattling tabloids or paternity suits, or worse, as Dianne had inadvertently taught me. So flings were eventually ruled out as well.

I was stuck. If love was the point, then I was screwed, because I couldn't even do *that* right. My career wasn't enough, I was apparently unable to have a real relationship, and those were the only two things I could possibly think of that would make it worthwhile to stick around.

Not that eighty-sixing myself was really a viable option either. My parents back in Reily would be pretty bummed, to say the least. And if I'd refused to let Dianne kill herself when her life was doomed anyway, then what right did I have to think I had a good enough reason to off myself? Unfortunately, that made it worse; I didn't even have death as an option. I was trapped in a pointless existence.

I continued to accept movie roles, and I booked up the next year with film projects, but I stopped doing pretty much everything and anything else. I was doing my job because I was an actor, and that was really the only thing I could muster the energy to do. No more drinks with Todd, no more dates or flings, no more volunteering that required me to actually leave my apartment and be with people. I started drinking again, knowing full well that this was a very bad idea, but I was so desperate I didn't care. I was slipping back into the hole I'd crawled into when Dianne had died. It was familiar and peaceful somehow, because I knew what to expect from it, and I knew how to do it and do it well. I didn't think I could mess up getting messed up.

I started shooting my next project, and I managed, like I had on *DC,* to get through rehearsals and tapings without letting my hangovers interfere with my work. I spent breaks apart from the rest of the cast and crew and went home every night right after wrap—no hanging around and socializing for me.

I eventually noticed that one of the actresses, Casey Greene, was always watching me. She was very attractive and had a no-nonsense attitude about her that gave her a reputation for being a bit cold and intense. I'd been feeling cold and intense lately, so she intrigued me. I finally accepted her invitation to join her for lunch one day, and we ate sandwiches from the catered lunch on the set away from the rest of the group. She was a tremendous flirt, in a cold and intense kind of way, and I finally told her I wasn't good at relationships, and if that was what she was hoping to find, it wasn't going to work.

Her response nearly made me choke on my ham and cheese. "I wasn't looking for a relationship, I was just hoping for a good time. No strings."

"Oh, I see… That can be messy, you know. It's a good time for a while, and then there's a falling-out and a leak to the press…" I was stalling because I didn't know what else to do. This was my chance, falling right into my lap. Too good to be true.

She shrugged. "There's no basis for a falling-out if there are no expectations."

She came home with me that night, and the next, and the next. She later moved in and became what she called my "roommate with benefits." No commitment, no expectations, just someone to hang out with when no one else was around, and someone to sleep with when we had the desire. I continued drinking, she didn't care, we continued working, and after the film wrapped up for good, we were back on separate projects.

This arrangement did not satisfy me the way I'd expected it to, but it beat living alone, so I stuck with it. My current project got stalled by a tech labor strike, so I started reading for hours on my balcony, ignoring everyone and everything else in my life. Casey would come home and either make or order dinner, and usually I'd tear myself away from my book long enough to eat. She told me she was getting worried about me but that in keeping with our no-commitment arrangement, she wasn't going to get on my case. "Just let me know if I can help."

The labor dispute was settled, we went back to work, and a couple weeks later we wrapped the project. My next project wasn't scheduled to start for another couple of months, so I was again stuck with a lot of time to fill. Books were starting to pale as an escape, and I began to run out of options to occupy myself.

Then one night I started watching TV, something I rarely did these days, and saw a special on spirituality and prayer and healing. I didn't normally put much stock in spirituality, but I was bored, and nothing else was on, so I kept watching. It was interesting, I had to admit. I started wondering if maybe I should look into some spirituality classes, like yoga or that mystical Judaism that Madonna was into. I was getting to the point where I'd try anything to get rid of the shadow that seemed to follow me everywhere. Unfortunately, I found that my tendency to be the king of flaw-finding wasn't limited to women.

Yoga was my first try, since it was so ubiquitous. I went to one of the yoga centers that catered to celebrities and sat in the back trying not to laugh at the names of the positions and the little chime the instructor used to signal the end of class. And they insisted on this whole "empty your mind" idea, but I couldn't—my thoughts were too persistent.

I tried t'ai chi next; a few former costars attended a class in Beverly Hills and loved it. It seemed like the next natural step from yoga and was actually kind of fun, but you had to string together all these movements, and my physical memory just wasn't good enough.

I gave up the body stuff and went into more mind-driven activities. Kabbalah came first; Madonna had popularized it to the point where it was simple to find a place to go learn. This I found fascinating for a while. But it was a lot of academia, and I had never been very good at school, so that was the end of that.

From there I moved on to studying crystals, but it didn't last long because I couldn't get past the idea that rocks had power. There was one very embarrassing moment when the instructor held up a green crystal and began cataloguing its strengths, but it reminded me too much of Superman's kryptonite, and I burst out laughing. I wasn't welcomed back.

Buddhism, Hinduism, Taoism…tried them, dumped them, moved on. I felt defeated. *Nothing was working.* What kind of a loser couldn't even get spirituality right? Of all the areas in life that one has to work with, spirituality ought to be the easiest—it's so enigmatic and nebulous, anything goes! But I couldn't get any of it to go anywhere, and it was only convincing me more and more that I was so inept at living that I shouldn't be allowed to.

GRACE

SUMMER CAME, and with it the kind of gorgeous weather California is known for. I completed my credential requirements and then found a job for the coming fall, teaching fifth grade at a school just ten minutes away. The days at Williams & Williams got increasingly difficult once I knew something better was just around the bend.

In my spare time I was in the process of reading the whole Bible, cover to cover, and doing a study with my small group. I also borrowed a couple books on theology and Christianity from the library. The others marveled at how much reading I was able to stuff into a week. "It's all just a matter of motivation," I explained, and it was. I never would have spent this much time learning how to be a better secretary.

The summer zipped by at light speed, and then suddenly I was stapling up bulletin boards in my classroom and attending first-year teacher training sessions. I had the names of my students now, all thirty of them, and couldn't wait to put faces to them. I was giddy with excitement; school started in a week, and I was finally going to teach!

In contrast to the blur of summer, the week before school started was slow as molasses in a Chicago January. With the help of the other fifth-grade teachers I'd planned the first three weeks' worth of lessons. I finished arranging my room, finished decorating, and was now spending my time reviewing my child psychology and teaching methods textbooks from college.

I'd met most of the teachers and hit it off with a couple of them: Gale was a third-grade teacher who dispensed invaluable advice about classroom discipline, and Amie was a new kindergarten teacher I'd gone out with a couple of times after we'd found out we were both new. We hit it off, so I invited her to the next girls' night, which would be the Friday at the end of the first week of classes. "A fitting time to party," I'd joked. "We'll deserve it for making it through the week!"

On Sunday night, Missy and I went out for dessert with a few other women from the Sunday night service. By that time all the excitement had worn off, and I was starting to get *really* nervous about facing thirty ten-year-olds in two days.

"They're just as nervous about facing you," Missy said. "They have no idea who you are. You're the mysterious new teacher, so they don't know whether you'll be a witch or friend or what."

I chuckled. "Who knows what I'll be—a panicky mess, if nothing else."

"We'll pray like crazy for you on Tuesday," Taylor assured me.

"Thanks, I'll need it. Just pray that I don't look as scared as I feel. They're like animals; they can smell fear, and they'll use it to their advantage." This got a laugh out of everyone, and I forced myself to laugh, too—if I didn't loosen up I'd be dead by the time school started.

The next day I attended the district's in-service at one of the intermediate schools, and then after lunch went back to my school to attend our own staff in-service. I expected all the other teachers to be mellow, but everyone was buzzing with anxiety about the next day's events.

We finished early, and everyone dispersed to their rooms. I surveyed my room a final time, pleased with the décor and the arrangement (finally), and snapped off the light to head home. I'd be here early in the morning, every morning for the next four months, so there was no point in forcing myself to stick around if I didn't have to. I stopped down at Amie's room to see if she wanted to catch coffee, but she was changing her first day's activities at the last minute and wanted to work. "See you bright and early!" I quipped as I left her room. She waved, looking harried, and I walked out to my car with a bounce in my step, forcing myself to be confident and calm, just as I had during the month before my move to California. I'd gotten through that just fine; I could do this, no problem.

That night I lay in bed and stared at the ceiling for six hours. I forced myself to stop looking at the clock every five minutes somewhere around 3:30 in the morning, and watched as the morning light crept into my window and across the wall and floor until my alarm went off at 6:00. I showered, dressed, and ate without really noticing what I was doing, and was amazed that I'd managed to coordinate clothes and pull myself together. As 7:30 drew closer, I felt surprisingly energized, and I hoped it would last the day.

I gave the room one final look. This big, bright room was *mine*. I was finally teaching! I stood before the bay of windows, staring out at the field behind the school, and prayed silently for confidence and calm—the two things I'd been faking all week and wanted to honestly feel rather than pretend.

I killed time until the bell rang at 8:30. The moment of truth. I took my place in the hall outside the door, along with the other teachers, and tried to look as calm and in charge as they did. "Good luck!" Gale whispered before the tidal wave of small bodies began surging down the hall. Their little faces looked along the wall at the room numbers which identified their new classrooms, and the eyes that finally landed on me spoke volumes: *Who are you?* I wondered if they could tell I was thinking the same question.

Finally the bell rang to signal the beginning of class. I stood and walked to the door, kicking out the doorstop and taking a deep breath as I closed myself into the room with my new charges. I walked back to the front of the room and forced myself to smile, even though my cheeks hurt already. "Well hey, everyone!" The chatter died down as students ended their conversations and turned in their seats to face me. *"Well hey, everyone"? Great opening line,* I chided myself. I mentally commanded myself to look confident as I launched into my introduction. Roll call followed, then class rules and a get-to-know-you game. I supervised them as they raced around getting signatures for classmate bingo, and I suddenly realized, "This is my class. These kids are mine for nine months. I'm a teacher!"

By the end of the day, I'd managed to cover everything I'd wanted to. I didn't seem to have made any enemies yet, which was a good thing. I walked them down to the front door and out to the circle drive where buses and cars waited to usher them home. I waved and smiled as they walked past me to wherever it was they were going, and once they were all gone I went back to my room where I shut the door, put in a Mozart CD, and literally lay on my back on the front table, legs dangling off the edge, and stared at the ceiling in a daze. I'd made it through the first day of school, no war injuries yet, and my brain was still functioning. All in all a very good day.

The quarter moved quickly and, thankfully, smoothly as well. After about a month we had a good routine down in the classroom, and my stomach no longer fluttered when I stood before the whole class to teach. They were all really great kids, and I knew I was lucky to have been blessed with such a relatively easy group my first year. I kept the women in my small group in stitches with stories about things the students did.

Unfortunately, I realized there was no way I could keep doing everything I was doing at the church. Small group, college band, rehearsals…on top of lesson plans and grading and all the other minutiae that come with teaching, it was just too much. I reluctantly dropped the college band, which gave me two more free nights a week. There was no way I was going to drop my small group, though;

those women were my family. Our weekly meetings were a boon to me and well worth the exhaustion I felt Tuesday mornings.

Before I knew it the holidays were upon us again. The Uptons invited me to their Thanksgiving and Christmas dinners, which I accepted gratefully. The students were more squirrelly than usual, and I was fighting for their attention every minute of the day. I was grateful for the short week before Thanksgiving, but even with a long weekend it seemed I was back in the classroom before I'd had a chance to catch my breath.

December was hectic. The church was gearing up for its Christmas Eve services and wanted to incorporate some singers and musicians from the Sunday night service. I was asked, and against my better judgment I accepted, even though it meant a lot of rehearsals for the next three weeks on top of the end-of-the-quarter madness.

That winter the rains began early. Usually they didn't start in earnest until mid-January, or so they told me, but the second week of December it was like living in a rain cloud. I've always enjoyed rain, so the weather itself didn't bother me. What *did* bother me was the traffic. Driving in inclement weather was nothing new to me, being from Illinois, but Californians seemed to forget from year to year just how hard it is to drive on roads that haven't seen rain in ten months, and as a result there were accidents galore closing down the freeways every night. Thankfully I didn't often have to use them, but as fate (if I believed in such things anymore) would have it, the I-5 was the fastest route to small group.

Monday night, two weeks before Christmas break, it was 10:30 —late for me because we'd celebrated Joy's birthday, and I hadn't wanted to skip out early—and thankfully there weren't a lot of cars on the road. It was pouring; I had my wipers on high speed, and even that wasn't helping all that much. I hadn't been feeling well that past weekend; I'd been battling a cold and not sleeping well, and I was stressed out about finishing everything before vacation, and how I'd fit it all in around rehearsals. In a nutshell, I was preoccupied and sleepy, and the rotten roads weren't helping either.

You can probably tell where this is going. I don't remember what happened or what I did or why. A swerve, a slamming of breaks, and I was sandwiched between two cars. It all took less than two seconds, but it turns out two seconds can grab hold of your life and turn it upside down.

JACK

DEPRESSION. IN RETROSPECT I know that's what I was experiencing, although at the time I didn't know it. I was forcing myself through work, just barely making it, and then sleeping the rest of the time. I'd given up on spirituality—I'd pretty much decided I didn't have a soul—I'd given up on sex, I'd given up on basically everything. The only reason I hadn't done myself in was because I didn't know a good way of doing it and didn't have the mental energy to really think it out.

I'd wrapped on my last project. Christmas was fast approaching, but the last thing I wanted was to be surrounded by my normal family, seeing Abby's new son and being reminded of how utterly alone I was. I made an excuse to Mom about why I couldn't come again this year, promised to call on Christmas Day, and generally executed a performance worthy of an Oscar by getting through the whole hour-long conversation without her realizing what a mess I was.

I slept away most of the following week, only to be roused on Thursday afternoon by a call from an old friend from *Every Other Night*. We'd been pretty good buddies back then, and in the first couple years after the show's demise. He'd called to see if I wanted to join him and some friends for a week of sailing off the coast of Mexico. I couldn't bear the thought of leaving my bed, much less my apartment, but he wouldn't take no for an answer. I exhausted my list of excuses before relenting and promising to meet him at the port in San Diego on Monday night.

I had absolutely nothing to do between then and Monday, yet I put off everything to the last minute and left later than I should have Monday night. After throwing some clothes in a duffel, I jumped in the car at 7:30 and headed toward the I-5. Adding insult to injury, a jackknifed semi had blocked traffic. We sat for a full hour before one lane was finally opened—hallelujah!—and cars slowly started trickling through like a leaky faucet. But since I was a mile back from the semi, it took another hour before I was through.

I blared my stereo as I screamed down the freeway, dodging cars right and left. I kept an eye out for cops, not caring to think how big the bill would be if I got a speeding ticket. But apparently they were all tied up with the semi. Then it began to rain, and even though I'd been out of Vermont winters for a decade now, my bad weather driving skills still kicked in. Sadly, most Southern Californians don't know how to drive in the rain, so I was forced to compensate not only for the slick roads but also for the clueless people around me.

After another hour I began to get nervous. I had never been any farther south than Newport Beach, so I had no idea where I was going. I had a vague recollection of the I-5 going all the way to Mexico, and I had a map that I'd hastily bought at the corner gas station but had yet to look at. I flipped open my cell phone and rolled through the numbers, my gaze flicking back and forth between the blue-lit screen and the shiny wet pavement.

The car in front of me slowed, then sped up again, then slowed… what was he doing? I downshifted into third as he evened out at a speed far slower than the flow of traffic. Cars were coming up fast on the right, so I didn't want to pass him; instead I slowed to allow some distance to grow between us, and then all hell broke loose. I was hit twice from behind, the second impact pushing me into the guard rail on the left. The airbag exploded from my steering wheel, and suddenly everything was still, and I could see cars stopping and drivers pulling out cell phones to report the crash.

The front of my car had crumpled, and a glance in my rearview mirror showed that the trunk was a lot shorter than it had been when

I'd left the apartment. There was another car scrunched up against the end of mine, but I couldn't tell how badly it was damaged. I opened the door with a shaking hand and tumbled out. I saw two cars behind me, the closer one pretty well demolished. I slowly walked along my car, feeling dazed and trembling with adrenaline. I lost my breath when I could finally see the driver whose car was now fused to mine.

A young woman was slumped forward as much as her locked seat belt would allow, with blood trailing down the side of her face. Shards of glass twinkled on her shoulder and in her hair as they caught the beams of approaching headlights. For a minute I couldn't move. It was like the worst case of déjà vu ever. The driver of the third car came out, limping and yelling that it wasn't his fault. I ignored him and walked to the place where his front end was crunched against the side of the woman's car. I looked around wildly, trying to figure out how to get to her.

I couldn't let this happen again.

"Move your car!" I shouted and waved my arms like a madman in the face of the approaching driver. "We can't reach her—your car, back it up!" He looked at me like I was mad. *"Go!"*

He back-pedaled, probably thinking I was crazed and would attack, yelling that it wasn't drivable, that it wouldn't move. He was right, it shouldn't have moved, but it did—only about a foot before it died, but that was all the room I needed to be able to reach in through the broken window and jab my finger to her neck. There it was: a faint pulse beneath my shaking hand. I shrugged off my flannel and pressed it against her head.

The woman stirred slowly and made a low, unintelligible sound. Her eyes opened briefly, looked into mine, closed again, screwed shut tight with pain. "Hey there, take it easy," I said, trying not to allow my voice to belie the terror I was feeling. "Just sit still, and you'll be fine, okay?" *Please let her be okay, please let her be okay.* Sirens began to scream off in the distance. I glanced around, looking for their lights. "I hear the ambulances," I told her; she was squirming, pinned in the seat. "They should be here any minute. Try not to move, okay? You might hurt yourself worse."

She slowed her movements, then she stopped moving—and then she stopped breathing. I stared at her, not knowing what to do. "Hey, hey there, come on, wake up," I said, gently tapping her cheek. The shirt was damp in my hand; blood had soaked almost the whole thing. "Come on, *come on, breathe!*" I was yelling, my whole body shaking. I felt again for her pulse, but couldn't find it. She was dying, or dead. "Oh God, don't do this to me!"

Suddenly a paramedic was beside me; I was pulled away as two firemen with tools began to work on the door of her car. I dropped the shirt and stumbled back, watching the vaguely familiar choreography of the rescue. Another paramedic came up to me and began speaking, but his words didn't register; my mind was locked on the woman in the car, my entire being willing her to be alive.

I was holding a thin Styrofoam cup of extremely hot coffee, but the heat wasn't registering. I was sitting in a curvy plastic chair, but the discomfort of its form wasn't registering either. The only things that *were* registering were the sharp pain in my sternum from the seat belt, the ache in my neck from whiplash, and the shape of the door to the trauma room. A cop had taken my statement earlier, and I had given it as best as I could remember, although there wasn't much I was sure of other than the fact that I got hit and now my car was in a pound somewhere, waiting for me to empty it of its contents before it was crushed and melted or stripped for its last useful parts.

I'd been there half an hour when the doctors and nurses began to trickle out of the room. No one seemed to know that I was waiting to hear what had happened, so I chased down a nurse who directed me to a doctor looking at charts at a reception desk. "I was in the accident with the woman you were working on," I said, motioning to the trauma room from which he had just emerged. "Is she okay?"

He looked at me and then the room, and said quietly, "She probably will be. But I'm afraid I can't discuss specifics with you unless you're a relative."

I shook my head. "Honestly, I don't even know her. I just wanted to know if she'd make it or not."

He nodded thoughtfully as he scanned the chart in his hand. "Provided she does all right for the next couple hours or so, she'll be moved out of the ER. We have her in an induced coma, though; she won't be talking anytime soon."

I went back to the hard plastic chair and sat down. I slowly finished the coffee, which had cooled to a drinkable temperature, but there wasn't enough caffeine to keep me awake. I jerked back to consciousness about thirty minutes later and went down to the cafeteria to get something to eat. I was just returning from a short walk outside when the doors to the trauma room opened and a bed was rolled out by two nurses. A young, pale woman with dark hair matted with blood lay on the bed, tubes and wires running all over the place like some freak science experiment. A steady beep emanated from a machine that one of the nurses was rolling along beside the bed as they disappeared down the hall.

I wandered back to the chairs and sat down again. Relief flooded through me. She was obviously stable, or they wouldn't be moving her. But now I was in an awkward position. No one had come for her yet, and I felt funny just leaving when she was all alone.

Two women ran past me into the ER and up to the reception desk. "We're the Uptons," the older woman said. They appeared to be mother and daughter. "We were called about Grace Winslowe. Is she all right? Is she still here?"

The nurse responded with something I couldn't hear and then motioned for them to sit in the waiting area. She walked away, then returned a moment later and sat back down behind the desk. The women watched the nurse, and any other hospital staff that walked by, with tense, anxious faces. The older woman put her arm around the younger one, and they bent their heads low and together and spoke quietly until the doctor I'd spoken to walked up to the waiting area and called for them. The women's heads bobbed up, and they stood and rushed up to the doctor. He led them down the hall and out of sight.

Grace Winslowe. Was that her name? I wondered if we were all here to see the same woman. I debated following them to see whose room they went to, but decided this was probably not the wisest course. I would just sit and wait for one of them to show up again.

It didn't actually take that long. About ten minutes later the younger one walked back to the reception desk and asked the nurse a question. The nurse pointed to the hot drinks machine hidden in the back corner of the waiting area. The young woman walked past me to the machine, rubbing a hand over her face. I stood and approached her as she waited for the machine to finish trickling her order into the cup.

"Excuse me, ma'am?" I startled her; she jumped and gasped, then slumped against the beverage machine.

"Oh, I'm so sorry—"

"No, it's all right, I'm just jumpy." She took a deep breath and gave me a half-smile. Then her eyes studied my face, and her expression changed. "Are—uh—you're Jack Harrington, right?" I nodded sheepishly. I realized that until now I had somehow managed to go unrecognized all evening, and I couldn't imagine how. She let out a small, embarrassed laugh. "I'm sorry, you must be sick of that; it just surprised me, that's all."

"That's all right; you're the first person to have noticed all night, so hey, bonus points for you." We chuckled a bit, and the machine beeped to remind her that her coffee was done. She wrapped her hands around the cup and plugged in a couple more coins. I took a breath. "Look, I'm sorry to approach you like this, but I think the woman you're here to see is the woman I was in the accident with. Her car hit me from behind, and I was with her before the ambulances came. They won't tell me how she is because I'm not family, but I wanted to make sure she was all right. Would you mind just letting me know what's going on?"

The machine finished pouring her second drink, and she spoke as she snapped a plastic lid on its top. "Um…yeah." She took a deep breath. "Collapsed lung, concussion, broken arm, broken leg, sprained neck. They seem to think she'll be all right, though." She stared down at the coffee cups in her hands as she spoke, and when she looked up there were tears on her cheeks. She tried to wipe them with the backs of her hands, still clutching the coffees. "Sorry," she murmured, her face reddening.

"No reason to be, believe me. I'm glad it looks like she'll be okay. Thanks for telling me…"

"Oh…I'm Missy. My mom, Jane, and I are good friends with Grace. She doesn't have family out here in California, and we've kind of hooked her into ours. Grace was on the way home from our Bible study tonight. I didn't even know she'd listed us as emergency contacts; they said she had it written in her appointment book."

I nodded, not knowing what to say. Finally I realized she was waiting for me to say something, so I stood back and nodded toward the hall. "Your mom is probably dying for her coffee." I winced at the inappropriate phrasing, but Missy didn't seem to notice. "When Grace wakes up, tell her I'll try to stop by and see how she's doing."

Missy smiled. "That's so sweet of you. I will tell her for sure. Thank you."

I nodded. "Take care. Don't burn your mouth on that coffee; it's hot enough to self-combust." I smiled, and she laughed a little as she moved down the hall. I watched her disappear around the corner, then realized there was no point in sticking around. I called a cab from the reception desk, and an hour later I was stumbling into my apartment. I downed a couple of the extra-strength Tylenol they had given me at the hospital and crawled into bed. I dreamed of concrete walls coming toward me at impossible speeds and of a woman whose face kept changing from Dianne's to Grace's and back again.

GRACE

THERE IS ONE THING I do remember.

I am down at the bottom of the ocean, where the water is like ink and the sunlight doesn't reach. I don't breathe, but somehow that's okay. Something is trying to pull me back to the surface, but it's far away and I'm tired and I don't have the energy to swim up. I lie on my back, the soft sand of the ocean floor beneath me, the water pressing in all around me, and I sleep.

Then there's blinding light and a heat that evaporates all the water, and I'm left on dry sand with a sky of pure white above me. The heat doesn't hurt, even though it is strong enough to turn the whole ocean to vapor, and it seems to be in me as well as around me. Then a sound envelops me: music unlike any I've ever heard before. It's not just that the melody is unfamiliar, but the instruments and meter—even the notes themselves are different. They seem three-dimensional, like you could grab each one as it floats into the atmosphere. I know without a doubt that I am in heaven.

The music changes. Now it is a voice speaking to me without words. I can't open my eyes to see the speaker, but I desperately want to; the light is so bright that it's hurting my eyes even while they're shut, and I know if I open them I'll go blind. The musical voice is outside me and inside me at the same time. As it enfolds me it creates images in my mind: the face of a man, scared, talking to me. I know this man needs my help, but I don't know what to do to help him, I don't know what is wrong.

The music changes again, so beautiful and tender and warm and rich that I want to cry for the sheer joy it creates in me: this music is mine, or maybe it's the other way around, that I belong to the music. That's it. It owns me. And then I understand: this man I see can't hear this music. He doesn't belong to it, to anyone, to anything. He wants to belong.

I want to gather the music in my hands, pluck the notes from the air like a bouquet of sound, and offer it to the sad man. I see him in my mind, and I see myself, hands outstretched, music flowing on the current of the air to surround him and hold him. I am desperate to do this; as the music builds and crests like waves on the ocean I know that it is telling me to do this.

Suddenly the music stops, the light is gone, and the water crashes in around me again. I am struggling for breath beneath its crush. I am freezing cold, my bones are like solid ice. I am desperately trying to swim back to the top, but the water is thick as tar, and I don't get anywhere. There are explosions of light that jerk through my body, and then the water begins to drain away and I can breathe again. I am still freezing, but I am exhausted, and again I sleep.

And then I awake.

There were strange voices around me, and at first they seemed far away, like someone had turned the volume down, and all I was catching were the really loud bits—little intelligible islands in a sea of muffled noise. Then the volume began to rise, slowly, until I felt immersed in the world again instead of simply listening to it. There were beeps, the sound of metal striking metal, and voices: low voices, loud voices that were far away and angry, crying voices, and foreign voices. But the two nearest voices were familiar.

And then there was pain.

It hit me just as I was feeling comfortable in the world again, no longer under water and not in heaven. It slammed into me as if it was dropped from the top of the world, and I could hear it as it made contact with my body: a crash and thud merged into one other-worldly sound. I couldn't figure out where the pain was coming from; there seemed to be a thousand focal points, but the shock waves rippling out from the epicenter all smacked together into one giant jumble of agony.

I listened to the voices speak for a while, but they talked as though I wasn't there, and I wanted them to know I was. I concentrated very hard and slowly opened my eyes. I was in a whitish room, with figures moving quickly on the other side of the window, and next to the bed were two women whose faces I knew. It took me a second to remember their names. They were talking and didn't see that my eyes were open. I tried to say hello, but it came out as a rasp and a dry cough. I realized there was a tube down my throat.

Their heads whipped around to face me, and they both broke out in massive smiles. "You're awake!" Missy squealed as she lunged for me and gingerly hugged me as best she could through the octopus of wires.

"I'll get a doctor." Jane leapt from her chair and raced from the room. Her body sped past the window, and I saw her pointing back to the room. A figure in white glided across the view and into the door. A doctor.

She shooed Jane and Missy from the room while she checked me out and removed the tube from my throat. After a few sips of water I was able to talk again, albeit with a lot of pain. "How long was I out?"

"Two days."

"*Two days?*" I was stunned. I was almost afraid to hear everything else that had happened. "Everything hurts."

"Well, there's a lot of you that's busted, so that's to be expected. How bad is the pain?"

"Bad." I felt dangerously close to crying. It seemed like it got worse every minute I was conscious. She adjusted a drip hanging on a pole and made a note on a chart. I tried to turn my head to look out the window to my right, but there was something around my neck preventing me from moving it. "Is my neck broken?"

"No. Your left arm is broken in two places. Your left leg is broken. But your neck is only sprained."

It hurt to talk, but I needed to know what was going on. "Anything else?"

"Concussion and collapsed lung. Looks like the seat belt didn't hold you back as much as it should have; your chest hit the steering column pretty hard."

I winced. "Yeah. Old car." How stupid had I been not to get that fixed sooner? I was lucky it locked at all.

"Lost quite a bit of blood from a gash on your head. Broke a couple ribs. And a wide assortment of cuts and bruises. But that's it."

"Thanks."

"No problem. Let me know if you need anything. I'll let your friends back in for half an hour more." With that she smiled and left the room.

Jane and Missy returned and plunked themselves back into the plastic folding chairs, looking at me expectantly as if I was about to deliver a speech or something. "What?" I tried to smirk, but it hurt to move my mouth that way.

They both chuckled. "Do you know what happened, Grace?" Jane asked.

"No. I remember...cake and ice cream." Shadows of memories danced at the edge of my mind, but I couldn't pull them forward.

"Apparently you rear-ended a car, and then you were hit and sandwiched in between."

I was shocked. "Is everyone else okay?"

"Yeah. The guy you hit was barely hurt, and same for the guy who hit you."

I let out a sigh of relief. "Thank God," I breathed. Something flashed in my mind as I said that, but I couldn't grab it fast enough to figure out what it was. "Is anyone suing me?"

"No. Although I doubt anyone would. No one knows what happened, I don't think. Everyone was sober, the road was slick, it was dark, it was raining…"

I tried to remember what happened after small group. I must have gotten in the car, driven to the freeway… I couldn't stand not being able to remember.

Missy had a funny grin on her face. "What?" I asked.

"Guess who you hit."

"Oh no…Paul?" How embarrassing it would be to rear-end your pastor!

"No."

"*You?*" She laughed and shook her head. "Well, who?"

"Jack Harrington."

I furrowed my brow, which caused an arrow of pain to pierce my head. "Ow. *Who?*"

"Remember *Desert Moon,* that movie about the Navajo girl?"

"Yeah."

"Remember the guy who played the homeless soldier who found her?"

"Yeah. Oh. *Oh.*" I closed my eyes and felt ill. "Jack Harrington, as in, *Jack Harrington.*"

"That would be the one."

I squeezed my eyes shut, which launched another arrow, but I didn't care. I couldn't figure out why they were smiling as if this was a good thing.

"He was here the night of the accident; we talked out in the waiting area. He seemed very concerned about you." Her voice turned coy and singsong, and my knee-jerk reaction was to roll my eyes, which hurt more than I thought it would.

The pain and exhaustion and probably the meds were threatening to pull me back to unconsciousness, but this news was enough to keep me present. "Oh, please. Probably just doesn't wanna sound like a bad driver. *National Enquirer* and all that—oh! Was it on the news?" I groaned and tried to pull the covers over my head. Southern California's news thrived on the spectacular, especially when it involved Hollywood's darlings. "This is a nightmare."

"Grace, honey, relax," Jane chuckled.

I sighed. All was quiet for a while, and then I thought of something. "How's my car?" Both heads shook. "That bad, huh?" Both heads nodded. I sighed. "That sucks. That was a great car. And now I have to get a new car…and insurance is gonna skyrocket…and my classroom! Oh man, my kids. My cat!" Tears were looming.

"We've been feeding her, don't worry. And everything else will work out, Grace, just take it easy. God will take care of everything."

I heaved a sigh as deeply as I could, which wasn't much since everything still hurt so badly. She was right, I knew she was. It was still hard to remember to trust, though. I was still so used to being self-reliant and expecting to have to take care of everything myself that it was hard to remember to just let go and allow God to do His thing. "Okay. You're right." I forced myself to unclench my fists from around the thin white bedsheet. "How long am I stuck here?"

Jane shrugged. "No idea. Depends. But I don't know *what* exactly it depends on. I'm sure they'll tell you after they've checked you out and done more tests."

I wrinkled my nose, which didn't hurt quite as much as I expected; the drugs must have started working. "Let's talk about something else."

So we did for another twenty minutes until the doctor strolled back in to kick the Uptons out. "Visiting hours start at eight tomorrow morning, ladies," she said as she riffled through pages on a clipboard. Jane and Missy dutifully stood and pulled on their coats.

"We'll come by in the afternoon after work," Jane said as she leaned over to give me a gentle hug. Missy did the same, then they both made their exit. After an hour of poking, questioning, and testing, it was determined that I would remain in the hospital until Friday, at which point, assuming no turns for the worse, I would be allowed to go home. I was finally brought back to the room and left alone, and I slept and dreamed of the ocean.

JACK

I WOKE UP WITH a raging headache, and my first question was, why on earth does my neck hurt so much? Then I remembered the evening before and groaned aloud. Why did these things keep happening to me?

The phone rang and nearly scared me out of my skin. My assistant was on the other end, asking where I'd been all day. "Here," I answered as I looked around wildly for the time. The clock on the night table read 2:47.

"I've been calling all morning."

"Slept through it, sorry."

"So what happened?"

"Got hit. Car that hit me got hit. Big mess. Car's totaled, I think."

"Yeah, it is. Cops called and told me where you could go claim the contents."

"Good."

"So what's your statement?"

"No statement."

"How's the girl?"

"Don't know. She was still out when I was there. I'll call today to check up on her. Any press?"

"Some. The usual news outlets, that's all."

I sighed, hoping they'd at least leave Grace alone. "Okay. Keep me updated."

"I will. You do the same."

"Okay. Thanks, Kate."

We hung up, and after a moment I picked up the phone to check my voice mail. Five messages, all from Kate, and one from the guy I'd been on my way to meet in San Diego. I called and left him a message explaining what had happened, then showered and dressed and called the hospital on a whim. Someone must have put in a good word for me, because they told me she was still unconscious, but stable. I felt myself relax with the news.

I spent the next two days nursing a whiplashed neck and buying a new car. News of the accident got around, and calls from Todd, Carl, and others kept my phone busy. Wednesday I called again; no change, call again tomorrow. When I did, my persistence was rewarded: she was awake, and she was taking visitors. I took my new car for a little drive down the I-5.

The hospital looked less busy during the day than it had the night I'd been there. I walked up toward the main lobby and stopped short. Could I really just waltz into her room? What was I going to say once I got in there? "Hi, I'm Jack, I'm the guy you hit." I didn't want her to feel guilty. "Hi, I'm Jack, how are you doing?" Awful, obviously; there was no point in asking that. So why was I here?

To make sure she was still living and breathing and *okay.* I needed to see her myself to dispel once and for all my fear at the possibility of another life lost in my arms.

And I wanted to warn her about the press. I didn't know if they'd try to talk to her, but there was no telling whether they would or not, and I didn't want it to scare her or come as a surprise. I hoped they hadn't contacted her yet.

It was chilly out, wet from the light rain; I'd forgotten my jacket and needed something to warm me up. I stopped in to the cafeteria and bought a coffee. I held it tightly and sat down at a small round table in the corner, staring out from under my baseball cap into the hall as doctors and nurses and visitors walked back and forth.

The coffee chased some of the cold from my body, and I was able to think more rationally. I knew what my objectives were in going to see her, but it still felt like a bad idea. Thing was, I had no idea why; I couldn't tell what would be "bad" about it, it was just this irrational feeling. I didn't like irrational feelings.

I downed the rest of the coffee and tossed the cup into the bin behind me. This was ridiculous. I'd just go, introduce myself, lay everything out on the table, and leave her alone. Quick in-and-out; I'd be home in an hour.

I marched myself, a man with a purpose, into the reception area. "I'm here to see Grace Winslowe," I said with more calm and assurance than I felt.

She entered the name into the computer and wrote down a number on a small piece of paper and handed it to me. "Room 253. Elevator is down that hall; take it to the second floor and go right."

I thanked her and moved on, keeping my gaze down and avoiding eye contact with everyone else in the hallway. I was afraid to attract attention, and it still amazed me that no one had recognized me the last time. I hoped my luck would hold again.

I entered the elevator and pressed the 2 button. No one else joined me. As I walked down the hall, quick glances into the open rooms revealed lots of shiny equipment with tubes and wires and strange, disquieting noises.

The numbers ascended, and then I was there. I stood next to the door, trying to dispel the urge to turn around and walk away. I peeked stealthily around the corner; she appeared to be sleeping. Great. Now what?

I passed by the room and found a water fountain where I drank enough to fill a fish tank before straightening and marching back toward the room. I entered slowly and stood in the doorway for an awkward moment before realizing she wasn't asleep at all, but humming quietly to herself with her eyes closed. I noticed earphones, then a yellow Walkman in her lap. I stared at her for a moment, realizing that I wouldn't have been able to describe her to anyone based on the events of that night; I'd been so scared I hadn't really *seen* her. She had long, blondish-brown hair, a strip of sunlight shining through the window illuminating red highlights. Her skin was pale, no typical California tan, and though her face was bruised and scratched, she looked like she could be pretty. Not gorgeous, but pretty. She looked young—twenty-five maybe? Twenty-seven?

I suddenly felt bad for just standing and staring when she didn't even know I was there, so I cleared my throat gently. Nothing. Her music was apparently too loud. I tried again. "Grace?" Her eyes opened as she pulled off the earphones. "I'm sorry to disturb you," I began, moving further into the room. "I'm Jack Harrington; I was in the accident with you a couple nights ago."

She nodded mutely, staring at me with a look that I couldn't name. It wasn't the usual "Wow, a celebrity!" face that I tended to get; it was more searching, confused. I wondered if she was coherent or still mentally fuzzy from the head injury, or from the drip of drugs beside her bed.

I was suddenly very uncomfortable. "I just wanted to…uh… come by and see how you were." She nodded and opened her mouth to speak, then apparently thought better of it and shut it again. This was really weird. I wished she'd at least say something. I kept talking to fill the silence. "I also wanted to let you know that the press might try to contact you—they also may not, they can be hard to predict, but I'm not going to comment, and you don't have to, either, unless you want to." Another nod; she looked distracted, but she was staring at me intently, and I didn't know how to interpret this. I shrugged. "Anyway, that's it. I'm glad to see you're doing all right. You, uh, *are* all right, aren't you?"

This seemed to snap her out of something, and she blushed and smiled. "Yes, I am, thank you." Her voice was quiet; I had to really listen to hear her. "I'm sorry I was staring." She flashed a small smile. "Thank you for your concern."

More awkward silence followed, and I felt desperate to leave. "Well, nice to meet you, Grace. Glad you're on the mend."

I backed up toward the door, preparing to leave, when she hastily called out, "Wait!" I stopped and looked at her expectantly. She had that look on her face again: somewhat distracted, but looking right at me, as if she was trying to see something in me.

She studied me, frowning slightly, and then suddenly she smiled with a look of recognition. She let out a light, "Ohhh," and she said, apparently more to herself than to me, a sentence that seemed born out of medicinal loopiness: "You're the one I'm supposed to save."

GRACE

THE WORDS WERE out of my mouth before I realized I was saying them, not just thinking them. I sat there, wishing for all the world that I could get up and run out. Judging from the look on his face, he was going to attribute this to the gash in my head and not take me at all seriously. But what else could I do?

The minute I saw him I had this incredible sense of déjà vu. But it wasn't because I'd seen him on television or in movies; I just knew somehow that this was a totally different thing. And then suddenly the memory of music and warmth and *heaven* washed over me, and I realized that I had seen his face in my mind when I had been unconscious. It was him I was supposed to…well, save.

The poor man probably thought I had either been rendered mute from the accident or was out of my mind, because all I could do was stare at him as I frantically thought about how exactly you tell someone that God has given you a message to give to them. It was totally and completely clear to me that this was the man, and I was supposed to help him, but I knew he would think me totally mad. What was I supposed to do? Surely God wasn't expecting him to take this seriously! But could I really just say, "Not now, God; maybe later"? I hadn't been a Christian for very long, but I was pretty sure that this was not how one worked with Him. I just wished He could have introduced us in a less painful way.

He looked at me with a face that said both "I *beg* your pardon?" and "How much morphine are you on, anyway?" I wanted to hide under the covers. I tried to laugh it off, which hurt, but I was willing to endure the pain to try to somehow salvage this encounter. "I know that's probably the most ridiculous thing anyone has ever said to you, and please believe that I'm *not* mentally unstable and I'm *not* delirious and that I *know* how bizarre it is for a total stranger to say that to you." I paused, thinking. "I don't know if I can even explain it, really. But I had this vision—except it wasn't a vision, it was more real than that, as though I was actually there—I think it was heaven, believe it or not, and…*God* was talking to me, except He wasn't exactly talking." I stopped and smiled, realizing I was probably making no sense at all. "I never put much stock in near-death experiences, but I guess maybe—"

"You stopped breathing."

I frowned. "What?"

The look on his face had changed. He still looked skeptical, but there was a hint of curiosity in his face now. "We were waiting for the ambulance. You were unconscious, then you woke up and tried to talk, and then you looked at me, and then you stopped breathing."

The image of his face, scared, looking at me while music swirled around me flashed in my head. Vision or dream or reality? "Then what?"

He thought for a minute. "Then the ambulance came, they pulled the door off your car, and they brought you here."

I winced. "And you're all right?"

He nodded and shrugged. "Amazingly, yeah. Some mild whiplash and overall ache, but that's it."

"And the other guy?"

"About the same as me."

"Your car? And the other one?"

He gave a small smile. "I was getting tired of it, anyway; this gave me a good excuse to get a new one."

I groaned and covered my eyes with my uninjured hand. "Oh… I'm so sorry."

He chuckled. "Seriously, it's all right. Don't worry about it; replacing it is no problem. And the other guy just had a bashed-up front end, that's all. Nothing bad. No one's fault, as far as I'm concerned."

I sighed and dropped my hand down to the bed. "What a mess," I said aloud to myself. It was quiet for a moment as I stared down at my lap, thinking about the implications of all this. It was very difficult to relax and not let any of it worry me, as Jane had admonished me to do.

I looked back at Jack, and he was watching me. I was suddenly very aware of how awful I looked. I could feel myself blushing, but he didn't seem to notice—or care, at any rate. Then he was aware of me watching him watch me, and he averted his eyes and looked past the bed to the machines beside me.

He grinned and said, "You're not going to start glowing and say something like, 'I'm an angel sent by God,' are you?"

I let out a laugh, but it only lasted a second before my ribs reminded me they were broken. I gasped in pain and let out a chuckle at the same time. Jack looked alarmed. "Oh, I'm sorry! Are you okay?"

I collapsed against the bed and tried to smile. "Well, I promise I'm not an angel, and I won't glow unless they've injected me with uranium or something." I grinned, then shrugged. "Take it or leave it; I'm just the messenger, you know? But I can't deny that it was God who gave it to me; I *know* it was Him. Don't ask me how, I just know."

"So what exactly was this…vision?"

I frowned in concentration. Could I even remember it all? "Until you walked in I didn't even remember it." I closed my eyes and tried to conjure up the images. "There was…water. The ocean, maybe? I could feel the pressure of the water all around me, and I wasn't breathing, but I didn't have to; I was just…existing." I took a deep breath, the memory unfolding fast and in such detail I could almost feel the water. "And then it all disappeared—evaporated—because of this heat. And out of the heat came music that was…" An incredulous laugh bubbled up inside me. "I can't even explain it; it *was* music, but not like the music we have, it was different, more than just tones." I stopped, feeling self-conscious and embarrassed. What must he think of me? But he was listening, or at least doing a good job of faking it. "And the music was talking to me, without words, just…impressions and sensations and thoughts. And then your face was in my mind, and you looked so…*sad.* And the music was so joyful that I wanted to give it to you, so you wouldn't be sad anymore…"

I stopped talking and opened my eyes. He had left the doorway and taken the seat next to my bed. I looked him in the eyes. "I swear to God I'm not crazy."

He laughed, leaning back in the chair and running his hand through his hair. "Forgive me if the thought crosses my mind."

I sighed and rubbed my eyes; this was giving me a headache. "Like I said, I'm just the messenger. I *know* this really happened, but I also know there's no way I can convince you of it. You have to decide whether or not to believe it."

"You keep saying you're the messenger, but I don't know what you think the message is."

I didn't know how to put it into words and told him so. "I know that doesn't help. Like I said, there weren't words, just this over-whelming sense of being *so happy,* and you being so sad. And I knew if you could just…hear God, I guess…" I shrugged. "I'm botching this, I know it. Until this year I didn't even believe in God, so for me to be saying this stuff is bizarre even to me." I smiled. "I don't know what else to tell you, other than to say that I was alone, and God took me in, and He's offering that to you, too. That's the bottom line, I think. Why He chose me to tell you, and why He chose this way, I don't know. But there you have it."

He was staring out the window. I picked at the sheet that was pulled up to my waist and waited for him to respond or laugh or leave or do whatever it was he was going to do. Finally he seemed to remember where he was, and he looked at me and smiled. "Well, thanks for the message. I'm glad to see you're going to be all right." He stood and straightened his shirt. "I hope you get out of here soon. What is it you do?"

The wall he erected with those words was almost tangible. I felt my heart sink. "I'm a teacher. Fifth grade."

"A teacher; great. Well, don't let those kids wear you out when you go back." He moved to the door. "Take care, Grace. Nice meeting you."

I nodded. "You too, Jack. Take care."

With a final smile he turned and disappeared out the door. I closed my eyes and let out a long, painful sigh. I'd done my part, there was nothing else I could do.

At least I could tell my students I'd met Jack Harrington, even if he did think me mad.

JACK

I NEARLY RAN out of her room and down the hall to the elevator. Being in the enclosed space of the elevator felt more comfortable than that room. Talk about crazy! I'd never met someone so delusional before. All that talk about God and "heaven"—and to think that some-one would actually think it possible that God, if He really existed in the first place, would send a message like that. The whole thing was completely implausible. Stuff like that just didn't happen.

I drove back to my apartment and grabbed a brew from the fridge before flopping onto the couch and turning on the TV. I flipped through the channels for a while before landing on a college ball game, but my concentration only lingered there for a little while. She *had* seemed pretty sincere, not your typical religious fanatic. And she'd been lucid; it didn't seem like painkillers talking. But come *on,* a mes-sage from God?

I shook the thought from my head and focused on the game. I wasn't going to spend my time dwelling on this obviously trauma-induced trick of the mind she'd experienced. I was glad to see she wasn't going to die; I didn't think I could handle being involved in anything else where I had to watch someone else's life end. With a final mental shove I rid my mind of all thought of the afternoon's nonsense and eventually fell asleep on the couch.

One good thing from all of this was that the depression I'd been in had apparently been chased away by the accident, at least for now. I was eager to get going on another project, so I started reading through the three scripts I'd been sent: one action, one drama, and one romance. I hadn't done any romances yet, so I read that first. It was a typical romantic comedy, pretty light on plot and heavy on sappy dialogue, but they'd already cast Alexis Giovanni as the female lead, and she would be great to work with. I enjoyed the script and made a note to consider it.

I kept an eye on the TV tabloids to see if Grace ever talked to the press, but the accident was apparently old news now that one of Hollywood's hottest couples had announced their divorce. The stiffness in my neck would occasionally remind me of the accident, but other than that I had effectively pushed the whole thing from my mind. It was over, no one was dead, life goes on.

I accepted the part in the romantic comedy, and by mid-January we were rehearsing. This was a new genre for me, and I enjoyed the stretch. The cast was great too; besides Alexis Giovanni, we were joined by Hannah Price, a contemporary legend I was privileged to finally meet. We were all talking over lunch one afternoon when she mentioned her daughter, who had decided to go into teaching. "No Hollywood for my girl," she laughed as she sipped her Evian. "She's got her father's reticence for the limelight. But she's got a great gift for teaching. I'm proud of her. She'll be broke, but her boyfriend does computer stuff, so hopefully she'll marry into some money."

This comment stayed with me that night. As I drove home I was reminded of Grace and realized she probably wasn't making that much—and now she had to buy a new car and probably deal with higher insurance on top of it. Could a teacher handle that financially? The car she'd been driving the night of the accident had not been in the best shape; it was an old model, boxy and rusted. Not the safest thing to be driving on the 5, surrounded by SUVs and minivans.

I arrived home, sorted through the mail, of which there wasn't much, and got ready for bed. I'd done a good job of forgetting about Grace, but now I was having a hard time doing it again. I couldn't chase away the image of her staring at me, her blue eyes reflecting something between compassion and resignation as I'd hightailed it out of her room. She was the one in the hospital, and yet she was trying to help me.

That night I couldn't sleep. I couldn't stop thinking about this woman, and I couldn't figure out why. Moreover, I couldn't explain the urge I was feeling to help her out. What did I care if she needed a new car? That's life, right? No one bought me a new car, and I was the least to blame in this whole mess. She'd caused most of it, and yet here I was thinking about providing her with another vehicle with which to wreak havoc on the California freeways.

I knew I was overreacting, but it *was* an unheard-of thing to do, buying a car for a stranger. I didn't want to draw any more media attention to the whole thing either, and if it got out that I was doing it, they'd want to know why, and then she'd get dragged into it too, and I didn't want to put her or myself through that. Although I could do it anonymously…

I went back and forth like this for hours before finally falling asleep. When I awoke I felt awful, but I also felt resigned to the fact that I simply had to help her out. There was no explaining it, no rationalizing it, but I knew that if I didn't I was going to be miserable, and I was done with feeling miserable.

I arrived at the set that morning as ready to work as I could be on three hours of sleep. Ella, my assistant on the set, met me with coffee. "You look fresh this morning," she commented sarcastically. "Insomnia?"

"Sorta. Thinking about buying a car."

"Another one? Didn't you just get one?"

"No. I mean, yes, it *is* new, but I'm not buying one for me. It's for a friend who can't afford it."

"Aw, that's so decent of you."

I smirked. "You make it sound like I'm not often decent."

She laughed. "No, that wasn't what I was implying, believe me. But listen, I've been thinking about selling mine, so if you're interested, let me know."

I perked up. "Is it in okay shape? Why are you selling?"

She shrugged. "I've had it awhile, and I'm bored with it. I get like that with cars; I need change. I usually trade them in, but I'll sell it to you instead, if you want it: 1999 Honda Civic, black, manual. Great shape, no problems, no major work."

I thought about it for a minute. Hondas were reliable, and I knew I could trust Ella to be honest with me about its condition. And they weren't fancy or sporty or anything else that might jack up the insurance. "How much you asking?"

"Haven't thought about it. Make me an offer."

"I wouldn't know what would be fair. Let me do some research, okay?"

"Sure thing."

I forced myself to shift into work mode and stop thinking about the car. Alexis arrived, and we ran lines while having our hair and makeup done. From there on out I was immersed in the work at hand.

We finished rehearsing late that evening, and I was on my way home when I remembered I'd wanted to check into pricing for Ella's car. I called Kate and asked her to investigate, all the while asking myself again if this was really a good idea. My internal debate continued long after I'd gone to bed.

The next morning I showed up early to check out the car. Ella gave me the keys, and I took it for a quick spin around the lot. It looked great and drove smoothly; I was impressed by how well she'd kept it up. After hearing back from Kate, I proposed a price. "What do you think? Sound fair?"

"Well, yeah, it does," she said. "I'd say you're being pretty generous."

I shrugged. "I don't want to cheat you, you know. What were you expecting, for me to bid low and make you haggle?" I grinned. "What have I done to deserve such a reputation?"

She laughed. "Oh, hush. I'm just surprised, that's all."

"When would you be willing to give it up?"

"How about Monday? That gives me the weekend to buy a new one."

"Great. Thanks, Ella."

"Thank *you*. And make your friend thank you as well; that's incredibly nice. I'll let you know when I get bored with my condo, too, just in case."

Monday I gave Ella a check and my approval of her new convertible with a killer stereo. That night, after rehearsal had ended, I stood in the parking lot and stared at my two cars, realizing I'd not quite thought through all the logistics. Now what? I didn't know where Grace lived. And how would I get home once I drove it out to her? She probably couldn't even drive yet, not that I wanted to be trapped in a car with her and her God visions. I groaned and sat on the hood of the Honda. This wasn't supposed to be difficult; I was just supposed to buy her a car and be done with it.

I left a note on the Honda to make sure it didn't get towed and then went back to my apartment. I fished out the phone book from its place in a cabinet, where it was buried under a number of other little-used items. It was only for LA County, and there was no Grace Winslow or Winslowe or Windslow anywhere in LA. Maybe Orange County, then.

I looked her up on the Internet and struck gold. Grace Winslowe, Rancho Los Lagos, Orange County, California. Her address and phone number were listed. Another site provided driving directions. She was only an hour away.

I turned off my laptop, then plunked down on my couch and

turned on the TV. I needed to formulate a plan and get this done before I changed my mind. I landed on some random sitcom and zoned for a while, thinking about what my options were, but the week of long rehearsals caught up with me, and I fell asleep.

GRACE

I AWOKE EARLIER than I'd planned Sunday and snuggled lower under the covers, the sound of steady rain reminding me of Chicago. It was my second full day alone at home, and I was grateful for the solitude. After bringing me back from the hospital nearly two months ago, Jane, Missy, or one of the girls from church had been around 24/7 treating me like the Queen of Sheba. It was fun to have a personal attendant, and sometimes two, but it didn't take long for my pride to be irritated at the idea of not being able to take care of myself.

The bruises were gone, the scratches mended, and my arm finally out of its cast. I'd been given a walking cast on my last visit to the doctor; he hoped that within another week or so I'd even be free of that. I was champing at the bit to be back to normal, and my patience for hobbling around was quickly growing thin.

I'd spent most of the previous day with my laptop actually on my lap as I reclined on the couch, going over my budget and trying to figure out how the heck I was going to afford a new car. Obviously it would be anything but new; with the small amount I had saved, I'd be lucky if I could afford a decent bicycle. A woman from church had called when I'd first come home from the hospital, asking if I was in need of financial assistance. While it was true that money was tight, I'd been reluctant to accept their help; my independence and pride were still too stubborn for me to take what I saw as a handout. I had a feeling I could figure it out on my own if I just went over the numbers enough.

I slowly sat up and stretched as I pondered what I'd do for the morning. I'd been back at work for a week, having eased myself back in with the long-term sub taking the afternoons, so there was a mile-high stack of papers to be graded. I knew I should dive into that, but the thought of grading math problems and history tests at eight in the morning on a weekend was just too much. I elected instead to have a very long shower and a very leisurely breakfast and then see how I felt.

It was 10:30 by the time I finished breakfast, and by then I was awake enough to decipher the students' handwriting, so I started in on the homework. A much-needed surge of mental energy helped me to rip through three assignments in the next hour, and I was considering taking a break when I heard footsteps on the stairs outside. I pushed my chair out from my desk and stood just as the doorbell rang, and when I peeked through the peephole I nearly fell over.

Jack Harrington was standing on my porch.

I unchained the door and twisted the deadbolt, then opened the door and, yes, it was indeed him. "Hi," I said with a voice that sounded more astounded than I meant it to.

He smiled. "Hi there. How are you feeling?"

"Fine, I'm fine, thanks," I stammered. I grinned at him like an idiot and could feel my face growing hotter and undoubtedly redder. "Do you want to come in?"

"Well, I don't want to interrupt you or anything—"

"Oh, no, you're not; I was just grading papers. Needed the break, to be honest."

"Well, I really can't stay; I just wanted to drop this off." He held out his hand, which held a plain silver key ring with two car keys and a lock fob from it.

I stared at them. "Huh?"

Now *he* was getting red, and wow, was it adorable; he ducked his head and raked his fingers through his hair. "Well, your car was totaled, and my set assistant was selling hers, so…" He shrugged and stood there still holding the keys out to me. "I didn't know which space was yours, so I parked it there…" He pointed to the spot directly below my door, and there was a shiny black Civic sitting there in the rain.

My jaw dropped. "You're kidding," I choked out around a laugh that escaped before I had the chance to stop it. "I— My gosh, it looks brand new! There's no way I can afford it— I mean, thank you so, *so* much for thinking of me, but there's no way I can buy it—"

"No, no, no, I didn't mean for you to *buy* it from me. *I* bought it for *you*." He shifted on his feet, looking uncomfortable. "I know you probably don't have the money for it, being a teacher and all, and I have plenty, so, you know…" He shrugged again and jangled the keys. "You gonna take these?"

I slowly took the keys from his hand and looked down at the car and back up at him. "Wow, Ja…um, Mr. Harr—"

"Jack."

I could feel my face glowing with embarrassment. "Jack, I don't know what to say. This is a total answer to—" I stopped myself before saying it was an answer to prayer; I didn't want to freak him out again. "Thank you. This is so beyond the call of duty; I can't thank you enough."

"It's manual; do you know how to drive a stick?"

I laughed. "Are you kidding? It's my favorite way to drive! Although I won't be able to for a couple more weeks. But soon…" The conversation died, and I couldn't think of a way to resurrect it. I was just too flabbergasted. I threw up my hands. "You've floored me. I don't know what to say. Are you sure you don't want to come in?"

He smiled. "Thanks, but a friend of mine is waiting down there to drive me home." He pointed to a black BMW purring in a spot a few yards away from the new car. *My* new car. "Glad you were home, though; I wasn't quite sure what I'd do if you weren't."

"This is just unreal. I don't know how to thank you enough."

"Well, I hope you like it. It's a good drive; the previous owner took excellent care of it. But if there are any problems with it, give me a call, and I'll get it straightened out, okay?" He reached into his pocket and pulled out his wallet, then extracted a business card.

I laughed. "You have a business card?"

He grinned. "Well, yeah, why not?"

"Because everyone knows who you are."

He grinned. "Ah, but not everyone knows how to get ahold of me." He reached out to shake my hand. "But now you do. Nice seeing you again, Miss Winslowe."

"Oh please; it's Grace. Thank you so much. I know there's probably no chance of it, but if there's *ever* anything I can do for you… I certainly owe you one."

He smiled and nodded. "I'll remember that. Take care." With a final smile over his shoulder he bounded down the stairs. He trotted through the rain to the BMW and slid in; it eased out of the space and roared like the Batmobile through the lot to the street.

I closed the door and fell against it, staring in awe at the keys in my hand. Jack Harrington, *the* Jack Harrington whose own car I had totaled, had just become the answer to my prayers and bought me a car.

God has a strange sense of humor.

JACK

"So what did she say?"

" 'Thank you.' "

"Well, I'd certainly hope so. Anything else?"

I laughed. "What else *should* she have said?"

"Oh, I don't know… 'Come on in and let me repay you'?"

I socked Todd on the arm. "You are so sick. She's a nice girl, don't talk about her that way."

He threw me a sidelong glance and shrugged. "Kiddin', buddy, relax. How do you know she's nice?"

I rolled my eyes. "You can just tell with some people, you know?"

"Well of course she's nice to you, you're *you*."

"So you think she would have thrown me off the balcony if I'd been some average Joe?"

"No, I'm just saying that she sees you and sees a celebrity that she can use to get her own ticket to fame. They all do, you know that."

I shook my head adamantly. "No, it was *definitely* not like that. Not at all. She was surprised and grateful, and that was it. No trying to get in—"

"Your pants?"

I glared at him. "I was going to say the spotlight. But not my pants, either. She was friendly and thankful and charming."

"Ooh, she's charming now?"

I thunked my head against the headrest and groaned. "Just drop it, okay?" Todd snickered but shut up. I stared silently out the window as we entered onto the 5 and headed north toward the city. It really was pretty amazing; in a way I could understand Todd's sick assumption that she would have thrown herself at me. Judging by some of my fan mail, there were many out there who would have done just that.

Maybe she wasn't a fan. This was a new twist. I'd never met someone who didn't like me. Not that I didn't think those people existed; I'd just never been faced with one. It was an odd realization. I mentioned it to Todd, who got a kick out of that possibility. Big surprise.

"You bought her a car?"

I pulled a beer from the fridge and walked to the sofa as I screwed off the top. "Well, yeah. So?"

"I don't know…it just seems…weird."

I sat down and turned on the TV, muting the sound and flipping through the channels. "Weird how?"

"Well, from a PR standpoint it's just interesting. I mean, are you seeing this woman, is she a friend—"

"She's a stranger I'm helping out, Kate, that's it. I'm playing her Fairy Godmother. Godfather. Whatever. It doesn't have to be a big deal."

"Well, it's not—to me. If the rags get wind of it—"

"Kate, I am *so tired* of wondering how the media is going to interpret my every waking move. I just don't care anymore. And besides, the only way they'll find out about it is if I tell them, or you tell them, or Grace tells them. Or Todd. And since no one is planning on doing that, I don't think it's going to be a problem."

"How do you know she won't?"

"Why *would* she?"

"Why *wouldn't* she? It's great publicity for her."

I laughed and almost spilled beer all over myself. "Kate! She's a *schoolteacher!* She's not some fanatic looking for some time in the spotlight."

"How do you know? Schoolteachers don't get fame at all; even more reason for her to grab it when she can."

I groaned. "You and Todd really ought to get together. I mean it. You're perfect for each other. You could sit around dreaming up conspiracies and waiting for the other shoe to drop on every situation you encounter while waiting for people to try to cash in on their relationship with you."

Kate sighed. "Look, I'm sorry. You understand why I worry—"

"Yes, I do, but I'm telling you not to. It's not the end of the world if someone gets wind of it, and no one is going to anyway, so just chill out." I took a swig from the bottle. "So what did she say?"

"Just that she wanted to thank you again. She was totally flustered when she found out the number was for me and not you. It took her a second to regroup."

"I didn't even think to mention the number was for my assistant. Sorry about that."

"I don't mind. She did sound nice, though. Very…polite."

I chuckled. "You sound surprised."

"Hey, I don't talk to many polite people during the day. I usually deal with the press. It was a nice change."

"Well, thanks for passing on the message."

"No problem."

"Talk to you later."

"Sure thing."

"Bye— Wait, hold on."

"What?"

"Did you get her number?"

"Yes, why?"

"Do me a favor. Call her back and give her my number here."

"Your number…like, your personal number?"

"Yeah. Wait, no, I take it back. That seems way too…I don't know. Having my assistant call is too impersonal. I'll just do it."

"You sure? Because, like, that's the sort of thing I'm supposed to do."

"Yeah, I know, but this isn't business. Never mind. Thanks, Kate. Later."

She made a weird noise that sounded like a cross between a sneeze and a snicker. "Bye, Jack."

I drained the bottle and got up. What had I done with the paper I'd written Grace's info on? I checked the pockets of my jacket and finally found it in one of them. I dialed the number. It rang four times and then went over to a machine.

"Hi, you've reached Grace Winslowe. Leave a message."

"Hi, Grace, Jack here. Uh, Jack *Harrington;* guess I shouldn't assume you'd know right away who I meant." *Great. I sound like an idiot.* "Listen, sorry about not explaining about the number on the card. I wasn't thinking. If you need to call me about the car or anything, you can call me here at my place. The number is 310-555-2853. Hope you enjoy the car. Take care. Bye."

I hung up and dropped the cordless back into its base and shook my head. "Uh, Jack *Harrington.*" She'd think I was totally stoned or something. I opened the fridge to look for something to eat. What did I care what she thought? I'd just bought her a car, she wasn't going to hate me, that's for sure.

I marched back to the living room and unmuted the television, then channel surfed till I found a football game. I ate my sandwich and stared at the screen, my eyes following the game and my brain in a completely different realm. A long time passed before I realized I'd spent it all thinking about her.

GRACE

"HE GAVE YOU a car?"

I held the phone a few inches from my ear as Missy squawked. "Ow. Quieter, please. And yes. How incredible is that?"

"He just stopped on over, dropped the keys in your hand, and said it was all yours?"

"Believe it or not! You were right, Missy; God provided."

She laughed in evident amazement. "That He did. What did you say?"

I laughed. "'Thank you,' about a million times. I even called him to thank him—"

"He gave you his number?"

"Well, that's the thing, he gave me his card and said to call if there was a problem with the car. So I called after he left to leave him a message and tell him thank you again. It was his assistant!"

"He has an assistant?"

"Apparently. I was so embarrassed. And she had no idea what I was talking about. It was awful; I felt so stupid."

"I'm sure you didn't sound as bad as you think."

"I hope you're right. Man, I wish I could drive, I want to test it out."

"We ought to take it for a spin tomorrow after work."

"Ooh, great idea! I wonder what features it has."

"You should read the owner's manual."

"Oh, now that's fun."

"Hey, never know what useful tidbits of information you'll learn."

"Whatever. Call me when you get home tomorrow, okay?"

"Will do. Have fun admiring your new ride."

"No problem there."

I grabbed my jacket, hobbled down to the car, and scrambled into the front seat to avoid the rain. I readjusted the seat to suit my outstretched leg and sat staring at the dash. It smelled faintly of vanilla.

I turned it on to look at the lights on the display. It had a full tank of gas. What a gentleman! I played around with the radio, changing all the presets and fiddling with the equalizers even though I didn't really know what they did. The owner's manual sat alone in the glove compartment; I pulled it out and started skimming. Dry reading, to be sure, but useful.

I stayed down there for twenty minutes, playing with my big new toy, then took advantage of a break in the rain to hobble back up to the apartment. When I went to the kitchen to make some tea, I noticed the answering machine was blinking.

"Hi, Grace. It's Jack." I nearly dropped the teapot into the sink. I missed the next part of his message because I was so surprised, and finally tuned back in when he apologized for not explaining that the number was his assistant's. How sweet! I wished someone was here to hear this. I grabbed the phone and called Missy. "No more waiting till tomorrow after work," I told her, "come over tonight for dinner. You'll never guess who left a message on my machine…"

Missy ran her hand over the steering wheel. "All righty then. Where should we go?"

"I don't know, just around. Go up to Joy's and see if she's home." Missy started the car and backed out of the space as I flipped through the radio presets looking for good driving music. "This is unreal," I murmured.

"I know; it's incredible." Missy suddenly squealed. "He sat right

here!" We both laughed, and she launched into an obsessed-fan routine. "Oh my gosh, he sat right here, my butt is right where his butt
was; his hands were on this steering wheel!" She kissed the top of the
wheel. "I'll never wash the interior of my car again!"

We laughed till we cried. "Stop!" I finally commanded, "You
shouldn't drive when you're laughing that hard."

"Should we test the antilock brakes?" Missy waggled her eyebrows
at me.

"Good grief, no, thank you." Missy chuckled, and we sang with
the radio the rest of the way to Joy's house, where we gushed all over
again as we told her what had happened. She called Taylor, and we all
had dinner and talked for a couple hours before leaving for the
evening. But once I crawled into bed, I hovered on the brink of sleep
for two hours, unable to drop into unconsciousness because of all the
thoughts pinging around in my head. Apparently I hadn't completely
scared him away with my bizarre message from God. I wondered
what he thought of all that. I wanted to ask him, but I was not about
to call him. I forced myself to be content with the fact that if he
wanted to talk about it, he certainly knew how to find me.

Later that week the girls and I had a valentine writing party. I had to
write them for my kids, which inspired the others to revisit the childhood tradition and write some too. We were sprawled around the living room with the *Sleepless in Seattle* soundtrack in the background.

"Gonna send a card to Jack?" Joy asked in a coy voice after a
music-filled spell of writing. They all snickered, and I felt myself
blush.

I snorted. "Sure, that'll be the day."

"You totally should, Grace. It could double as a thank-you card."

I rolled my eyes. "You're out of your minds."

"Oh, come on," Missy coaxed, "what if he's up there in LA,

thinking about how much he likes you, and how he wishes he could have some sign that you like him too?" She was really getting into it. "And then this card arrives—the sign he's been waiting for! And he drives down here in a limo and sweeps you off your feet, and you fly to Bali to get married. All because you sent him a simple little note."

I was snickering in spite of myself. "Missy, you're leaking melodrama all over my clean carpet; knock it off."

"So...gonna do it?"

"Sure," I said sarcastically. "Yeah, I'll write him one right now. What should I say?"

Joy jumped into the action. "Happy Valentine's Day, you gorgeous hunk, you, thanks for coming to my rescue, your devoted Grace." She blink-blinked innocently, and we all dissolved into laughter.

"Oh, *please*," I groaned. "You guys are awful."

"Well, if you write the card we'll leave you alone." Missy smiled sweetly over the top of her mug of hot chocolate.

"Forget it, ladies. I'm not gonna do it."

Missy sighed and shrugged. "Big mistake, but okay."

We went back to our cards, and I marveled silently at how out of hand the other girls were getting with this whole thing. It was all just a bizarre fluke, something I'd get to brag about for the rest of my life, the closest I'd ever get to living a storybook romance—but that was all. I had no expectation of ever meeting up with Jack Harrington again.

JACK

SHOOTING WAS FINALLY COMPLETED on *Destiny Awaits,* and I was savoring the ability to sleep late and lounge around in bed as long as I wanted. But when I saw the clock change to 11:00 a.m., I reluctantly got up, figuring I ought to do something more productive than lie in bed all day. As I ate a brunch of leftover Chinese, I flipped around on TV and ran across the film, *Grace of My Heart.* Seeing the name in the small yellow box on the bottom of the screen instantly reminded me of Grace, and suddenly the dream I'd been in the middle of when I had awakened was clear as day in my head.

I'd been dropping off the car at Grace's apartment again, but this time I'd gone in and sat at her kitchen table. She'd taken the keys from me, then sat down and started laughing. "What?" I'd asked.

"You actually came back. After the scene in the hospital I thought for sure you'd never come back."

"You did say some pretty bizarre things."

"Ah, but they're not bizarre to me. Only to you. If you believed, they wouldn't be so weird."

"Believed what?"

And then I'd woken up.

I hadn't given the scene at the hospital a whole lot of thought recently, although every time I ran across one of those televangelists on TV, I wondered vaguely if she thought the same way they did. And yet whenever I *did* think of that day, I could remember exactly what she had said. I had a hard time believing that someone who seemed as normal as she did would really think that God worked like that, if there even was a God. It seemed a bit fanatical to me. But then again, it had been a long, *long* time since I had darkened the door of a church, and I didn't remember much of what I'd learned at the church my parents had dragged us to a few times a year when I was growing up. Maybe it wasn't that fanatical. Maybe it was pretty normal, and I just didn't know it. Either way, it didn't seem like something I was willing to buy into. Heck, I'd tried all those other religions to no avail. Why would this one be any different?

I finished eating, then showered and dressed before trying to make the apartment presentable. Kate was stopping by sometime after noon, and it was 12:30 by the time I finally got the place looking decent. I'd been pretty sloppy lately, which wasn't typical of me, but I'd been preoccupied and distracted, and when I got like that, I tended to get messy. Too much brainpower was being diverted to the Grace issue for me to think about being tidy.

Kate arrived a little after 1:00, a cardboard box in her arms. "All right, let's see what you've got here," she said after settling into an armchair. She handed me a bundle of fan mail, a stack of scripts, and an envelope of business mail. After that she whipped out a calendar and ran down a list of interview requests, charity invitations, and a few other issues that needed my attention, and after an hour we had everything squared away.

When we were done, she fidgeted a bit in her seat and then stared me down. "So tell me about this girl."

I shrugged. "What's to tell?"

"Well, you gave her a car."

"Yeah."

"And?"

"And what?"

"So that's it? You gave her a car, said, 'Have a nice life,' and that's the end of that? Not gonna call, not gonna write, just...let it lie?"

I raked a hand through my hair. Why did this conversation make me uncomfortable? "Well, yeah, I guess. What's the big deal?"

She seemed to study me for a minute. "Permission to speak freely?"

I laughed. "Always."

"I've known you for, what, three years or so now, right?"

"Yeah."

"I've seen you jump in and out of a lot of relationships. And don't think I don't know about all of them; I've got my sources." She smirked and winked, and I laughed, feeling sheepish. Kate did have a remarkable talent for seemingly reading my mind. "And even with Dianne, whom I know you were in love with, I never saw you do anything that big and selfless and be so concerned." She shrugged. "Something in your voice changes when you talk about this woman, and I'm willing to bet she's on your mind a lot more than you would readily admit."

She leaned forward, not letting me avoid her gaze. "You've had a rough couple of years, Jack. If you think you've found someone who could lighten the load a bit, I'd go for it." She threw up her hands and smirked. "Or just ignore me completely, and tell me to shut up and get back in my place."

I laughed, glad for the escape. "And your love advice column starts next week in the *LA Times,* right?"

"Yeah, and once the mail starts pouring in I'll have to start charging for these private sessions, so take advantage of it now when I'm still dispensing it for free." She winked as she stood and headed for the door.

I walked her out and gave her a hug. "Thanks, Kate. You're a good friend."

She smiled, her tone light but still serious. "I care about you, Jack. I don't want to see you hurting anymore, that's all." She descended the stairs and turned out of sight.

I walked back to the apartment and pulled a beer from the fridge before sitting back down on the couch, surrounded by mail and scripts. I thought about what Kate had said, trying to decide whether it had any merit.

Truth was, Grace fascinated me. When I'd first seen her in the hospital, I felt only concern, but mostly because of the circumstances. The second time, I'd been curious. She'd seemed harmless enough, but once she'd laid on all that God talk, I'd been more than a bit wary of her. But that morning when I'd dropped off the car at her house, she'd been so friendly, and so sincere and *normal*…if she hadn't said anything about God in the hospital I would never have pegged her as religious.

And she hadn't gushed or gotten all giggly when I'd shown up either. I rarely met women who didn't get tongue-tied or star-struck when they met me for the first time. She'd been totally cool—or as cool as someone could be when a celebrity appeared on her doorstep and gave her a car.

She was unusual. I couldn't deny the fact that I was tempted to come up with other ways to see her. I just wasn't sure it was a good idea.

I tried to clear my head and halfheartedly started in on the stuff Kate brought. I scanned the scripts, then moved on to the fan mail. I only got through a couple before realizing it was pointless; I wasn't really concentrating on anything right now. I just couldn't get Grace off my mind.

Then I started wondering if I could come up with any other excuses to see her again. Not that I would necessarily make use of such an opportunity, even if one presented itself. But what if…?

My eyes fell on the marketing packet Kate had left with me for *Destiny Awaits*. It contained the release dates for trailers and the movie itself, as well as the premiere information. It wasn't a megamovie of any sort, so the festivities were not going to be anything ultraexciting or unusual. But it would still be nice to go with a date.

Hmm.

Here was my chance. Was I willing to take it? I drew up a mental list. Pro: I'd get to see her again. Con: the media would see her too. Pro: it would be better than going by myself. Con: rumors would run rampant. Pro: maybe something would come of it. Con: maybe something would come of it.

I stood and walked into my bedroom to riffle through a stack of papers. I pulled a sheet from the middle and stared at it. Her phone number. I brought it back into the living room with me, where I sat back down and began to think.

Then it struck me that she might already be in a relationship. Wouldn't *that* suck: to call and make a move and then find out she's already got a boyfriend! I wracked my brain, trying to think of anything I'd seen or she'd said that would tell me one way or the other. I couldn't come up with anything.

Ah…but the night of the accident two women had come in for her. No one had mentioned a boyfriend or husband or fiancé or anything like that. I couldn't remember seeing any diamond or wedding band on her finger—not that I'd been looking, either. But certainly he would have come to the hospital that night, if there was a he in the picture at all. He would have been there during visiting hours.

I laughed aloud and shook my head. This was nonsense. I'd just call, ask her point-blank if she wanted to go, and if there was already someone in her life she'd say it, and I'd thank her anyway and hang up. How could I be expected to know?

I picked up the phone, dialed all but the last digit, and then took a deep breath and hit the last button. I couldn't remember when I'd last felt nervous about talking to a woman.

One ring. Two rings. The beginning of a third, and then a click as the line was picked up. I heard laughter in the background. "Hello?"

"Hello, is Grace there, please?" My voice sounded salesmanlike to my ears. Why couldn't I just talk normally?

"This is she."

"Grace, hi; this is Jack. Harrington."

"Oh! Jack. Hi!" The laughter on the other end of the line suddenly went silent. "How are you?"

"Good, thanks. How's the car? Driving it yet?"

"Yes, it's fantastic. I can't thank you enough."

"It was my pleasure. You're all healed up now?"

"Oh yeah, I'm fine. Everything's in working order."

"That's good; I'm glad to hear it." I took a deep breath. "Well, the reason I'm calling is because I have a movie coming out next month, and the premiere is on April 15. I was wondering if you would like to join me as my, ah, guest." I choked at the last second and couldn't bring myself to say date. I was starting to wish I'd scripted this out.

For a moment there was silence on the other end. Then she said in an endearingly awestruck voice, "Oh my goodness, are you serious?"

I swallowed down a chuckle, not wanting her to think I was laughing at her. "Yes, I'm entirely serious. I know it's quite a ways down the road, but I wanted to make sure I got the offer in before your calendar filled up."

She laughed and said dryly, "Yeah, fat chance of that. Wow, I am so… I would *love* to go. Is there anything special I need to know, or do, or…whatever? How exactly does this work?"

"Ah, well, let's see… There really isn't anything special. Red carpet starts at six, so knowing what the traffic going into the city is like on weeknights, I should probably be at your place by 3:30. Would that be all right?"

"Wait, hold on a second. I need to grab a pen and write all this down, or I'll forget." I heard a thunk as the phone was set down, and I forced myself not to laugh when I heard someone in the background squeal. "Okay, 3:30, April 15. Got it."

"Is that all right?"

"Are you kidding? That's fine. Perfect timing, in fact; I'm on spring break that week. But I'm sorry you'd have to come down that early in the day, though. Kind of sucks for you."

I laughed a bit. "Don't worry about me, that's okay. I'll read on the way down or something."

"Read while you drive?"

"Well, the driver will be driving, I'll just be sitting there watching the less-than-scenic scenery of greater LA pass me by."

"Oh. Driver. Right." I could almost hear her blushing. For some reason it made me smile. "Um...what do I wear?"

"Nothing ultraformal. The theatre is almost always freezing, though, so you may want to make sure you have a wrap or something."

"All right..."

"And afterward Alexis is throwing a bash at her house in Beverly Hills. I need to at least show my face, but if you'd rather not go, I can always bring you home first. I'll leave it up to you."

Silence for a moment. Then, "Alexis? Like, Alexis Giovanni, that Alexis?"

"Yeah, she's in the movie."

"Would it be...okay, this is going to sound really lame, but...is it okay for me to be there? I mean, I don't know anyone, it's not my— I mean, I'm not an actress, or in show business or anything— I can't believe I just called it show business, that sounds so 1950s, sorry..." She let out an exasperated sigh. "Do you have any idea what I'm try-ing to say?"

This time I couldn't help but laugh. She joined in, albeit weakly, and I could sense she was already feeling out of her element. And understandably so. I gave her points for being as calm as she was. "Yes, I know exactly what you're saying. And no, there's no reason why you shouldn't be there. I get to bring whoever I want, actress or not. But if you don't feel comfortable, you don't have to go. And you don't have to decide right now; you can tell me what you feel up to after the movie is over."

She sighed. "Wow. I don't know what to say; this is just…amazing. Thank you so much for asking me, Jack."

"Thank you for saying yes."

GRACE

I SET THE PHONE back in its cradle and turned slowly to face the room where Joy, Taylor, and Missy were sitting. The movie we'd been watching played on with the sound muted; no one had paid it the slightest attention since I'd answered the phone. As if on cue we all screamed at the top of our lungs and dissolved into laughter. I threw myself onto the couch and hugged a pillow to my face, shrieking and laughing.

"What did he say?!" Joy gasped. "*What* is happening at 3:30 on April 15?"

I calmed myself down and tossed the pillow aside and sighed. "Well, first he said hello." I giggled. "Actually, it's kind of funny; he said, 'This is Jack. *Harrington.*' Like I wouldn't know! And then he asked how the car was, and how I was—"

"Typical guy to ask about the car first," smirked Taylor.

I laughed. "Oh, be nice!" I sat up and felt my face splitting with a huge grin. "And *then* he asked if I would accompany him to a premiere next month!"

"Oh, my goodness!" Taylor breathed. "For *Destiny Awaits,* right? I've seen the trailers. Oh, wow; this is like Cinderella for the new millennium!"

Missy snorted. "Yeah—except she doesn't have any oppressive stepsisters or stepmothers or a fairy godmother—but other than that, yeah, totally Cinderella."

Taylor rolled her eyes. "Fine, it's a general, nondescript fairy tale for the new millennium, that better?"

"So what else?" Joy asked.

"He's picking me up in a limo. And afterward there's a party at Alexis Giovanni's."

More hoots and hollers followed, and in the end we were all sprawled around the floor, giggling spastically. But the more I thought about it, the more unsure of the whole thing I became. "Oh man. I'm never gonna look the part. I'll need to get a new dress! What on earth do you wear to a premiere?!"

"Don't you have any old prom dresses or anything?"

"Oh yeah, sure, pink sequins are just the right thing; good thought, Missy." I pelted her with a pillow. "Seriously, you guys, you know me, I'm not the dress-up type; I never wear makeup, much less get all dolled up. I don't know how to do 'dolled up'!"

"We'll take care of you, don't worry. You'll be stunning."

"I don't know if I *want* to look stunning. I mean, not too stunning, anyway. Stunning isn't me. I just want to be me, you know? Can I do that with a celebrity?"

"You're stressing way too much, Grace; calm down," Joy advised. "It's a month and a half away, you have plenty of time to get everything sorted out, and it'll all be fine. Don't worry."

I sighed and flopped my arm over my eyes. "Oh, the drama." I sighed. "You know, I really wish something *interesting* would happen to me; life is just so dull these days."

I wasn't letting myself dwell too much on the premiere, because the minute I did I went into a full-blown panic. I still couldn't believe I was going. I couldn't believe he was even talking to me after what I'd said to him in the hospital. I wondered if he would bring any of that up, or if God would prompt me to broach the subject again. I almost hoped neither would happen, that it would never come up in the conversation, because I was still so new to the Christianity thing myself, I didn't know what I would say if he asked me about it. And even Jane and Missy had been unsure what to make of it when I'd told them about my experience.

I finally decided there was no use worrying about it anymore. Whatever was going to happen would happen whether or not I was ready for it. Might as well just hang on and let the roller coaster continue.

One Saturday afternoon in late March, Missy, Joy, and Taylor picked me up and whisked me to the mall for dress shopping. We worked out the most efficient dress-shopping strategy ever created: I pointed, they found the right size, and once we'd amassed more dresses than we could carry, we schlepped everything to the biggest fitting room we could find. We took a lot of breaks—fast shopping burns a lot of calories, after all—and after a total of two mochas, a brownie, a cheese croissant, a hot flavored pretzel, and twelve stores, we finally found the perfect dress: a floor-length, black satin number in a mandarin style, with cap sleeves and little flowers embroidered into the slinky material. It fit beautifully, was neither too dressy nor too casual, and was very comfortable, and we all agreed instantly that it was The Dress. We also found a black satin wrap and shoes I felt sure would permanently reform my foot, and after a very full day, we went home to order pizza to celebrate.

There were about two weeks left before the premiere. I'd started looking critically at myself, trying to figure out if I was being neurotic or if I really was going to look absolutely ridiculous standing next to one of the most beautiful men in the world. I'd always had pretty simple taste; jeans and T-shirts were my favorite outfits. Would I really be able to pull off even a somewhat-glamorous look for this premiere? Or would I just look like a jeans-and-T-shirt girl stuck in a nice dress?

I was flipping through a *Cosmopolitan* magazine one afternoon— an impulse buy from my recent grocery trip—and one segment on hair caught my eye. I'd worn my hair past my shoulders for years, a minor rebellion against my mother who always cut my hair into a blunt pageboy when I was growing up. I'd dyed it various shades of red or brown all through college, but after graduation I gave up doing anything remotely exciting with it and just let it be. I'd never been very good at doing fancy things with it; ponytails tended to win out over anything more stylish. As I flipped through the magazine, with the hair section displaying pictures of celebrities with short hair, I started thinking twice about my long, boring locks. I grabbed the phone to called Missy for the name of her stylist.

"Ooh, what are you gonna do?" she asked as she looked it up.

"Short."

"Short? How short?"

"*Short.* Like, remember Winona Ryder's hair in *Girl, Interrupted*?"

"*Wow.*"

"Told you! Gimme the number; I need to make this appointment before I lose my nerve."

I called the salon and made an appointment for Wednesday evening. That would be exactly two weeks before the premiere, and that way I'd have time to buy a wig or something if I looked awful. I ripped out the photo and stuck it in my purse so I was sure not to forget it.

In the back of my mind, I didn't really think *it*—the premiere— was going to happen: he'd call and apologize, and I'd be horribly embarrassed, but I'd at least have another interesting story to tell my grandkids someday. Or something would happen—the movie would be pulled, or he'd start dating someone, or he'd be sick, or I'd be sick. It just seemed too good to be true. I could not be this lucky.

Because I was 99 percent positive I wouldn't actually get to go, I refrained from telling anyone except the girls, and I swore all of them to secrecy. I didn't want to get sympathetic looks from people when the whole thing fell through. But apparently I was a lousy actor because a lot of people asked me the next few weeks if I was all right; apparently I looked "distracted" and kept "zoning out." "Don't mind me," I'd say smoothly, "I just have a lot on my mind these days. Should have it sorted out in a few weeks."

Wednesday evening I left school both nervous and excited. I found the salon easily and settled into the waiting area to kill the last few minutes before my appointment. Missy had warned me that it was a pretty expensive place, but her mother had been going to this stylist, Dinah, since before Missy was born, and she was worth the money. Missy had told me of a time in high school when she'd been obsessed with a particular look, but when she'd brought in the picture, Dinah had gently told her that the style would look awful on her. Her alternative, however, ended up being Missy's favorite haircut ever, and she swore to give Dinah her business for life.

A seven-month-old issue of *People* sat on the table. I flipped through the pages, scanning articles and pictures to see if there was a hairstyle I liked better. Toward the end was a montage of photos from a slew of charity events, and there in the middle photo was Jack, dressed in a black tux with a red ribbon pinned to the lapel, standing behind a podium handing a small gold statue to a teenage boy. The caption read:

> Hollywood AIDS Project spokesman Jack Harrington presented the annual HAP AIDS Awareness Award to Warren Michaels, a Los Angeles high-school senior who raised over three hundred thousand dollars through fund-raisers over the past year to donate to AIDS research. Michaels was diagnosed with AIDS in 1994. Dianne Wallington, Harrington's one-time girlfriend and coworker on the network drama *Deep Cover,* was diagnosed with the disease in 1999; she died in a car wreck in 2000. Harrington has been the spokesman for HAP for two years.

I stared at the picture and began to read the article again when I heard someone call my name. Dinah was smiling from the hallway. "Are you ready?"

"I think so, yeah." I stood and set the magazine down, then pulled the photo page out of my purse.

Dinah led me to a station in the back. I was getting more nervous every second, so I forced myself to relax as I sat down in the swivel chair and handed her the page. "I've never had my hair shorter than this," I said as I indicated a length that fell right below my jaw. "I saw this photo, and I don't even know if it would look good on me, but that's the kind of thing I want to do: short, easy to deal with, not a lot of work. But still feminine."

Dinah stood behind me and looked at me in the mirror. She took the picture and stared at it intensely for a moment, then back at me, her eyes slightly narrowed and her red lips pursed. She ran her hands through my hair, and after a minute looked up and smiled. "Love it. I think it'll look great on you. Fantastic choice!"

I sighed with relief. "I'm so glad you think so. This is a huge decision. I haven't cut my hair since college, and I have kind of a big event coming up."

Dinah chuckled and patted my shoulder comfortingly. "You'll be gorgeous, don't worry. Let's get you shampooed."

Missy opened the door and her jaw just about fell off her face. "Oh…my…*gosh.*"

I bit my lip and smiled. "Is that a good 'Oh my gosh' or do I need to shave it all off and start over?"

Missy grabbed my arm and pulled me into the house. "Mom!" she yelled. "Come look at Grace!"

Jane scurried in from the kitchen, a dishtowel still in her hands. "Oh my heavens," she said when she registered the new look. "Grace, I can't believe how much it changes you. It's wonderful! Oh, not that you didn't look lovely before—you know what I mean. Do you like it?"

I nodded furiously, laughing. "I *love* it!" I howled. "I can't believe I didn't do it sooner!" I ran my hand over the back of my head. "My neck is cold, though. It's never been exposed like this before."

"It's so *short*...but I love it, Grace, I really do. You are gonna *so* look like you belong in Hollywood."

"There's one more thing I want to do, though; you're gonna have to help me, Missy."

"What's that?"

I raised my eyebrows. "Dye it."

"Oooh, sounds fun. What color?"

"Something...dark."

"Black?" Missy and Jane chorus.

"No, not *that* dark. But dark, dark brown. I think the contrast would look really cool with my skin. I'm so...*not* tan."

"You're getting bold with your newfound beauty, aren't you?" Missy teased.

I laughed and glanced at the hall mirror near the front door. "Every time I see myself I have to look twice. I can't believe that's *me*." I grinned and said in a little voice that sent Jane and Missy into gales of laughter, "I look *goooood*."

"You sure do, girl," Missy said. "Let's go get some coffee or something so you can show off your hair to the world." She grabbed her coat and purse from the table beneath the mirror and followed me out the door.

We went to a small coffeehouse down the street and sat on a ragged couch near the window. A table filled with magazines sat before us, and it reminded me of the magazine I'd read at the salon. "Did you know his girlfriend had AIDS?" There was no need to clarify who "he" was; there had only been one guy in our conversations lately.

She frowned and shook her head. "Don't think I knew that, no. 'Had'? Did she die?"

"In a car accident, yeah."

"Ah, I think I remember that. He left *Deep Cover* not long after, I think. Did you ever watch that?" I shook my head. "Good show. Anyway, I vaguely remember hearing about the accident. He was there and saw it happen."

I shuddered. "Wow, can you imagine?" I sipped my mocha and stared out the window. My free hand absently went to the back of my newly bared neck, which was registering every breeze and shift in temperature that occurred. It was going to take a while to get used to that.

"He must have freaked when you guys were in that accident," Missy suddenly said. "It's only been a couple years since she died. Wouldn't that totally suck? To see someone die in an accident while you're right there, trying to help—and then have it happen again?"

I hadn't thought of that. It *would* be pretty horrific. "That's why he's doing it," I said, the light suddenly seeming to dawn. "He's all, you know, trying to make up for what he couldn't do for her."

Missy made a skeptical face. "You think so?"

I shrugged. "Missy, why else would he be doing all this? I mean, come on, I am *not* anything special compared to the people he knows. I'm not saying I'm not quality; I'm just saying it doesn't make sense. I mean, do you know of any actors who haven't married actresses? Or at least someone who's famous for something? It doesn't happen. There has to be some reason for it, and that must be it. He's still tormented by what happened with what's-her-name, and he's found someone he can make it up to, in a way." I sipped my mocha and thought it over. "That must be it. Honestly, it doesn't make sense any other way."

"Well…"

I looked at Missy. "What?"

"What if he's actually interested in what you said at the hospital?"

My stomach turned over. "Do you think he might be?"

She shrugged and drained the rest of her mocha. "Nothing is impossible."

"Oh man." I leaned my head back against the couch cushions and groaned. "That's almost worse."

"How do you figure? That would be awesome!"

I sighed impatiently. "Well, yes, in theory. It would be great if he wanted to know about God, yes. But not from *me*. I hardly know anything myself!"

"Well yeah, but"—she lowered her voice and leaned in toward me—"you were obviously good enough for God to choose you to talk to Jack about it in the first place."

"Missy, for all I know I was high on morphine when I said all that. I mean, how ridiculous is it to think God really would have done that? I am *not* the ideal person for something like that."

Missy smirked. "Since when does God *ever* use the ideal person for anything? Moses, Rahab, Paul, Peter, Ruth—"

"Fine, fine, whatever, you win," I groused.

"I mean, you *do* have to admit it's pretty miraculous that he'd want to talk to you again after you threw something like that out there the first time you met him, right? And not only does he talk to you, but he buys you a car, he invites you to a freakin' *premiere*… You have to wonder, don't you, at how unlikely that all is?"

"That's what *I* have been telling *you*," I reminded her.

"Yeah, but you think it's unlikely simply because you're not some model-perfect beauty goddess. I think it's unlikely because most people would have thought you were off your rocker to say something like that. And yet it's happening."

I sighed and clutched my stomach as it danced the jitterbug. "Yes, it is."

JACK

"SO YOU'RE DRIVING down to get her and then coming back? Do you have any idea how horrendous traffic is gonna be? For all the gas that'll take you'd probably save money hiring a helicopter."

I laughed. "Now that would be a heck of an entrance. But a bit incongruous for the opening of a romantic comedy, don't you think? Let's save that for the opening of *Nine Lives.*"

Kate chuckled. "All right, it's your call. Anything else?"

"Nope, I'm good on my end. You?"

"No, I'm fine for now. If anything last minute comes up I'll call, but everything should be fine. Have fun tomorrow."

We hung up, and I went back to reading the script I'd started just before Kate's call. I was having a hard time concentrating though and ended up having to start over from the beginning. I was three pages into it the second time around when I realized I just wasn't focused, so I tossed the script on the couch beside me and got up to change for a jog on my treadmill.

This would be my sixth premiere, but it was only the second one I'd ever been nervous about. Usually I was excited to see the finished product on the big screen. Besides tonight, the only one I'd ever been nervous about had been my first, and that was only because I'd been ignorant about the process. Now I had it down pat: arrive to cheering crowds, get blinded by camera flashes, wave to the onlookers, submit myself to a couple on-the-spot interviews, slowly make my way into the theatre, watch the movie, feel relieved that it turned out well (usually), and then reverse the process and go home.

But this time would be very different. The entire process would be the same, but I'd be with someone who had never experienced any of it before. People would ask questions about who she was, and the sharp ones would make the connection pretty quickly. She'd probably get more attention than I would.

But I couldn't figure out exactly what was bothering me. I didn't worry that she'd mess anything up, or that she'd be poorly received by the press. She might not be Hollywood beautiful, but she *was* pretty, and all done up for the evening she'd probably look great.

I did wonder whether or not she'd like the movie. I was proud of it, and I knew the director and other actors had been pleased with the outcome. But it was, in all honesty, a chick flick, so the chances of her not liking it were pretty small.

So what was the deal?

That evening Sean, one of the guys Todd and I hung out with, came over to watch the Lakers game, and during a commercial break he asked if she was still coming to the premiere the next evening.

"Yes, she is. And for some reason, I'm extremely nervous."

"Seriously?" He chuckled.

"Yeah. Bizarre, isn't it?"

He sipped his beer and thought for a minute. "Well, not that bizarre. I mean, you barely know her. It's gonna be a long drive back up to the city from her place. Could be awkward. She's an outsider to this whole thing; she may think it's awesome, she may think it's ridiculous." He shrugged. "First-date jitters."

I laughed and almost spilled my beer. "First-date jitters? This isn't a date, though."

Sean rolled his eyes. "Then what is it?"

Good question.

Sean could practically see the wheels turning in my head. "How deep is *your* denial, buddy?" he laughed as he stood from the couch to head for the kitchen.

"Well— But it's really *not* a date." Sean glared at me from the fridge. "I'm serious! A date means you're interested in dating someone. A date is a precursor to a relationship. Or at least sex. This isn't any of that."

"Well then, what *is* it?"

"It's— Quick, the game's back on." Sean grabbed another beer and lunged back to the couch. Lakers were up 45 to the Pistons' 38 with two minutes to go, and Sean was a die-hard fan.

"So what is it?"

"Hold on, I'm still thinking," I mumbled around a mouthful of popcorn.

"Don't hurt yourself."

All right. So what was it? I was convinced it wasn't a date. But if it wasn't a date, there weren't a whole lot of other things it could be.

I considered the ramifications of calling it a date. Would it be that bad? I'd have to stick by her during the evening and not flirt with anyone else. I could do that. I'd have to call her, or something, after it was over, since that was the protocol. But I wouldn't have to ask her out again, just call and thank her for coming and sign off with a non-committal "Take care, thanks again." And if we had a good time, then the door was open to more dates. I could handle that.

Now. If it wasn't a date, then what else could it be? Why had I extended the invitation in the first place?

I had wanted to see her again.

Why had I wanted to see her again?

There was something there I couldn't put my finger on.

Sean looked at me, an eyebrow cocked.

"Okay, yeah. It's a date."

I buttoned my jacket and pulled the sleeves taut as I walked to the mirror in my walk-in closet. Looking good, as usual. But I was still nervous. I caught myself more than once wondering what she would be wearing.

Ever since I'd resigned myself to the idea that this was a date, things in my mind had gotten worse, not better. Now I was experiencing flashbacks to my first homecoming, my first prom, my first date ever—none of them had been disasters, a fact that I was trying to pull some comfort from. And those were all before I'd been named one of *People*'s "Top 25 Most Beautiful People." There was no reason why this date should not be fantastic.

It was a long, uneventful drive down to Orange County. Only a couple delays on the 405, and we made it in pretty good time, considering it was a Friday afternoon. Coming back up was going to be hell. I hoped hard the conversation came easy.

We pulled into the parking lot of her complex, and the car slid to a soft stop. I spotted the Honda a couple parking spots down; seeing it made me somehow more nervous. I took a deep breath as I walked up the stairs to her balcony, sneaking a glance into her front window to see if she was there but just getting my reflection. I rang the bell and forced myself to relax; I was terrified that my tension would be written all over my face.

The door opened, and a gorgeous woman in an Oriental-inspired dress stood in front of me. I was about to ask if Grace was home, assuming that this was her roommate or a friend, when I realized it *was* Grace. She'd cut her hair drastically, and it was darker, but it was definitely her. And she was stunning. "Wow!" was the first thing out of my mouth, and I was instantly embarrassed. *Brilliant; great start, Harrington.* She blushed and ducked her head, and I chuckled. "Sorry; the filter between my brain and my mouth is apparently out of order. But you do look *amazing*."

She looked back and smiled, obviously self-conscious. "Thank you."

"Are you ready to go, or do you need a minute?"

"No, I'm ready." She reached back to a table by the door and took hold of a small black purse and a satin shawl. She locked the door behind her, and I led the way down to the car. A dog-walking neighbor paused to watch from the other side of the street, and I wondered for the umpteenth time what Grace would make of all the attention. I didn't know her well enough to guess. I realized I didn't know her at all.

The driver opened the door and helped her into the car, and I settled in across from her. She folded her shawl and placed it in her lap, then shot me a sheepish grin. "I'm just going to apologize up front in case I do something completely idiotic tonight. I haven't the foggiest idea what to expect, and I am terrified I'm going to embarrass you. So, if that happens, forgive me." She shrank back a bit in her seat, her gaze steady on me.

I chuckled and shook my head. "Believe me, you have nothing to worry about. This isn't nearly as big a deal as everyone makes it out to be. So little happens there's hardly any time to screw anything up. Care for a drink?" I motioned to the wet bar that ran the length of the limo and slid down the seat toward the minifridge. Even if she didn't want one, I was definitely going to need one; I was suddenly just as worried I'd be the one doing something idiotic.

GRACE

I AM IN A STRETCH limousine with Jack Harrington. *It's actually happening. I'm really here. There's even a refrigerator! Oh my gosh, he's talking to me. Be casual. Be witty. Be articulate.*

"Oh, no thanks. This dress is the most expensive thing I've ever purchased; drinking in a moving vehicle would just be begging for a giant spill."

He didn't look as dressed up as I had expected: white collarless shirt and a jacket, nondescript (but probably expensive) slacks. I began to panic. Was I overdressed? Did I look like I was trying too hard? I was too upset to even think before blurting out, "Is this dress overdone?"

"Um…overdone?" He looked confused.

My face felt so hot I could have toasted s'mores by it. "I mean, am I overdressed? Is it too much? You're not as dressed up as I thought you'd be, and I don't want—"

"Oh! No, your dress is fine. It's great. Really, it's perfect."

I smiled with relief, but inside I felt so tense I thought I'd explode. I wracked my brain for something else to say. "So what's the game plan for the evening?" *Game plan? Real classy, Winslowe.*

"Well, provided the traffic does what we're expecting it to do—which is to lock us in a near standstill for the last hour and a half of the drive—we should get to the theatre around six. Then we'll do the whole meet-the-press thing, which basically means smile and wave in the face of all the flashbulbs, say some innocuous pleasantries about the rest of the cast and the filming experience to a few reporters, then get inside and watch the movie. Afterward there's Alexis's party, if you're feeling up to it. But if not it's no big deal. It can be a lot to take in, especially when it's your first time."

"Wow." *You've got to come up with something better than 'wow.'* "So I might see myself in next month's *People,* eh?"

He chuckled and nodded. "I've seen myself in there before and not even remembered having the picture taken. A bit unnerving." I laughed with him, but it sounded high and chirpy. I felt like dying.

Silence ensued for a moment and I thought desperately for something to say. "So," I started, "the movie, what's it about exactly?"

He launched into a description of the plot, which led to tales of mishaps and bloopers on the set and then tales of mishaps and bloopers on other sets, and for a whole fifteen minutes all I had to do was nod and laugh. It was a relief.

But then he stopped, and we sat there again, both of us staring out the windows. He sipped his beer, and I fiddled with the fringed edge of my wrap. "So you teach, right? Fifth grade?" I nodded. "So how's that going this year?"

"Pretty well, actually." I told him about my kids, about the goofy things they did and said, the trials and tribulations of a first-year teacher, all the while watching for boredom on his face. My life was certainly not as interesting as his. It also didn't take as long to talk about; I found myself falling silent not too long after starting to talk.

This was absolute agony.

JACK

THIS WAS ABSOLUTE agony.

I could tell she was nervous, but the worst part was that I was so nervous myself I was having a hard time making her feel comfortable. All the suave charm and flirting that I usually employed seemed to have dried up completely. I couldn't think of anything to say. I wanted to relax and just be myself, but I'd never done that on a date before and didn't know if I was even supposed to. Wasn't that the whole difference between going on dates and steadily dating someone? When you date, you charm, you flirt, you're on your best behavior, and you never let them see who you really are, since that would send them running. You save that for after you've started sleeping together, after you feel attached and it's harder for them to just one day stop returning your calls.

The other weird thing was that, while she was obviously nervous, she wasn't nearly as star-struck as women usually were. She just seemed shy, not in awe of me. What was wrong with her? What few non-celebrity women I'd come in contact with always gushed and fawned and made themselves completely available to me for whatever purpose I might want to use them. *That* I knew how to deal with. This shy, demure stuff boggled me. I was completely out of my element.

We tossed the small-talk ball back and forth for a while longer until I thought to turn on the radio. That gave us a new topic, and we discussed bands and songs and albums for quite a while, but the underlying tension was still there, thick as cement. This was worse than any other date I'd ever been on, and we were only an hour into it. I prayed to the gods of time and conversation that they'd save us from ourselves.

GRACE

GOD, HELP ME. I was exhausted from scrambling for more conversation, from trying to be witty (and feeling sure I'd failed miserably), from forcing laughs, and I was dying for something to drink. Why had I turned him down? I felt stupid changing my mind, but my mouth was like cotton.

I was figuring out in my head how to ask without sounding stupid when a glance out the window revealed why we'd been moving so slowly for so long. Three mangled cars were blocking the two left lanes, and a slew of emergency vehicles and uniformed people surrounded them.

"Oh, God," I murmured, leaning forward and staring out the window. My breath fogged the glass, and I polished it with the corner of my wrap. A shiver coursed through me as I glimpsed blood on one of the windshields, and I sank back in my seat, eyes closed, and prayed hard in my mind. *Protect them, God. Give wisdom to the medics and doctors, don't let them die if they don't know You yet, give their families peace—*

"Grace, are you all right?"

My eyes flew open, and I could feel myself blushing. "Oh, goodness, sorry. Yes, I'm fine. Sort of zoned out there for a second." I gave a small smile and forced myself not to look back at the wreck.

Jack glanced from me to the window and back. "Flashbacks?"

"Pardon?"

"Flashbacks. From the accident."

"Oh! No." I shook my head. "I don't remember any of it at all, still. I only know what you told me. You?"

"What, remember it?"

"No, flashbacks."

"Ah." He looked back out the window again, his hand coming up to rub his cheek and chin. "Not of *that* accident, no…" He suddenly smiled slightly. "But that's a very depressing story, so we'll leave that for some other time." He slid back along the seat to reach the minifridge. "You know, we're barely moving. Are you sure you don't want something? If you spill, I'm sure we can find some club soda or something."

Thank you, God! "Well, sure, I might as well. What's in there?"

He tugged the door open and slouched forward to root through the cans and bottles. "Let's see…Coke, Sprite, white zinfandel, Chardonnay, Miller, water…think that's it."

"Sprite, please."

He pulled out a small can and a bottle of Miller and shut the door. He opened the can and handed it to me, then twisted the cap from his bottle. "Shall we toast?"

I laughed. "I'm lousy at toasts, so if we do you'll have to say it."

"Oh all right." He made a show of thinking hard, then hoisted his bottle. "To a memorable evening and favorable reviews." I laughed and clinked my can to his bottle.

We sat in silence for a while more, watching as the traffic zipped by. Now that we were past the wreck, traffic was moving more quickly. "So how far is the theatre from here? Will we still make it on time?"

"Oh yeah, we should be okay. We're still about forty-five minutes out."

Forty-five minutes! *Lord, what else are we going to talk about for that long?* The thought of it almost made me sick. I didn't know how much longer I could do this. "So are you working on anything else right now?" Inwardly I gave myself a pat on the back for thinking of that; I'd read in a *Cosmo* article once that guys loved talking about themselves. It was probably doubly true for celebrities.

He started talking about some action movie, *Nine Lives,* and then mentioned a banquet for an organization he volunteered with.

Without thinking, I made a sympathetic face and nodded. "Oh, the Hollywood AIDS thing, that's right."

He raised his eyebrows slightly. "You knew that, eh?"

"Oh…well, I saw this really old issue of *People* the other day with a photo of you giving some high-school boy an award—HAP or something."

"Oh yeah, that's right. I remember that."

I watched his face carefully, looking for signs that I'd crossed into a touchy subject. "What does HAP stand for?"

"It's the Hollywood AIDS Project. Great organization. It's good to know my time is well spent there. Acting is fun; I love movies and television and…I don't know, all of it. But it's not going to change the world. Working with HAP makes me feel like I'm doing something worthwhile with myself."

I didn't know what to say to that. I nodded in agreement and sipped my Sprite, hoping he'd keep the conversation moving. I was afraid to ask anything else about the organization; I didn't know where the line between innocent curiosity and delving into personal territory was. When he failed to keep talking, I resolved not to say anything until he did and busied myself with the view out the tinted windows. We'd slowed again. The next exit sign was for the 101 freeway, which told me nothing since I'd never been up here before. I wondered how much farther we had to go. I hadn't worn a watch, and there were no clocks in the back of the limo, so I was completely clueless. It made me nervous not knowing the time.

I was trying really hard not to give in to the temptation to think of him as belonging to some higher class than me. Granted, celebrities are the closest thing Americans have to a royal class, but that doesn't make them any different from anyone else; they're just better known than the average Joe. And like I'd told the girls the night before, he's just a regular guy underneath all the stardust and celebrity. If I could get myself to see past the fame, it would go fine. So if this were a date with anyone else, how would I be acting? The problem was, if I were on a date with any other person, that person would most likely be someone from church, and I wouldn't feel so nervous about slipping up and mentioning church or God or my beliefs. My whole life had become wrapped up in those things, so it was hard to think of subjects to talk about that didn't include those topics.

But if that was who I was, and that was what my life was all about, then no one could possibly expect me *not* to talk about those things, right? That would be like expecting Jack not to talk about making movies, or discussing the people he hung out with, who just happened to be very famous people. It was his life, and there was no reason why he shouldn't have been mentioning those things. And if he could be candid about that, then I could be candid about my Christianity. So there!

"You all right over there?"

JACK

SHE JUMPED. I quickly apologized for scaring her, but she shook her head and smiled. "No, that's okay. I didn't mean to zone out again. I'm sorry." She blushed and smiled. "I'm fine, thank you. Did I not look all right?"

I shrugged. She didn't, actually; her face had registered about five different looks in the past two minutes, none of them reflecting any sort of enjoyment of what was going on around her. But I didn't want to embarrass her, so I said noncommittally, "You just looked...I don't know, conflicted or something."

She grinned. "I guess that's better than 'tortured.'" We chuckled, but then she became serious. "Yes, conflicted would definitely describe it. But I'm not being a particularly entertaining guest, so I'm sorry for going off into my own little world there." She sipped her soda and smiled apologetically as she glanced out the window. "So where exactly are we? I haven't been this far north yet."

"You haven't?"

"Nope."

"How long have you lived here?"

"Oh, let's see...a year and a few months. Moved out the first week of December."

"And you still haven't been up here?"

She smiled and shook her head.

"Amazing! I thought everyone did the Hollywood tourist thing the minute they moved to Southern California."

"Well, all my friends have grown up here, so the Hollywood thing isn't a big deal for them. I just never thought about it, really. Although whenever I hear about some star living in LA, it always catches me off guard. I'm like, wow, Keanu Reeves lives, like, an hour away from me!" She grinned. "I actually haven't even been up to LA, either."

I rolled my eyes, but inwardly I was cheering. This was an actual conversation! "You're kidding! The greatest city in the world and you've never been there?"

She laughed. "Same thing. None of my friends think it's a big deal, so I've just never gone. I wouldn't know where to go, anyway. I don't usually like going places I've never been before, especially big cities with scary freeways and traffic." She made motions of being frazzled and stressed out. "Too much pressure. Besides, LA drivers are horrible." A second later her eyes grew wide and she stared at me. "I totally didn't mean that."

It took me a second to understand what she thought she'd implied, and I laughed. "Oh, no offense taken here, believe me. I agree with you. We're the worst." I grinned and winked, and relief was written all over her face.

She shook her head and covered her eyes with her hand. "I don't know how many more times I can stick my foot in my mouth like that."

I realized then how many times I'd seen that look of embarrassment and fear on her face in the past hour, and felt awful that she was so nervous around me. What had I done to make her so careful and cautious? She'd never seemed intimidated the other times we'd talked. I wracked my brain to see if I'd said or done anything to make her uncomfortable, but I couldn't think of anything. "Don't worry about it, honestly. You really haven't stuck your foot in your mouth at all, I promise. Now, to answer your question, we're just coming into LA. We'll get on the 101, and then exit onto Hollywood Boulevard. That's about fifteen miles from here, so in this traffic it'll take…oh, who knows, I won't even try to guess."

"And where exactly are we going? What theatre?"

"Grauman's Chinese Theatre."

She grinned and her eyes grew wide. "The one with the handprints?"

"That would be it."

She laughed. "Oh wow. I *so* get to brag about this for the next ten years."

I smiled. "I'm glad you're excited. It's weird to see all this through someone else's eyes; I've done it so many times it's not a big deal anymore."

"You're kidding! I can't imagine how this could ever get dull."

"Well, it doesn't get *dull*, but it does get tiring."

She clapped her hands to her ears and squeezed her eyes shut. "Stop ruining my illusion that celebrities' lives are always glamorous!" Then she winked and took a sip of her soda.

I shook my head and grinned, relieved she seemed to be relaxing. "Aren't you the Queen of Sarcasm."

She nodded solemnly. "It's a gift. I've cultivated it over the years and raised it to an art form."

"I'll bet."

It was a little after six when we finally pulled up to the theatre. The street was teeming with paparazzi and media, and as our car slowed to a stop in front of the theatre, Grace seemed to revert back to the timid girl she'd been at the beginning of the evening. She shrank back into the corner of the seat, staring unblinkingly at the crowd milling around on the sidewalk. "Oh my," she murmured, as Alexis emerged from the car in front of us and the flashbulbs went nuts. It was like noon with all the cameras and the lights outside the theatre. "No one is going to talk to me, are they?"

I shrugged. "I honestly don't know. They might ask your name or something so they know what to put in the photo captions."

She drew in a deep breath as our car began to creep forward to the opening in the barricades that lined the sidewalk in front of the street. "I really don't have anything to be nervous about, do I." As she said it, she drew her wrap around her shoulders and watched Alexis move toward the theatre with her husband—her third, a television producer—in tow.

"'Course not," I replied. "All you have to do is smile and follow me and tell them who you are if anyone asks." The car slowed, and her eyes widened even more as a valet reached for the door to let us out. I extended my hand. "Stick with me, kid." I grinned and winked, and she flashed a weak smile as the door opened and we emerged from the backseat.

GRACE

I TOOK HIS HAND as the door opened, and then I couldn't see because there was so much light in my eyes. I moved to the door and tried my hardest to be graceful as I got out, but I'm sure a recording of the event would show me fumbling to get my feet planted. Jack helped me out of the car, then released my hand as he moved toward the walkway lined with photographers and media. I walked after him, feeling at once ignored and the center of attention.

I was afraid to look directly at anyone, in case they took that as an invitation for an interview. *Please don't talk to me,* I chanted in my head as I shadowed Jack. I kept my eyes averted and almost ran right into him when he stopped halfway up the walkway. A woman with a familiar face asked him about the movie, and as he responded he casually reached over and took my hand. A frenzy of flashbulbs exploded. I was grateful for the connection, not knowing what I was supposed to be doing during the interviews. I suddenly realized it might look incredibly rude for me to not at least look engaged in the conversation, so I stepped in closer to Jack and tried to look available without intruding.

"And who is this with you tonight?" the bubbly voiced woman asked, then thrust the microphone back toward Jack. I looked quickly to her and then Jack, trying to appear nonchalant but positive I was coming off like a deer caught in headlights.

"This is Grace Winslowe; she's a friend of mine who was kind enough to join me for the evening," Jack answered smoothly. I smiled at her as he continued talking, then watched as she pulled the microphone back to herself and began to say, "Miss Winslowe, what do you—"

My heart stopped as I realized she was asking me a question, but then Jack began to walk away, pulling me along with him and calling over his shoulder, "Enjoy the movie!" to the reporter. I looked back at her with what I hoped looked like an apologetic "Gotta run, sorry!" kind of expression and not the "I'm so glad I didn't have to answer you!" kind. She watched us move on for about half a second, then turned her attention to another actress who had just arrived.

As we approached the theatre, I leaned in to say, "Excellent timing."

He laughed. "I was afraid for a second there that you were going to freeze."

"I probably would have. I didn't even realize at first that she was talking to *me!*"

We were stopped a second later by another photographer, and Jack smiled and talked to him as though he knew him as he snapped our picture over and over. Another reporter took advantage of the fact that we weren't moving and pounced with microphone in hand to ask the same questions the first reporter had started. This time I smiled and tried to look charming. When she asked what I thought of all the festivities, I replied, "It's wonderful. I feel honored to be here."

"Is this your first premiere?" she asked.

"Yes—and it's a little overwhelming." She and Jack both laughed, and I could tell the difference in his demeanor as compared to the ride up; the glitz and glamour facade was on full force.

"Have fun tonight, and good luck with the critics!" she said as Jack steered us back down the red carpet.

"Hey, you're a natural!" he said with a grin as we passed more reporters and photographers.

"Oh yeah, I could do this all day," I said, fake-smiling so much my jaw hurt.

He laughed. "Well, I think you're pretty much in the clear now."

"Good. Now what?"

"Now we go in and get a seat and hang out with everyone else until the movie starts."

"Ugh…hang out with everyone else, eh?"

"Yep. Want popcorn or anything?"

I shook my head. "Don't think I should eat. Too nervous."

He laughed. "*You're* nervous? Your first romantic comedy isn't about to be unveiled to the merciless critics. Try that sometime and *then* talk to me about nerves." He winked at me as an usher opened the door for us, and we entered the theatre.

Once inside I felt less threatened. There weren't any reporters in here who might put my incoherent sentences into print, so all I had to worry about was not making a fool of myself and Jack in front of countless other famous people. If the drive with Jack had been that uncomfortable, what would it be like with them? Then a question popped into my head.

"What are you going to tell people when they ask how we met?" I whispered as we entered the dimly lit theatre and moved toward the seats.

He chuckled. "She ran into me one day down in Orange County."

I laughed. "Are you serious?"

He shrugged. "Sure, why not? And if they press the issue, I'll just say you made an impression."

I groaned. "That's a terrible, terrible joke. And a gross under-statement. Didn't I *total* your car?"

"Well…yeah, but they don't need to know that." He smiled. "I'm just messing with you. If they ask, I'll tell them what happened. Are you comfortable with that?"

I nodded. "Sure. Easier than trying to be coy all evening. I'm not good at that."

He chuckled. "Yeah, coy doesn't seem like you."

"So…tell me, what exactly *did* happen? I mean, car accidents and large expensive gifts and invitations to movie premieres don't usually go hand in hand."

Instead of answering, he steered me toward a knot of people. I could see Alexis sitting next to a tall, older man, her back to me. I recognized her French twist from when I'd seen her walking toward the theatre as we got out of the car. Jack leaned over and finally answered, "I was in a smash-up on the freeway with this really intriguing woman that I thought I ought to get to know a little better." He smiled and then walked in front of me, taking my hand and pulling me behind him as we moved into the row behind Alexis. As a group they turned in their seats to greet us. I shook hands with Alexis and her husband and five other people I recognized, and I wondered if Jack was finding his thought to be worth the trouble.

The movie was standard romantic-comedy fare: funny and sweet, and thoroughly enjoyable. When the lights came up at the end of the credits, I stretched lazily and smiled at Jack. "Not bad, Harrington."

He smiled that white-teeth smile that I had just seen illuminated larger-than-life onscreen. "Thanks. Would you mind going over to some of the critics and convincing them of that for me?" I laughed and shook my head. "Humph, well then, what good are you?" he mock-pouted before winking and retrieving my purse for me from the floor. As he handed it to me, he leaned over the armrest and whispered, "Are you up for that party at Alexis's? Or would you prefer to go home?"

"It would be such an inconvenience for the driver to have to come all the way back to get you after dropping me off, I'll just—"

"Wait. Huh?"

"What?"

"The driver!" He laughed, then swore. "Grace, I wouldn't send you home alone! I'd take you back, *I'd* go with you—how rude would *that* be, to just send you home?" He shook his head. "No, if you want to go back, I would go with you. And it would be no big deal, honestly. The party will go on forever, I'd make it back and still have more than enough time there. I just want you to be comfortable, that's all."

"Oh. Well…would *you* be comfortable with me there?"

"Why wouldn't I be?"

"I don't know. Because I'm not part of this crowd, or"—I waved my hand to indicate the event we were in the midst of—"I have no idea what to expect, what to do—you know better whether or not I'd fit in."

"Personally, I think you'll be great. I would love to have you come."

I shrugged and smiled. "All right then, I will!"

"And whenever you want to leave, we'll leave. No big deal."

"Okay. Thank you."

"Thank *you*." He smiled, then stood and held out his hand to help me up. He led me out of the aisle and into the lobby, trading comments and greetings with people along the way. Once in the lobby we were ensnared in a conversation with a small group of critics and reporters whom he seemed to know on a personal basis. We stood and talked with them for half an hour—I could hardly believe it when I found myself pulled into the conversation. They were friendly and not anywhere near as forceful as the reporters outside the theatre had been. Jack explained our connection, which they all agreed sounded like a movie script itself. "Hmm, good idea," Jack said. "Don't mention it to anyone else; maybe I'll try writing for a change!"

This triggered some in-joke to which I was obviously not privy, and for a while I was totally lost in the conversation. I allowed myself to mentally depart from it and take in what was going on around me. Actors in knots, rogue photographers in the corners, theatre staff, security…there were people everywhere, and I was one of them, I was a part of this world tonight. Unbelievable.

"Uh-oh, I've lost my date," I heard Jack lament. I blushed and turned back to the group, who were all grinning and beginning to pull on their coats.

"I can't blame her; you're boring her. Can't believe she's still here. Better make up for it, Harrington," one of the older gentlemen chided, then extended his hand. "Miss Winslowe, a pleasure to meet you. I hope you enjoy the party at Alexis's."

"It was nice meeting you, too," I said, shaking his hand and smiling. The others followed suit, and then filed from the lobby into the drizzle that had begun.

"I'm sorry."

"Good heavens, why?"

"You were totally bored."

I laughed. "Good grief, Jack, I don't expect you to baby-sit me. And you can't expect me to mesh with everyone here. Or *anyone* here, for that matter. But that's fine, I'm okay with that." I thought briefly of Taylor's comment and smiled. "This is the modern-day version of Cinderella at the ball, and I'm just happy for the opportunity. I can handle the fact that I'm a complete outsider."

Jack laughed and pulled a cell phone out of his jacket. "Okay, Cinderella, whatever you say." He dialed the driver and told him we were ready, then slapped the phone shut and dropped it back into his pocket before pulling on his overcoat. "It will take us about twenty minutes to get to Alexis's place. Do you want to get something to eat on the way there? You haven't eaten in a long time."

I was touched by his concern. "Thanks for thinking of that, but I think I can make it."

We moved closer to the doors to watch for the car. The little group of smokers were dousing their cigarettes and eying the rain, which had picked up and was turning into a full-fledged downpour. "That's one of the things I love about California," I said as I watched them. "No smoking inside public buildings."

"It's a pain when you're a smoker," Jack said ruefully. "But once you quit you appreciate it."

"It took me a month after I moved here to stop requesting non-smoking when I went to restaurants."

"Where were you from before that?"

"Chicago. Suburbs, anyway. Grew up there, went back after college."

"Family still there?"

I felt the uncomfortable twinge that always pinched my heart at the mention of my family. "My mom is, yeah. But there's just my parents, no one else, and they're divorced, and we don't talk much, so even if they were there, it wouldn't be enough of a reason to stay or go back." I shrugged, hoping that would be the end of it.

"That sucks."

I smiled a bit. "Yeah, I guess it does."

Our car pulled up, and a doorman pushed open the lobby door as he saw us approach. "Oh man," I muttered as I pulled my wrap tight around my shoulders, but Jack stopped me from venturing out from underneath the eaves and pulled off his overcoat. He held it up over both of us and grinned.

"Ready?"

I chuckled. "Okay!"

We made a mad dash for the car as the driver quickly got out and whipped open the door. I jumped in and scurried to the far end of the car to make room for Jack as he tumbled in and just barely missed getting caught in the slamming door.

I settled into the corner of the car and wondered if it would be tacky for me to check my hair and makeup. I decided to take my chance. As I pulled a small compact from my clutch, I asked, "So where are you from? Are you a California native or a transplant like me?"

He grinned. "No, I'm from about as far from California as you can get and still be on the continent: Vermont."

"Ah, so you *do* know what real winters are like. Whereabouts?"

"Reily; it's a small little place about an hour southwest of Montpelier."

Satisfied with my appearance, I snapped the compact shut and tossed it back into my purse. "My Vermont geography is completely nonexistent. What is it like out there: mountains, forest?"

"Mountains, mostly, but forest, too. Lots of good skiing. Tons of little B&Bs and ski lodges and stuff."

"So you spent your youth on the slopes?"

He laughed. "Not as much as you'd think. Did some, obviously, but I wasn't that into it. Not like most people were, anyway. What does one do for fun in the suburbs of Chicago?"

I mused. "Not much. I rarely went into the city; it made me nervous. And the suburbs were typical suburbs: all malls and movie theatres and bowling alleys. There's a lot I never did. I think I see and do more when I'm a tourist than when I'm trying to get to know the place I live in. As I said, I still haven't gone into LA to do anything, or even spent much time at the beaches. Haven't gone to the mountains, either, or down to San Diego. But if I was only in town for a week I would have gone everywhere."

Jack leaned back against the seat and grinned. "When I first moved out here I spent weeks exploring. I was going to auditions as often as I could and working lame jobs to pay the rent, but whenever I was free I went somewhere new. You really ought to get out there and look around."

"Teaching doesn't allow for much free time. I tend to bring the office home, as they say, nearly every night *and* weekend. Plus I wouldn't know where to go, and I don't want my friends to feel obligated to play tour guide."

We were entering Beverly Hills at this point, and my attention was drawn to the sprawling and sometimes bizarre homes that lined the boulevard. "Whoa," I breathed as we passed a massive home; it looked like it belonged on a Southern plantation. "I can't imagine living in a place like that. You'd get lost!"

"Wait till you see Alexis's place. It's about the same size." I gaped at him, and he laughed. "Don't worry, we'll leave breadcrumbs for you from the front door." I smirked and shook my head, going back to gazing out the rainy window at the beautiful homes.

We were soon pulling into the circle drive in front of Alexis's house, and its beautiful columns and spacious tree-filled yard almost took my breath away. "This is another thing I miss," I sighed. "Big front yards with lots of grass and trees and flowers."

"Wait till you see the back."

The rain had slowed to a mild drizzle, and a doorman came down to the car with a huge umbrella to accompany us to the front door. The door opened, and the sound of music and conversation wafted out to meet us. I tried not to look as awed as I felt as I surveyed the décor of the massive open front room. A broad staircase in the center of the room led up to the second floor and split into two branches that wound gently upward. A crystal chandelier hung over the center of the room and threw sparkle everywhere. Art in ornate frames hung on the museum white walls, and the marble floor was polished enough for me to see my stunned face in detail.

Alexis chose that moment to appear from nowhere bearing two glasses of champagne. She handed one to each of us and then lightly embraced us in turn. "Welcome! You're just in time; dinner is going to be served in just a few moments in the back. Make yourselves at home!" With that she flitted away and disappeared through a door in the back corner of the room.

"I don't know how *anyone* could be 'at home' here," I confided under my breath. "It's like living in a museum. I'm afraid to touch anything."

Jack snickered. "Really? You don't see yourself decorating with crystal and authentic art?"

"That's *real?*" We were both eying a large abstract that I'd thought looked an awful lot like a Picasso. I shook my head in amazement. Just then a waiter appeared from the door into which Alexis had disappeared and announced that dinner was being served. We fell in with the rest of the crowd that began to file through double doors in the back of the room. My jaw dropped again as we entered the dining room. It was the size of a small banquet hall, with solid-looking wood tables surrounded by chairs with velvet upholstery. Gorgeous place settings adorned the tables, and exotic flower arrangements sat in the center of each. Jack led me to a table where we joined two other couples we'd sat near during the premiere. I was instantly nervous again, worrying about what I should or shouldn't say if these people started asking me questions. I sat back in my seat and tried to look distracted and not interested in conversation. Jack was immediately laughing and talking and generally the life of our table's party; I was grateful that all the attention was on him.

Waiters came around to distribute salad and more champagne. I still hadn't touched my first glass; I'd never been big into champagne or wine. A wet bar manned by two bartenders was located along the far wall, and I had a sudden craving. Jack apparently noticed me staring at the bar, because he leaned over and said, "I'm going to go grab a beer. Do you want something?"

My craving won out. "Bailey's on ice, please." He smiled and excused himself from the table. I began to eat my salad, thankful to finally get some food and wondering what the main course would be. Then I realized someone was talking to me. I blushed furiously at my lack of attentiveness and smiled at Madison Grey, one of the supporting actresses I'd seen in numerous other movies. "I'm so sorry, I'm a little out of it. What were you saying?"

She grinned. "It's overwhelming, isn't it?" I nodded. "I was just asking how long you and Jack have known each other."

"Oh, not long; just a few months, really." *Get over here and save me, Jack!* I shoved another forkful of salad into my mouth to put off having to talk again.

Suddenly Madison's eyes widened. "You're the woman from the accident, right? When was that…December?" I nodded, chewing slowly and slightly relieved that someone had finally made the connection. "And now you're going out, how romantic!"

I shook my head and swallowed. "Oh, we're not going out, this is just a friends thing."

She gave me an odd smile. "Really?"

"Well, if we're dating, he forgot to send me the memo."

She laughed. "Wow; I would never have guessed you two were just friends."

I was about to ask her what she meant when Jack returned with our drinks. Grateful for the distraction, I sipped long and slow from the glass, trying to decipher Madison's comment.

"Not harassing my date, are you?" Jack asked Madison good-naturedly as he sat back down.

"Oh heavens, no, just asking how you two had met. I just figured out that she was the one from that accident you were in."

"Ah, we finally have a winner!" He grinned. "We should have brought a prize for the first person to get it."

Waiters came around to clear the tables, and then carts were wheeled out bearing covered dishes, which were placed before each guest and unveiled with a flourish. The chef had prepared a copy of the same meal shared by the main characters in the movie on their first date, a pivotal moment in the plot. This garnered applause from the mostly inebriated crowd.

As I ate I tried to estimate how much money had gone into this little soiree. Filet mignon for well over a hundred people, champagne, bar, waiters, chef, flowers…it boggled me. I smiled as I thought of what interesting math story problems I could create from this. But at the same time, it made me slightly ill to think of what a waste it all was. Even this house…all the art, the crystal, the furniture. Multiple families could live for a year off what it probably took to furnish and decorate the place. I couldn't comprehend how much money that would be. I was barely making ends meet, but I didn't need anything more than what I already had, so it was fine. How could people justify it?

JACK

Grace had been chewing the same piece of meat for about a minute. I leaned over and whispered, "Having an out-of-body experience or something?"

She blushed and swallowed. "Just thinking."

"'Bout what?"

She shook her head as she cut another piece off the filet. "Nothing."

I went back to my meal, pondering her obvious lie. I hoped Madison hadn't said anything to upset her; she had a tendency to say more than she ought to, and I knew Grace had been worried about people's reaction to her. But it also had been a long night, especially for someone who had never experienced anything like this before, so I told myself she was just tired and left it at that. It was surprising how much I was starting to care how she was.

Dessert was served a little later, and by then I could tell Grace was fading. She sat back in her seat observing but not engaging, and while she'd been doing this most of the evening, I could see fatigue written all over her. Knowing we had a long drive back to Orange County, I asked her after the dessert dishes were removed if she wanted to go.

"Only if you won't be offending anyone by leaving so soon. And only if you don't want to stay."

I shook my head. "These things are all the same. Everyone will mingle for a while, drink some more… I'll probably be doing myself a favor by leaving now."

She smiled and nodded. "In that case, yes, I think I want to leave. Either that or else lead me to a bedroom and let me sleep."

I laughed. "That's not a bad idea. I think this place has eight of them; she ought to include nap time in the evening's agenda."

"And pancakes for everyone in the morning."

"There you go—a giant slumber party." We laughed, and I stood and addressed the rest of the table. "We're exhausted, and we're going home."

"So soon? Party's just getting started," Madison said in a singsong voice that revealed just how much she'd drunk that night. She waggled her eyebrows and danced a little in her seat. "You two could do a little cha-cha-cha…" She winked.

I held out my hand to Grace to help her from her seat and rolled my eyes at Madison. "We're not really the cha-cha-cha-ing type, Mad. But hey, don't let us stop you." Grace and I bade good-bye to the rest of the table and headed toward Alexis to thank her for the party and say good night.

"Thanks for coming," she gushed as she stood and hugged us both. "Grace, honey, welcome to the crowd, I hope you had fun. Be good to her, now, Jack." She smirked and wagged her finger in mock admonishment. "You could redeem yourself with this, you know. No more lovin' and leavin'."

I was stunned by Alexis's impropriety, and I didn't even have to see Grace's face to know it was red. I slapped on a smile and said good night to the rest of the table, then steered Grace toward the door, fuming and trying to figure out what Alexis had been hoping to do with that remark.

When we arrived at the front door I called the driver and pulled on my coat, then apologized to Grace. "I have no idea what she was thinking, saying something like that in front of you. I'm sorry."

She shrugged and pulled her wrap around her shoulders. Her cheeks were still flushed. "I'm not offended; it's your life. It doesn't affect me." She smiled, but it didn't reach her eyes.

"Well, I know that, but I don't want you to think I'm some play-boy—well, I sort of was there for a while, I'll admit that, but I'm not now. And it put you in an awkward position, and that's not right either."

"They all think we're dating."

I was caught off guard. "Huh?"

"I think they think we're going out. Madison was all surprised when I said this was just a friends thing." She yawned and then grinned apologetically. "I shouldn't have had that drink; alcohol always makes me sleepy."

I chuckled. "You can sleep in the car on the way back."

"And make you sit there all by yourself? No way."

The doorman escorted us under his enormous umbrella to the car. It was a relief to be out of the crowd and back in the privacy of the limo. Grace settled into the seat, and I could see she felt the same way. She was watching the houses again as we drove through the ritzy Beverly Hills neighborhood.

I tried to think of something to say to start the conversation again. The first topic that came into my mind started with a question I'd been wondering about for weeks: now that she was off the pain medication, did she still think she'd had a message from God about me? I debated whether to bring it up. I wanted to, but at the same time, I didn't want to end the evening on an uncomfortable note. It would be a long, tor-turous ride home if it didn't go well. She seemed to have loosened up a bit, and I didn't want to put her back on the defensive. I wracked my brain for something else to say, and finally came up with something. I asked her what she'd been thinking about earlier.

"During dinner?"

"Yeah, when you checked out."

She chuckled and rubbed her eyes. "I'm sorry about that. Was I catatonic for long?"

"No, I doubt anyone else noticed."

"But you did."

I shrugged. "I was watching to make sure you weren't uncomfortable."

"Really? That was sweet. Thank you."

I grinned. "You're welcome. Now tell me what you were thinking."

She opened her mouth to speak, then suddenly stopped. "I don't want to offend you."

"Offend me?"

"Yeah. I think what I was thinking applies to you, too, but since I don't know you well, I can't be sure. But I don't want to inadvertently criticize you."

"But what if you're right? Then it would be good of you to criticize me, so I can fix whatever it is I'm doing that I shouldn't be doing."

She smiled. "That's diplomatic of you."

"Hey, I'll say anything at this point just to find out what you were thinking."

"It wasn't that big a deal, really."

"All the more reason why you can tell me."

She laughed and shook her head. "Incorrigible! Okay, fine. But just remember you asked for it, okay?" She sighed and fidgeted in her seat. "I was looking at all that food, and the flowers, and the hired help, and the string quartet in the corner, and then thinking about the furniture, and the art, and the crystal, and the gold plating, and the marble floor, and the massive house itself, and wondering how much it all cost. I mean, I can't fathom the amount of money that went into that party, much less her house. And the premiere itself! And what it took to make the movie…I mean, it's *just* a movie, it's *just* entertainment. And then you think how much it is to *see* a movie these days, and how many people will see this one, and all the other movies out there…millions and millions of dollars surround this movie alone.

And when I student-taught I had kids in my class who came to school half an hour early for breakfast because their parents couldn't afford cereal. The imbalance of resources is mind-boggling."

She straightened, warming to her subject. "And to what end? Is Alexis happier than me because she makes about a hundred million dollars more a year than I do? Is she content? Is anyone in Hollywood content? Or do you spend all you have on cars and houses and jewelry and art and then demand a higher salary for your next movie because ten million isn't enough to live on in a year?" She stopped talking and clapped a hand to her mouth. "I mean 'they,' not 'you'; like I said, I don't— Oh my." She sighed. "I've said way, way too much. I'm so sorry." She leaned back in her seat and closed her eyes. "I'm sorry. That was very judgmental. I'm not usually like that, honestly."

Well. This was awkward. Truth be told, I was defensive, but she definitely had a point. It was pretty sad just how much money was pumped into this business.

"I mean, maybe I'm wrong," she said. "Maybe Alexis sponsors, like, a hundred Ethiopian kids a month and donates to every charity on the planet and I just don't know it because, you know, why would I? I'm not saying you're bad or she's bad or anything like that…" She lost steam and cast her eyes toward me. She looked miserable. "Jack, I'm sorry," she said in a small voice. "Please forgive me."

I shrugged. "What is there to forgive?"

"I insulted you."

"You spoke your mind."

"I didn't have to."

"I asked you to."

"I didn't have to be so blunt."

"True." A small smile crept onto her face. "But what you said was pretty straight up. This can indeed be a greedy and self-centered business."

She sighed and closed her eyes. "I had such a good time tonight, Jack. I'm sorry I ruined it."

"Nothing was ruined. I'm glad you had a good time. I was afraid you'd be overwhelmed."

"I was." She smiled. "But it was fascinating. Not many people from the outside make it in. I finally have a juicy story to tell my grandkids."

I laughed. "What, no wild days of your youth to recount?"

She smirked. "Do I look like someone with a shady past?"

I grinned and shook my head. "Not really, no."

We both fell silent, lost in our own thoughts. She stared out the window, but I stared at her, her face lit up by streetlights as we passed through their beams. What did she think of me? Did she totally disapprove of me, my lifestyle, my career? What had she thought about the movie? I hadn't asked her because I hadn't wanted to put her on the spot and make her think she had to compliment it. And, as with all the other times we'd interacted either in person or over the phone, she'd surprised me by being utterly normal and not at all star-struck. Even around the others at the theatre and party, she'd been levelheaded and natural. No gushing, no posturing, no shallowness. On the way up I'd been a bit put out at her lack of it; now I was impressed.

I watched her fall asleep, her head rolling back to the headrest. I slouched down in my seat, the activity of the evening starting to catch up with me. We were about half an hour from her condo, and then suddenly I was jostled awake as we drove over the speed bumps in her parking lot. "I'm sorry I fell asleep," she said, groping for her clutch which had fallen to the floor.

"Don't be; I did too."

We pulled in front of her building, and the driver came around to open the door. We both got out, and I walked her up. She fumbled for her key and, finally finding it, opened the door and leaned against the frame. "I'd offer you a nightcap, but I think all I have is milk and Tang."

I laughed and shook my head. "I need to get home and crash. But thank you anyway."

"Thank you again, Jack," she said. It struck me then how sincere she was. Guileless. I didn't know guileless women still existed. I took a chance and planted a quick kiss on her cheek.

"Thank you for accepting my invitation, Grace. Sleep well."

"You too. Good night."

"Good night."

I was halfway to the stairs and her door was half closed when I blurted out, "Can I call you?" The door creaked as it opened again, and she giggled. I tried to sound wounded. "What's that for?"

"I'm sorry. It was just so cute and old-fashioned." She composed her features and smiled. "You most certainly may call me."

I didn't end up sleeping on the way home. I couldn't stop thinking about her.

GRACE

THE PHONE WAS RINGING. Half-asleep, I groped along the nightstand, feeling for the cordless. "Hello?"

"It's 11:10, Grace, I can't believe you're still sleeping!"

"I didn't get to sleep till, like, after 2:00."

Missy huffed. "Well, Joy and I did breakfast to pass the time while we waited for you to call, but we couldn't wait anymore. You *have* to tell us *everything*, preferably right now."

I rolled onto my back and stretched, slowly opening my eyes to the assaulting sun streaming between the blinds. "You guys can come over if you want and cook me breakfast."

She laughed and relayed this to Joy, whose laughter could be heard in the background. "Got pancake mix and milk?"

"Yeah."

"We're on our way."

I hung up and dropped the phone to the floor beside the bed. It would take them at least ten minutes to get here, so I allowed myself a few more moments of warmth beneath the covers. I thought back to the party, to the premiere, to the kiss on the cheek, and to Jack's parting comment. Did he really want to call me? *No, he was just pulling your chain because he's a jerk.* It was just hard to believe. The vast majority of the women I'd seen last night were ten times more beautiful than I, and more eloquent and interesting. And most were definitely interested in Jack; you could tell by the way they stared at him when they talked or the way they found reasons to touch him. How did people stay sane in that industry?

This thought brought to mind the way I'd gone off about money.

The memory of it made me groan aloud and pull the comforter up over my head. What had come over me? What was I thinking? Yet another reason why it was difficult to believe he'd really want to see me again.

I was in danger of drifting off, so I forced myself to get up and throw on some sweats before the girls got there. I padded into the kitchen for some juice, then sat in a half-asleep daze until they arrived. They'd picked up Taylor on the way over and paraded into the condo, then simultaneously assaulted me with questions and tore my kitchen apart to make me pancakes.

"Cooking spray?"

"Pantry, second shelf."

"Was the movie any good?"

"I liked it, yeah. It's really cute."

"Who did you meet?"

"Where's the flipper?"

"Flipper?"

"You know, to flip the pancakes with."

I laughed and pointed. "That drawer. And I met pretty much everyone who was in the movie, and a bunch of the crew. I can't remember all their names. Some critics, too."

"Alexis Giovanni?"

"Yep."

"Madison Grey?"

"Yep."

"What are they like?"

"Beautiful, nosy, and loose-lipped."

They laughed. "How so?"

"They all thought we were dating and kept making comments."

"Yikes, sounds awkward."

"It was."

"Whisk?"

"Isn't it in with the flipper?"

"Oh yeah, you're right."

"Okay, give us a play-by-play, starting the moment he picked you up."

"Oh my, let's see…well, first off, if I do say so myself, I looked *good.*"

Missy smacked her forehead. "Oh yeah, we know! We forgot to tell you: we saw you on TV!"

I blinked. "What?"

"It was on the news. They showed part of the premiere, when people were arriving and stuff, and they interviewed Jack. I taped it— where's the tape, you guys?"

"Must still be in the car." Missy tossed Taylor her keys, and Taylor ran out the door and was back in what seemed like mere seconds.

"Sheesh. You're fast when you're excited." I gave her a wry grin. She shoved the tape into the VCR, and all pancake production halted while we gathered in the living room to watch. She fast-forwarded to the end of the weather segment that came on before the entertainment report.

"…and we should see an end to the rain by Tuesday."

"Thanks Mike. Well, despite the rain the stars were out tonight for the premiere of *Destiny Awaits,* a new romantic comedy starring Jack Harrington and Alexis Giovanni. Our Melissa Thomas was there."

The picture changed to the premiere and, indeed, there I was on the arm of Jack Harrington. "Oh my gosh," I breathed. "That's me!" The girls giggled. It was like an out-of-body experience, getting to watch myself. I looked surprisingly calm. I could see other people in the background, and remembered my view of the scene when I'd been there. It was slightly disorienting.

"You look like you've done this a million times, Grace," Joy marveled.

"I should get an Oscar." They laughed. "Seriously! I can't even tell you how nervous I was. It was terrible. I could hardly enjoy it, I was so afraid someone was going to talk to me."

"Did anyone interview you?"

"This Melissa chick started to, but Jack rescued me, thank heavens."

Missy smirked. "Dang, girl, you two look good together." I stared at us and realized she was right.

"Did he say anything about your dress or how you looked?"

I grinned and crushed a pillow to my chest. "Yeah. He said, 'Wow,' and that I looked amazing." They squealed with delight.

"Did he ask you out again?"

"He asked if he could call me." More squealing. I smacked them all playfully. "Knock it off," I laughed. "Y'all sound like three-year-olds."

We watched the tape a second time, then went back to the kitchen to finish breakfast. I told them about the agonizing ride up, and the party, and how everyone thought we were a couple.

"But the ride home was the worst," I groaned. "Oh, you guys, it was so awful. I totally went off for no good reason about money."

They looked baffled. "What about money?" Taylor asked. "Like, how ugly the new money is?"

They laughed. I smirked and shook my head. "I went off about how celebrities have all this money and how they misspend it and how spoiled they are. You guys should have seen Alexis's house! She had a *real* Picasso! And fed filet mignon to, like, a hundred people! *And* the house was massive, with real marble floors and real crystal chande-liers…it was all such overkill!" I sighed and drizzled syrup on the pancakes Missy set in front of me. "I don't know why I did it, but I did. He was cool about it, and he'd begged me to tell him what I was thinking in the first place, and I warned him I might offend him, so in a way it's his own fault. But *still*." I shoved a forkful of pancake in my mouth.

"But he still wants to see you," Joy pointed out, "so obviously there was no permanent damage."

I shrugged. "I think he was just trying to be polite. I mean, it would have been a little weird if he *hadn't* said something like that, you know?"

"No, I think 'Talk to you later' is the kind of thing you say to be polite; you don't ask someone if you can call them. That's genuine," Missy countered. I had to admit she had a point. I stuffed more pancake into my mouth to avoid answering.

"So now what for the rest of the day?" asked Taylor as she idly spun the butter dish on the table.

Missy snickered. "Jack Harrington movie-fest?"

I rolled my eyes. "I don't need no stinkin' movie-fest," I said loftily. "I can talk to the real thing."

They dissolved into laughter as I finished my pancakes.

JACK

THE STRESS THAT always accompanies the opening of a new movie had melted away after seeing the critics' response to *Destiny Awaits*. Overall the press was positive, and I spent the next week basking in the glory of having made another hit. Box office returns so far were excellent, and I was receiving a number of scripts in the romantic comedy genre. I contemplated doing another after finishing *Nine Lives*.

But always in the back of my mind was Grace. It was the strangest thing: I admitted to myself now that I was definitely attracted to her, but it was something different that was truly *drawing* me to her. I had yet to put my finger on it. Seeing her in the company of people like Alexis and Madison highlighted how different she was from the women I was used to. It wasn't just the fact that she wasn't a celebrity or that she wasn't fluent in the industry languages of schmoozing and flirting. There was something deeper that made her stand out compared to those other women. Damned if I could figure out what it was.

I'd asked her if I could call her, but now I wasn't sure if I should. She'd been pretty brutal on the way home; maybe she wasn't interested in seeing me again. Although, I reminded myself, she had been very apologetic. I could understand her point of view, but she didn't understand what it was really like in this business. Not that she'd be expected to understand. But would she be willing to set aside her views? She didn't seem like the compromising type, so I doubted she would. But if that had been the case, she could easily have declined my request to call. Unless she felt obligated.

This was giving me a headache. It wasn't supposed to be this difficult. Did I like the woman or not? Was I going to make a move or not? *Just make a decision and stick to it,* I told myself.

Of course, there was also that whole God thing.

I'd been half expecting her to bring it up that evening, but when I thought back to that first conversation in the hospital, I realized there had been nothing pushy about her. She'd stated what she'd had to say, and then left the ball in my court. She hadn't badgered me or talked my ear off about it; she had just spoken her mind and left it at that. It was a gutsy thing to do, especially when she had no idea what my response would be.

Perhaps this was what was so alluring. She was so confident about what she believed. The God thing, the money thing...she didn't mince words. I got the feeling there was nothing hidden about her, no facade or pretense. What you see is what you get, as they say, unlike my world where everyone has a secret or an ace up their sleeve.

So where did that leave me? I didn't necessarily agree with her on what she said, but so what? She was honest and open and...*authentic.* What a refreshing mix!

I sat in this reality for a week or so, reading scripts, working out, and replacing the furniture in my apartment because it was old and starting to bore me. A couple scripts captured my attention, but no gears would start turning for another month or so on any of them, so I had some time on my hands. Frankly, the working out and reading and shopping were just distractions to stop me from driving right down to Orange County and parking myself on Grace's front step. But then after a while I realized I didn't have a good reason *not* to drive down there—other than the fact that it might look a bit forward. So finally I dropped the distractions and called her.

Of course, this being a Wednesday morning, she was at work; I'd forgotten that most of the world worked on daily schedules and didn't have this much free time. I left a message asking her to call when she got the chance, and then sent myself out for a jog.

"H'lo?"

"Jack?"

"Yeah—Grace?"

"Yeah, hi. I got your message. How are you?" I could hear the smile in her voice, and it made me smile, too.

"I'm doing all right; you?"

"Doing well." She laughed. "Saw *Destiny Awaits* again last night with some friends. It's very strange to watch you up there."

I laughed. "I never quite get used to it, either."

Silence.

"So…you called because…"

"Oh yeah, right. Well, I called to see what you're doing this weekend."

"Um…nothing. Wait. Sunday night I have church at seven, but other than that I'm open. What's up?"

"You said you hadn't seen the city yet, right?"

"Yeah."

"Well, I had such a good time seeing the premiere through your eyes that I thought it would be fun to see the city the same way."

I could picture her eyes twinkling. "So you're offering to be my private tour guide?"

"Absolutely. I'm better than Fodor's or Triple A, because I'm interactive."

She laughed. "You crack me up. I would love to. Thanks so much. Should I meet you somewhere or what?"

"Let me give you directions to my place; you can meet me here on Saturday, say around ten, and we can take my car."

"Sounds like a plan; hold on while I get a pen."

We got the directions squared away and then chatted a bit more about the recent lousy weather. After we hung up, I went out for another jog. Talking with her was giving me a lot of energy.

GRACE

"WHAT DO YOU think? Good idea or bad idea?"

The women all put on their thinking faces, and I waited impatiently for their response.

"Could go both ways," Missy said. "The fact that he wants to see you means he's interested, so obviously the Christianity thing isn't putting him off. Maybe that's *why* he still wants to see you; maybe this will give you an opportunity to talk with him about God. But on the other hand, maybe he thinks a relationship with you is like a relationship with anyone else in Hollywood—low commitment, high intimacy—and he thinks this is just the next step toward sleeping together or something."

"I think you need to lay down some boundaries this time, Grace." This came from Joy.

I wrinkled my nose. "So soon? I mean, what if he's just thinking, 'Hey, a new friend to hang out with,' and there's no desire on his part to move it any deeper than that? Then I'll feel like an idiot for assuming he *does* want to go out; it'll look like I think I'm all that or something."

"But then at least you'll know where you stand. You need to figure out what the expectations are on both sides so neither of you is taken by surprise or put out."

I groaned and buried my face in my hands. "Dating was so much easier when I wasn't a Christian." They chuckled. I sighed and raised my head as I mused, "'Course it was a lot more painful, too."

"What are you going to do if he *does* want to date you?"

I winced at the thought; I knew what I *should* do, but I wasn't sure if I was ready to accept that. "Honestly, you guys, he's not going to want to. Just think of the logistics! I'm down here, he's up there—and that goes for both geography *and* society—he's, like, five years older than me... If it really comes to that, then I won't do anything rash. I'll deal with it *if* it becomes an issue, but I don't think there's any point worrying about something that *isn't* going to happen." I put a note of finality in my voice to deter them from pursuing it further; I really just didn't want to think about it right now.

The one thing I *did* want to think about was how to make things less uncomfortable than they were the night of the premiere. Bottom line was, I couldn't *not* be me. I couldn't try to be sophisticated and fancy when I wasn't. If he was going to get to know me, I was going to have to start *being* me. I wanted him to drop the facade and be himself, too, but there wasn't any way I could force that. I just hoped that by being myself, I'd encourage him to do the same.

Saturday came quickly, and then I was zipping north on the 405 toward Hollywood. The whole way I rehearsed how I would tell him that I didn't want to pretend to be something I wasn't, and it made me more and more nervous the closer I got. As I wound through the side streets toward his condo, I breathed a prayer for God to calm me down, and when his building came into sight, I waited for my stomach to do flips, but instead felt the tension melt away. *Thank you!*

I parked in an empty space and buzzed up to his apartment. The door unlocked, and I climbed the stairs to 205. The building was beautiful, and I had a feeling the apartments would be bigger than any I'd ever seen.

"Welcome to my humble abode," he said cheerily as he opened the door to let me in. "Can I get you something to drink?"

I was right; these were amazing. His apartment was, anyway. "Thanks, but I'm fine. Great place you've got."

He grinned, looking proud. "Thanks! You should have seen the old furniture; I just replaced it a couple weeks ago, and already the place looks 100 percent better." He grabbed his jacket from the back of a leather recliner. "Ready to go?"

I licked my lips. "Actually, before we leave, can we talk a minute?"

"Yeah, sure." He pulled out a chair at the kitchen table and motioned for me to sit down.

I took a deep breath. "Remember the drive up to the premiere, how…awkward things were? At least, they were awkward for me; maybe you were fine…"

He chuckled. "No, I know what you mean. It was a bit…weird."

I took a deep breath. *Here we go.* "Well, here's the thing. I was really uncomfortable that night—not because of anything you did or said, so don't feel bad, okay? It's just that I was trying *so hard* to be the kind of person I thought you tended to be with, and I was so afraid of making you think I was a total idiot or something. And the truth is, I'm not a glitzy person, and it's way too exhausting to try to act that way. So, from now on, I'm just going to be who I am, and if I embarrass you or something, then that's probably just a sign that your world and my world are really incompatible." I stopped and sighed, then gave him a small smile. "Okay, speech over. Are we cool?"

A slow smile spread across his face as he nodded. "Absolutely, Grace. Thanks. I'm really glad you feel that way, and that you told me. And by the way, you did a very good job of being glitzy that night."

I could feel myself blush as he winked and stood. "Shall we?" he asked.

"Yeah!"

We made our way to the garage and settled in his BMW. The leather was so soft I was afraid my nails would tear it, and I folded my hands in my lap just to be safe.

"So how's that car treating you?" he asked as we headed out into the street.

"Fantastic. Thank you yet again."

He nodded. "I'm just afraid it's going to suddenly fall apart on you one day. I'd feel terrible if it turned out I'd given you a lemon."

"Well, even if it did that would be all right; at least I would have had this long to not worry about it."

"True."

"So where are we going? What's the plan for the day?"

"Well, since this is your first time, we have to do all the truly touristy things, like get a good view of the Hollywood sign, go down Rodeo Drive, go to Santa Monica Pier, go through Beverly Hills—it looks a lot different in the daylight."

I grinned. "Sounds great!"

"Did you bring your camera? There are sure to be plenty of Kodak moments."

"Oh…I didn't even think of it!" I frowned. "I can't believe that."

He shrugged. "That's all right, we can stop and get a disposable. My treat; part of the whole Harrington Tour Experience." He grinned and waggled his eyebrows, making me laugh and wish again that things could work out.

And with that we were off. We stopped at a gas station close by, and I ran in for a camera, and then from there we headed into Hollywood Hills. Conversation, unlike the night in the limo, was easy and nonstop as we drove through the narrow and twisty roads that led to what was supposedly the best vantage point for the Hollywood sign. After getting several pictures, we made our way back down the hills, getting deliberately lost and taking twice as long to get back to the main road, just so we could check out the houses along the way. From there we went into Hollywood, where we found parking in a public lot and walked to the Chinese Theatre. Before we got out, he fished around on the floor of the backseat for a moment before finally finding a beat-up Angels cap and pulling it down low over his eyes.

I frowned as he locked the car. "Is this going to be a hassle for you?"

He pocketed the keys and came around to my side of the car. "What do you mean?"

I glanced up at the cap. "Doing the whole incognito thing must mean you expect to get blitzed."

He shrugged. "Goes with the territory. I don't usually try to hide myself, but I don't want you to get all mixed up in that. It wouldn't be fair to you." Then he smiled. "Unless you *want* to be mobbed by strangers."

I laughed. "Eh, maybe next time. I'm not really in a mobbing kind of mood."

He led me out to Hollywood Boulevard where most people were looking down at the names on the sidewalk and not into the faces of those passing by. It was weird seeing all this again in the daylight and without scores of photographers and celebrity-watchers. We got to the theatre and measured our hands against those of the people famous enough to get a block of cement all their own. Judy Garland was a perfect fit for me, and for the rest of the afternoon, I was subjected to comments about my dog Toto and getting high on poppies.

After that we went back to the car—as it turns out there's not much to do in Hollywood—and then drove out to Beverly Hills. The houses there were amazing, and we oohed and aahed our way down the streets. I was reminded of my diatribe on money, but he didn't mention it, so I guessed we were all right.

A little before noon he asked, "So how hungry are you?"

I grinned. "Not very, but now that you've mentioned eating, I'll be starving in about five minutes. My stomach is voice activated."

He laughed. "Well, I have reservations at a place just off Rodeo. Do you like Italian?"

"Love it—but are we dressed up enough for a place that requires reservations?"

"Oh sure; it's not really fancy, just very popular."

He maneuvered the car into a turn lane, and soon we were cruising down toward the infamous Rodeo Drive. All the stores I'd heard about but never been in—Escada, Harry Winston, Armani, Tiffany—lined the street like an elegant strip mall for the filthy rich. Jack noticed my stares and asked, "Somewhere you want to go into after lunch?"

I had a good laugh at that. "Oh sure; my teacher's salary makes it easy to afford a Gucci wardrobe. Chalk dust wipes right off of leather, you know; it's very practical."

He laughed. "Well, you can always browse—"

I snorted. "I'd walk into one of those places, and they wouldn't even give me the time of day. It's so obvious I'm not part of this culture it's laughable."

He turned and looked me over carefully as we waited for the light to change. "I don't know; I think you underestimate yourself." He winked and then turned his attention back to the traffic, leaving me to laugh and shake my head incredulously.

"You're incorrigible."

"Is that a good thing?" The smirk in his voice was unmistakable. I laughed again and gave up.

We pulled off Rodeo and onto a smaller side street with more shops and a few restaurants. He pulled up to a valet standing near the curb who opened the door for me and helped me out. Jack handed him the keys, and I nearly melted as he smiled and placed his hand on the small of my back to steer me through the door.

I could still feel the weight of his hand on my back as we were seated and given our menus. I suddenly worried that I was flirting without realizing it. What if I was sending him signals I didn't intend to send? I'd never been good at this game, and the last thing I wanted was for him to think I was a tease.

"Grace?" I jumped and nearly dropped the menu, jolting out of my little world of inner angst. He chuckled and smiled apologetically. "I'm sorry, I didn't mean to surprise you like that. You were just really quiet for a bit there. Seems to be a habit."

I could feel my face burning as I shook my head and smiled slightly. "I'm sorry; my mind just started wandering."

"Uh-oh; I'm that boring, hmm?"

"Yes. Watching paint dry would be more entertaining." I winked, then shrugged. "Sometimes my thoughts get the best of me. Don't take it personally."

"I'll try not to. Now, what are you thinking of ordering?"

I forced myself to be normal as I perused the menu and we discussed the specials and dishes he'd had here before. Our waiter came to take our order, and as we were waiting for our salads, a woman passed the table, then backtracked and stared at Jack.

JACK

"JACK? OH MY gosh, haven't seen you in ages!"

I nearly choked on my Coke. "Penelope! Wow, great to see you!" I stood to deliver the requisite hug, hoping I'd submerged my shock before it had a chance to register on my face, and then introduced her to Grace. "This is Penelope Jones; we worked together on *Deep Cover*. Penelope, this is Grace Winslowe."

Penelope shook Grace's outstretched hand, and I saw her check Grace out with the kind of subtle judgment women so often use on each other. I hoped Grace didn't notice. Then Penelope turned back to me, resting her hand on my shoulder. "I saw *Destiny Awaits* the other night. I loved it! Guess there's no point in hoping you'll ever come back to *DC* now that you've successfully transitioned to the silver screen, hmm?"

I chuckled and shook my head, wishing she'd get her hand off me and get out. "Don't think so. But I have to admit, I miss the set schedule sometimes. Not often, but sometimes."

"I'd gladly trade it for the success you've stumbled into. Don't forget us, okay?" She winked then turned to Grace. "Pleasure to meet you, Grace. Take care, Jack." She smiled at us both and then went on her way.

I tried not to look as relieved as I felt. I hadn't seen Penelope since my last day on the set of *DC,* and every time I saw her, I was reminded of the night I'd woken up and found myself in her bed. While I'd never been particularly proud of the fact that it had happened, I was suddenly ashamed, and the whole time Penelope had been talking to Grace and me, I'd been terrified of her saying something about it. I didn't feel like I could finally breathe again until I saw her disappear out the door.

"You all right?" Grace asked.

"Yeah. Why?"

She shrugged as she reached for another piece of bread. "You looked for a second there like you were ready to bolt out the door."

I chuckled and shook my head. "I was just surprised to see her, that's all. I really haven't seen her in years."

Grace nodded, apparently appeased, and then the food arrived.

We managed to make it through lunch without any more awkward moments and then headed for the pier in Santa Monica. The weather was perfect for a day at the beach, and the sand was crowded with sunbathers and kids running through the surf. We walked down the pier and stopped at a small arcade. "I believe I see Skee-Ball back there," Grace said. "You probably don't know this, but I'm the reigning Skee-Ball queen of the Midwest."

I arched a brow. "Oh really? And when did you win that prestigious title?"

"Chuck E. Cheese's, 1989. I'm still undefeated." She cracked her knuckles and shined her nails on her T-shirt.

"Hmm. Sounds like a challenge."

"Oh, no; I would never lure someone into a game they can't win. That would be mean-spirited." There was no mistaking the twinkle in her eyes.

I laughed. "That does it. Come on."

We bought tokens and staked out two lanes. We declared the first round a practice session, and had we been playing for keeps, I would have won. But then, once we started playing for real, she completely creamed me on every round. I demanded two rematches, and lost both times. At the end of my humiliating defeat Grace pressed three dollar bills into my hand. "You shouldn't have to pay to get your butt kicked," she said with mock sympathy. I was torn between kissing her and strangling her.

From there we strolled around downtown Santa Monica, occasionally stopping to window-shop or go in to look around. In a secondhand bookshop Grace went overboard in the children's section, and as she paid for her books, I wandered back outside into the sunshine. I'd been trying all day not to overanalyze or critique how things were going, but I couldn't deny the fact that I was having an incredible time. She seemed to be having a good time too, and I couldn't help but wonder if there was potential here. There were all sorts of snags we'd have to work out, but if the day so far was indicative of what our relationship would be like, then I was willing to make it work.

There was one thing that bothered me, though, and it was the one thing that was always in the back of my mind whenever I thought about Grace: the God thing. It hadn't come up yet in conversation, save for passing comments about something she called her "small group" at church or the service she went to on Sunday nights. I started wondering if maybe that whole hospital thing had been injury-induced, or the result of too much morphine. Part of me wanted to bring it up, but if it *had* been spoken out of a state of temporary mental unbalance, I didn't want to embarrass her.

"Ready?" she asked, bag of books in hand.

"Indeed. Coffee break?"

"Definitely."

We meandered up and down the streets until we happened upon a small coffeehouse. We played chess at our table as we slurped blended mochas. I made up for my Skee-Ball loss, then we sat silently for a while, people-watching and flipping through year-old magazines that cluttered the small end tables between the couches along the wall.

"So, what's the rest of your weekend look like?" I asked during a silent spell. "Lots of schoolwork?"

She chuckled as she stirred her drink with the straw. "Well, Friday was the due date for government essays, so I have thirty papers to read and critique tomorrow."

I winced. "Sounds painful."

"It can be. But other than that I don't have anything else to do. I'll go to church and hang out with Missy and the gang after the service." She paused for a moment and then continued. "They're doing a big summer concert thing and need more people to sing, so I think I might audition for that."

"Hey, that's cool," I said noncommitally. "Are you nervous?"

She shook her head. "No. I sang with their college group for a while and I think the leader from that is helping coordinate it, so he'll be able to vouch for my talent—or lack thereof, whatever the case may be." She grinned and sipped her drink, looking out the window at a group of teenagers traipsing toward the beach in skimpy outfits and flip-flops.

This was my window of opportunity. A question about religion would be completely natural, fitting with the conversation. But I hadn't thought long enough to know what question to ask: *So, God— you're really into that, aren't you? What religion are you, anyway? So what made you think I had to be saved from anything, and why do you think your god can do it?* None of them seemed like a segue into a comfortable conversation.

We both stared out the window, me trying to figure out a way to bring up that day in the hospital, and she oblivious to the mental jumping jacks I was going through. I took a breath and finally blurted, "So do you remember the day I saw you in the hospital?"

GRACE

I NEARLY CHOKED. It was the last thing I expected him to ask. Did I remember it? Did I remember staring into the face of a man known all over the Western world and telling him he needed God?

I could feel my face burning as I nodded. "Not something you forget," I said, hoping my voice only sounded shaky to me. I jabbed at and stirred what was left of my slushy mocha and forced a grin. "Bet that's not the line you usually hear from women when they meet you for the first time."

It was just the thing to say to break some of the tension; we both laughed, and I inwardly breathed a sigh of relief and thanked God for the words.

"True. Bonus points for originality."

I avoided his eyes as I smiled and slurped some more mocha, waiting for him to continue the conversation. I didn't know what I was supposed to say. This wasn't just uncharted conversational territory; it was *unimagined* territory.

"So," he finally ventured, "do you still believe what you said?"

I took a ridiculously long pull on my drink, finishing it off as I stalled for time and prayed. Eventually I drew a breath and looked him in the eyes. "I do. I can't deny it; I do. If someone had said the same things to me that I said to you, back before I believed in God, I know I would have blown them off and thought they were out of their mind. So I understand if that's how you feel, and I don't take it personally." I smiled, hoping to diffuse some of the weight of the conversation. "But at the same time, I would hope that you'd realize I'm *not* crazy, and I *do* have my head on straight, and that I wouldn't have a motive for making it up." I shrugged and dropped my hands in my lap, waiting for his reaction.

He was silent for a minute, then spoke. "You're right, it sounds ridiculous." He grinned slightly, I think in an attempt to soften his statement, but it came off looking smug. I tried to give him the benefit of the doubt. "But everyone's entitled to his opinion—and *her* opinion. And far be it from me to say what you did or didn't experience." He shrugged. "It's all good."

I slapped on a smile, but inside I was completely withered. I suddenly wanted to be home. I wanted to be with Missy and Joy and Taylor and not here with this man who thought I was a simpleton. I wanted to yell at God for making me look like a fool in front of the most incredible man I'd ever met. All the fun and warmth of our time together came crashing down in a black cloud of frustration as I wondered despairingly how much longer the day would last.

Apparently my emotions were visible on my face. "I've made you completely uncomfortable, haven't I?"

I shook my head wordlessly, then looked up with a small smile. "Not uncomfortable exactly, no. I don't blame you for not believing me." I shrugged helplessly. "So now what?"

He sat back in his chair and readjusted the cap on his head, glancing around idly and then finally sighing. "I don't know. Does this completely eliminate all possibility of friendship?"

I leaned in closer, frowning. "No; why would it?"

"Well, if you're into this God thing, and I'm *not,* then where does that leave us?"

"Well…I was into God when we left this morning, and when we went to the premiere, and I'm assuming you've been *not* into God pretty much all that time, too, so it leaves us where we've been all along. Doesn't it?"

He looked as baffled as I felt. "Well, yeah, but…you don't think there's anything wrong with that?"

"With what?" I felt like I was missing half the conversation.

"With us not agreeing on God."

"N-no."

"No what?"

"No there's nothing wrong with it. Why would there be?"

"Well, because you think I'm some heathen or something."

I laughed. "I do?"

"You don't?"

"No! You don't believe in God, and that's your choice. I don't think it's a good choice, but I can't force you to change your mind, so oh well. That doesn't make you some evil person in my eyes or anything. Hanging out will give me the chance to show you what my beliefs are about."

"So now I'm a project?"

I leaned back in my chair and groaned, covering my face with my hands. This was so much more difficult than it needed to be. "No!" I sighed and righted myself, then leaned across the table and said frankly, "Look. You're cool. I like hanging out with you. I would like to continue hanging out with you, if you also enjoy hanging out with me. I'm a Christian, it's true. And you're not. And while I think that's a shame, it doesn't mean I can't be with you, or shouldn't be with you. It means we'll disagree on things, and that I'll pray for you, and that I'll say things you'll think are flaky, and I'll think you're just misinformed, but it does *not* mean I'm commanded to stay away from you. Now…is this all clear?"

He stared at me for a moment, then smiled and shrugged. "Crystal."

JACK

THINGS WERE AWKWARD for a while, but by the time we had returned to our sightseeing tour, things were almost back to normal. Part of me was still annoyed for bringing all this up; the day had been going fine, and there had been no reason to ruin it. But the other half of me was glad it was out in the open and each of us was clear on where the other stood. I didn't want anything to do with God, but I definitely wanted something to do with Grace. I wasn't sure what exactly I wanted to do with her—well, I had some ideas, not that I thought she'd go for them—so for now I was content just being with her.

After we finished our coffee, we went to Venice Beach and meandered down the boardwalk for a while, but it had been a long day and we'd both pretty much reached our sightseeing limits. After half an hour we made our way back to the car, and by the time we were back on the 405, the sun had almost completely set.

The drive back to my apartment was uneventful and pretty quiet, but not in an uncomfortable way. I was trying to think of ways to talk her into staying for a while, maybe ordering something in for dinner, but when we arrived she immediately pulled her keys from her bag and planted herself by her car.

"Jack, thank you *so much*," she said. "I can't tell you how much I appreciate you spending your day like this."

I didn't like the way this sounded. I chuckled slightly as I moved next to her. "That sounds like the kind of thank-you you get after tutoring someone all day in physics or something. I wasn't trying to do you a favor, Grace, I was hanging out with you because I like to hang out with you. You make it sound like it was a hassle for me or something." I couldn't help the note of irritation I could hear in my tone.

She rubbed her eyes and gave me a weary look. I was instantly contrite. "I'm sorry, Grace; you were sincere, I know you were. I should just be glad you didn't jump into your car and race off without a backward glance."

She rolled her eyes. "Like that would ever happen to someone like you."

"Like me? What does that mean?"

"It means no woman in her right mind would ditch you. I'm still amazed you haven't ditched me."

I kissed her. I leaned over and kissed her full on the mouth, and it took me a second to realize I'd done it, but then I was kissing her, and then suddenly I *wasn't* kissing her, and I knew I'd just made a really bad move. Her eyes were big and she didn't say anything, just stared at me with a look of surprise.

"Guess I shouldn't have done that," I said. "I'm sorry."

She moved past me and opened the door, then turned on the car and backed out. I watched her drive away, then ran upstairs to jump on the treadmill to expend some of my anger before it sent my fist flying into a wall.

GRACE

THE PHONE RANG. I let the machine get it, and when I heard it was Missy, I swung an arm over to the bedside table to pick up the cordless. "I'm here."

"I can't believe you didn't call me!" Missy yelled. "How was it? When did you get home? What did you guys do?"

"He kissed me," I said.

"*What?*" The volume made me yank the phone from my ear.

"Ow, you're loud. Knock it off."

"Sorry, sorry… Oh, Grace, what happened? What did you do?"

I sighed. "Drove home."

"Huh?"

"I broke off the kiss and got in my car and drove home."

"But what did you tell him?"

"Nothing."

"At all?"

"Nope."

"What did he say?"

"That he guessed he shouldn't have done it, and that he was sorry."

"And you didn't say anything?"

"Like what, Missy? 'Take me now?' Because that's what I wanted to say. I nearly *did* say it." My voice was shaking with the effort it took not to cry; I'd been doing that most of the night. "That's why I didn't say anything; I knew if I tried to talk I'd say something I shouldn't. I can't tell you how badly I don't want to be a Christian right now, Missy. I don't want any reasons to not call him and throw myself at him. Yesterday was *so perfect,* except for the kiss—actually, that *was* perfect—and except for the really uncomfortable discussion about God—"

"You talked to him about God?"

"He asked if I remembered our first conversation."

"Ah."

"I felt like an idiot."

"But you did the right thing."

It was exactly what I didn't want to hear. "Who cares?!" I exploded. "He doesn't want God, he doesn't think he needs God, he doesn't believe in God; the whole thing was pointless! It didn't matter! He doesn't care! God put me in this ridiculous situation, and now I've made a fool of myself in front of Mr. Right who, just my luck, I can't be with because *he's not a Christian!*"

Missy was quiet, and I felt rotten. It should have been easier to deal with by this time, but it wasn't. "Sorry," I muttered. "I don't want to talk anymore. I'll call you later." I hung up the phone and dropped it to the floor, then yanked the covers over my head and hid for another hour until I could no longer put off the papers that needed grading and the dinner I really needed to eat. There were two messages on my machine that must have been left while I was sleeping. I hit the Play button as I rummaged through the freezer for something I could microwave.

The first message was a hang-up. The second was Jack. "Grace, hi. It's me, Jack." He sounded tired, subdued. "Listen, I just wanted to apologize again. I really don't know why I did that. Um…please call me, okay? Please don't be mad at me. I know I was totally out of line; I should have asked or—well, I should have just left well enough alone, is what I should have done." He sighed, sounding frustrated. "Look, please just call me, okay?" He left his number and hung up.

I microwaved my dinner, then picked at it until it was cold again.

I was hungry, but I didn't feel like eating. I was tired, but I'd been in bed all day. I had a stack of papers to grade, but I could barely put two thoughts together. My mother had once described these as the symptoms she'd experienced when she'd fallen in love with my father. She later described them as the symptoms she'd experienced when she'd fallen out of love with my father. I had no idea what they were signaling for me. I warmed up my dinner a final time, forced myself to eat, and then pulled the papers out of my bag and graded until eight, then went back to bed. I didn't even think about the fact that I'd skipped church for the first time.

I tried to pray once I was in bed, but I couldn't. That's when I figured out what was wrong: I was angry at God. Angry He had led me into this, angry He had allowed things to get this far when He knew He'd forbidden me to be with someone who didn't believe in Him the way I did. A sliver of me wanted to reach out to Him and ask Him for His help, but the rest of me wanted Him to mind His own business and leave me alone.

That moment, buried under the covers, turned out to be pivotal, because it was the moment I made the decision to take my own road. It wasn't exactly a conscious resolution, but more of an opening of my mind to the things I had been denying myself out of obedience to God, an embracing of the options that had originally been out of bounds. Someone was whispering to me that I was exempt from these rules, that God would not blame me for following after that which He told others to run from, and even though I knew that voice wasn't from God, I chose to listen and to believe.

JACK

I'D BEEN WORKING for most of the evening on a HAP fund-raiser when the phone rang for probably the twentieth time that day. Kate had called five times because she kept forgetting things during our previous calls. Sean called three times, twice to try to talk me into going clubbing that night, and the third time to tell me he'd decided to ditch the club scene and to ask if I wanted to watch the Lakers game at his place. Mom had called just to say hi, and, strangely enough, so had Abby. I was tired of talking to people, so I let the machine pick it up, but when I heard Grace's voice, I nearly broke my ankle diving out of my chair.

"Screening calls?" she asked with a touch of bemusement.

"It's been Grand Central Station here today; just didn't want to talk to people anymore."

"Ah, but you picked up for me?"

"You're a different story."

"Well, I'm flattered."

I could hear the beguiling smirk in her voice, a tone I'd heard in the voices of countless women over the years, but never in hers. I was confused. "So," I finally ventured, "you called back. I was starting to think I'd never hear from you again."

"I know; I'm sorry it took me so long." The flirt was gone from her voice; she sounded like the old Grace. "I just had to think for a while, you know?"

"Yeah, I understand. Listen, Grace, I really am sorry about...what happened. I swear to God—oh, sorry—I swear I have no idea what came over me."

"It's okay, honestly. I'm sorry I just took off and then avoided you like that. I was just so shocked, I didn't know how to respond."

"So, now that you've thought about it, what's your response?" I held my breath.

I could hear her take a deep breath. "Well…I really want for us to be friends. I really enjoy your company, and I'd like to see you again. Beyond that I don't know."

I almost laughed out loud I was so happy. "As long as you're not dropping me like a bad habit, I'm up for any arrangement you want to impose."

She returned my laugh. "How about I impose dinner on you? Here at my place, 6:30, Friday?"

"I'm up for that."

"I'm glad."

"Thank you for asking."

"Thank you for accepting. See you then?"

"You bet." We said our good-byes and then I stood, phone in hand, trying to comprehend this turnaround. It was the last thing I'd expected. I was on the brink of trying to analyze this sudden change of heart when I decided I didn't much care what had caused it. The fact that she wanted to see me again was enough.

Grace sat across from me on the other end of the couch, absorbed in a story she was telling me about one of her students, and while I was doing my best to listen, I couldn't help but be aware of how fast I was falling for her. We'd been talking for nearly three solid hours, completely comfortable, flirting and yet at ease, and the only thing that was stopping me from kissing her again was the memory of her reaction the first time. I tried to remember if I had felt like this about Dianne, so totally immersed in her, every thought somehow connecting itself to her, and I was almost sure I hadn't. It was baffling and intense and not a little disquieting, and yet completely inviting.

And there was something different about her tonight. She seemed more open, more engaged than in the past, although she'd been warm and friendly since the beginning. It drew me to her all the more.

I poured another glass of wine and sipped it slowly, watching her over the rim of the glass as she leaned back and stifled a yawn. "I'm incredibly boring, I know," I said sadly, setting down the glass and slumping in my corner of the sofa.

She chuckled and shook her head. "I was up at six this morning for school; I'm never very fun on Friday nights. I should have asked you over for tomorrow night instead."

"Nonsense," I laughed. "You're plenty fun. And a fantastic cook."

"I swear that's the only dish I know how to make; I'm the most undomestic woman in the country. I live purely on boxed foods that require less than five minutes of microwave preparation. My mom always joked that I'd need to marry a chef or I'd die of malnutrition."

I threw my hands up in defeat. "Well, that puts me out of the running. I live off of Taco Bell and McDonald's."

"Yes, but you're rich and famous; you could just hire a chef."

I slapped my forehead. "Of course! Why didn't I think of that?" I winked at her, and she shook her head, laughing.

"You're incorrigible."

"So I've heard. It's your own fault; you incorrige me."

She groaned. "Oh sure, blame it on me…"

We continued like this for another two hours, flirting and teasing and trading barbs in between bouts of real conversation. The bottle of wine I'd brought disappeared quickly, and soon Grace was in danger of falling asleep sitting up.

It was almost physically painful to admit aloud that I ought to go. "Look at you, you're nodding off practically in the middle of your sentences," I countered when she argued that she was fine.

She stood and stretched. "It's the demon liquor," she stated.

"Well, next time I'll bring some Red Bull or something."

I stood and walked to the door, and she meandered over behind me. And then *she* was kissing *me*. I didn't know what to do, so I didn't do anything. Besides kiss her back, anyway.

It felt like forever before I finally pulled away and stared at her. "Well, that was unexpected," I ventured.

She smiled coyly and shrugged. "You only live once, right?"

I didn't know what to make of this. "Why the sudden change?"

"I realized I'd be crazy to let you slip by. We're obviously a great match. Why not give it a chance?"

I was floored. Completely confused and completely head over heels at the same time. I wanted to kiss her again, but then the terrible thought struck that this might all be alcohol-induced, and the last thing I wanted was to take advantage of her poor judgment. "Listen, Grace, call me tomorrow, okay? And tell me then whether or not you meant this."

She frowned. "Why wouldn't I mean it now?"

"Because you yourself said alcohol affects you, and I don't want you to do anything you're going to regret."

She flashed a small smile. "That's very gentlemanly of you. To-morrow's answer will be the same as tonight's, but I'll put your mind at ease tomorrow if that's what you want."

"It is."

"Then consider it done." She backed away from the door and opened it, smiling all the while. "Have a safe ride home. I'll call you tomorrow."

GRACE

I COULDN'T SLEEP. The adrenaline rush I'd experienced the second I moved to kiss Jack had long since subsided, leaving me with a heavy stomach and a slight headache. But I'd done it—the thing I'd been dying to do since day one. I wished he hadn't thought it was just the alcohol, although I suppose I never would have had the courage to actually go through with it had I been stone sober. But I'd made the decision to kiss him the morning I'd invited him over. This was hardly a spur-of-the-moment maneuver.

All I could think about was the amazing conversations we'd had, how thoroughly at ease we'd been, how *right* the whole thing felt. I had no trouble imagining us together; we definitely clicked. Once I'd finally decided to give this a chance, the trepidation and self-consciousness I felt when I was around him had dissolved into confidence and wit and flirtation. I loved that side of me. I felt sexy and strong and intelligent and clever. That didn't happen often.

Once I finally rolled from bed and woke up a bit, I called Jack and got his machine. "Hi, it's Grace. I still mean it. Talk to you later." The ache in my head was quickly being replaced by a glow in my gut.

Missy called that afternoon to ask if I felt like meeting her to go for a jog. I agreed, forgetting momentarily the way I'd blown up at her. I remembered as I stood waiting at the park, and threw my arms around her when she arrived. "Missy, I am *so sorry* about the other day. I was just so frustrated with everything."

"It's all right. I can't begin to imagine what this has been like for you. How are you now?"

"Great." I smiled as we began to jog. I had this amazing surplus of energy, and the run felt good.

"Wow, what happened?"

Later I would see what I was doing as total deception, but at the time I simply thought I was saving myself the hassle of convincing Missy that my unconventional method of evangelism was valid. It hadn't taken me long to justify to myself my blatant disobedience through spin control: I wasn't defying God; I was breaking away from the church's archaic standards in order that I might win another soul for Christ. Allowing oneself to fall in love with an unbeliever wasn't detrimental for the believer; it was beneficial for both parties, since the believer would surely win out in the end.

Similarly, I had convinced myself that he was on the road to Christianity and that, with my guidance, he would change his mind about God; it was simply a matter of being patient and waiting for him to accept the inevitable. He'd continued to talk to me after knowing how I felt about God, hadn't he? That, to me, was proof that he was interested. That was all I needed.

And so, in that spirit, I answered her, "We talked, and he's starting to come around."

Her eyes bulged. "Are you serious?"

"Well, I wouldn't expect a conversion in the next month, but I think it's just a matter of time. Keep it under your hat, though, okay?"

"Sure, sure. When did all this happen?"

"We had dinner again last night, and we talked for ages. Fantastic conversations. He's so intelligent. Had a great time."

"Dang, girl. That's amazing."

"Yeah. So how have you been this week? I've been a lousy friend and I'm sorry; tell me everything I've missed the past seven days."

I deftly changed the conversation to avoid any more discussion on this delicate topic, and for the rest of the afternoon, we jogged and hung out and put the nasty business of my short temper behind us.

When I got home that evening, I had a message from Jack asking me to call him.

"Watcha been up to?" I asked.

"My usual Saturday routine: worked out, read scripts, relived last night a million times, and hoped against hope you were serious."

"I was. Didn't you get my message this morning?"

"Well, yeah, but I couldn't believe it."

"Why not?"

"Why do you think?"

I chuckled. "Yeah…I suppose bolting when you kissed me wasn't the best way to show my affection." He laughed. "I'm sorry about that, I really am. But I've thought about it and I want for this to become whatever it is it's going to become. I mean, we're not talking about anything serious, for heaven's sake. We're just exploring the *possibilities* of a relationship, right?" I marvel now at how adept I was at convincing myself as I tried to convince others.

"Well…yeah. I mean, you're right, we're not looking at a lifelong commitment, just the opportunity to develop our friendship."

"Precisely."

"I'm up for that."

"Great!"

"So now what?"

I giggled. "Beats me."

"I hate that we live so far apart."

I sighed. "I know, it sucks. Newport Beach is a lot closer, and I think some famous people live there; if you moved in, you wouldn't feel out of place or anything."

He got a good laugh out of that. "I'll keep it in mind."

We talked for two hours. Whenever the subject veered toward philosophy or religion, I took the opportunity to inject my Christian thinking and defense. We actually did have a pretty good discussion about faith, but nothing monumental. That was all the justification I needed. Obviously he was interested in spiritual things; what kind of Christian would I be if I didn't do everything in my power to walk him through that journey?

At the end of the night we reluctantly wound down our conversation and pondered what our next move would be in the exploring-the-possibilities-of-a-relationship game. Eventually we landed on the idea of another day of sightseeing, this time in San Diego. After we'd laid down some of the plans for that trip, we said our good-byes and hung up, and I dragged myself off to bed in hopes that I'd actually sleep.

After church the next evening the girls and I went out for dessert and talked about the upcoming summer concert at church. Auditions were that week for the vocalists, and as I told the girls about this, I realized the rehearsal was scheduled for the same weekend as Jack's and my San Diego trip. I wrinkled my nose and frowned at the realization of the conflict, and since nothing gets by them, they all wanted to know what I had planned.

I waved my hand in dismissal. "It's not a big deal, I can change it."

"What is it?"

Why was I so reluctant to tell them? "I was going to go to San Diego that Saturday. I haven't been there yet."

"With who, just by yourself?" Joy asked.

When I hesitated, Missy's eyes got big, and she grinned. "Ooh—were you going to go with Jack?"

Joy and Taylor whooped as I shrugged and tried to act like it wasn't a big deal, mostly because I desperately didn't want it to be a big deal. It would be, after all, the fourth time we'd hung out. How long would it be before it wasn't such big news?

"Just to see the city, not for any fancy stuff," I explained as I played with the remainder of my dinner.

"What's with you two, anyway?" Joy finally asked. "Are you guys dating?"

I shrugged and waved my fork. "We're hanging out. That's it. No agenda, just trying to get to know each other like two normal people."

"You still don't think he'll want to date?"

I chose my words carefully, being sure not to commit to anything one way or the other. "Does it really matter if he wants to or not?"

It worked. "Wow. I'm impressed," Taylor sighed as she rearranged the food on her plate. "I don't think I'd have that much willpower. Although I know someone who converted her boyfriend, so I guess it *can* work sometimes. But what if it didn't? That would be heartbreaking."

"Or worse—what if they dragged you down, away from your faith?" Joy added.

I frowned, confused. "Why would that happen?"

"Well, for example, if he doesn't want to go to church with you and thinks you're wasting your time there, maybe you'll eventually stop going so it doesn't annoy him. And then pretty soon you stop hanging out with your Christian friends because he complains that they're boring or too religious or something…and then soon you don't have anyone to help you stay strong in your faith, and you're just trying to keep the peace, and then eventually you drift away altogether." She shrugged. "Just one possibility."

I hadn't actually considered that. Somewhere in the back of my mind little red flags were beginning to wave, but I decided I would simply not allow such a thing to happen to me.

How blind I was not even to realize it had already begun.

JACK

THERE WAS DEFINITELY a change in Grace starting that evening at her house. It didn't take long before kissing was just a warmup for later activities, and though I never asked her to actually sleep with me, we definitely explored the gamut of intimacy. It was the first time since Dianne that I'd felt like I actually *loved* a woman I wanted to sleep with, and I didn't want to jeopardize anything. I didn't think religious people would be okay with what we were doing, but she seemed okay with it, so I figured there must be some exceptions I wasn't aware of. Religions were always filled with crazy rules that didn't make sense; maybe there were some crazy exceptions as well.

I decided not to think about it at all. I'd progress however I wanted and leave it up to her to put a stop to things or change the course we were on. But I couldn't entirely shake the feeling that things weren't quite kosher.

Over the next few weeks we continued the phone calls and weekend-long dates. I was reading scripts and planning on accepting one soon, and I knew that once I was on a new project, our time together would be limited. I wanted to get in as much time with her as I could before that, which is probably why I agreed to attend the concert with her at her church.

I was reluctant to do so when she first asked, knowing how much of a stir it would cause. But she promised anonymity and friends who would shelter me from the rest of the congregation. Plus, she would be singing, and I was eager to see her perform.

We decided the Saturday afternoon performance would be the least crowded and thus the best for me to attend, and while she would have to stick around for the seven o'clock performance until she'd completed her part, she promised I could take the keys to her place and go hang out there until she was done. I liked that idea; I could surprise her with dinner when she came back, since I'd already learned cooking was not her forte.

Saturday morning I awoke to dense fog and a great desire to stay in bed for the day. But I dragged myself out and forced myself to be productive for a few hours before heading down to her church, an hour from my place. She'd explained the night before where I ought to park: a small lot toward the back of the building used only by the staff. Just as I shut off the engine at 3:45, she came out of an unmarked door and ushered me in. I could hear music in a far-off room as she motioned to an office in the middle of the hall. Inside we sat down in a receptionlike room. "This is the associate pastor's office. I told him what was up and he offered to let us hang out here. I need to go get ready for the concert, but Missy and her mom ought to be here any minute. I think you met Missy at the hospital."

I thought back and then nodded. "The coffee girl; yeah, I remember."

"After the service starts they'll bring you out into one of the back sections. The view is fine, and it'll be empty back there. That way you won't get mobbed." She grinned.

"All right, sounds fine. Good luck; I can't wait to hear you sing." I stood as she did and reached over to kiss her, but she pulled back and reached for the doorknob. "Gotta run. Enjoy the service!" I chalked up the strangeness of her smile to nerves. Then she left the room, shutting the door quietly behind her.

I sat down and stared at the door, wondering if I'd misinterpreted that last second. Had she not noticed the kiss, or had she not wanted to?

The door opened again, and two women entered, smiling shyly.

I stood and extended a hand. "Nice to see you again," I said to the younger one. "Missy, right?"

She nodded, shaking my hand. "Glad you were able to make it. This is my mother, Jane."

I shook Jane's hand as well, then motioned to the door. "Have things filled up out there?"

"Not too badly, no. We've reserved a few seats in the back, and from here we'll be able to hear the orchestra start. Once they do we'll head back there and sneak in after the crowd has died down." Jane opened the door slightly, making it easier to hear the activity down the hall. We all sat down, and Missy began to chuckle. "Kind of a shame we can't announce your presence. That would be the most exciting thing this congregation has seen in a long time."

I smiled. "I'm just glad there're no paparazzi down here. I would hate to bring that kind of chaos to this poor, unsuspecting church."

"That happen often?"

I shrugged. "Kinda comes in waves. I haven't done a project in a while, so I'm not as hot a commodity right now. Had my film just opened last week I'd be a lot more closely watched."

Missy and Jane were easy to talk to, and we chatted for a few minutes until we could hear strings and horns beginning to play down the hall. "Ah, that's our cue," Jane grinned.

Missy stuck her head out the door and looked down the hall. "I think the coast is clear," she said. Then she snickered. "I feel like James Bond." She led us to a stairwell that wound up to a vestibule where music was audible through a large wooden door. She opened it and peered in, then we followed her in.

Missy led us to a row of seats with programs placed atop the chairs. The sanctuary had not filled more than three-fourths of the way back, so we were well isolated from the rest of the crowd. Just as the orchestra was finishing their song, we slipped into our row and joined the applause that resounded from the crowd in front of us. I smiled as the singers streamed on stage to take their places.

There was Grace, second from the end, looking beautiful. I tried to ignore the fact that this was a church and just watched her as she sang. The words to the song were projected on a screen to the left, but I wasn't as interested in the words as I was in the woman singing them. I listened for harmonies where her voice would soar above the others, smiling to myself when I could recognize hers among the rest.

When their first song was over the lead singer welcomed everyone and began to talk about God in relation to the lyrics of the songs. This brought me back with a thud to the reality that I was in a church and not a theatre. I felt uncomfortable until the orchestra started another song, and then I felt really uncomfortable when everyone else seemed to know it and the whole congregation started singing along. I could hear Missy and Jane singing beside me, and I was mildly annoyed that I couldn't hear Grace anymore. I didn't even try to sing, since the song was completely foreign to me, and instead watched Grace as she belted out the tune from her place on the stage. So far the program was impressive, for a church. The orchestra was actually quite good, and the singers were obviously talented. Nothing like the church I had been sporadically dragged to as a child, with an organ in the front and a choir of twelve voices that never blended.

Another song followed, and then another, and then the majority of the singers, including Grace, filed off the stage along with the orchestra. The lead singer remained along with a guitarist, and I settled lower in my seat, wondering how long the acoustic interlude would go and trying to determine whether I could get away with a quick nap. Then the singer opened a book—a Bible, I presumed—and began to speak.

I didn't bother listening at first, but then I heard a sentence that caught my attention. "If you're looking for a place where you can be real, be open and honest about your life and your struggles, and meet others who will be the same with you, then I hope you'll give us a try." That didn't sound to me like church. I waited to see what else he'd say, but another song started, and I was left to contemplate what I'd heard.

If this guy was to be believed, then this church was full of people like Grace, people who didn't try to be something they weren't, people who didn't hide behind money or success—or the illusion of it. People who were real, like he'd said. It was hard to believe people would be willing to be like that with each other, because it sounded dangerous. Being real meant not hiding, and so much of my life was spent hiding something—my self from the media, my frustrations with life, my faults and quirks from people who might not like me otherwise. Could I be where I was now if I was totally honest with everyone? It seemed like an awfully risky proposition.

But then I thought about Grace and her friends. She talked about Missy and Joy and Taylor all the time. She didn't hesitate to call them her family. She told them everything, as far as I could tell, and they in turn did the same with her. I'd never had such close friends. Todd was the closest I had, and there were a thousand things I'd never tell him. Sean wasn't too bad, but we weren't *real* friends, just hang-out friends. I couldn't imagine discussing spirituality with him. On Mondays that's all Grace and her friends did: talk about God. As strange as it sounded, it had a certain appeal; at least they recognized that it meant something to them, that it was important. For a while there I'd thought it was important too, but had had no one to talk to about it. Maybe things would have been different if I had had someone.

Maybe now I did.

The acoustic thing was over, and a different guy was taking the stage. He looked like a surfer, and couldn't have been over thirty. "I'm Greg Baylor, one of the pastors," he said. The name rang a bell; I wondered if this guy was the pastor for the service Grace went to on Sunday nights. "If you're ever looking for a place to hang out on Sunday nights, I'd encourage you to check out our service—" I was right. At this some cheering erupted toward the middle of the crowd; the rest of the audience laughed, and Greg pointed and waved. "Ah, some of my fellow Sunday nighters making their presence known," he explained. "Anyway, I've been asked to come up and talk a little bit before we finish up, but I know you all came to hear this great music, and not me. And so, for that reason, I'm going to make you a promise. I am only going to talk for ten minutes, and then the fantastic musicians will come back up here and close out the concert. And since I'm only going to talk for ten minutes, I would like to ask you to listen—really listen—to what I have to say, and think about how, if at all, if might affect you.

"So, that being said, let me tell you why we"—at this he waved his hand to indicate the people who had been on stage, and the people in the audience—"are here this afternoon." And for the next nine minutes and thirty-four seconds—I timed him—he outlined what this whole Christianity thing was about.

I was riveted.

GRACE

"GRACE, YOU LOOK positively green. Are you all right?"

I stopped pacing. "A friend is here at the concert. He's not a Christian."

Rochelle, the alto who stood to my right onstage, reached out to squeeze my hand. "That's wonderful! You should have told us; we could have prayed for him before the service."

"Who's this?" asked William, one of the cellists.

"Grace has a friend here who isn't a believer."

"Hey, that's great, we oughtta pray for him."

Word spread, and suddenly seventeen musicians and singers were bowed in prayer. This sense of camaraderie warmed my heart, and I momentarily lost my anxiety.

I'd been prowling around the room where we waited between performances since the minute we'd left the stage, which had been about six minutes. Others were watching the stage on a closed-circuit TV, and others were grabbing dinner from the buffet, but I wasn't hungry, and I was too nervous to watch the concert, although why exactly I was nervous I couldn't explain. I think I wanted to be able to claim ignorance if someone onstage said something I couldn't explain or said something offensive. Not that I'd ever known anyone here to do such a thing, but there might always be a first, and I didn't want to witness it if it happened today.

I was also nagged by the fact that I'd ducked his kiss on my way out. Something about kissing in church didn't seem right. I wasn't sure why I thought it was wrong, or if I even thought it *was* wrong, or if I was just projecting "God doesn't approve of sexuality" myths onto the church.

"Closing remarks coming up," was stated from within the TV crowd. Everyone stood and straightened clothes and hair and lined up near the door. I took my place along with them and ached another prayer as we made our way up the back stairs.

Back on stage I was grateful I knew the songs well enough to sing them without thinking. I was a mess inside. I was beginning to regret my decision not to listen to the message; now I wanted to know what kinds of questions I was in for.

We finished the last song, and as the orchestra played a post-lude, the singers filed offstage and down into the room below. After a few minutes of discussion we all drifted back up to the sanctuary, and as everyone else went to the lobby to stretch their legs and meet up with friends and family, I snuck back to the associate pastor's office.

"You did great!" Missy squealed as I entered. She and Jane both hugged me, and Jack smiled warmly. "What's the game plan now?" Missy asked.

I did some quick math. "I have about twenty-five minutes left before the next concert starts, but that's not enough time to do any-thing, so Jack, if you want to go back to my place to hang out, I can give you the keys."

He stuffed his hands in his pockets and rocked a bit on his feet. "Well, now, I don't know. I might just stay and watch the next ser-vice, too."

I nearly fell over. "Seriously?" Missy and Jane looked just as stunned.

He nodded. "That Greg guy was really good. Very interesting. Do you think he'd be able to talk after the next concert?"

"Actually, if you want, I could go see if he's free right now. That way you can talk to him now and then again later if you think of more questions. It wasn't a very full crowd, so he probably just went back to his office once everyone left. Want me to check?"

He seemed to hesitate for a moment and then nodded firmly. "Sure. Thanks."

The second I was outside the room I nearly screamed with astonishment. I dashed to Greg's office just down the hall and knocked with a shaking hand.

A voice from within the office beckoned me to enter, and I found Greg with his feet propped up on his desk, reading *Rolling Stone*. "Ah, Grace! Hey, great job up there. What's up?"

I shut the door behind me and took a deep breath. "Jack Harrington is here; you knew that, right?"

His feet hit the floor as he motioned me to a seat, smiling. "Yeah; did he attend the first concert?" I nodded. "And?"

"And he liked it. I think. He wants to go to the next one, anyway—and he wants to talk to you."

Greg's eyes bulged as he let out a laugh. "Fantastic! Absolutely, send him in."

I dashed back to the associate pastor's office, then paused outside the door to take a deep breath, not wanting to seem flustered. I opened the door and tried to be casual. "He's in his office, which is right down the hall. He said he has some time now if you want to talk before the next concert."

Jack seemed to waver again, but then headed for the door. "Okay."

I led him down the hall. "Greg, this is Jack Harrington," I said smoothly as Greg advanced to shake Jack's hand. He showed Jack to a chair and I quickly left the office, then half flew back to the other room where Jane and Missy were praying.

"Oh my gosh, oh my gosh, oh my gosh," I mumbled as I collapsed into a chair near the door. "Can you guys believe this? Tell me about the concert; what did he do, what was he like?"

Jane and Missy sat down and smiled. "He didn't really say anything," Missy said, shrugging. "He seemed to enjoy it, though. He definitely listened to Greg's message." She giggled. "Man, Grace, how great would this be."

"I'm going to keep praying," Jane announced as she settled back in her chair and closed her eyes. Missy nodded and did the same. A faint smile played on her lips and I watched her, feeling jealous that prayer was not the first thing on my mind the way it was for these two. I tried to follow their example, but my mind was racing; I couldn't concentrate long enough to pray an entire thought before my imagination was wandering to visions of Jack and me together. This would make everything perfect.

After a few moments I realized I needed to get back to the sanctuary. "Gotta run, ladies," I said quietly, hating to disturb their reveries. I left and went quickly to the room beneath the stage where the musicians were preparing for the next concert. I grabbed my purse from beneath a table and fished out my lipstick, all the while wondering what Greg and Jack were talking about. I couldn't wait to hear the story.

Rochelle was suddenly beside me and whispering conspiratorially, "So what did your friend think?"

I grinned back. "He's talking to Greg right now," I whispered back, jabbing a finger upward, indicating the pastors' office area upstairs. She laughed and put an arm around my shoulder.

"That's fantastic. We'll keep praying."

"Thanks." I quickly put on a fresh coat of lipstick before tossing the tube back in my purse, then took my place by the door just as word came for us to go upstairs. I forced myself not to think about what was going on with Jack and to focus on the task at hand.

JACK

A SOFT KNOCK on the door interrupted our discussion, and a voice from outside said, "They're starting the last song, Greg."

"Thanks, Paul!" Greg called out. He shot me an apologetic look. "Looks like I need to go do my job," he said. "Are you still staying for the second concert?"

I nodded. "I will, thank you. Will the last rows be as empty as they were before?"

"I'm not sure; depends how many people show. But if you wait until I'm talking, people will be less likely to notice you. And you might want to just stand in the back, although I'd hate for you to be without a seat for that long."

I nodded. "Well, as long as you stick to your ten-minute promise, it won't be too bad." I stuck out my hand. "Thank you for your time, Greg."

"Of course!" he said with a vigorous handshake. "Feel free to come back here after the concert if you want; I'll have to meet and greet the congregation afterward, but after that I'm all yours." He led the way out the door and down the hall, making sure I knew where I was going before moving in the opposite direction toward the stage. I found my way to the sanctuary and risked a peek inside. There was a small section of empty seats in the back corner, so I ducked my head, dashed to the cluster, and settled into a chair just as Greg arrived at the podium. I caught a glimpse of Grace as she disappeared off stage right, and wondered vaguely whether Missy and her mom were still here somewhere. I felt bad that I hadn't gone back to them after talking to the pastor, but I really wanted to hear his message one more time.

I listened intently to his words, linking them with the explanations he'd given down in his office. Most of what he was saying made sense, although I wasn't sure what I was supposed to do with all this information. Well, that wasn't entirely true; Greg said exactly what you were supposed to do with it, but I wasn't sure if I could—or even if I wanted to. This seemed like an awfully big decision to make based on an hour of conversation and two rounds of a sermon. He offered to lend me some books if I wanted them, and I was considering taking him up on it, but then I realized that reading those in public—or on the set, at least—would cause quite a stir. I was not the religious type; anyone who had worked with me before knew that. Was I willing to open myself up to the ridicule and questions and cynicism of my coworkers?

I absorbed every word for the second time. He finished and was heading offstage, so I began to stand to go meet him back at his office, when Grace appeared again in the stream of singers returning to the stage. In the mental gymnastics I'd been doing I'd forgotten she'd be singing again, and seeing her made my heart jump. I stared at her and realized that I really—

Loved her? Wanted her? What did I 'really'? I watched her sing, forgetting my intention of sneaking out to talk to Greg again, and realized that, if I didn't love her already, I definitely was on my way there.

The last group of songs ended, and I discovered I'd missed my chance of getting out while people were distracted. I hastily angled for the exit before the people in the rest of the section did. I was just outside Greg's door when Grace was suddenly beside me. "Hi!" I said, grabbing her hand and pulling her in with me. "I missed your first set," I said apologetically. "I didn't leave here till it was almost time for Greg to preach again."

Hands on hips, she shook her head in mock rage. "I don't think I can forgive you for that," she said, eyes twinkling. "Seeing me sing songs you've already heard me sing once should have taken priority over your eternal soul, and you know it."

I took her hand and pulled her toward the two chairs in front of Greg's desk. "I did watch the last songs, though, and you did beautifully."

"Thank you," she said with a prim nod of her head as we sat down. "And the message? What did you think the second time around?"

I let out a huge sigh and ran my hand through my hair, settling back in the chair and gathering my thoughts. "I have a lot to think about," was all I could manage to say. She nodded silently, and I could tell she wanted to dig deeper but was holding herself back. I raised her hand and kissed it lightly. "Thank you for inviting me."

The shy smile I was used to seeing stretched across her face. "Thank you for coming." The mischievous glimmer in her eyes had been replaced by the glow that had always been there before the night she'd kissed me. I'd missed it.

The door opened, and Greg entered, Styrofoam cup of steaming brew in hand. "Ah, so we *do* meet again, Mr. Harrington!" he laughed. "Would have brought you coffee if I'd been thinking. My apologies."

"No problem; not much of a coffee drinker, to be honest."

"Well, that's probably a good thing. Grace, can I get you anything?"

"No, thanks, Greg, I'm fine."

He took his seat behind the desk and propped his feet on the desk blotter. "Well, my duties here are done, so if you have any questions, Jack, I'm more than willing to tackle them with you."

I nodded and thought for a moment. "I think I'm good for now, but thanks for the offer. And thanks for the help you've already given me, I really do appreciate it."

"Not a problem, Jack." He reached into a drawer and withdrew a business card. "If you ever have any other questions, you can call me here. I'd be glad to talk with you anytime."

I accepted the card and tucked it into my pocket, impressed with his generosity. I turned to Grace. "Is there more you need to do, or are you ready to go?"

"I've got a reception thing, for all the musicians. I think it's supposed to be about half an hour or so. But I'll leave as soon as I can."

"Well, how about I go back to your place and make you dinner?"

She smiled. "You know me, I'd never turn down a free meal." We bade Greg good-bye and slipped through the hall and out the door, where Grace offered to walk me to the car.

Neither of us said much on the way out, and once we were at the car the awkward silence persisted. I felt as if there was so much to say, but I didn't know how to start. The look on her face was a cross between sadness and confusion and something else I couldn't decipher. I wanted to ask her what was wrong, but something about her posture and face caused me to hold back my thoughts. "This is silly," she finally said. "I'll see you in, like, forty minutes."

"Yeah, you're right. Have fun."

"Drive safe."

Once more I debated kissing her, but before I could move she just smiled and headed for the building. When she left, there were tears in her eyes.

GRACE

THE THANK-YOU PROGRAM was a nightmare. I couldn't keep my mind on what was going on. When I realized it was finally drawing to an end, I slipped out as unobtrusively as possible and practically ran to my car. I didn't want to socialize or talk about my anonymous friend; I just wanted to get home.

I jumped into my car, and under the cover of darkness that had finally fallen, tears suddenly cascaded down my face. My soul *hurt*. Seeing Jack in church gave me so much hope, and yet somehow I knew there would be no eternal change made today, and the uncertainty of whether or not there ever would be was agony. Every minute I spent with him sent me deeper into what I was pretty sure was love. The thought of ending our relationship made me want to curl up and bawl. But when I analyzed our behavior, how intimate we'd become, I couldn't deny I was setting myself up for trouble.

I felt trapped. It was my own fault, and I knew how to get out, but I felt frozen the way you are in a nightmare, with the eighteen-wheeler barreling down on you and your feet rooted to the concrete. I wasn't willing to give him up, pure and simple. I'd found someone amazing who made *me* feel amazing, and I was not willing to cut myself loose. There had to be a way to plant my feet on the slippery slope of intimacy and prevent our relationship from progressing too far until…

Until what? What was going to happen that would allow us to tumble down that slope in wild abandon? Marriage? That was what I was supposed to wait for, and yet I knew that I didn't want to marry someone who didn't love God the way I did. And I had no guarantee that Jack would ever feel that way.

But hadn't God brought us together? Hadn't He gotten Jack to church? Why would God bring us together if we weren't supposed to *really* be together?

I felt like my heart and mind were on the verge of exploding. I wanted to scream and rage and cry out of sheer frustration. Then the sound of voices floating through the night air startled me, and I realized the other musicians were starting to exit the church. Resigning myself to being decisionless, I quickly started my car and snaked my way out of the lot toward home.

When I entered the apartment, the scent of something delicious hit me, and I was suddenly hungry. Jack, however, was nowhere in sight. I dodged Joker as she darted between my legs and went toward the bedroom, calling his name, and ran smack into him.

He looked sheepish. "I was looking for your music," he explained as he held up a stack of CDs. "I hope that's all right; I wasn't snooping or anything."

"That's fine." I couldn't help but laugh at the look on his face. "You look like you've been caught with your hand in the cookie jar. Are you *sure* you were just getting CDs?"

He smirked and pushed gently past me toward the kitchen. "*Yes.* Are you hungry?"

"Famished. You?" I followed him out and flopped down on the couch, kicking off my shoes and stretching.

"The same. You didn't have much in the way of food, though, so I had to improvise. How does a really late—or really early, depending on how you see it—breakfast sound?"

"Sounds as good as it smells. What are you making in there?"

"Well, let's see…we have bacon, waffles, hash browns—"

"Are you serious?!"

"—eggs, toast, and, yes, I'm serious. I never joke about breakfast.

And since it's the only kind of food you have, you apparently don't either."

I laughed. "You're priceless."

"Actually I'm seven million for lead parts, but for cooking I'm a lot cheaper. And more useful, some critics would insist."

That cracked me up. He waggled his eyebrows and turned his attention to a steaming pan on the stove. "Put in one of the CDs," he said over his shoulder. I got up and shuffled through the jewel cases he'd left on the kitchen counter, selecting an Ella Fitzgerald collection. Jazz filled the apartment, and I flopped again onto the couch, watching as Jack jockeyed from one pan to another. I felt on the edge of exploding, dying to know what he'd thought of the concerts and what he and Greg had discussed. I closed my eyes and listened to Ella crooning and Jack buttering toast. The sheer normality of it all— relaxing on the sofa, breakfast cooking, Jack at home in my kitchen— was at once perfect and begging for disaster. This was too good. It couldn't possibly last.

It was Jack's turn to lounge on the sofa while I cleaned up and did the dishes. "It's only fair," I'd insisted after we'd finished eating. "You cooked, I clean. That's how it always works."

It didn't take much to convince him, and now I could feel his gaze on me as I scraped dishes. I avoided his stare, focusing too intently on the sink and trying not to look flustered. Ella was finishing up the last song on the CD, and I could sense the unavoidable silence creeping up on us. I couldn't think with him watching me like that, and I *really* needed to think. What was going to come next? What were we moving toward? Why couldn't he just give in and get God so we could get on with it? And why was I having such a hard time doing what I *knew* I needed to do?

The last song was beginning to fade, and not able to bear the thought of silence, I glanced over at the stack of CDs on the counter. "Come pick another disc; that was the last song."

He slowly got up and ambled over to the counter, looking each one over carefully and then loading a soundtrack. I finished up the last of the dishes and dried my hands before collapsing into an armchair next to the couch. Desperate to start a safe conversation, I finally asked what form his next project was taking.

"Action," he responded. "And shooting in Ireland for part of it."

"Oh, how lucky. Ever been there?"

"Nope. You?"

"No. That would be incredible. How long would you go for?"

"Don't know for sure; probably a couple months or so. Maybe less; depends on how fast we work and if the weather cooperates."

"Send me a postcard."

"How about coming with me?"

I blinked. He was serious; I could tell.

"Jack, I can't just up and—"

"We're going in July; you wouldn't be back in school by then, and you wouldn't even have to stay the whole time."

My head swam. This was too much. I groped for excuses. "You'd be rehearsing and filming the whole time; I'd be bored out of my mind."

"You could film too; you could be an extra. And you could go sightseeing; you wouldn't have to sit around the set all day. I'll figure out a way to get a day off, and we can hang out. It would be perfect."

This wasn't a spontaneous idea; I could tell he'd been working on it for a while. I stared back at him, knowing in my heart that I couldn't say yes. This was it, the moment of truth. The can of worms was in my hand, and I found myself pulling back the lid.

"Asking a girl to accompany you to overseas filming isn't something you do lightly, Jack, at least not in my world."

"I'm not doing it lightly, Grace, I mean it. I've given it a lot of thought."

"I'm not saying you haven't. But…that's a request you save for someone you're serious about."

The perfect setup. My audacity amazed me. I waited for him to state his intentions, whatever they might be. My tone had implied that I assumed he wasn't serious; if he wanted out, he could easily admit I had come to the right conclusion.

His stare was so intense I nearly looked away. For a moment I thought he was blushing. He took a deep breath and said, "I *am* serious about you, Grace." He dropped his gaze for a split second before recovering and saying, "I want to make this work."

The words sent me reeling. He saw my incredulity and hurried to fill the silence. "I know it's inconvenient, and that the God thing throws a wrench in the works, but it's the truth, Grace. I didn't see this coming, and I don't want to hurt you, and…and the look on your face is kind of scaring me because I don't know what it means, and I don't know if I've just destroyed everything or…or what," he faltered, his hand raking through his hair as his eyes roamed the room before coming to rest on my face again. He looked as panicked as I felt.

I swallowed and cleared my throat, stalling. A nervous laugh broke from my throat. "I don't know what to say," I squeaked truthfully. I'd wanted honesty, but now I didn't know what to do with it.

"This isn't a proposal or anything, Grace, I'm not asking you for a response—although I do want to know where I stand. I just wanted to make sure you knew how I felt."

I took a deep breath and forced myself to look him in the eye. My thoughts were so scrambled I could hardly tell one from the other. But beneath all the chaos was a single impression that I knew in my heart was from God, and with what little presence of mind I had left, I flung up to heaven a prayer for strength.

"It's not where you stand with me that is the problem, Jack. It's where you stand with God." Where the words came from, I didn't know. But the chaos ceased as abruptly as it had begun, and I knew I was doing the right thing. "The 'God thing' does more than throw a wrench in the works. It doesn't matter how much I care for you, or you for me; the bottom line is that without God in the center of it, it wouldn't work the way a solid relationship should work. And I can't allow either of us to subject ourselves to that kind of heartache."

Relief like I'd never felt before cascaded over me like rain. The words that had needed to be spoken for so long were finally out there, irrevocable, clear as crystal, and unable to be ignored. There were tears on my face, but I didn't actually cry until he stood and walked out the door.

"You broke up with him?"

Grace nods. "I had to," she whispers. Jack fell asleep in the middle of her narrative, and she's been trying not to awaken him. "And I don't know where the strength came from to do it—well, I mean, I know where it came from, but it wasn't from me."

"Did you have any kind of feeling you'd eventually get back together?"

"Nope."

"So you were really okay with the fact that he might never come back, that you'd just cut loose the most eligible bachelor on the planet?"

She nods and shrugs, then leans forward to make sure I clearly hear her. "You have to understand, Jada, that I trusted God knew what He was doing. He'd brought us together for something. As long as I did what I knew I was supposed to do, I couldn't go wrong, even though it looked on the surface like I was making a huge mistake. The things the world sees as logical aren't necessarily logical when seen from God's perspective, and since I can't see what He sees, I just have to trust Him when He tells me what to do."

I can't help shaking my head. "That's an awful lot of trust."

She flashes a small smile. "Maybe so, but He led me right." Jack rouses from his nap and, after sipping his water, picks up where Grace left off.

JACK

I DON'T REMEMBER the first ten minutes of the drive home. The look on her face—so serene and confident as she shoved a knife into my chest—was before me like a ghost until I got to the freeway. Then the other drivers got a taste of my wrath as I wove in and out of lanes doing eighty.

I couldn't believe what had just happened. I'd been absolutely convinced she felt the same way I did; had I known she didn't, I would never have said anything. And all that crap about God—it hadn't stopped her lately, so why was it stopping her now?

All the things I wished I'd said filled my mind as I sped back to LA; the words are never there when you need them. I almost went back to demand an explanation, but frankly I didn't want to talk to her. And I wasn't sure an explanation would help anyway; it wouldn't change the fact that I loved her and she didn't love me. Or at least didn't love me enough to look past her God.

I drank a twelve-pack of beer in front of the television that night. After the third can I allowed myself to acknowledge that she was probably right. Religion was practically her whole life, but it had no place in mine. I still didn't understand why it hadn't mattered the last couple months, but I didn't care anymore either. The point was that this was now reality, and no amount of anger on my part was going to change it.

I started shooting *Nine Lives* two weeks later. It felt good to be on the set again, where I knew exactly what was coming and I always had the right words to say because someone gave them to me. I didn't have to think on my feet; I just slipped into character and allowed my mind to take a break from reality. It was a very physical role, and I pushed myself in the action sequences like a man possessed. At night I crashed hard, sleeping like the dead until makeup call the next morning.

More than once in the following month I had to stop myself from calling her to try to reconcile or at least figure out what was going on in her mind. I had a hard time believing two minutes of conversation could destroy a friendship and romance and potential long-term commitment. I hadn't been ready for a relationship in a long time, and then I was not only ready but actually willing to commit—and to someone outside the industry on top of it. I'd felt in my heart that it would have worked, that it had promise. But it turned out it didn't matter what I thought.

Shoving my hand in my jeans pocket one morning, I found Greg's card in the pocket. I'd forgotten about his willingness to talk and wondered now if the offer still stood, considering Grace and I were no longer... Well, we hadn't technically been anything in the first place, so perhaps that wouldn't be an issue. I stuffed it back into my pocket to be dealt with later.

This was only one of many too-perfect-to-be-coincidental events that occurred that day. In one of the first scenes, shot on a hotel room set, I opened the drawer of the nightstand to make sure my prop was in there and saw a Gideon Bible. "Who put this here?" I asked with far more surprise in my voice than the situation warranted.

The prop guy came over, looking defensive. "I did. What's the matter?"

"Why is it here?"

"Dude, it's a hotel, hotels always have Gideon Bibles, haven't you ever noticed?"

"Oh yeah." I felt like an idiot. My face betrayed my embarrassment, and the prop guy changed his tone and covered for me: "Well, but then again, maybe they figure the cheap hotels need 'em more than the ritzy ones. You probably haven't been in anything less than a Ritz-Carlton in ten years." He winked and headed off the set, and I was suddenly reminded of Greg's blunt words during our conversation: "All have sinned, Jack; just because you have it made here doesn't mean you have it made in heaven."

The caterer that afternoon was setting out sandwiches as I passed by, and the song she was humming sounded familiar. It played in my head—I could hear the harmony, and then instruments—and when I came back past her again, I caught her singing the words under her breath, words I'd heard Grace sing at the concert. They'd done that particular song twice; once in the beginning of the service and once at the end. The caterer caught me staring; I apologized and hurried back to the set.

The fourth thing occurred as I was driven home that night. The 101 was clogged, as usual, and as we crept along I noticed the license plate of a car next to me: GRACE4U. I couldn't help smiling—*Don't I wish,* I thought—and then a second meaning emerged. Greg had talked about grace a lot that afternoon in his office. His words came back to me as the traffic finally thinned and I neared home, and even once I was in bed searching for sleep the concepts he'd so clearly illustrated for me hovered at the forefront of my mind.

I spent the night wide awake, a luxury I couldn't afford when I was in midproject. As I stumbled out the door that morning, my hand found the business card again. On the way to the studio I called Greg's office and left a message for him. Five hours of staring at the ceiling had convinced me that I needed to get this God business sorted out, regardless of the impact it would have on Grace's and my relationship. I needed to decide one way or the other what I was going to do about faith, because apparently it just wasn't going to go away.

GRACE

I WASN'T SURPRISED when I didn't hear from him. That night he left I sobbed myself to sleep, alternately railing at God, myself, and occasionally Jack. There was no consolation in knowing I'd done the right thing. As the days came and went, I prayed he would call, then prayed he wouldn't, then prayed for permission to call him myself. Nothing doing. How could such a short friendship leave such an enormous hole?

School ended, and I was relieved for the break. I started meeting with the girls again every week; during my short fling with Jack I had stopped attending our Bible study. One night I spilled everything to Missy, not because I wanted someone to know, but because I knew keeping it secret would only make it easier to do again. It was a relief to get it off my chest, but at the same time it brought back the memory of him more strongly than anything else had, and the ache that had finally started to subside came back with a vengeance.

I filled the first half of the summer with a community art class and volunteering at church. The second half I took a course toward my master's degree, and it struck me one day as I studied in the library that Jack was probably in Ireland at that very moment. My heart ached at the thought of his invitation to join him there.

The beginning of school crept up on me, and I threw myself into teaching to try to occupy my mind. I started singing with the band at church again and working with their drama group as well. First quarter sped by, and when I thought back to the beginning of the year, it seemed as though everything with Jack was a dream. Had I really gone to that premiere with him? Had I really kissed him? Had he really said he was serious about me? Was that *all* that had happened, and if so, why did it take so little to tie me in such a knot? Surely it was all just an elaborate daydream. Nothing like that ever happened to people like me.

Things started well, but the second quarter steamrolled me. Struggling students and nervous parents drained every ounce of my energy, and the momentum from the beginning of the year was squandered in parent conferences and meetings with administration. I plodded along, hardly aware of what day it was, not to mention the month, and then suddenly Christmas break was nearly upon us.

The last week of school before break completely knocked me out. I hadn't realized how hard I'd been pushing myself until I almost didn't make it to the last day, having been bowled over by a nasty flu.

By the time the day was over I could barely think, I was so feverish. I drove home with a raging headache and fell into bed with my clothes still on and a Christmas corsage from one of the students still pinned to my blouse. I succumbed to a deep, feverish slumber that was plagued by convoluted dreams: my students storming my apartment, Joy and Missy cooking dinner in my kitchen with Greg doing karaoke in the living room, Jack on the big screen staring down at me in the front row and reaching out his hand. He was holding the keys to my car and telling me he was taking it back.

The jangle of the phone roused me that evening. Still half-asleep, I picked up. A ringing in my ears interfered with the voice on the other end; it took two rounds of, "I'm sorry, *who* is this?" before I finally heard "Kate Gordon, Jack Harrington's assistant."

I forced myself to sit up, wincing against the jackhammer banging inside my skull. "Um...okay," I said, not sure what she expected.

"Jack isn't there, is he?"

Huh? "Why would he be?" was my baffled response.

"Well, I don't know, but I've been looking for two days, and I'm running out of ideas. Has he contacted you?"

I was so confused I wanted to cry. What was she talking about? "I haven't talked to Jack since June. Why can't you find him?"

"If he contacts you, have him call me, okay?"

"Yeah, all right, but why can't you find him?"

"Because he's left without telling anyone where he was going." She swore. "Look, don't tell anyone about this, okay?"

"Who would I tell?"

"I don't know—just don't, all right? Tell him to call me." She hung up.

I dropped the phone and lowered myself back onto the pillow. Trying to form thoughts was like trying to swim through Elmer's glue. Where was Jack? Why didn't he tell anyone he was leaving? The small part of my brain that still functioned was worried, but the rest of me was too sick to care. I surrendered to the smothering sleep that rolled over me and dreamed of Jack zooming past my apartment while I screamed at him to slow down. There was a phone in my hand, and it started ringing. I stared at it as it smiled at me, its numbers curving like lips. When I talked to it, the mouth formed by the buttons moved. I surfaced from sleep with the phone in my hand and a faint voice emanating from the earpiece. Utterly confused, I held it to my ear. "Hello?"

"Grace?"

"Yeah?"

"What's wrong? Are you all right?"

I didn't recognize the voice. "I'm sick. Who is this?"

"It's Greg, from church. Are you sure you're all right? You weren't making sense when you answered the phone."

I groaned. "I'm sorry, Greg. I'm sick, and I was asleep and dreaming. I woke up with the phone in my hand." I giggled. "I didn't say anything embarrassing, did I?"

He laughed. "Don't think so. Listen, I'm sorry to bother you, especially since you're sick, but I wanted to know if you'd talked to Jack recently."

Two times in one day? Did I dream that first call, or had I really talked to Kate? Why on earth was everyone asking me about Jack? And why was I still in my school clothes? I stood shakily and began to clumsily change into sweats and a T-shirt as I tried to form coherent sentences.

"Um…no, I haven't."

"You don't sound sure."

I sighed. "Well, it's just weird, that's all." I told him about Kate's call, forgetting it was supposed to be confidential. "Have *you* talked to him?"

"Well, actually, yes."

My stomach did a little flip I hadn't felt in a while. "When? What happened?"

"Well," he hesitated, "pastor-congregant discussions are sort of the same as doctor-patient relationships, you know? Don't think I should really go into details."

"Oh. Okay." My mind was running a mile a minute, but unfortunately the flu kept getting in the way of any of it making sense. I struggled to pull my sweatpants on as we talked. "Should I be worried?"

"I don't think so, no."

"Okay." I was too tired to care what was going on anymore, especially if Greg wasn't concerned; I wanted to hang up and go back to sleep.

"Listen, Grace, if you happen to talk to him, tell him to call me, okay?"

"Yeah, okay."

"Now get some sleep, and get better."

"Yes sir." I hung up and dropped the cordless phone to the floor atop the pile of my school clothes. I was just pulling the comforter over my head when the doorbell rang. I groaned. I was on the verge of weeping; I just wanted to sleep. I stumbled down the hall, every muscle aching and my teeth chattering. Was it my head pounding or someone at the door? I braced myself against the wall as the room swam and, unconcerned with who might be on the outside, pulled open the door and hung on the knob while my eyes struggled to get the face into focus. It finally stopped moving, and there was Jack.

He was smiling until he got a good look at me. "Grace, what's the matter?"

"There you are," I said, relieved that he could start taking his own messages so I could sleep. The blinding pain in my head got louder. "Call everyone," I slurred before stumbling to the couch and passing out.

JACK

IT WASN'T EXACTLY how I'd hoped things would work, but now that Grace was asleep on the couch, it was a mercy. I realized I hadn't thought at all about what to say to her.

I carried her back to her bed, piling on the blankets and pulling the shade to block the glare from the streetlight outside her window. Her cat emerged from beneath the bed and leapt to the top, curving herself around Grace's head and purring.

I shut the door and returned to the living room, where I sat on the sofa and stared out the window. It had been six months since I'd been in this room, and the emotions of that day were still vivid. I could see her face, serene as she delivered the verbal blow that almost literally knocked the wind out of me. Being on this side of things made it easier for me to imagine how difficult that conversation must have been for her; at the time I'd been too selfish to respect her strength of character. But a lot had happened in those six months. I hoped she'd give me another chance.

One evening in early July I called Greg and left him a message asking him to call me before I left for Ireland. What he'd said before had intrigued me, but I'd been working hard to convince myself that it was myth, and yet every turn brought me face-to-face with what Grace would have called a "glimpse of God." I felt like I was being stalked by Him. I needed to turn and face Him and figure out what it was He wanted from me so I could get on with my life.

When Greg called, our conversation turned quickly into a one-sided diatribe—by me. He listened with incredible patience and never once tried to counter my lame arguments. After a lengthy monologue

I concluded that I'd made a mistake in calling him, I was sorry to have wasted his time, and it was obvious to me that the whole thing was a well-written farce. My arrogance swelled my head momentarily, and for a second I thought I'd hit upon clarity for the first time. And then, with a simple question, Greg muddied my waters again.

"How confident are you in your beliefs, Jack?"

I asserted boldly, albeit untruthfully, that I was just as confident in them as he was in his. Even as the words came out of my mouth, I knew they weren't true, and a part of me begged him to give up and go away so I could stay safely in my cocoon of self-imposed ignorance.

"Would you consider yourself an intelligent man?"

The question was asked without challenge or condescension. I answered that yes, I would, but what did that have to do with God?

"Okay then," he said, "I'd love to know your view on some of the evidence we Christians look to as support for what we believe and why. How about this: I'll send you a summary of what I believe and the reasons why I believe, and you send me back your response, okay? That is, if your schedule permits; I know how busy you are."

The earnestness in his voice told me he was serious, and this wasn't just a mind game. He honestly wanted to know what I thought. The idea was interesting, and I saw the opportunity to outline, for myself, exactly what I believed. I'd never given much thought to these things, and I was discovering that it was hard to verbalize and organize them on the fly when I'd never truly considered them before.

And so I shortly found a package containing three books and a two-page letter from Greg.

Five months later, I awoke to the sound of a woodpecker drilling through a pine outside my window. The room was awash in sparkling sunlight glinting off the snow outside; a blurry glance at the clock told me it was closer to lunch than breakfast. I tried to remember what food I'd purchased on my way up the mountain the afternoon before, and whether any of it would make a good first meal of the day.

I shuffled to the kitchen and rummaged through the sack of groceries, still where I'd first set it down on the table. I settled for two granola bars and a lukewarm can of Mountain Dew. Breakfast of champions.

I'd called Sean the day before to ask if anyone was at his cabin this weekend. He'd once offered it to me on a "Call me anytime" basis, and I decided my current situation required a little vacation. He'd dropped the keys off at my place along with directions and a warning to make sure I lowered the thermostat to 50 degrees before I left.

The past five months had put my mind and heart through the wringer. I'd left for Ireland in August and taken one of Greg's books with me, thinking if I happened to find time, I'd perhaps give it a whirl. I ended up finishing the whole thing on the flight over, taking notes and marking up the book as though I'd be tested later. I reread it during my breaks, making more notes and coming up with more questions and, unfortunately, more reasons why my views on life and spirituality didn't quite work the way I'd thought they did. After returning from Ireland, I devoured one of the other books, giving it the same brutal treatment as the first. I began to e-mail Greg, arguing and feeling sure I'd finally stumped him, but his answer would come back, and *I'd* be the one who was lost for words. I kept waiting for him to gloat or push me to give up, but he never did. He simply sent his response and then left me alone.

Four months of this didn't seem to get me anywhere. I finally decided I needed to go somewhere to clear my head, somewhere I could escape from the everyday activity and surroundings of my life and give myself a little break. Sean's cabin came to mind, and here I was. Of course, rather than allow myself to completely leave behind everything that had been hounding me for the past two seasons, I lugged the books along, reasoning that a new perspective would help me crack the shell of this religion thing and give myself all the reasons I needed to ditch it once and for all.

Rather than zone out in front of the TV after I arrived, I grabbed one of the books and started rereading it. By the time I felt ready to put it down, it was well past midnight. My head churned with the evidence I read, the notes I'd made in the margins after reading Greg's e-mails, and the little questions I'd written but could now answer for myself. I didn't know what to think of the arguments against God that I'd always heard. Greg seemed to refute them all. I lay in bed, exhausted yet convinced I wouldn't sleep. My mind wouldn't stop working long enough for me to drop into unconsciousness, or so I thought—but then suddenly it was morning.

When I awoke, thoughts of skiing were quickly forgotten when I spied the book on the coffee table. After breakfast, I threw myself on the couch and picked up where I'd left off. By two I'd finished and started the second book for the third time; dinnertime came, and I read while eating Pasta-Roni. I debated calling Greg, but then I realized there probably wasn't much more he could tell me; I'd asked him nearly every question a person could ask, and I'd read the books multiple times. How much more information did I really need? What I needed to do was organize my thoughts and ideas, sort through it all instead of just reading it over and over.

In my mind I drew up a flow chart. Step one. God: Yes or no? If yes, move on, if no, game over and go hit the slopes.

I thought for a minute.

God.

Yes.

I let this statement sit for a while, turning it over and looking at it from all angles. Lots of people believed in God, didn't they? Maybe not the one I was thinking about, but a god of some kind, somewhere. I could believe in God and not be tagged as a fanatic.

I took a deep breath. Level one cleared.

Step two. Truth: relative or absolute? If it was relative, then I was done, but if it was absolute, then only one religion was going to work, and I needed to figure out if this was it.

I sat on that one for a while. Mathematics: absolute. Two plus two always equaled four, whether you liked it or not. White couldn't be black; the grass couldn't be the sky; a cat couldn't be a dog. Those were absolutes. But they weren't ideas, they weren't emotions, they weren't decisions—those were different, weren't they?

I thought about people who killed because they said God told them to. If truth was relative, then we had no right to tell them they were wrong. I couldn't imagine being okay with what they did, but if I didn't want them imposing their beliefs on me, then could I impose my sense of right and wrong on them?

I thought about the business world, about hearing my father tell stories over dinner about stealing clients from rival companies and fudging expense reports and how handy statistics were for telling people anything you wanted to tell them. "It's how business gets done," he'd say. Everybody's doing it. How bad can it be when every-one is in on it?

I thought about Penelope Jones, about sleeping with her when Dianne was still alive. We were still living together, but I'd distanced myself from her and her illness and looked for my own comfort. Right or wrong? Black or white? Relative or absolute?

I thought about Dianne's face, the look she'd given me when I'd come home that next morning, and how I'd convinced myself she didn't know what had happened. But she knew. Of course she knew. I thought of the night a few weeks later when I'd found her passed out, unconscious, a failed attempt at suicide that had as much to do with my betrayal as with her disease. If I'd told her outright about Penelope, would she have said it was no big deal, it was my choice, my life, go ahead and do whatever you want? Relative or absolute?

I knew the answer already. She had given it without the question even being asked.

I had been wrong. And not simply by my own standard, because my standard at the time had given me the green light. In my eyes I hadn't been wrong. But that didn't matter. Just because I believed I was justified didn't mean I was.

Moonlight shone on the snow outside, and I stared out the window for a long time, eyes fixed unseeing on frosted trees outside the window, my unwanted memories pulling me into a whirlpool of personal history. Lies told, women used, promises broken. My thoughts ranged beyond my own actions and flickered through newscasts from years gone by: planes hijacked and crashed, ethnic cleansings, computer viruses unleashed simply because someone had the power to do so.

Truth?

Absolute.

My skepticism is apparently obvious because Jack asks, "Whatcha thinking, Jada?"

"I don't understand how you could use logic to help figure out religion. I mean, spirituality isn't supposed to be logical."

"According to whom?"

How could this man always be so exasperating? Sometimes I pitied Grace. "According to everyone! That's the point!"

"Yeah, that's what a lot of people think, and yet you can't really explain why, right? Because there's no real reason. People just don't want to admit religion should be logical because then they can't just do whatever they want and claim it's okay."

I try to counter him, but find I can't. "Fine, whatever, go on." I'm getting to the point where I want to just finish this project and get out of here. These two keep making me very uncomfortable.

With this revelation came a fear I'd not expected. I'd always thought I was a good person, and yet look at what I'd done! I wasn't as good as I'd deceived myself into believing. I wanted to fix it, to fix *me*. I didn't like the thought of being someone who willingly hurt other people, but my actions told a different story. My transgression against Dianne stuck with me because I'd loved her—think of how many people I had wounded without ever knowing it, because I didn't care about them enough to notice. The realization that I was capable of cruelty frightened me.

I felt a nudging, almost physical, toward the third book Greg had sent: a compact, leather-bound Bible, still in the small box the books had arrived in. It was the only one I hadn't opened yet. Mental flow chart forgotten, I picked it up and noticed the small sticky notes peeping through the tops of the pages and clustered toward the back, labeled 1, 2, 3. I unsnapped the clasp, opening cautiously, as if something inside might jump out. The leather binding creaked in that way new leather bindings do, and I marveled at how thin the pages were. I turned them, long, confusing names catching my eye, tiny numbers and footnotes dancing in the margins. I made my way to slip one, where a sentence was underlined in red. *"For all have sinned..."* Sin. An archaic-sounding word, but it captured the way I was feeling, the hopeless distance between me and anything really and truly good. God.

Careful not to tear the delicate paper, I made my way to number two. Another underlined sentence. *"For the wages of sin is death..."* I thought of Dianne, how my actions played into her demise. I thought of the victims of power-hungry people and their wars. So true, I mused. Their actions—their *sin,* I thought, testing out the word—caused the deaths of so many.

It took a moment to figure out the verse was referring to the death of the sinner, not to the death of other people because of sin. It was referring to me.

"But the gift of God is eternal life through Jesus Christ His Son."

Greg had mentioned this verse. I remembered a picture he'd sketched at his desk on a piece of printer paper: a canyon with a man standing on one side and God on the other, with a cross in the middle bridging the gap between them. "The death of Christ gave us access to God, if we want it," he'd said. "Just walk across."

Too simple, I thought.

I turned more pages. Sticky number 3. Another red-lined verse. *"Everyone who calls on the name of the Lord will be saved."* A verbal version of crossing the bridge.

I felt a twinge of panic. I couldn't do this.

I looked up, out the window at the trees, dusted in snow fine as talc, like arrows pointing skyward. Heavenward.

My eyes dropped back to the book in my hands. They continued down the page, catching phrases here and there that intrigued me. I continued to read. The numbers got in the way at first, but after a while I didn't see them. A new section, labeled First Corinthians. I continued to read. Second Corinthians. A verse with a different kind of number. A note in the margin. A reference? I took a guess at how it worked and found myself in Matthew. Red-typed words, the tag *Jesus said* coming before them. *His* words.

I read more.

The room began to grow lighter, the sun slowly rising and casting butter-yellow rays onto the floor. My eyes dry and tired, barely open now, but still reading, six pages left. Angels and thrones and churches and judgments of fire and earthquakes. The makings of a first-rate horror movie. I fell asleep on the couch with the image of an endlessly sunny world full of music and a man in the center on the throne of gold, casting a never-ending light.

I'd been at the cabin for three days and was beginning to miss civilization—or what little of it I usually interacted with. I'd read nearly the whole Bible over the past two days, and while the first section bored me some, the second section fascinated me. I couldn't get enough of it. But I didn't know what to do with it.

I analyzed over and over the few prayers I'd heard Greg deliver, trying to determine the etiquette and structure before attempting one myself. It appeared far easier than I thought it ought to. But there had been in Matthew, in red ink, a prayer that sounded vaguely familiar, that Jesus said was the way to pray. I tended to think Jesus would be the authority, but Greg didn't stick to that formula, and I started to wonder if maybe he wasn't as smart as I had thought him to be. But could he really get something wrong when the "right" way was right there?

Jesus seemed like a cool guy, and until I read Revelation I thought praying would be no big deal. But then I read that last book, and the image of Him there scared me, and suddenly I wasn't as eager to launch into a conversation with Him unless I really knew what I was doing. Until now I'd managed to hold off calling Greg because I'd wanted to do it all on my own, but this was too important to botch. I pulled his number from my jacket pocket and drove down to town where I could use a pay phone. Sean hadn't installed phones at the cabin.

He sounded surprised that I was calling. I hoped I wasn't intruding too much on his good graces. "Won't take too much of your time," I promised. "Just need some clarification on prayer, and I'm not near my computer to e-mail you."

"Okay, go for it," he said. I could almost imagine him shoving his chair away from his desk and propping his feet on the blotter.

"I've been thinking about how you prayed at the services, and the times we talked. And then I read Matthew, and Jesus said to use the Lord's Prayer. So what's up with that?"

He chuckled. "An excellent observation. Did you like Matthew, by the way?"

"Yeah, actually. The whole second section—New Testament, right?—is pretty cool. Except Revelation. I don't get all that, and it kinda freaked me out."

He laughed outright. "That's pretty common. It can be a difficult book for even the most learned Christians. We can talk about that one sometime, if you'd like. But I'm glad to hear you read it.

"Now, the prayer thing. Here's the deal: the Lord's Prayer isn't a magic charm; the form and words aren't special in and of themselves. It's the principles they symbolize that are important: worshiping God, confessing our sins, thanking Him for His blessings, and bringing our needs and desires before Him. The way we do those things can vary, and we don't always have to do them every time we pray. But if you want a balanced relationship with God, you need all those parts on a consistent basis. Does that make sense?"

"Uh…" I was still processing, wishing I'd brought pen and paper with me in the car. "I think so."

"Bottom line is, just talk. And then, just listen. Don't worry about the words or the structure. He knows what's in your head, anyway; trying to be fancy won't impress Him, and not being honest isn't going to fool Him. That just puts a wall between you both, because you're not being completely open."

I was ruminating on this for longer than I realized, because finally he asked if I was still there or if he'd totally lost me. I assured him that I understood, I thought, and just needed to think a little more. "Sounds good," he said. "Call again if you need anything."

"I will, thanks."

We hung up, and I drove back to the cabin, my mind churning the whole way. The "just talking" part I was pretty sure I could handle; it was the "just listening" part that confused me. Listen to what? God wouldn't actually talk to me, would He? Then I remembered my first encounter with Grace, her firm belief God had talked to her through a vision. I'd thought she was nuts; now I almost hoped for the same thing.

Back in the cabin I opened the Bible again to Matthew, reading the prayer one more time before deciding it was now or never. I opened my mouth and shut it again.

I feel stupid doing this. I'm not going to talk out loud; I'd feel like an idiot. I feel stupid doing this at all. Even talking in my head isn't too much better than talking out loud.

Just do it already, what are you waiting for?

Okay, yeah, just do it. Okay. Deep breath. God? I think I want this, although I don't really know how to qualify what "this" is. I want what Grace has, and Greg. It makes sense, in some weird way. I think it's right. I'm not entirely sure, but I'm pretty sure. So…what do I do?

Just ask.

I don't know what I'm supposed to ask for.

Jesus.

The thought was amusing. It sounded like ordering off a menu. *I'll have the Jesus, please.* I smiled in spite of myself.

But then it made sense, the things in the New Testament about receiving Christ and having Him with you, and I realized that that's what you were supposed to do—to get Jesus.

Okay. I want Jesus. I want whatever it is He can give me. I thought of the image of Him in Revelation, the burning eyes and the sword, His intensity and strength. It still roused a mild sense of fear. I didn't want Him to know what I had done, and in a painful realization it occurred to me that He already did. I feared His response to my…my sin. The word seemed to fit better now than it had the first time I'd used it.

"I'm sorry." The words came out of my mouth before I had time to think about not saying them. "I was wrong. I'm sorry. Forgive me."

There was a warmth in the pit of my stomach, but not really my stomach—deeper than that. My soul? "I didn't mean to— I mean, I did mean to, but I thought I was justified; I didn't think it mattered." The warmth seeped into my bones. I felt almost lightheaded, but at the same time the world around me seemed to have sharpened in resolution; the color of everything seemed richer and deeper and truer. The words kept coming. "For Dianne and Penelope and every lie I told to get a part and every dollar I wasted and every mean thing I've ever said…" There was an energy that seemed to grow and expand and vibrate inside me. "And I have so much. Why do I have so much? Why did you let me get so much when you knew I'd waste so much? This career and fame and money." I was nearly laughing at the sheer volume of it all. "My health, my life, my family, my friends, Grace— God, Grace! You saved her! She could have died, but You saved her. Without her this wouldn't be happening."

It was like seeing one of those cornfield mazes from above. When you're in it you don't see the patterns, but when you're above it it's so obvious. I saw the past five years of my life, all the dead ends and hiccups and tragedies that had led me to where I was now, and the intersection of my life with Grace's and how everything changed because of that one rainy night. Like I'd been living with my eyes closed for all these years and had opened them, finally, for the first time.

"Thank You." The words were woefully inadequate. *Thank You?* Was that the best the English language had to offer? But I could think of nothing else. "Thank You, thank You, thank You. Why me? Thank You."

I was standing—when had I stood from the sofa?—and staring out the window at the trees, blindingly bright in the late morning sunshine. I had to go. I had to tell Grace.

It wasn't until later that I realized I hadn't been carrying on a conversation with myself in my head. God had been the One talking to me.

GRACE

SOMETHING SMELLED REALLY GOOD. I roused slowly, the dull ache in my skull growing more intense. I could hear voices somewhere and was pretty sure they weren't just in my head. I took a deep breath and reluctantly opened my eyes. The room was dark. My shades were drawn—I never drew them, I always forgot. Had I done that? The voices, I now determined, were coming from the living room, and sounded a lot like Missy and Jack.

I sat up, and stars danced before my eyes for a moment before my vision cleared and I felt safe to stand. I pulled on a sweatshirt and shuffled into the living room where Jack and Missy sat. Their conversation stopped as I appeared, and their faces told me how awful I looked. Jack looked different, although I couldn't tell why. He smiled hugely. "Good evening," he chuckled, a teasing lilt in his voice. "Have a nice sleep?"

I frowned and tried to figure out what time it was. "How late is it?"

"Only eight," Missy responded. "Are you hungry? Jack made dinner."

What had smelled heavenly upon my return to consciousness now made my stomach churn in an unpleasant way. "Um...no." I felt myself sway slightly on my feet.

"Drink something, anyway; I'll get you juice." She stood and walked to the kitchen, grinning like an idiot. Why were they so happy?

"Everyone's been calling here for you," I mumbled as I fell onto the sofa and curled into a corner. I still felt half-asleep. "Greg, your assistant..." I yawned. "Where have you been?"

Jack smiled. "Been out thinking. Went to Sean's cabin in Big

Bear. Had it out with God and some ghosts from the past." His smile nearly burst his face. "I did it, Grace."

I stared at him while the meaning of "it" came into focus. Suddenly I knew why everyone was so happy. I didn't even try to say anything; the lump in my throat sprang up before I could get anything out. I stared at him in shock. Missy stood back in the kitchen; I could see her wiping her eyes with her sweater sleeve.

All I could do was stare. The last six months I had slowly and painfully purged from my heart any kind of emotion toward him, forcing myself to pray that his soul would find God and that I would be freed from the longing to be with him. And now here he was, claiming to have found faith, and that corner of my heart that I knew would never really be free of him was swelling and taking over and assuming all now would be as I had once hoped it would.

A little squeak made its way through my constricted throat, and I let out a choked laugh, tears pooling and stinging my eyes. He laughed, and Missy laughed and finally made it back with the juice, and I forced myself to calm down and drink so I would have more time to think of what to really say, because "Take me now!" just didn't seem appropriate, no matter how heartfelt it would be.

"Wow." I shook my head and laughed again. Jack smiled self-consciously, one of the few times I could recall seeing him anything less than entirely self-confident. "This is amazing. I can't believe—How? When? *Why?*"

"The short of it is that I finally got it. The long of it is, well, long, and"—he shrugged—"I don't know. It just sort of all came together." He spread his hands and shrugged again. "And here I am."

"Here you are, all right," I murmured, the drained juice glass still in my hand. I resisted the urge to say, "So now what? Busy Friday?" I was determined not to be the one to make the first move. And why was I even thinking about moves? The man had just committed his life to God, and I was busy planning dates. *Get your priorities straight, girl.* "So who else knows?" I asked, leading myself away from the slippery slope forming in my head.

"No one," he replied. "I haven't talked to anyone. I came straight here. I need to call Greg. And Kate, apparently, although I don't know what I'm going to tell her." A shadow crossed his face, and I wondered if he'd thought at all about the ramifications of one of Hollywood's leading personalities claiming Christianity. Even though I'd prayed for it for so long, I'd never once thought to pray for the way he would handle the fallout. I launched an arrow prayer as he continued. "Did Kate say why she was calling? Or Greg?"

I shook my head slowly; the throbbing ache had momentarily passed with the news of Jack's conversion, but was now coming back with a vengeance. "Honestly, I don't remember much of either conversation; I was so out of it. But I don't think either of them said anything specific, other than to have you call. They were both pretty concerned about not having heard from you, and not being able to find you."

Jack nodded slowly and stared at me, and I found myself staring back, and feeling suddenly shy and embarrassed. I looked awful, I was sure. And I was beginning to remember all the very unchristianlike things we had done while we'd been together, and I felt found out, exposed as a hypocrite, and very afraid to talk to him about anything remotely close to the subject of us.

And that's when Missy decided to make her exit.

"You sure?" I implored with what I hoped was a convincing nonchalance. "Did you have enough to eat?" My mind raced, looking for reasons to convince her to stay, but the look on her face told me she'd have none of it. Missy was no fool; she knew there were things we needed to discuss that wouldn't come up while she was there, and in her ever-so-thoughtful manner she was getting out of the way. Little did she know how much I dreaded them.

She hugged Jack and me and moved for the door. "Grace, call me if you need anything," she said as she shrugged into her jacket. "Jack, congratulations." She smiled, gave a little wave, disappeared out the door, and crossed the balcony to the stairs. I watched her until she was out of sight, and kept staring out the window until I could hear her car start and back out. I didn't want to look at Jack; I didn't want to talk about anything. How unfair that he should be the one to finally see the depraved condition of his soul but that I would be the one suffering the guilt!

An awkward silence settled around us. I forced a yawn, then a weak cough; maybe he would have mercy on me in my frail condition and leave so I could sleep. But no. He remained, and I wracked my brain for a way to segue into the inevitable conversation that lay waiting for us.

"So now what?" The words were out before I could actually decide whether or not they were suitable. As good as any, I figured. At least we could cut to the chase.

He chuckled. "Well," he said, leaning forward, elbows on knees, hands clasped in a businesslike manner, "I don't know. Any ideas?"

I shook my head and shrugged. "I don't know."

More silence. What to say? Where to go with all this? The suspense was unbearable, but the conversation required to get to the bottom of it all was just as bad. I tried to remember what had happened when I told Missy and the others I'd made my decision about God. What had been their reaction? What did they say? I was at a loss.

"I guess this changes things a lot, doesn't it?" he asked in a halting sort of way. I'd been staring into that middle distance, and when I finally focused on him, I saw he'd lost the glow he'd had when I'd first come out of the bedroom. Now he stared down at his hands looking almost worried. I wanted to ease his mind, but I didn't know how or even if I should. I'd never seen him unsure; angry, yes, hurt and confused, yes, but even in those times he had retained a kind of control and sureness that seemed to hold him together. But this was different, and I ached knowing my blank face and virtual silence were the cause.

"Jack," I said. Great; now that I'd started a sentence I'd have to end it. He waited for me to continue, expectancy on his face. I sighed and frowned and rubbed my forehead; it hurt to think. "I'm sorry," I finally said. "You must think I don't...that this is no big deal to me or something. That's not true at all. This is amazing. Completely amazing. But also completely unexpected. That's why I'm so..." I shrugged. "I just don't know how to react. Because you're right, this *does* change things. And I don't know what I'm supposed to do with that change." I stole a glance at him, having averted my eyes and focused instead on the ends of my sweatshirt sleeves bunched together in my fists. I was afraid to look at him for too long.

I could see him nodding out of my peripheral vision. He sat back in the chair and blew out a sigh through rounded lips. "I guess I thought we'd just pick up where we'd left off," he admitted.

"Is that why you did it?"

Silence for a moment. I feared he would say yes, that the whole thing was a hoax to get back into my good graces. *Please, God, let it be real,* I begged.

"N-no."

"You don't sound convinced."

"Well, I'm not, entirely. But I know that it wasn't you I was thinking about when I made the decision. No offense."

I laughed. "None taken." I smiled at him. He smiled back. He still looked sad, but some of the tension was gone now.

His voice was low, soft as suede. "Grace, I still want to try to make this work. The God thing was in the way before, and I understand now why you had to end it and why it wouldn't have worked. But I get it now, and I believe it, and…well, now we're on the same page. Isn't that enough?"

The weight of his stare was like being buried under quilts and blankets, suffocating and hot. Everything I'd worked on over the past six months, listening to God, seeking out the direction He had laid out for me, learning and reading and trying my level best to be what He wanted me to be, were put to the test in the asking of this one simple question. Was this what God wanted for me? Was it really enough that he believed what I believed? I wanted it to be; more than anything I wanted for God to nod and give me the thumbs-up, a wink and a smile and a gentle nudge. But I knew better than to expect anything like that.

"What will Kate say, when you tell her?" I forced myself to look at him, to continue to look at him as he thought and responded.

He frowned, not seeing the relevance of the question. "I don't know," he stammered. "I hadn't thought about it." Seeing I was not accepting this answer, he shrugged and continued. "I suppose, um…she'll probably be surprised."

"When the next script comes in, and it requires behavior or scenes you don't think God would approve of, what will you do?"

The light dawned. His eyebrows arched as he sat back on the couch, his back straight. "Um, well…I guess I would…look for a better way to play the scene? Suggest changes?"

"Everyone wants to know what you think, Jack. Do you know— I mean, have you ever *really* considered—the power you have over people? What your opinions can do? What your endorsement or condemnation can cause?

"If you're serious about God, Jack, if you're serious about believing in Him, and following Him, and allowing Him to determine the course your life will take, then you're setting yourself up for a lot of gossip, and rumors, and snubbing, and cold shoulders, and outright denouncements of friendship, because people do not like to be told that they have made the wrong choice with their lives, and your decision for God is going to hold a mirror up to a lot of people who would rather not see the reality of their decisions. If you're willing to go through with that, then we are on the same page, and it is enough. But if not, then we're where we were in June."

JACK

I FELT STABBED. Of course I knew and understood the outrageous amount of attention and importance people gave me. But I was embarrassed to admit I had not considered the effect my beliefs would have on my career and my image in the eyes of the public.

What *would* Kate say? She was my link to the public—to the press, more important—the one responsible, whether I liked it or not, for shaping my image. Her lack of support might cost her her job, as she well knew, but she was talented and could easily find employment with someone else.

What would my friends say? I thought of Todd. He would laugh and make a joke—make a lot of jokes, who was I kidding?—and never really be okay with it, although he would claim to be and never mention it again. Sean…I had no idea how he would respond. All around he seemed like a decent guy; I couldn't remember him ever making disparaging comments—at least not about people's religion. Other than those two, and Kate and Grace, I could think of no other people I would really call friends.

But most important, what would the directors say, the ones who held my fate in their hands along with the scripts they sent me? How much was my name in the opening credits worth to them? Would they ask that I lay my beliefs aside for this one scene, this one theme, this one line? Would they send scripts at all?

Surely I was overreacting. Surely I was allowing this to take on far more importance and authority than it really did.

But still…

"It's not *that* extreme, is it?" I asked in a way that projected more confidence than I really felt.

Grace cocked one eyebrow. "Just how delusional are you?"

This was not comforting. I stood and began to pace with nervous energy. "No, really, I mean, think of all the people in Hollywood that are outspoken about their religious faith, and they're still working. Richard Gere, John Travolta, Shirley MacLaine—"

"She's working?"

"Okay, yeah, not her, but the others."

"They get laughed at. Mocked. Sure, they get jobs, but they're the butt of jokes as well. Plus, their beliefs don't interfere with the roles they play. But God isn't just an idea you pull out on the weekends and in your spare time; or at least, that's not what He's meant to be. He should be influencing every decision you make. If you force Him into a box and limit His influence, you're reducing your relationship with Him to a fair-weather arrangement. No earthly friend would stand for that kind of relationship, and He won't either. If you're serious, you're going to have to face the fact that you're gonna get flak for it, and possibly lose your career as you know it."

I sat down again, hard, rubbing my eyes. "That's an awful lot to risk on someone I don't know very well."

Her lips curled slightly. "Which one of us are you talking about, Him or me?"

I shot her a rueful smirk. "I suppose it goes for both of you."

She shrugged and unfurled herself to stand. "I'm far less concerned about our relationship than I am about yours and God's. But remember, this isn't a typical relationship. This isn't the occasional dinner and a movie and a walk on the beach. This is *God*. And while He'd much rather you be devoted to Him, He can handle it if you're not. But what He *really* hates is when you're in the middle, lukewarm. Make your decision and go with it, but don't oscillate." She was tottering toward the kitchen as she said this, where she slowly opened the refrigerator and pulled out the juice. I watched her unsteadily pour and return the container, then shuffle back to the sofa.

"Don't take this the wrong way, but you really do look like hell."

"Thanks, love. You're a doll." Slow sips of juice, a halfhearted waggle of the eyebrows to let me know no harm done.

I sighed. "Look, you need to sleep, and I obviously have some calls to make. Can I maybe come back tomorrow or Sunday?"

"Sure. What are you doing for Christmas?"

"Staying home, why?"

"Why don't you come to church with me for one of the Christmas Eve services, and then come over afterward and we can talk? I ought to be better by then; that way I'm more likely to have my head on completely straight."

I chuckled. "For not having it on straight tonight, you sure were shooting accurately."

She shrugged and yawned. "God can use anyone, lucidity is not required."

"Say that again?" Kate's voice squeaked. This was not going well.

"I said I've, um, decided to become a Christian." I really wished there was a better term I could use; *Christian* seemed to conjure the worst images in people's minds.

"Why, Jack?"

"Long story. But that's the bottom line. I just wanted you to know."

"Who else knows?" Her PR gears were already spinning.

"Grace, her friend, that's all so far."

"Who else are you telling?"

I sighed. "Well, at this point, the pastor I've been talking to, and that's about all, but people are gonna find out eventually."

"And this doesn't bother you?"

"No. Should it?"

She made a noise halfway between a laugh and a snort. "How many Christians have you met in Hollywood, Jack?" The way she said the word made it sound like a racial epithet.

"None. Your point?"

"That *is* the point."

Todd simply laughed. This was at least expected. "Guess I'll have to start stocking a lot more juice and soda, huh?"

I laughed, confused. "Why?"

"You still gonna drink?"

"Why wouldn't I?"

"Wow, dude, your brand of religion is a lot cooler than my aunt's. No drinkin', no smokin', no dancin'…lemme tell ya, holidays at her place were like hell on earth. I think maybe that was the point, though, to show you just how bad it could really be. Scare you into church. Going to church, too?"

"Well, yeah, eventually I guess."

He shook his head and slammed down another shot. "Good luck, dude. My aunt wasn't too keen on the whole movie thing either. Hope your crowd isn't like that."

Not surprisingly, Greg was a bit more excited. His face lit up. "Jack, that's fantastic. I'm totally stoked!"

"Well, I'm glad someone is."

"Grace isn't?"

"Well, she is, but I think she questions my sincerity."

"What makes you think that?"

"The fact that I'm uncertain of it myself."

"Ah, gotcha. And why is that, you think?" I relayed our conversation to him, along with Kate's and Todd's reactions. "Yeah, I can see how you'd be worried about whether or not this was the right thing. But let me ask you something. Do you think what you believe is true?"

For once I felt I could answer with certainty. "Yes."

"And do you think God can and will take care of you?"

"Yes."

"And what is more important: following God or following your career?"

The truth hurt, but it was still truth, regardless of how much I didn't like it. "I guess I *have* to say God if I said yes to all that other stuff, huh?"

He shrugged. "Well, no, you don't have to, but that would be kind of like saying you believed one plus one equals two, but you were still going to put down three as your answer. See what I'm saying?"

I groaned inwardly and rubbed my face. "Bottom line, Greg, is that I don't know that I believe enough to take that big a risk. Frankly, I barely know the guy, you know? For all I know He's some giant shyster in the sky who puts on a good show for newcomers like me and then yanks the rug out from under them." Some of the stories from the Bible I'd read seemed to confirm this for me, but I didn't want to bring them up right now. "I mean, that's a lot of change all at once: having to say I believe in God, and Jesus, and having to give up so much—"

"What are you giving up right now?"

"Huh?"

Greg shifted in his chair. "What are you giving up?"

It seemed obvious to me. "Um, my *life*."

"And how much control have you really had over that?"

"Well," I said defensively, "I made all the decisions; that's a lot of control, if you ask me."

"And how was that working for you?"

This conversation was ticking me off. "Look, Greg, I don't like to rub it in, but do you know how much money I make? Do you have any idea what kind of life I live?"

"Ah, so your job *is* your life, that's all there is to it."

"No, it's not *all*, but it's a big part."

"And you choose the roles?"

"Yes!"

"And you choose how well they do?"

"Well obviously not—"

"And you decide how the critics are going to judge the movie and you, and how the public perceives you?"

I rolled my eyes, "No, but even so, I've been—"

"And what about every other aspect of your life, Jack? How about your friends? your family? What about all the other women you've been linked to in the past? How is all that going? You exert a fair amount of control over them? over their existence and the way it affects you and your life?"

I wanted to deck him. "What's your point, Greg?"

"My point, Jack, is that you have long enjoyed the illusion that you were the captain of the ship, but in reality you've been lucky that your dreams and desires have, for the most part, lined up with what has actually happened. You've had very little control, Jack, but you're afraid of giving that up, because you're afraid that God may want different things for you than what *you* want for you. Sure, God can have control as long as His plans and yours match up. But you're not ready for the possibility that your life is not what God has in mind for you and that He might ask you to leave it."

As usual, he was right. How did he do that?

Greg leaned toward me, elbows on knees, staring me down. "If you were honest about giving Jesus your soul, then your eternity is sealed. All that's left now is to make this life count for as much as it possibly can. And I'm not saying He's going to yank you out of filmmaking; it's an industry that could definitely use someone like you. But it may be that He has other things lined up, and while that's a scary thing to admit, it's also exciting to think that your life could be even more effective, even more productive, than it is now, and that what you do with it will last far beyond you and have an impact you can't even imagine."

He stood and clapped me on the shoulder as he moved for the door. "Stick around and think as long as you want," he said. "I'd stay, but I'm getting the feeling you need to think alone for a while and hash all this out with God." His office door closed behind him, and I stared out his window to the parking lot and the field beyond, not really seeing them, but trying to decide how much of what he had said I believed.

GRACE

I PRAYED ALL WEEKEND that I would feel better by Christmas Eve, and as Tuesday morning dawned I found myself much improved. I'd slept soundly for the first night in almost a week, and awoke with energy and excitement about the holiday—and Jack.

I cranked up some Christmas music on my stereo, belting out the "Hallelujah Chorus" and the usual carols at the top of my lungs as I showered and dressed. I couldn't believe this was already my third Christmas in California. Part of me still longed for a white Christmas, but the lights on the palm trees didn't look nearly as funny as they had two years ago.

I hadn't heard from Jack whether he was actually coming. I prayed God would solidify his faith and help him deal with the consequences. I shouldn't have expected it to be as easy for him as it was for me; he had a lot more at stake.

Joker was pulling ornaments off the tree after lunch when I heard footsteps on the balcony. "Come on in!" I yelled as I tried to drag her out from where she hid beneath the tree. I heard the door open as I made a lunge for the cat.

"Merry Christ— Grace? Where are you?" Jack asked.

"Under the tree, over here."

He laughed. "What are you doing?"

"Trying to get Joker. She keeps knocking down the ornaments and drinking the tree water out of the stand." I finally got hold of her back legs and pulled her out; she mewed and howled the whole way and took off for the bedroom after squirming out of my grip. "Blasted cat," I mumbled before grinning at Jack. "Merry Christmas! Want some eggnog?"

"Sure. Sorry I didn't call before I came over."

"That's all right; I couldn't remember if we'd decided you were coming for sure. I was expecting almost anything."

"Ah. Then I should have come with the sleigh and reindeer like I'd been planning." He shook his head in mock disappointment, and smirked.

"I certainly hope a Santa suit would have been involved."

"Oh, definitely."

"Well, next year, right?" I grinned and handed him a glass of eggnog, then poured one for myself.

We sat on the couch, and he produced from his pocket a small box wrapped in red paper. "Merry Christmas."

My shoulders sagged. I'd been too unsure of where we stood to risk getting him something, and being sick I hadn't had a chance to shop anyway. "Oh, Jack, I didn't—"

"I didn't expect you to; don't worry about it. I saw this when I was in Ireland and it had you written all over it." He shook it a little; I could hear a faint rustle inside. "Open it."

I took the package and tore off the paper. A red-lidded box appeared, and inside was a silver Celtic knot cross on a delicate chain. "Oh Jack, my goodness, it's beautiful…" I pulled it from the black velvet board and opened the clasp before handing it to him to put on me. It dangled down my blue sweater, the perfect length. "It's gorgeous, Jack, it really is. Thank you." We hugged—our first physical contact in six months. It was harder to let go than I thought it would be, but I pulled away and looked down to admire the cross again. "Missy will be jealous; she loves Celtic knots."

"Eh, I'll get her one next time," Jack said with a dismissive wave.

I sat back and fingered the cross as I spoke. "Well, the first service isn't until six, so we still have about five hours to kill. What do you want to do?"

Jack reclined into his corner of the couch, thinking. "Well, let's see…a movie?"

"I could do that. What's playing?"

"Um, *Jolly Roger, Dream State, Countdown to College*—"

I rolled my eyes. "How festive." Then I remembered an ad I'd seen in the paper. "Oh—there's an art theatre down in Dana Point that's showing *It's a Wonderful Life* all day today. Let's go see that!"

Jack grinned. "I'm game."

We filled three hours altogether, then came back to my house to eat. A little before six we left for the church. The plan was to get there late so we could sneak into the back and not be spotted. Missy and Joy promised to save us seats, so after watching from the shadows to make sure no one else was walking in, we slipped into the building and down the hall to the sanctuary, then stole across the back to the empty seats tagged for us on the end of the last row. We had only missed a couple carols, and as we settled into our seats, the senior pastor, Paul, took the stage to give his message.

I rolled my program over and over in my hands as Paul spoke, trying to determine at each point he made how Jack would take it, think of it, what he would believe about it. I hadn't realized what a racket my fidgeting was making until Jack gently stilled my hand with his and flashed me a curious smile. I bit my lip and forced myself to be still. I noticed later he'd never let go.

We stood to sing the last few carols of the night, and halfway through the second one he leaned over and whispered, "Did they rewrite these lyrics?"

I stared at him, baffled. "Um…no. Why?"

"They're all about Jesus. Have they always been about Jesus?"

It took a second to realize he was serious. I tried not to laugh. "That's how they've always been! You're just really hearing them for the first time, that's all." He grinned and shook his head in amazement.

When they started "Silent Night," I tugged his sleeve and whispered up to him, "This is the last song. Do you want to slip out?"

He thought for a minute, then shook his head. "If I'm gonna be coming here, people are gonna have to get used to seeing me. We'll just leave when it's over."

Coming here? He was planning on coming here?

And with that, the lights rose, Paul bade us all good night, and people began shuffling up the row toward the doors in the back. Missy looked over at me in surprise. "You guys didn't leave."

I shrugged. "He didn't want to."

We sat and talked, deciding what to do for the rest of the evening, and it wasn't until we were on our way out that I heard someone behind us say to her husband, "Call me crazy, but I think that's Jack Harrington up there!"

Her husband snorted. "You're dreaming, Lucy."

Jack and I stifled a giggle as we threaded our way through the cars. The couple behind us continued to bicker, oblivious to how their voices carried, and as we climbed into my car Jack yelled back, "Merry Christmas, Lucy!"

I laughed until I had tears in my eyes as the stunned face of Lucy stared at us as we sped away.

JACK

FOR WEEKS I FELT like a completely different person, and I seemed to see the world in a new way. I saw the way things were interconnected, the way people reacted to God without even realizing it, including myself. Greg had given me a book when I saw him after my "conversion," which is what everyone kept calling my weekend in Big Bear, and it talked about the basic beliefs of Christianity. I devoured it in two days. Grace and I talked about it on the phone in the evenings, and I was constantly amazed by how much she knew when she'd only been a Christian for a couple years. "It's not me coming up with these answers," she'd laugh. "God's giving them to me. Trust me, I don't know *that* much!"

Even after I'd finished the book and we'd exhausted all the topics in it, Grace and I still talked every evening, sometimes about God and the rest of the time about whatever it is people usually talk about when they're in love. I wasn't working on anything, and I'd begun thinking about taking a break for a while. I was tired of shooting, and with things moving the way they were with Grace, I wanted to free myself up to be with her more. We'd talked long and hard in the week between Christmas and New Year's, and after praying about it—the first thing I ever prayed about specifically—we both felt like dating was a possibility. I officially asked her out on New Year's Day, and even though we'd been together such a short time, in my heart I knew it was only a matter of time before I got up the courage to propose. She had six months left of school, and then, if I wasn't working, we'd have the summer free. The possibility of spending more than just weekends together and evenings on the phone was exciting to both of us.

As the weeks wore on, I felt myself losing that shiny new feeling. It wasn't pretty. I felt sluggish, but not physically. Almost depressed, but not quite. All the crap that existed in the world before my Big Bear experience was still there, and my trust in God was already fraying a bit at the edge. One of Grace's students lost her mother to cancer. One of the people on staff at the church was in a car accident and possibly paralyzed for life. An armed robbery six blocks from my apartment ended with the death of a liquor store owner and left a wife and three kids. The world disgusted me now. It sucked before, but for some reason it sucked more now. I felt a desperation for people that I hadn't felt before, a longing to tell them what I knew about God. But who was I going to tell?

Kate was still a bit wary of my beliefs—and of me, in a way—and I tried not to make her more uncomfortable by bringing up God or church, or even Grace. We'd always had a good working relationship, but now things were strained. Todd had stopped making any effort to hang out with me, although he always accepted whenever I made the first move. Sean didn't seem to care either way, but his apathy was almost as frustrating as Kate's and Todd's obvious discomfort. I hadn't brought it up with my family yet, and based on the reactions of the people I worked with, I was nervous about how they would react.

Grace, try as she might, didn't know what to say to help me. All her friends had been Christians—they'd been the ones who'd introduced her to God in the first place. They'd been happy for her. I was jealous.

And Grace herself was one of the issues that was causing me no small measure of concern. We were spending more time together than ever, both in person and on the phone, but a subtle change had taken place in her over the past few weeks, like she was slowly stepping back from me. We talked about all kinds of things, and she never told me any subject was off-limits, but she seemed to shy away from sharing what she felt, what she was thinking. I tried to pinpoint what was happening, but I couldn't define it, and I didn't feel I could say anything until I knew precisely what to say in case I was the one building up walls and not even realizing it.

Things blew wide open one night when I broached the subject of my friends and their reactions. Over dinner at her place I asked for her insight. We talked about the people she worked with, their views of Christians and of her specifically, and how her kids would even talk to her about God sometimes.

"What about your mom?" I asked between bites of steak. "Have you told her you're a Christian? Or your dad?" My mom had called recently, asking if I would be able to come out for another visit sometime soon; maybe I could get some pointers for how to break it to the family.

Grace shook her head and said abruptly, "Never told them," busying herself with the green beans, and something in her face told me this was going to be a tender subject. When she didn't elaborate, I pushed a bit further. "Are you afraid to tell them? I mean, you could tell *me*—"

"I just didn't, that's all." Words quickly said, laced with the end-of-subject tone. "But your family sounds cool," she said. "I'm sure they'll be great."

I shrugged. "Maybe. I don't know; they've never been that big into religion. How about your parents? Religious, atheist?"

"Undeclared. And why all the interest in them?" Snappish tone. I was on thin ice.

"Just curiosity, Grace. You never mention them." That was no exaggeration; save for mentioning that her parents were divorced, she'd never once told me about them.

"They're not worth mentioning."

"Ouch."

"What?"

"That doesn't seem like you. I've never seen you express that much disfavor for someone before, much less two someones."

She folded her arms on the table, and her face took on a bitterness I'd never expected to see in her. "Dad lives in New York with a woman I've never met, and Mom lives in Chicago and is married to a guy I met once and instantly hated. I haven't talked to him in five years or her in three. They divorced after he cheated on her, and neither of them has done much to deserve my respect or my affection. I don't know what they're doing, or who they're with, and to be perfectly honest, I don't care."

She stalked to the kitchen with her plate and dumped the rest of her meal into the sink, then slammed the plate onto the counter and headed for her room. The door thunked shut, and I remained where I was, left in utter amazement that someone so sweet and kind could harbor such resentment and never mention it. I didn't know she had it in her.

I knew better than to go after her, so I cleaned the dishes and settled down in the living room to channel surf. An hour passed. Then another. I perused her video collection, determined not to go anywhere until we'd talked again, and popped in a Disney movie I'd last seen in the theatre when I was eight. I made some popcorn and got comfortable on the couch.

Sometime after ten the door to Grace's room opened. I quickly turned down the volume and listened for her footsteps, hearing instead a small, tired voice say, "You're not leaving, are you?"

"Nope." Silence again, and then her steps down the hall. She dropped into the armchair and stared at me sullenly. I turned off the TV and settled sideways on the couch, waiting patiently for her to speak.

"I'm sorry."

"It's all right."

"No, it's not. I shouldn't have walked out like that."

"You were mad; it's okay."

"It's *not* okay. I wasn't mad at you, and I shouldn't have taken it out on you like that. You were just curious, and I…" She looked like she might cry. I nudged the tissue box on the coffee table closer to her with my foot, and she grinned slightly.

We were silent for a while, and after a bit I got up and filled her teakettle with water, having noticed in recent months that she made tea whenever she was stressed. She was staring out the window, looking distracted, and I was suddenly afraid I'd overstepped a boundary somewhere, that I should have simply left her alone and gone home. I set the tea on the coffee table and asked quietly, "Should I just go?"

She looked up quickly, as if I'd startled her. A look of vulnerability? fear? crossed her face. "Do you have to?"

"No, no; I can't tell what you're thinking, or if you want me here. I don't want to push you." I sat down and took her hand.

"I'm sorry, Jack." She rubbed her eyes with her free hand and shook her head. "This past month, with all that's gone on… I've been thinking a lot about my parents and feeling horribly, horribly guilty. And mad. And abandoned. It's stupid, really, because *I'm* the one who left Chicago and shunned what few attempts at contact my dad made over the years, and it's wrong and I shouldn't have, but they shouldn't have divorced, either, and…" Her voice trailed off, and she blushed, then shook her head, looking embarrassed. "Listen to me, I'm totally babbling, this is ridiculous."

She stood abruptly and ran her hands through her hair, looking helpless. Feeling very much the clumsy, bumbling guy, I stood and pulled her to me and wrapped my arms around her. She started to cry into my shoulder, and I found myself thanking God for her and asking Him to tell me what to do to help her. I'd never spontaneously prayed like that before, and my thoughts turned from Grace to God, and I was once again amazed at what had transpired in the last year. I was astounded by the way He worked, and the hunger I'd experienced after Big Bear—the emotional and spiritual mountaintop I'd been on—began to awaken again, thanks to this woman He'd led me to know. I held her tighter, kissed her hair, and, for the first time, prayed for her.

GRACE

I COULDN'T SLEEP.

I tossed and rolled and sighed and counted sheep and breaths and heartbeats and finally, at 2:47 a.m., gave up and turned on the light. I propped myself up on pillows and tried to read, but my mind kept wandering, and I couldn't keep my place.

Jack had touched a nerve, and I hadn't been prepared for the reaction it had triggered. My subconscious had been wreaking havoc lately, haunting me with dreams of my parents and nightmares with shapeless terrors that left me feeling panicked and exhausted in the morning. I hadn't been prepared for the way Jack's conversion would alter our relationship. Everything should have been great, except now there were nameless fears holding me back from him, from opening up to him and allowing him into these dark places that were forming in my mind.

And then he'd asked about my parents.

Sleep was obviously not coming, so I tried to untangle the knot of fears and hurts and memories in my head. As far as I could decipher, there were three major threads creating this mess: Richard Winslowe, Daphne Winslowe, and Their Divorce. I forced myself to think about this mess, about the events leading up to their split—memories I'd locked away years ago and never allowed myself to revisit. My spirit bucked like a spooked colt; I nearly ran to the living room to watch TV and give my mind something else to do. But I forced myself to stay put and examine the events and people that were threatening to ruin one of the best things that had ever happened to me.

My parents had been married young, while Mom was still in law school and Dad was working sixty hours a week to establish himself. Babies hadn't been in the plan, and I grew up hearing how inconvenient the timing was and how many sacrifices my mom had been forced to make to be the Supermom she thought she had to be—"but of course it was worth it for you, honey!" For twenty years my dad was a workaholic who never made it to my school musicals or choir performances because of "last minute issues," but my mom made it to every single one "even though the briefs/the witness lists/the first draft of the closing arguments are due in the morning and I'll have to stay up till 2:00 to get them done." She never let me forget how much effort it took for her to be a mom and a lawyer, and I grew up wondering which she'd rather be if she had to choose. I never asked because I was afraid how she might answer.

My senior year of high school our family unraveled. My father was promoted and went from working sixty hours a week to working eighty and traveling every other week. But my mom became convinced that the traveling was a cover-up for an affair. She obsessed about it, going through his drawers and closet and meticulously picking apart his cell phone bill, although I don't think she even knew what to look for. Then one afternoon I came home from school to find her screaming into the phone that she was onto him and that she'd ruin him if he didn't straighten up. She nearly dropped the phone when she finally noticed me standing there, abruptly hung up, and began making dinner as if she hadn't just destroyed my tender teenage psyche. I went out to my car and drove to a nearby forest preserve, where I sobbed and listened to the radio for three hours before driving home in the dark. She'd gone to bed and left my dinner on the kitchen table.

My father denied my mother's charges and tried to meet all her demands: cutting back his hours, coming home for supper so we could "eat together like a normal family" (although I didn't know any other kids who had their whole family at the table for dinner), and even firing the secretary he'd had for six years because Mom was convinced the woman was out to steal him. Mom went off the deep end, and no one could figure out why. Then one afternoon I was rummaging through her drawers in search of nylons and found a four-page letter from her mother, dated six months back, spilling the secret she'd kept for nearly forty years about her husband's affair and subsequent abandonment of my mother and her sisters. I was shocked. Mom always told me her dad had died of a heart attack when she was three; apparently that was what her mother had told her as well. But no, he'd run off—with his secretary.

I called Dad at work and told him about the letter, convinced he'd be able to fix things. He promised to talk to her once he was able to come up with a convincing reason for why he knew about her parents' situation. But as the weeks wore on he did nothing, until finally I, armed with the wisdom of one semester of high-school-level psychology, told my mother I'd found the letter and thought maybe she was projecting her anger toward her father onto Dad, and that perhaps she needed to talk to a therapist instead of taking it out on him. She slapped me—the only time she'd ever hit me—and told me never to go through her things again, and never again to tell her what to do.

A week later she filed for divorce. A week after that my father admitted he was having an affair and moved to New York. Two months later I graduated, packed up, and moved to a university three hours south of Chicago, where I lived for four years without going home for holidays or vacations. Dad paid the bills—part of the alimony settlement—and Mom flew down to visit for a weekend every once in a while. In between classes and parties and midterms and club meetings, I worked hard to be completely self-reliant, to convince myself I didn't need anyone else to make my life work, and to convince myself that my parents' actions had nothing to do with me.

For nine years I'd done a fairly good job of building these myths, but now I was feeling helpless, raw with need, and utterly abandoned by the two people who were supposed to love me most in this world. And I was beginning to fear that Jack, the man I wanted so much to love and be loved by, was going to screw me over—that I would be mistreated the way my mother and her mother had been. And if my father had found someone else, how much easier would it be for Jack?

Then the thoughts I'd so effectively pushed away since first falling for Jack began to resurface. He was rich. He was famous. He was a celebrity. Women all over the world lusted after him. Why would he stay with me when he had all those options?

I thought of all the women he'd starred with, the women he'd kissed and touched and seen nude take after take—and would continue to kiss and touch and see nude if he continued acting. And why wouldn't he continue? And how could I ever come close to competing with their sculpted bodies and perfect faces? It was too much. I'd never make it.

I slid further under the sheets and dissolved into tears as the roots of my fears were finally laid bare. The bottom line was that I couldn't compete, and I didn't trust him to love me forever. One look at the marital statistics of celebrities proved the point; he came from a culture that discarded marriage like yesterday's newspaper. The fact that he was a Christian now didn't ease my fears. He was only human; he'd never be able to resist the seduction of the women he was surrounded by.

I fell asleep as dawn was breaking, exhausted from thinking and crying, with visions before me of my mother's face the day my father left.

JACK

I DIDN'T HEAR from Grace for a week.

The day after our explosive dinner I called and left her a message, and then forced myself to find something else to do besides calling again and again until she answered. I prayed for God to calm my anxiety when she didn't call back by that evening, or the next day. Tuesday I called in the evening, a time when she was almost always home, and again got her machine. I realized that the issue was not that she wasn't home, but that she wasn't answering. I was hurt, but tried to remember that she was obviously in the throes of some family flashbacks that were eating away at her, and that this probably had nothing to do with me. It worked for a while.

Wednesday I nearly drove down to her place to camp out on her balcony, convinced that something was desperately wrong. I dreamed that night of the accident, our accident, blood on her face and her crumpled car, and woke up shaking. It was irrational, I knew, to think anything that serious had occurred; I'd have heard about it, somehow, by now. But the dream stole my sleep for the rest of the night.

Friday came around again, and still no Grace. I sent her flowers with a silly note, hoping to melt her a bit and elicit some response. Knowing she wouldn't receive them until she got back from school, I drove into Beverly Hills to window shop, kicking myself for not being able to remember when her birthday was, or even whether she'd ever told me. I looked into the shops I passed, seeking something that suited her that I could buy as a gift, and remembered the day I'd brought her here for lunch. I'd offered to take her into the shops after lunch, and she'd laughed, saying something about how she'd never be given the time of day by the staff because she was so obviously not the type. After passing five shops I realized she was right—these clothes would never suit her. She would never have to try that hard.

I continued walking and found myself inside Tiffany. The concierge greeted me at the door and asked if there was something specific I was looking for. I opened my mouth to say, "Nothing," and was surprised to find myself suddenly saying, "Engagement rings." She nodded and led me to a case that ran the length of the room, introducing me to an elegant woman in black named Anya who stood behind the counter. Anya explained the various cuts and settings after I admitted my diamond ignorance, and by the time the concierge had returned with a flute of champagne, I'd already decided what to buy. After three sips of bubbly and a few thank-you checks written to the staff to make sure my purchase wasn't made public, I was on my way out with a small blue box, wrapped with white ribbon, and a ridiculous grin on my face that I simply couldn't shake.

I went home, intending to change clothes and call Grace one more time, but found a message waiting for me on my machine. "Hi, Jack," said Grace's voice, and I almost laughed with relief. "I'm sorry I haven't called. I've been a mess. Oh, thank you for the flowers, they're beautiful. Joker keeps trying to eat them, though, so they're stuck on top of the fridge for now." A pause, two starts and stops of her voice. "Um…I…we really need to talk. I can't tonight, but can we meet tomorrow night? I can come up there if you want, since you've been coming down here so much; I feel bad about you having to always drive all that way. Let me know if that's all right. Talk to you later. Bye."

All the happiness I'd felt on the way back from Tiffany, the sheer joy at the thought of seeing her face when I gave her the ring, was sucked out of me. She'd sounded awful, and it wasn't hard to read between the lines. No "I miss you" or "Can't wait to see you." This was a disaster. Everything was crumbling.

I sat down with the phone in my hand, trying to get myself to call her but not able to push the speed dial. I tried not to panic. Had I done something? Said something? Other than that night over dinner, I couldn't recall ever having a conversation with Grace where I said something that set her off. I'd seen the latest *Us* and *People* magazines and knew I wasn't in them, so it couldn't be some wild accusation or rumor. Not that it would matter; we always laughed together over the ridiculous claims made by the gossip columnists, the way they mis-construed meetings of celebrities and their friendships and conversa-tions and chance run-ins.

I took a deep breath, forcing myself to relax. I called her house—getting, of course, her machine. "Hey, Grace, it's me. Of course we can meet tomorrow. Come on up, and I'll make dinner and we can talk about whatever it is that's been bothering you." I took a deep breath. "I hope you're okay, Grace. I've been worried about you. I'll pray that things are okay by tomorrow, all right? I'm a little nervous about it—your message didn't sound very encouraging. Have I done something? If I did, then I'm sorry, whatever it was. Just tell me so I won't do it again." Another deep breath, and then I took a huge risk. "I love you, Grace. Sorry I'm saying it for the first time to your machine instead of you, but I wanted you to know now. All right, your machine will probably cut me off in a minute, so I'm outta here. Take care tonight. See you tomorrow. I love you, Grace."

I hung up and dropped the phone to the floor. My hand was shaking. I'd finally said it! We'd been so cautious, but it was so obvi-ous we were in love, I simply didn't want to put it off any longer.

I looked around the room and resolved to make Saturday night the most special night Grace had ever had. Flowers, dinner, music— I'd sweep her off her feet if it killed me.

GRACE

MISSY GAPED. Joy gaped. Taylor gaped. I cried.

We'd been out to dinner, my idea to try to get my mind off Jack and the inevitable. The plan was to have an evening with my friends, get to bed early, and then spend tomorrow rehearsing the lines I'd composed for ending things with Jack.

When we'd gotten to my place, I'd checked my messages while the others lounged in the living room, and by God's grace they'd not heard the first half of his message. But those golden words caught their attention, and then we were all circled around the answering machine, staring at the little black box that had projected Jack's voice into the air and told me he loved me. *He loved me.* I was speechless. I felt like water, like I'd literally splash to the floor if I let go of the counter.

"Oh, Grace," Missy breathed. "Oh…wow." She looked at me, saw my tears, and mistook them for signs of happiness and not the horror and dread they truly were. She hugged me and laughed. "This is so wonderful!"

I shook my head, not knowing how to tell her it was all wrong. "It's too much," I said at last, not knowing what else to say.

"What will you wear tomorrow?" Taylor asked, taking my hand and pulling me toward the bedroom. "Let's get you ready for tomorrow night!"

"It's just dinner. At his apartment, not even a restaurant."

"Girl, when a guy like him tells you he loves you, nothing is 'just dinner' anymore."

My thoughts were in shambles as Joy and Taylor raided my closet.

Outfits were coordinated on the bed, my jewelry box brought in from the bathroom and rummaged through for the right earrings, shoes lined up like Rockettes waiting to dance. Only Missy held back from the fashion party, sitting instead on the chair in the corner and watching me watch the other two girls parade in and out of my closet. Joy and Taylor were good friends, but Missy knew me best; I could tell she was seeing right through me.

"Movie time!" she finally sang. "Grace looks tired and needs to get her beauty sleep, so let's put the movie in so she can get to bed before midnight." The others acquiesced and we moved to the living room. They pulled *Lady and the Tramp* out of the DVD player, and I nearly cried again, remembering the night one week ago where everything had fallen apart. We'd rented some romantic comedy, but I had to force myself to pay attention and laugh in the right places. At one point I finally excused myself, supposedly for the bathroom, but instead I retreated to my room and slumped on the bed, exhausted from acting normal.

Missy came in after me and perched on the side of the bed, not saying anything for a while. Finally she broke the ice. "Something's up in that head of yours, Grace, and it's eating at you, I can tell. You don't have to tell me if you don't want, but if it'll make you feel better to get it out—"

"I'm breaking up with him." Silence. She nodded slowly, thinking. More silence. This wasn't helping me. "Well?"

She shrugged. "Well what? I'm not going to offer advice when I don't even know what's wrong. Did he do something?"

"No."

"Say something?"

"No."

"Not *do* or not *say* something?"

I sighed. "No."

"Something fundamentally wrong with him that God can't fix and you can't live with?"

"No."

"Is it worth it for me to keep guessing or should I just give up?"

I shrugged. "It's nothing that *has* happened. It's something that *might* happen. That *will* happen." Hearing the words out in the open instead of shut away in my head gave them a new perspective, and for the first time I wondered if I wasn't maybe overreacting just the tiniest bit. But I'd thought about it so much, and it seemed logical... "It's all just too good to be true, you know? It has been all along. This isn't a film script with a neat and tidy ending. It won't turn out all rosy. They never show what happens *after* they fall in love, you know? Like, after Cinderella and the prince get married—then what? He snores, and she can't cook, and he's uncommunicative, and she's needy, and they never show the fallout that happens when someone amazing marries someone average. He's amazing. I'm average. He's multi-million-dollar picture deals. I'm thirty thousand a year after taxes if I'm lucky. It's a disaster waiting to happen, and I don't want it to happen to me."

"So you're ending a relationship because of something that *might* happen to it later?"

This was irritating. "Look, I know it sounds stupid, but yes, that's why, and while it doesn't make sense to you, it does to me. You wouldn't be able to understand."

"Gee, thanks."

"I'm serious, trust me. You've been blessed with a whole family. I wasn't that blessed, and I don't want to go through what my parents went through, and put my kids through that kind of hell. This will save a lot of heartache in the long run."

Missy nodded. "Well," she said, "if you think this is what God is leading you to do, then of course you have to do it. I'm just...really surprised." She paused and then shrugged and stood. "Joy and Taylor will think we're conspiring against them; wanna go back and finish the movie?"

I nodded and followed her back to the living room, but this time I didn't even try to engage. I sat on the sofa and stared at the TV, not seeing it, but thinking instead about what Missy had assumed about my decision. She didn't even ask if I'd prayed; she just took it for granted that I had. But in reality, it had been a while since I'd automatically prayed about anything. I missed those days.

God, I am absolutely and utterly terrified of what is happening with Jack. I don't want to be like my mother. I don't want for my marriage to be like my parents'. I don't want to watch a movie and see my husband kiss another woman, or go to the grocery store and see a picture of him with another woman, or be constantly compared to other women.

He would do that?

How couldn't he? When he's surrounded by beautiful women with perfect bodies and goddess faces, how could he not come home and look at me and think, Eh, average.

If he loves you, he'll think you're more beautiful than all of them put together. Real love does not give someone up just because there are prettier options.

Then why did my dad leave?

Because his love was not real.

How do I know Jack's love is real? How do I know I can trust him? How do I know he won't leave me?

You can't know. But you can trust Me to guide you. You can trust Me not to leave you. And you can know My love is real and will not fail you. Follow Me, Grace, and stop trying to form your own future.

Tears coursed down my cheeks, unchecked and, thankfully, unseen by the other girls. I wanted to kill my father for the way he had made me so afraid, so independent. How dare he screw me up so badly!

I knew God wanted me to trust Him, but it was *so hard*. It scared me nearly senseless to think of committing myself to a relationship with Jack and therefore giving myself over completely to him. But how could I admit this to him, when it would mean admitting I didn't trust him? After everything we'd gone through, after finally getting to the place where we could pursue our relationship, how could I tell him no and hurt him like that?

The movie was coming to a close; I quickly forced my emotions back beneath the surface and wiped my eyes. The ending was a tear-jerker, thankfully, so my streaky mascara didn't seem out of place. We said our good-byes, and they filed out, leaving me blessedly alone to contemplate tomorrow's confrontation. Suddenly the door opened, and there was Missy. "Sorry; I think my keys are here somewhere."

I stood to help her look, and then she smiled. "Oh, hey, here they are in my pocket." She winked impishly. "Now, for the real reason I came back…"

I laughed and rolled my eyes. "Good grief, you didn't have to contrive something!"

She shrugged and grinned. "A little scheming now and then doesn't hurt." She leaned against the wall. "You have thirty seconds to tell me the real reason behind all this."

"Missy, I *did*. It won't work."

"You don't know that."

"I *do*."

"Grace, knock it off." I blinked. Missy's voice never sounded like that. "You're panicking, and I can sort of understand why, but truly, this is ridiculous. Don't let your insecurities and fears get in the way of God's plan. Is *He* telling you to end this, or are you taking His job out of His hands?"

I sputtered something unintelligible, flustered by this rare show of aggressiveness, before finally finding my tongue again. "Missy, think of the odds!"

"Grace, stop trying to justify your fear!" She took a deep breath and headed for the door. "Let me remind you of something you said back when all this started, when you were getting ready for the premiere. You told us, 'He's just a regular guy, underneath all the stardust and celebrity. If I can just get myself to see past the fame, it'll go fine.' I thought you were crazy at the time, and now I see you were right. Now *you* just have to remember it." She closed the door behind her and jogged down to the car. I heard the door slam and the car back out and drive away, and I stood in the living room, fury and fear and desperation wearing ruts in my heart.

I'd arrived ten minutes early, but I was fifteen minutes late. I couldn't seem to get myself out of the car.

He's just a regular guy underneath all the stardust and celebrity. If I can just get myself to see past the fame, it'll go fine. The thought came to me unbidden, and I tried to believe it. Who was anyone, really, once you took away what made them popular or famous? Just another guy on the street. Big deal. *Just a guy* was the key phrase I had to remember here.

My cell chimed beside me, making me jump. Jack's number lit up the LCD. "Hey," I answered, trying to sound light. "Just pulled in; sorry I'm late."

"No problem. On your way up?"

"Yep, just shutting off the car."

"Okay, see you in a sec."

I hung up, let out a shaky sigh, and shut off the car. No going back now. Out of the car, walk to the door, buzz the intercom, walk up the stairs, and his door opened before I even had a chance to knock.

Candles everywhere. In the center of the room sat a table draped in white linen, set with white china and ornate silverware. A champagne stand was beside the table, and a single red rose lay across one plate. Soft music wafted from the stereo in the corner, a Billie Holiday CD I had once mentioned as being one of my favorites. The door closed behind me and there was Jack, devastating even in khakis and a white button-down. Another rose was in his hand. He smiled, and for the first time he looked almost shy. He leaned over cautiously and kissed my cheek, then held out a flower. "Hi."

"H-hi." Amazed that anything came out. "This...this is"—I shook my head and sighed—"beautiful. I'm speechless."

He took my hand and led me to the table, pulling out my chair and pushing it gently in beneath me. "I hate to jump right in, but I'm afraid the food will get cold. Are you hungry?"

I nodded, my mind racing. What was all this for? I bit my lip to stop myself from voicing the question and ruining the magic of the moment. He placed the rose alongside the one on the plate, then filled our champagne flutes half-full. After placing them back on the table, he walked to the kitchen and reemerged a moment later with a silver tray on which lay servings of roast beef and vegetables, dinner rolls, and salad. Finally finding my voice, I chuckled and said, "If I weren't so dazzled I'd say something witty about your culinary abilities."

He flashed a sheepish grin as he carefully transferred food from the tray to our plates. "I'm tempted to take credit, but in all honesty, I had nothing to do with the food. I hired a chef. But I did pick the champagne."

Hired a chef? For a little define-the-relationship dinner? What did he have up his sleeve?

I grasped the champagne flute, hoping he couldn't see my hand shaking, and took a swallow. Any resolve I may have had on the way up had drained away at the sight of all the candles and the look on his face of eager anticipation mingled with cautious hope. I felt completely adrift. I cried out silently to God for direction.

He sat down and bowed his head, then prayed out loud for the first time. I knew I shouldn't stare, but I couldn't help myself. "God, thank You for Grace. Thank You for our friendship. Thank You for using her to lead me to you. Bless this food, and this evening. Amen." He looked up, catching my gaze, and I quickly lowered my eyes to my plate, feeling myself blush. He picked up his fork, and I followed his lead, grateful to have something to occupy myself with, but I couldn't bring myself to eat.

"You said you loved me." The words were out before I had a chance to review them in my head; apparently my filter was out of order. Thankfully they came out tinged with amazement rather than accusation.

He froze in midchew, then nodded slowly and swallowed. "I did." Pause. "Should I not have?"

I set down the fork, resigned to the fact that I wasn't eating anytime soon. "No. I mean, no, you shouldn't *not* have— I mean, it's fine that you did." I took a breath and slowly sighed, trying to calm myself. "I just wasn't expecting it."

He set down his fork, his eyes locked on mine. "I meant it, Grace. I wasn't trying to manipulate you or trap you or make you feel like you had to say it back. I just thought it was about time I stopped simply thinking it and finally said it. If you don't—"

His voice faltered, and everything changed. Suddenly he was just this regular guy trying to tell the woman he loved how he felt, and bracing himself for the possibility that she didn't feel the same way. My heart ached for him, for the risk he was taking and the effort he had put into making this night so amazing.

"If you don't love me, or you're not sure, that's okay." His eyes flickered down and back to mine, nervous. He was *nervous*.

My eyes stung. Tears pooled and blurred my vision, then spilled to my cheeks. His face clouded with uncertainty and—was it possible?—*fear*. I wanted to reassure him, calm him, but nothing came out. He came beside me, knelt, and gently smudged the tears from my cheeks with his hands. "It's okay if you don't, Grace." There were tears in his eyes.

He was crying for me.

JACK

SHE WASN'T SAYING anything, and I didn't know what to do. I'd never felt so helpless—or such a fool. I'd jumped the gun, read her completely wrong. She didn't love me, she didn't want to be here, I had ruined everything.

Her hands came up and took mine from her face. They were cold, trembling. I held them tightly, afraid if I let go she'd jump up and run out and leave me. *Please, God, don't let her leave me.*

"I'm afraid you'll leave me." Her voice quivered, her eyes were bright with unshed tears. My mind raced, searching for reasons that would cause her to think like that.

"Why? Why would I ever do that?"

"I'm not a star. I'm not beautiful." Words tumbled like a landslide. "I'm average and regular, and I'm not a celebrity. I'm not cut out to live the way you do. I'm not glamorous or fashionable or rich or used to being around people who are." She pulled her hands from mine; I was too stunned to respond. "But you're surrounded by women every day who look like goddesses, and women throw themselves at you. I can't compete with that, Jack! I can't be like them! And you'll get sick of me and leave me for one of them." Her voice faded to a whisper, and she looked suddenly stunned, as if she couldn't believe what she had just said. Then her shoulders shook, and she covered her face with her hands.

I wrapped my arms around her and searched for the words to say. *God, give me the words.* "You're right about all but two things: first, you *are* beautiful; and second, I would never, *never* want another woman over you."

Her voice, muffled, "How do you know?"

"Because I would choose not to. I would *promise* not to. And I think God will help me keep that promise."

She pulled away and looked at me through red eyes. She stared hard, as if able to read my mind through my eyes. "Really?" I nodded. She swallowed and quickly wiped her cheeks with her hand. "People promise that all the time. My dad promised my mom—didn't work."

"He didn't ask God to help."

"What if you change your mind?"

"What if you change *yours?*"

She laughed. "Oh, please."

"Hey, I'm serious! You may get tired of me. Of everything that comes with being me." These were fears I had never voiced, even to myself, but they had lodged in my heart over the weeks. "You may get sick of the press, the rumors, the gossip, the parties. Or you may go to one of those parties and meet someone else who seems more exciting, who has more potential. Or you might meet someone normal, who has a nine-to-five office job and golfs on the weekends—"

She kissed me, her arms slipping around my neck and pulling me close. My head swam. I was pretty sure this was a good sign.

She broke the kiss, leaned her forehead against mine, her eyes closed. She looked, finally, at peace. Leaning back, she opened her eyes and smiled. "I love you."

My heart stopped, and the chaos in my head ceased. "Really?"

She nodded, then smiled. "Yes!" She laughed, her shoulders shaking, tears running afresh. "I *love* you!" She stared at me. "I love that you honestly think I would ever want to leave you. I love that you bought this CD simply because I told you I liked it. I love that you hired someone to cook to impress me. I love that you broke fire codes and lit a hundred candles in your apartment. And"—she brought her face close to mine, her arms around my neck again—

"I'd love you even if you hadn't done any of that and were as average as me."

"You're not average."

"There's nothing wrong with it. I am indeed."

"I don't think so. You're wondrous. You're wonder*ful.*"

She giggled. "You're silly."

"I'm in love."

"So am I. Now what?"

I grinned. "Close your eyes." Dutifully, she sat up and shut them. "Put out your hands." She held them out, giggling again. Taking her hand, I kissed her palm as I slipped the ring on her finger. She gasped as her eyes flew open, staring in shock.

"Oh! Oh, Jack… Oh, *Jack.*"

"I love you, Grace. Will you marry me?"

GRACE

"GRACE, YOUR PARENTS are here."

Missy and Joy popped their heads into the ladies' room where I was fixing my hair. The rehearsal dinner was to start in fifteen minutes, and I'd come here not so much to inspect my appearance as to hide out. Honestly, it was my parents I'd been trying to hide from.

Neither of them had attended the rehearsal itself, which had actually been a relief. For them to agree to come to the dinner had been a shock. While I'd done my best to reconcile with both of them over the phone and through letters, seeing them in person was still going to be tough.

I took a deep breath and left the ladies' lounge for the foyer of the country club—the Upton family had a membership and organized the dinner for us—and there they were, my mother and my father, looking intensely uncomfortable with each other. I slapped on a smile and resolved not to let anything ruin this weekend.

"Mom! Dad!" I reached out for them both and pulled them in for a group hug. "I'm so glad you were able to make it. Come on in, and let me introduce you to everyone." Without allowing them a chance to protest, I pulled them toward the dining room.

Everyone was welcoming and warm with them, as I knew I could trust them to be. Jack was charming and even nervous about making a good impression, and the Uptons took them under their wings and drew them into conversation. Now there was only one nerve-racking thing left to get through this weekend: the wedding itself.

☆

I forced myself to stay calm. "This dress is way too expensive to start sweating in," I told myself aloud. "Save that for when you actually have to walk down the aisle." I adjusted my veil and checked my mascara one more time. The girls rolled their eyes and continued fixing their makeup. T minus fifteen and counting.

The door opened, and my parents walked in. My mother wore a pale blue dress, her long hair swept up in a french roll. I couldn't remember ever seeing her in a dress and not a suit. My father came in after her, looking uncomfortable in this room full of women. I wanted to cry. I willed myself not to.

"Oh, baby," my mother sighed. I stood and came over, then hugged her and felt the tears start. When my shoulders shook, she sniffed and laughed, "Oh, honey, your makeup!"

My dad stood apart from us, obviously clueless about what to do. My mother and I pulled apart, and I hugged him, too. He returned it stiffly, patting me gingerly on the back.

I dabbed at my eyes with a tissue—there were four boxes scattered throughout the bridal cottage since we girls had been afraid of floating away on a flood of tears—and sighed. "I was a fool to think I wouldn't cry. It's all right, I have fifteen minutes before the ceremony starts. I'll calm down and get it back on by then." I motioned to the couch and wingback chairs. "Take a seat?"

We sat, and Mom fussed over my dress, smoothing and tugging out folds lest I wrinkle before the Big Moment. "Are you enjoying California?" I asked.

"It's gorgeous, but I don't think I'd get anything done knowing the beach was only twenty minutes away," Mom said.

Dad nodded and shifted in his seat. "It's hot."

I grinned. "It's August; you weren't expecting that?"

He looked flustered, and I felt sorry for him. He'd never been much of a talker, with me or my mother, and while I didn't know what to say to him either, I at least felt peace about him being here. He obviously didn't. Impulsively I bounded out of my seat and kissed his nose—one of the few games we had between us when I was a child—and headed for the makeup table. "Don't worry, Pops," I chided, "it'll cool off once the sun goes down. That's only in about two hours. I promise you won't melt."

After reapplying my makeup, Mom and I sat back down, and I did my best to keep the conversation going. Jane popped her head in at 6:00 sharp. "Greg wants to know if you're ready."

I grinned and nodded. "Think so, yeah."

My parents stood; Mom hugged me, and Dad smiled faintly again, looking eager to be out of the room. "See you in a minute!" I said, bouncing on my toes with nervous energy. Mom looked on the verge of tears again and quickly left the cottage.

Dad meandered toward the door and winked. "Nice work, Grace." I beamed. The highest compliment, coming from him.

Jane came back in, followed by the girls. "Everything good?" Missy asked.

I nodded, then heard the violins starting to play the prelude. I could feel my heart twirl, and I shook my head. "I *was* okay…" They laughed and hugged me, then grabbed their bouquets and lined up at the door. Jane, who had graciously offered to put her love of details to work as my wedding coordinator, left to stand beside the bridge that led to the spacious, ceramic-tiled patio where the ceremony was being held. Taylor and Joy walked out together at their cue from her, their blue and silver dresses swaying with each step as they disappeared from my view. I took a deep breath and blew it slowly out through pursed lips; every second was making me more nervous.

"Gonna make it?" Missy asked. I nodded and flashed a tense smile. She frowned. "Dang. I was hoping I'd have to fill in for you or something."

Our laughter cut the tension mounting inside me. "Sorry, you'll have to get your own. The one out there in the tux is taken already." We giggled like little kids, giddy with the magic of the occasion. "How did Jack look?"

She grinned conspiratorially. "I heard him talking to Todd over by the fountain. He said he felt like he was going to throw up, he was so nervous. He said it's worse than auditioning!"

I laughed. "Oh, poor thing!"

She smiled. "Yeah, but then Todd pointed out that the audition was over ages ago, and he got the part, so what was he nervous about? And you know what he said?"

"What?"

"That he hoped he never thought that way, because as long as he lived, he didn't want to ever stop being his very best for you."

"Oh, Missy…"

"Hey, don't cry again. We don't have time to do your makeup!"

I laughed and blinked furiously, trying to get the tears back in before they spilled onto my freshly powdered cheeks. Missy snatched a tissue from the box and pressed it into my hand, then moved to the door just in time for her cue. "See you on the other side," she said over her shoulder, and then I was left alone to wait.

JACK

TAYLOR AND JOY GLIDED over the bridge and down the aisle between the ribbon-bedecked folding chairs, looking beautiful in the dresses Grace had chosen. As they crossed in front of me, they grinned and waggled their eyebrows almost in unison, and I stifled a laugh. They were incredible friends to Grace—Missy, too—and had become the same to me over the past months. I couldn't help but marvel over the warmth and affection they bestowed on me, nothing like the hollow adulation that fans and celebrity-hunters showered on the stars they chased.

Next, Missy glided toward me, looking almost as euphoric as a bride herself. She smiled at me as she crossed, and just before moving out of my view, she winked and stuck out her tongue, exactly the sassy kind of gesture I might have expected from her. I smirked and shook my head at her antics, catching the puzzled look on my parents' faces in the front row. I grinned at them and winked, which sent my mother back to her purse for a tissue; the poor woman had been a basket case all weekend. She and Grace got along exceptionally; we'd flown out to Vermont over Easter to spend the holiday with my family and give everyone a chance to meet, as well as to tell them about God's new role in my life. The God stuff was met with shaky acceptance, but they fell in love with Grace immediately. She'd had no trouble fitting in, and there were times when it felt like I was the outsider marrying in.

The violinists ended the prelude and began the song Grace had chosen for her grand entrance. All the guests craned their necks to see past the bridge to the bridal cottage where she appeared, seeming to levitate. The sight of her took my breath away. She glowed, as though she were illuminated from within. She floated over the bridge and to the back row of chairs, and then, as everyone stood for her solitary walk down the aisle, her eyes locked with mine, and I could barely keep from running up to kiss her then and there.

She slid in beside me, handing Missy her cascade bouquet of roses, and as I took her hand, I whispered, "Can I kiss you yet?"

"Hold your horses, cowboy," Greg admonished.

"How fast can we make this ceremony?" I asked.

"Cut the music, and we can be out of here in ten minutes."

"Not soon enough; go straight to the vows." The wedding party laughed along with us, although I don't think any of them realized how serious I was.

After that everything moved so quickly I felt as though we must have left something out, and then suddenly I had a ring on my finger, and Grace, my wife—*my wife*—was before me, eyes like blue stars shining up at me, and I heard the words I'd been waiting for all day.

"You may kiss the bride."

The guests, led by an enthusiastic wedding party, whooped and cheered and applauded as I dipped my beloved and delivered a flawless kiss, my first as a married man. So far matrimony was tops. Greg introduced us to the crowd, who stood and clapped some more as we came down from the small stage to dismiss the rows to the hors d'oeuvres tables on the far balcony. It was a small party, family and close friends only, and thankfully no leaks to the press had brought crashers.

The last row of guests having been dismissed, the staff began clearing the chairs away to set up the tables for dinner. Missy appeared with a tissue and pressed powder to give Grace a touch-up. "Now you know how I feel on the set between takes," I chided as Missy fussed over her. "Want a job, Missy?"

She smirked as she dabbed Grace's nose. "Thanks, but no. I don't relish the idea of applying makeup to people all day. Especially guys. No offense."

"None taken, believe me. Wish I could get around it."

"Anything else you need, girl?" she asked Grace as she snapped the compact shut.

"Nope, I'm good—oh wait, yes there is." There was a gleam in her eye. We both saw it and laughed. "Hey!" she protested. "Quit laughing, it's a serious request."

"Anything for my married friend," Missy quipped.

"Okay. It's easy, really. Just keep people happy till we get back."

I looked at her in confusion. "We're going somewhere?" She raised her eyebrows at me. "Ah, we're going somewhere. Gotcha."

Missy laughed and saluted. "Consider it done. Don't ruin your dress." She winked and moved quickly toward the stairs leading to the balcony.

I turned to my wife and pushed back a stray lock of hair. "So where are we going all of a sudden?" I teased in a knowing voice.

She smirked and lightly smacked my arm. "Now don't get any ideas, there's no time for *that*." She hooked her arm through mine and led me toward the bridge. "I just wanted a moment away from the crowd to be with my husband."

"Now, would that phrase 'be with' have any other, more biblical meaning, by any chance?"

She threw her head back and laughed, a sound that was like music to me. I couldn't believe how much I loved this woman.

"No! Not"—she added quickly—"that I wouldn't want to skip the rest of this fiesta and get on with the more private festivities, believe me. But when you factor in dinner with sixty people afterward, it's just not as appealing."

I frowned and nodded. "Ah, yes, I see the logic of that. A bit awkward." I pulled her in through the cottage door, out of sight, and kissed her with more passion than I'd felt free to exhibit in the ceremony. "But I'm going to find it awfully hard to make conversation with those people for four more hours," I murmured after.

A slow smile crept across her face. "If you do, I'll make it worth your while."

I laughed and kissed her again. "Deal."

It seemed more like four days until we were able to make our escape. We were sent off in a shower of rose petals and bubbles and arrived twenty minutes later at the Ritz, where our room had been lit with candles and strewn with roses at my request. The only big event that remained—other than the obvious Big Event—was the honeymoon, and Grace still didn't know where I was taking her.

"If I guess it right, will you tell me?" she asked sleepily for the umpteenth time at 2:00 a.m. I removed the champagne glass from her hand and set it on the night table before pulling her beside me and turning out the light.

"No, and if you don't go to sleep, you're not going to be awake enough to enjoy it once you know."

She nestled her head on my chest and kissed my chin. "If you loved me you'd tell me," she purred.

"I am a master at keeping secrets. Don't even try it."

"Oh, you're not fun."

I wrapped my arms around her and kissed her hair. "That's not what you said an hour ago."

She laughed. "I was wrong."

"Yeah, you'll be singing a different tune when we get to the airport."

"Tell me the tune, and I'll sing it, baby."

"Okay, how about, 'Good Night, Sweetheart'?" She breathed a laugh, and I knew she was about gone. I took the few minutes left before sleep caught up to me to mentally run through the list of things I'd told Missy to pack for Grace, in case there was something I'd forgotten. Her passport was the only truly important thing; any forgotten items could be purchased once we got there. France was hardly a third-world country.

GRACE

PARIS WAS HEAVEN on earth. At first I thought this because of course it's *Paris,* and of course it's wonderful, but then after coming home and living married life in California, I discovered it was heaven because the American paparazzi didn't live there.

I came to loathe cameras. I couldn't escape them: at the beach, at the grocery store, at the mall. Everywhere we went, it was just a matter of time before we'd spot one pointing our way. It took months before I got used to seeing photos in *Us* magazine of myself lugging shopping bags to the car with Jack, and even longer before I could just let myself live my life without worrying what might be caught on film.

We bought a house in Beverly Hills a month after the wedding. It was like living in a neighborhood of castles: everyone stayed inside, and the moats of fences and impossibly green lawns kept the world at bay. Not the kinds of houses you ran to when you needed a cup of sugar or someone to have coffee with.

I left teaching. I couldn't handle the thought of nosy parents and bragging students and teacher's lounge gossip. Besides, it wasn't as though we needed the money. But I got bored when Jack went back to work, and for the three months he was working, I languished at home, missing my job and my friends and my church. It was like moving to California all over again: all alone in a new place.

Jack was to start a second project after finishing the one he'd begun after our honeymoon, but when he saw what a mess I was, he pulled out and stayed home. For the first few weeks it was wonderful. No responsibilities, no stress, just me and my guy getting used to married life. Then we started getting on each other's nerves. He was messy. I was nitpicky. He was moody. I was clingy. We exasperated each other, and I began to wonder if we'd made a big mistake. The fears that had almost led me to leave him completely—the fear he'd leave me, he'd find someone better—resurfaced and wreaked havoc for a week or so, and it was then that we decided we needed to find a compromise. Obviously having all the time in the world to spend together wasn't necessarily the best thing for us.

So Jack started on another film that was scheduled to finish just before our first anniversary. The first part of the process wasn't nearly as time intensive as the actual shooting, so we still had our evenings and weekends together. I started volunteering at HAP to keep myself busy, and it allowed me to work with Jack on something as well. But once the project began to prepare for shooting, I tagged along to watch.

"It's 'Bring Your Wife to Work Month'!" he announced when we arrived at the first blocking session. The crew got a kick out of it, and I tried to make myself as useful as I could, despite the fact that the work going on around me was as foreign as space shuttle construction. But even as I helped out at the catering station, or gave the wrangler a hand, I couldn't help but feel there was something else I could be doing here. I just didn't know what it was.

About two weeks into the process I began to see what purpose God might have for me here. One morning as the crew prepared the sound stage, I noticed a young woman with severe, black-from-a-bottle hair hovering near one of the directors, a reporter's notebook in her pale, ring-bedecked hand. I watched her as she took furious notes, shadowing the director and occasionally dashing away only to return a few minutes later to confer with him or hand something over. It was hot on the sound stage, and I could tell she was uncomfortable in her black turtleneck.

Acting on impulse, I sidled over to the catering table and grabbed a bottle of juice, then meandered back toward her and waited for a moment when she didn't seem busy. I found my chance when the director called for the cast to meet with him and disappeared; she seemed to wilt as he walked away, and I could see she was tired.

"You've got to be sweltering," I said as I came up beside her. "Have some juice before you collapse, you poor thing." She took the bottle, looking startled, and I stuck out my hand. "Grace Harrington."

She smiled and shook my hand. "Nice to meet you. Thanks so much for the juice. I keep meaning to get myself something, but I forget. Oh, sorry—I'm Zoe, by the way." She flashed an embarrassed smile, then drained half the bottle.

I laughed. "Wow, good thing I got to you when I did!"

She grinned and blushed, holding a hand to her forehead. "Note to self: the sound stage is *really* hot."

"First time here?"

"Yeah. Snagged an internship with this production company, but when I got here they kind of shoved me off on Zach. I'm just sorta doing whatever he needs me to do, and trying to learn as much as I can about film in between trips to the snack bar and quests for random props." She rolled her eyes and smirked. I liked this girl.

"You still in college?"

"Yeah, senior at UCSD."

I gaped. "You don't commute all the way from San Diego for this, do you?"

"No!" she laughed. "I have the semester off for the internship. I'm subletting a room in a house in Long Beach."

"You have friends living there?"

"No, just a sublet thing I found through the paper. Surf shack, falling apart, but dirt cheap, which is good, since this isn't paying me anything."

I frowned. "Doesn't sound ideal."

She shrugged and took another swig of the juice. "Eh, it's not *ideal*, but it's not as bad as it could be. Gotta sleep somewhere, right?"

"Do you have any friends up here?"

"No. The neighbors are all beach bums; not my crowd. I don't know how much time I'll have to hang out with people anyway, with the hours I'll be putting in here."

"Sounds lonely." I knew exactly how that felt. Ideas began to take shape. "Hey, why don't you come to dinner with us tonight? We're just barbecuing."

"You and?"

"My husband, Jack."

She did a double take. "Jack Harrington is your husband?" I nodded. "Oh, I…I wouldn't want to impose—"

"You wouldn't, trust me. Besides, cooking for one sucks."

"I just—wow!" She waffled. "Are you sure that's all right?"

"Completely," I assured her. "I remember how isolated I felt when I first moved here. People were kind to me, and I couldn't possibly forgive myself if I missed the opportunity to repay the favor by passing it on to someone else."

"Wow," she said again. "Thank you. I can't tell you how—"

"Zoe!" Zach's voice boomed from the other side of the sound stage.

"On my way!" She grinned and squeezed my arm. "Thanks, Mrs. Harrington."

"It's Grace!" I laughed as she sprinted toward a palm tree, under which numerous directors had huddled. Hearing people call me Mrs. Harrington never failed to make me laugh.

Jack sauntered over and planted a kiss on my cheek. "Making friends?"

"Yep. That's Zoe. She's Zach's new assistant, sort of. An intern with the production company, but they passed her on to him when she showed up this morning. I invited her to dinner tonight."

He raised his eyebrows. "Oh really? It's not like you to invite near-strangers for dinner."

I shrugged and smiled. "I know, but I think God's starting something there."

"Ah," he said with understanding. "Then invite away!" With that, he kissed me once more and turned back to the rehearsal.

That night at dinner, Jack and I did our best to make Zoe comfortable, although it was obvious she was a little overwhelmed. I'd finally stopped seeing Jack the way the world did, and I forgot sometimes how intimidating it could be just to hang out with him. He was just Jack, my husband, the guy who left dishes in the sink right next to the dishwasher, the guy who was able to lose a pen ten seconds after picking it up, the guy who sang television show theme songs (badly) in the shower in the morning to wake me up.

In the weeks that followed, I made it a point to connect with Zoe every morning when we first arrived on the set. We'd spend her breaks together, and I'd invite her over whenever I could. It was clear to both Jack and me that God had set us in her life for one reason or another, and we continually looked for ways we could show her our friendship and faith. Her internship was only for the length of the project, and we wanted to make every day of it count.

One morning, during the first week of shooting, we arrived before Zoe did—which never happened. Zach seemed annoyed but not concerned; she had apparently called in to say she'd be late. When she did show up, she hardly acknowledged me and went straight to work. Her spark and energy were completely missing, and I watched her drag herself from one duty to another, seeming to avoid me on purpose as she moved around the sound stage. The pace at which Zach and the other directors drove the crew and actors on set was grueling, and unfortunately meant we had little time to talk anyway. She disappeared at lunch, showing up again only when everyone else had gone back to work. I sat in Jack's chair, trying to focus on the scene being shot but instead finding my thoughts turning back to her. *God, I finally prayed, what is going on with her? Is there something I should do?* I gave up trying to follow the action on the set and immersed myself instead in prayer.

While filming days are always long, this particular day seemed like it would never end, and as it wore on I could see Zoe becoming more frazzled and unlike her usual self. It took all the willpower I had not to seek her out at dinner; I knew I hadn't somehow offended her, or she, honest and straightforward as she was, would have come out and said something. I talked to Jack over our sandwiches about what I'd observed, and we prayed together before he went back to work. I retreated to his chair to watch the action and pray some more.

Shooting wrapped for the evening at 12:30 a.m., and as we came out of Jack's room, we found Zoe waiting for us, slumped against the wall. Before either of us could speak, she asked quietly, "Can I please come home with you guys?" I could see tears in her eyes, even though she avoided looking either of us in the face.

There was no need to even confer with each other. She received a double yes, and the three of us walked out to the lot without another word. Once at the car, she collapsed in the backseat and fell asleep at once. Jack dozed off as well, but I spent the half-hour drive home in fervent prayer for Zoe.

The next morning I took a chance and asked Jack to tell Zach that Zoe was sick and staying home. It took both of us to even wake her up when we got home, and when the alarm went off at 4:00 a.m., I couldn't imagine getting her up. I said good-bye to Jack and then set myself up in the kitchen to do chores that had been piling up since before preproduction. It wasn't until nearly 11:00 that Zoe staggered in with a slightly bewildered look on her face.

"Hi!" I chirped. "Want some breakfast? Or lunch?"

She looked around and blinked. "How did I get here?"

I grinned. "Between the two of us, we managed to lug you upstairs. Your eyes were open, but I'm pretty sure you were still asleep. Jack told Zach you weren't coming in; I hope that's all right. You obviously needed to sleep." I was itching to ask why but knew enough to keep my mouth shut.

She slowly nodded, digesting this. "Coffee?"

"Coming right up. Take a seat." I waved to the barstools along the island and started a fresh pot. I'd never been much of a coffee drinker, but I had quickly learned that tagging along with Jack when he was working required some kind of energy boost.

Zoe slipped onto a stool and rested her chin in her hand. I fought to keep quiet, not to fill the silence with chatter or inquire after her bizarre behavior yesterday. As I prepared her coffee, I prayed frantically for God to guide me in dealing with whatever was going on.

It wasn't until her coffee was half gone and I'd become immersed again in my tasks that she came and sat across from me at the table. I stopped what I was doing and looked at her expectantly, wanting her to know she had my full attention. Her face was clouded with anxiety; it was etched in every feature, and I longed to tell her everything would be all right.

"Remember the appointment I had last week, that I left for before lunch?" I nodded, remembering how Jack and I had teased her about a clandestine affair she must have been having. "It was for a biopsy." She squirmed in her seat. "I have cancer."

I stared at her in disbelief. It just seemed so unlikely. She was so healthy! A vegetarian to the extreme, an exercise fanatic who went for jogs at 4:00 in the morning before work. I nearly laughed. "It's got to be a mistake, Zoe," I stammered.

She shook her head, slowly turning her mug on the tabletop.

"What kind?"

"Breast. My mom had it, my grandmother had it, my aunt had it—"

"And survived?"

"Mom died nine years ago, my aunt four years ago, my grandmother twenty."

"Oh, Zoe." I was stupefied. "How bad?"

"They think we've caught it pretty early; they have to do more tests to be sure."

"When?"

"This weekend."

I slid from my seat and moved to the chair beside her, wrapping her in my arms as she broke down. "I've done so much to make sure it wouldn't happen to me," she sobbed into my shoulder. "I thought I could escape it or something. I can't believe it's happening to me!" Anger and fear radiated from her; I could feel the panic she was barely holding at bay in her tiny frame.

Oh God, I prayed, *spare her, heal her, give her strength and courage and let her survive. Give her peace; let her feel Your grace and protection.*

She sniffed. "Thank you."

I let go and sat back, smiling sympathetically. "What for?"

"For praying for me."

"How did you know?" I clapped a hand over my mouth. "I wasn't praying out loud, was I? I didn't mean to!"

She laughed. "No, don't worry." She shrugged. "I could just feel it. There's a power, almost, that just seems to kind of"—she made ocean wave motions with her hands—"flow out of you."

I blinked, embarrassed. "Really?"

She shrugged and reached for a napkin on the table, dabbing at her eyes. "It's cool. I've never met anyone who was that close to God before."

"Oh, Zoe," I sighed, laying a hand on her arm. "It's only by God's grace that I'm close to Him. It hasn't been that long that I've even cared about God, much less been close to Him. But it's so amazing." I smiled. "Jack and I have had the most incredible experiences because of it." Something prompted me to cut the conversation short, and I stood suddenly and moved toward the kitchen. "And I'll tell you all about it sometime if you want, but first we have to feed you because you can't beat cancer on an empty stomach."

Zoe laughed, the bright, deep laugh I was used to hearing from her. She wiped the tears from her eyes and finished her coffee as I rummaged through the cabinets. "Sadly, I don't cook, and Jack only does when he's really motivated, so unless you can work magic with eggs, celery, and oatmeal, we're going to have to go out. Why don't you run and freshen up, and I'll loan you some clothes. How does the pier sound for lunch?"

"Sounds good. You rock." She came over and hugged me, a tight embrace that told me we had crossed to a new level of friendship. She retreated back upstairs, and after I heard the shower start, I went to my closet, praying through tears for this girl who had become so precious to me.

JACK

ZOE'S UNFORTUNATE NEWS turned out to be only the first in what seemed to be a sick demonstration of just how much life can suck. The onset of filming—the most stressful aspect of the whole process—brought an onslaught of tragedy. One cameraman lost his baby daughter to SIDS, the head of costume design lost her mother in a car accident, and a member of the lighting team fell off a scaffold and broke both legs. It seemed as though every day brought another depressing story or tragic event. But in the midst of it all, Grace and I became the rocks to which everyone wanted to anchor their floundering boats.

Zoe began sharing with others on the staff what was going on with her, and specifically the way Grace had prayed for her. The two of us had always made it a point to pray before our meals and before I went back to work, and while we had never tried to be showy about it, we didn't try to hide it, either. Suddenly people started pausing as they passed us while in prayer, watching from a polite distance and hidden behind script books or soda cans as though merely pausing to admire, say, the postlunch disaster that was the catering table. We started praying a little louder to make it easier for everyone to eavesdrop.

Not until one of these "innocent passersby" let slip an "amen" when we finished did we even acknowledge what was happening. This slip of the tongue caused an uproar of guilty laughter from the small crowd that had assembled, and I finally threw up my hands and said, "Good grief, people, no point in all standing around alone when we could be meeting all this crap head-on together. If you want to pray with us, just come over." Twelve of the twenty or so that were there came up to us at dinner, asking if they could sit with us when we prayed. By dinner the next day we had thirty people gathered around our table, saying nothing while we prayed but obviously engrossed in it.

By the end of shooting, Grace had a following of about ten women from various departments who sought her out on their breaks to ask her to pray with them, to give them advice, and, most important, to tell them about "this whole God thing." When we finally wrapped, there wasn't the usual sense of relief and eagerness to move on with the process; instead, people seemed disappointed that we'd no longer be together. So the two of us proposed a weekly party at our house for those who had expressed interest in our beliefs and had been tagging along with us the past few weeks. Twenty-eight people promised to come, and we marveled at how God was using us to influence this tiny corner of the industry.

As time progressed, Grace and Zoe became closer, a godsend for Zoe since she was otherwise alone in her battle against the renegade cells trying to take over her body. She'd begun chemo with gusto, determined to channel every bit of energy into willing the cancer to die. Two weeks into the treatment Grace insisted Zoe move in with us, before the adverse side effects began to hit. Zoe hesitated at first, afraid she would be imposing, but we both insisted that she allow us to care for her in one of the few ways we could. She finally relented, but only after making us promise not to alter our lifestyle any to accommodate her. This was hardly necessary; she had practically an entire wing of the house to herself, and none of us were forced to see each other if we didn't want to. She and Grace spent the mornings talking through Zoe's questions about God and faith, and Grace always accompanied her to the hospital for her treatments. Grace was always a wreck after these trips, but she refused to let Zoe know and instead spilled her grief to me.

One afternoon I came home from a HAP meeting to find the

two of them singing in the kitchen with the radio on full blast and the makings of a cake strewn about the island. It took them a moment to notice my presence, but once they did they shrieked and rushed me, both talking at once and completely incomprehensible. The words they spoke a mile a minute finally sank in: Zoe had become a Christian.

I whooped and laughed along with them, squeezing Zoe in a bear hug and joining their carousing. As soon as the cake came out of the oven we struck out for Zoe's favorite restaurant to celebrate. It was a much-needed bright spot in our lives, which had become dominated by cancer research and hospital visits and a general feeling of dread.

Two nights later we had our third house party, which had grown to forty people. Zoe made no secret about her decision, and most of the evening was spent with people asking her what had made her change her mind about God. The air was electric with curiosity on the part of our guests, and anticipation of the next decision on ours. We prayed like crazy over the following week for the next house party.

Zoe's chemo sessions lasted for six weeks. Try as she might to prove "mind over matter" true, as the sessions progressed she began to suffer the side effects we'd dreaded. The last session found her weak and frail, with her black cropped hair nearly completely gone, and her already-slim figure frighteningly gaunt. Her spirits were high, however, and we waited with bated breath for the doctor's findings after her postchemo exam. We prayed before it. We prayed after it. We prayed for three days as we waited for the results. Grace and I, at Zoe's request, accompanied her to the doctor one Wednesday morning to hear what he had to say, and we both wept as much as she when the doctor declared the treatments a success.

I was on my way home from postproduction voice-overs a month later when I ran, quite literally, into Todd. I'd gotten the sense that he'd been avoiding me, and try as I might to keep in contact with him after the wedding, he pretty much disappeared. I could tell by the look on his face that he didn't really know what to do in my presence. I acted as though this was all lost on me and invited him to dinner at our house that weekend. To my surprise he accepted.

That Saturday he showed up with a bottle of wine and flowers for Grace, the first chivalrous act I'd ever seen him undertake. He was doing an excellent job of masking whatever apprehension he felt, and doing an equally impressive job of curbing his language and avoiding his usually ribald and shady humor. But no amount of acting could have masked his thoughts when Zoe joined us in the kitchen just before dinner. She'd planned on leaving the house before Todd arrived, despite our insistence that she was welcome to join us, but her afternoon nap had lasted longer than usual. I introduced them and cajoled Zoe into taking a seat, which she did, and then sat back and watched Todd fall in love.

Grace pointed out that a suspicious amount of smoke was seeping from the barbecue and joined me as we raced out to make sure dinner wasn't spoiled. We kept our backs to the kitchen windows as we muffled our laughter.

"I've never seen someone so obviously smitten," Grace giggled.

"I'm afraid he's far, far beyond smitten," I replied, flipping steaks and turning veggie kabobs on the grill. "That's full-blown infatuation. Borderline obsession. Do you think Zoe is catching the vibe?"

"I don't see how she could miss it; he's practically levitating." We shot surreptitious glances over our shoulders to the kitchen windows, where we could see Zoe chatting and Todd staring. "For an actor he sure is doing a lousy job hiding his feelings."

I smirked. "I've never seen him like this. Ever. He's usually James Bond when it comes to women."

Grace sighed. "Poor guy." Then she snickered. "He'd have his hands full with her; she's a real firecracker. Ooooh, this is gonna be fun!"

Over dinner the conversation was light and aimless, rarely more than superficial chitchat. Even so I was able to catch a clue here and there that Todd was not the guy I'd gotten drunk with at the beginning of my career. He seemed more grounded, more stable—hard to believe knowing how he'd lived. I was itching to ask him straight-out what was going on, but forced myself to let him decide when to open up. Dinner was finished, plates cleared and dishes piled in the sink for later, and we were just settling down in the living room when the phone rang for Zoe. After she excused herself and dashed to her room, Grace concocted a convincing reason to leave as well, and Todd and I danced around the obvious for five minutes before he finally brought up Zoe.

"She's fascinating," he said with a nod toward the staircase she'd ascended earlier.

I nodded. "She is. Grace and she are a riot together. It's interesting living with two women who both have so much energy. I think Grace sort of sees her as the sister she never had."

Todd toyed with the glass in his hand. "How long has she been here with you guys?"

I thought a moment. "Two months? Three? I forget when she moved in; right after she started treatment."

He gave me a puzzled look. "For what?"

I mentally kicked myself; she obviously hadn't mentioned the cancer. Apologizing to her ahead of time in my head, I explained the circumstances that had led to her moving in with us.

Todd shook his head in disbelief. "She looks fine; that's incredible."

"Well, a month ago she was bald and about twenty pounds lighter. She really bounced back after the chemo ended, although her hair is taking a while—that was a wig you saw tonight. She has about six of them; she and Grace kept buying them, just for the heck of it. Blond, redhead, you name it. She's still recovering, though; sleeps a lot." I grinned. "She meant to be gone by the time you got here, but her nap got out of hand." I took a leap. "I take it you're glad she didn't leave."

He reddened—I'd never seen Todd embarrassed before—and chuckled. "Wow. That obvious?"

"Billboards are more subtle."

He laughed, shaking his head and swirling the drink in his glass. "Oh boy." He looked at me. "Would you mind if I asked her out?"

I grinned and shrugged. "It's not my place to mind. Although, I *would* have to kick your butt if you did anything to hurt her. But other than that, go for it."

The conversation ended, and we both zoned out for a bit. I started imagining Zoe and Todd together, thinking how good she'd be for him when he broke the silence with an unexpected statement.

"I was talking to Dave Croft the other day and he said he'd been here with a bunch of other people to, like, pray and stuff."

I nodded. Dave had been one of the first on the set to join us for prayer, and one of the most reserved members of our impromptu Bible study. I was curious to know how he and Todd had hooked up, but I avoided the question for fear it would take us away from a more important discussion. "Yeah, there are about forty of us who get together once a week. Grace and I host it, and we just talk and read the Bible and pray." I mentally threw God a look of panic and a plea for help.

Todd drained his glass and twirled the ice silently for another minute before stating, "My mom died three months ago."

I blinked. "Oh wow, Todd...I'm so sorry."

"She started going to some church about a year ago and telling me about it. She sounded a lot like you did when you first told me you'd started believing in God. She'd had Parkinson's for a while; we pretty much saw it coming. She'd left my dad a list of stuff she wanted me to have, and one of the things she gave me was her Bible. It was all marked up, notes in the margins and stuff. She put a letter in the front, asking me to read it. So I started to." He'd been studying his glass while he spoke, but now he looked right at me. "Do you really believe all that?"

Slowly, I nodded. "I do. It took a lot of convincing at first, but it makes sense to me now. Well…to be honest, it made sense almost from the beginning, but I was too stubborn to admit it. If you believe it, it pretty much demands that you change, and I didn't want to change." I shrugged. "But eventually I quit fighting it, because it took a lot more energy to be in denial than it did to relent."

He frowned at his glass, thinking. I prayed like mad. "I don't see why my mom got such a raw deal then, if she believed. Why would God have let her die if she was so faithful?"

I was out of my depth, and I knew it. I shot up a prayer for how to respond, then suddenly Zoe was bounding down the stairs, oblivious to what had been taking place. God's timing was, as usual, impeccable. She stopped short when she realized the mood was more serious than it had been at her departure. "Am I interrupting?"

I stood and motioned for her to take my seat. "Not at all. Quite the opposite, in fact. I think Todd has some questions you'd be better at answering than I."

GRACE

THAT NIGHT MARKED the beginning of a roller-coaster relationship between Zoe and Todd. The two of them spent two hours that evening discussing Zoe's cancer, Todd's mother, and how God fit into both scenarios. Later that week Todd took Zoe out on a date, although Zoe confided in me that she was apprehensive given that he was not a Christian. Another date the following week made Zoe even more unsure of this new relational development. When she came back at midnight and found me still awake in the living room, reading, she threw herself into the sofa beside me and groaned.

"That man," she began in measured tones, "drives me absolutely nuts."

I smirked. "Oh yeah?"

She smacked me on the arm. "Not in a good way."

"Uh-huh, you just keep telling yourself that." I winked. She glared. "Okay, so what did he do?"

"One minute he's an absolute prince; the next he's a horror. Completely inconsistent. Same with his reaction to God; one minute he's totally into it, sounding like he's going to take the plunge, but the next minute he's bad-mouthing the whole thing and saying it's all a crock. What is his issue?!"

"You should talk to Jack. He's known Todd a long time; maybe he can shed some light on it. Same with the God stuff; Jack was sort of the same way; maybe he can give you some insights into what he's thinking."

Zoe did just that, and continued to see Todd a couple times a week. Jack and I knew it was only a matter of time for both of them.

"A matter of time" turned out to be six long months of Zoe returning from dates and being annoyed, frustrated, irritated, and yet inexplicably driven to go out with him again.

"Look, are you guys dating or what?" I demanded one night after a particularly long play-by-play of yet another frustration-filled date.

"Um"—she bit her lip—"I think so."

"Well, if he bothers you so much, why do you keep going out with him?"

"Because," Zoe began, then stopped. She frowned, thought a moment, and then shrugged. "Because I feel like God keeps telling me to." Then she winked and said with a wicked smile, "Besides, he's hot."

During this time Jack and I had continued to host our weekly Bible study, and to our surprise, Todd began to attend as well. One night, as guests began leaving, Todd led Zoe to the backyard, where they stayed until nearly eleven o'clock. Jack and I were shutting off lights on the ground before retreating upstairs for the night when the two of them burst through the back door.

"He did it!" Zoe shouted, throwing her hands up and spinning on the tiles before wrapping her arms around his neck. We cheered and demanded the details. It was well past midnight before Todd left to go home. Zoe and I sat in her room for another half-hour, giggling and talking like schoolgirls, before I forced her to go to bed to at least try to sleep. An amorous Jack met me in the bedroom, and try as he might to distract me, something in his eyes told me he was hiding something.

Indeed he was. He wasn't the least bit surprised when, a week later, Zoe came home from a date with a diamond on her hand.

Sometimes beautiful things happen to cushion us before life falls apart. One of those beautiful things was Zoe and Todd's wedding, which we hosted the following June. It was weird having the house to ourselves again after Zoe moved out, but it started us thinking about when we might begin filling the house with mini-Harringtons.

The second week in September Zoe and Todd came for dinner, as they often did, but the minute they walked through the door we could tell something was wrong. We didn't even make it past the foyer before Zoe choked out that the cancer was back. We spent the evening trying to be as jovial as possible, but the conversation kept coming back to chemo and mastectomies. A week later she began her treatments again. Todd was in my position now, putting on a brave face for Zoe but spilling his guts to Jack when they went out to give Zoe and me space during our girls-only nights.

In October I discovered I was pregnant. I was afraid to tell Zoe because I felt guilty for having so many good things in my life when hers was going so badly, but of course she was elated when she found out she would be an honorary aunt. She helped me decorate the nursery on her good days, and two months later she was once more declared cancer-free.

I did not do pregnancy well. The first trimester was a nightmare. I was sick as a dog half the day and exhausted all the time. Jack was taking a break from working, and he became my chef and masseuse and "gopher." After the first trimester passed things began to get better, and we took a week's vacation in Jamaica at the end of January to live it up while we still could. We returned to discover Zoe and Todd were also expecting; she, however, would go on to have the world's easiest pregnancy, and I was only half joking when I told her I despised her good fortune.

The rest of my pregnancy progressed without issues, and one late June morning I awoke from a nap with a start. I hollered for Jack, and he was down the stairs faster than greased lightning and had me in the car almost before I could take another breath. By 11:46 that evening, we had a daughter.

As I held this miracle in my arms, a feeling of unworthiness swept through me, and I contemplated how far I had come and what God had done in me and through me and around me. I was humbled beyond words, imagining myself prostrate before the throne of heaven, thanking God with words my human mind could not know. I floated through the next six months on this cloud of awe, feeling as though God Himself had borne me up into His arms and carried me through them, infusing me with strength and perseverance.

Life truly did seem perfect.

How was I to know how quickly it would all come tumbling down?

Bree seems to know instinctively when she is being discussed. She appears from nowhere, having been playing in the other room for the past hour, the minute Grace begins talking about her pregnancy. "She either has the hearing of a hawk or ESP; we haven't figured out which one," Grace jokes. Oblivious, Bree crawls up onto Grace's lap. "Tell me more about when I was a baby," she coos.

"Not now, doll, a little later, okay? Your bedtime story."

She considers pouting, but then changes her mind. "Juice please?"

Grace smiles at me. "Excuse me," she says with a grin before taking her daughter by the hand and heading for the kitchen. Jack watches them go, a smile slowly replacing the dull look of preoccupation he has worn for the past twenty minutes.

He's been getting worse. Had we not been so far into the process, I don't think I could have continued these last few weeks. It's truly horrible watching someone's body slowly deteriorate while their mind is still so sharp.

"Guess I'll pick up the thread," he offers, shifting slowly in the armchair he spends most of his days in.

"Only if you're up to it," I remind him. I'm terrified he'll suddenly keel over in the middle of my interview. I hate it when Grace leaves us alone; I wouldn't know what to do if something happened. I hope she gets back soon.

Jack gazes out the window for a minute, and I begin to think he may be zoning out. He does this a lot these days too: staring out into space, not talking, not reacting, while Grace and I talk. Then out of nowhere he'll make a comment, and you realize he's been listening all along. I watch him closely, and then, without turning his gaze from the window, he begins to speak.

JACK

HELL BEGAN WITH A COLD that wouldn't go away.

I came down with a virus the week after New Year's. We'd gone to Vermont for Christmas, showing off the new Bree Emma Harrington to her extended family. A week there had exhausted both of us, and when we got back we both came down with a typical winter cold. After a week and a half of sneezing and coughing Grace finally recovered, but I continued to ache and cough and occasionally flare up with a fever. Convinced it was just a bug, I weathered it and kept my distance from the baby and Grace. After three weeks it was still there, and Grace convinced me to go to the doctor. He prescribed a killer antibiotic and sent me on my way.

The giant pink pills seemed to do the trick, and I was back to myself within a week. Unfortunately, I was sick again within a month with the same thing. The doctor prescribed another megapill that again seemed to work for a while. Within a month it was back.

Tests, tests, tests. I gave up what seemed to be a pint of blood for a whole smorgasbord of tests one Tuesday morning; three days later a nurse asked me to come in the next morning to discuss the results, adding, "It might be good for Mrs. Harrington to join you." I fought the temptation to worry and fret over the test results. How bad could it possibly be? Cancer didn't seem nearly as frightening now that we'd gone through it with Zoe; I felt I knew that routine pretty well. I was pretty sure tumors didn't present like the flu—what else was there? Surely my imagination was getting the best of me. It wasn't going to be that big a deal.

Zoe and Todd took Bree for us the next morning. It was a beautiful April day, two weeks from Easter, and the jacarandas were blooming. Despite the aches I'd become almost accustomed to in my head and joints, I was feeling pretty good.

Dr. Patton had been recommended by my agent; he was not only an excellent physician but also discreet and trustworthy—the bulk of his patients were industry folk. His office was located a block off Rodeo Drive, and we were ushered into a mahogany-paneled office on the third floor as soon as we arrived.

That was the first clue that things might be worse than we thought. Not the standard exam room, but his personal study. I forced myself to relax. Grace's hand was shaking in mine as the doctor entered.

I'll never forget that room: thick beige carpet, red overstuffed chairs, a color-loaded Cézanne on the right-hand wall, the sunlight coming in the window and illuminating a stack of medical journals on the floor in a corner. The room was burned into my memory the moment Dr. Patton's deep, grandfatherly voice delivered the diagnosis: HIV.

Absolute silence. A constriction in my throat; I couldn't breathe. Grace's hand withdrawing from mine as she wrenched out a sob that split my heart in two. My mind reeled, mental vertigo produced images and memories that fragmented and spliced together into a fast-forward riot that documented my life. At the end of it, the memory of the last time I'd gone to the clinic for a three-month workup, the tradition I'd begun with Dianne and given up during one of my bouts of depression. It had not been a conscious decision. I think I believed at my core that it would just never happen to me. Denial is a strong, strong drug.

Dr. Patton offered to give us some time, then slipped quietly from the room. I couldn't look at Grace. I stared out the window, watching palm trees sway in the gentle Pacific breeze, listening to Grace as she cried, not knowing what to do about anything.

I don't know how long we sat there, neither of us talking or even looking at the other. Finally, her voice trembling, Grace whispered, "I should be tested."

I hadn't even thought about the possibility of Grace having contracted it as well. And Bree... It was too much. My few tests, after Dianne had told me about her status, were always negative. I had quit worrying about it. Now I couldn't bear the thought of either one of my precious girls being sick because of my carelessness. Rage like I hadn't known since Dianne's death crashed like a tsunami, and I jumped to my feet and stormed out the door.

All I could think about was how ashamed I was, of how I had jeopardized my wife and child. I hated myself. I hated Dianne. I could think of nothing that soothed my spirit or cooled my blood. I found myself at our car, and my first thought was to drive it into the wall at the end of the parking lot. It seemed, for about ten seconds, to be the most logical thing to do—I certainly deserved it. Then Grace's face was before me, and I couldn't bear to do it. I felt completely powerless, there was nothing I could do to fix this. With a shout that resounded through the concrete structure, I slammed my fist into the pillar beside the car. I barely felt it. Again. My knuckles bled. Again.

How could God do this to me? How could God see this coming and not stop it? Why me? Why would He let me marry Grace and father a child and put both of them at risk when they had done nothing to deserve it?

I heard Grace scream somewhere behind me, and it snapped me back to reality. Through tears I saw her running down the aisle, and suddenly pain surged through my hand. I stared at it, bloody and crumpled, incredulous. All at once, I was afraid of myself.

Grace's arms were around me, her face against my chest, her whole body shaking. I held her with one hand, my other hanging limply at my side. Pain throbbed through my entire arm, and I was glad. It was the only thing I wanted to feel. Not love, not hope, not peace. Pain was all I deserved. I silently cursed God and felt my heart go cold.

GRACE

SOMETHING BROKE THAT DAY besides Jack's hand. We couldn't talk anymore; we couldn't connect. Jack retreated into his head somewhere, and I could do nothing to pull him out. He stopped sleeping at night and would sit outside on the deck doing nothing. Sometimes I joined him, but he wouldn't acknowledge me, and I could sense he didn't want me there, so I'd go back to bed and cry myself to sleep. He would wander around the house or sit in the den in front of the computer without using it, and after a couple of days of this he would crash on the bed and sleep around the clock. Then it would start over again.

So far Bree and I tested negative for the virus. Our medicine cabinet became a small pharmacy, and our grocery list looked like something out of a hippie-vegan cookbook: sprouts, soy milk, vegetables I'd never heard of and didn't know how to prepare. Articles from the Internet were strewn about the house, underlined and highlighted during manic episodes where Jack would suddenly burst into action and channel all this strange behavior into an attempt to figure out some way of beating the insidious illness inside him. These rare bouts of energy were the only times I was able to get him to engage. I took shameless advantage of them, asking him questions I already knew the answers to and suggesting treatments we'd previously discarded just to hear him talk. But eventually the energy would run out, and he'd end up yet again on the deck at 3:00 a.m.

The worst part was that he wouldn't tell anyone, not even Zoe and Todd. They were so wrapped up in their new family that they didn't seem to notice that we'd stopped calling or inviting them over, and though normally I would have been offended, instead I was relieved.

I tried to keep the atmosphere happy for Bree. She was getting mobile now, and she kept me busy chasing her all over the house. I read to her, took her to the park, played with her in the pool, always inviting Jack to join us—begging him—but he would simply shake his head and murmur, "Not now."

This was our life for two months. Easter came and went; we didn't even notice. Greg called, and some of our Bible study friends— I'd canceled it without explanation via e-mail after we got the diagnosis—and Zoe called once or twice, but the calls went straight to voice mail, and Jack deleted them instantly. I was beginning to feel like a prisoner. Jack made no attempt to seize what time he had left, and I felt as if Bree and I were being sucked down into the black hole he was creating. I was going stir-crazy; I needed adult conversation about something other than alternative medicine's latest offering for HIV treatment. Every day while Bree napped I pleaded with God, physically fell to my knees in our bedroom and sobbed into the comforter for Him to reach down and fix this mess. I wanted my husband back. I wanted my life back.

One morning in June I completely lost it. I hadn't had a decent night's sleep in weeks, and the house was a disaster: random items strewn everywhere, dishes in the sink, baby toys on the floor, in the hall, in the bedroom… I hadn't cleaned in ages, and it was obvious. I'd canceled the housecleaning service, in no mood to have them there, and never rescheduled. And housekeeping had never been my strong suit. I tried to clean, but Bree kept getting in the way, and I could feel myself getting to the point where the next words out of my mouth to her would be in a voice I'd sworn never to use with my children, so I deposited her in her crib for an early nap and retreated to my room.

I slumped beside the bed, tears running down my cheeks as I tried to muster the energy to pray. I just couldn't do it. I felt like I'd been awake for a year, like my very soul had been drained from me. Bree was crying, but I couldn't get myself up off the floor to go to her.

"How could this be in Your plan?" The words were out of my

mouth before I realized I was speaking out loud. "Why are You doing this to us?"

Nothing.

"I can't do this anymore. I feel like I'm losing my mind!" My voice was rising. "How can You just stand there and watch? Why don't You *do* something?"

I didn't think I had any more gut-wrenching sobs left in me, but they rose again out of the pit of my stomach, and with them a fury I'd never experienced. *"Do something!"* I screamed, throwing a pillow from the bed and not even flinching when a lamp hit the floor. *"Why don't You do something?"*

Jack was in the doorway. I don't know how long he'd been there, but all of a sudden there he was, with a look on his face I couldn't begin to decipher and could barely even see through the tears streaming from my eyes.

I wanted to shake him, to punch him and kick him and yank him back to life. Yet I felt rooted to the floor, unable to move, so I yelled instead. I'd never yelled at Jack, never raised my voice.

"You're killing me!" The words flowed, unchecked. "You've already left and you're not even dead! I can't do this anymore. I can't take this anymore. If you want to die then do it, but don't take us down with you!"

Silence. Not even Bree was crying anymore. The sting of the words I'd shouted still hung between us, and for the first time in months, Jack seemed to be looking at me and actually *seeing* me. The weight of the words I'd chosen overwhelmed me, and I buried my face in my hands, utterly ashamed that I could be so cruel.

Without warning his arms were around me, pulling me to him, his face in my hair as he cried his apologies. Then, for the first time in two months, he kissed me.

JACK

THE FOLLOWING EVENING we invited Todd and Zoe over for dinner. I was sick with nerves when they arrived, dreading the likely "It's about time you called" comments and trying to keep the conversation light until after the meal was over.

The kids were asleep in the living room when we broke the news. Todd, of course, knew about Dianne, but Zoe did not, and I explained the whole sordid mess to try to fill the shocked silence that ensued.

Zoe spoke first. "April? You found out in *April* and you're only telling us now?"

I shrugged. "How do you tell someone that, really? I'm sorry, honestly, but I could barely bring myself to admit it, much less let anyone else know."

More silence as the news was digested, then Zoe's hand flew to her mouth as she murmured, "Oh, Grace, what about you?"

"Clear so far," she said, trying to smile. "And Bree, but"—she looked at her hands—"no guarantees."

Todd stood and walked to me, and with his face an inch from mine said, "I could kill you for not telling us sooner." He stared me down, and I saw tears in his eyes, something I never would have expected from him. He shook his head in silence and threw his arms around me. Zoe sprang from her seat and sat down beside Grace, both of them bursting into tears.

After a while all was silent, and then finally Grace stated, "I think we all really need some dessert." This lightened the mood, and after pie was distributed, the girls moved into the kitchen and Todd and I went to the deck. Todd threw back another half glass of wine—"This demands the excessive consumption of alcohol," he'd stated after eyes had been dried and pie eaten—and asked what my plans were.

"Plans for what?"

He shrugged. "Everything. Work. Grace. Bree. HAP."

I chuckled ruefully. "Boy, there's an irony, eh? From HAP director to HIV statistic."

"Irony? I'd say Divine Providence if anything. You probably had a far better understanding of the disease when you were diagnosed than most people. And the money you raised may save you."

Todd and Zoe left early but promised to have us over soon and to pray for the talks I would have to have with the women of my past. They needed to know they were at risk, and since Hollywood's grapevine was sure to find out the story eventually, I wanted to make sure I told them first. I asked Kate to arrange meetings with each of them individually, and the closer I got to those meetings, the more panicked I became. I was seeing more clearly every day just how far-reaching my stupid choices were. I prayed fervently that no one else's lives would be ruined from my behavior.

Casey Greene, my ex "roommate with benefits," was first. We met up at a bistro in Beverly Hills, where a nice chat with the maître d' guaranteed the tables around would remain empty. I hadn't talked to her in years, and she was naturally curious as to why I had wanted to meet. I pleaded with God to make it go well—although "well" is an awfully high expectation when you're telling someone they might have HIV. She called me a few choice words, promised to leak the story, and left ten minutes into our meeting.

Alannah was the next meeting two days later. She beat me to the punch by telling me she had HIV. My heart stopped. I'd brought down someone else's life. I could hardly stand to look her in the eyes—until she told me she'd contracted it from her ex-husband. Ex now because he'd failed to mention his HIV status before their Vegas wedding.

Penelope Jones was the last meeting. Of the three of them, Penelope was the only one no longer acting. She'd gotten married and dropped off the Hollywood radar to pursue motherhood. We shared baby pictures and described our spouses—she remembered Grace from the lunch where she'd run into us. Something about her set me at ease, and I didn't feel the stress I had with the other two.

"So there's another rumor I've heard," she said as she tucked away the photos of her three daughters. Instantly I panicked. Had Casey already leaked the story? "Word on the street says you've become a Christian."

This took me by surprise. Penelope was the only one who'd brought it up; I'd mentioned it to Alannah, but Casey hadn't given me the time. The stress was back, and I braced myself for a barrage of insults. "Yeah, I am. Grace is, too; she's the one who led me to God."

She smiled. "I could tell something was different the minute you walked in. I am too."

I nearly laughed. "Seriously? How did that happen?"

She related her story of her husband working six months ago with a guy named Jesse North. Jesse had been one of the crowd that had attended our house meetings. Jesse and Penelope's husband, Craig, had hit it off, and one thing led to another. I told her about Jesse's connection with us, and she cracked up. "Small world!"

The conversation faded for a moment, and then Penelope sat back in her chair and seemed to assess me with a small, guarded smile. "So I'm guessing there was some reason other than reminiscing that caused you to call me."

I took a deep breath. "Yeah, actually, there is."

"Not so good, eh?"

I let out a sigh and shook my head.

"Well, I've been bracing myself for two weeks now, so lay it on me before I crack from the suspense."

Telling her was almost worse now that I knew she was a Christian. Remembering my sordid past was not something I enjoyed doing, and to remind someone else of *their* sordid past, when they were probably trying just as hard as I to forget it, was more painful than I'd expected.

I closed my eyes, not able to bear looking at her when I said it, and in as low a voice as I could get away with, told her, "I have HIV." I slowly opened my eyes, and I think actually flinched, although you'd have to ask her to be sure; it certainly felt like it.

She didn't speak, didn't yell, just stared at me with a look of disbelief. A soft, "Ohhh" escaped her lips as the implications sank in, and tears formed in her eyes. She bowed her eyes, brushing tears from her cheeks as she murmured, "Oh God," over and over.

My heart ached, and I said the only thing I could think to say, as meaningless as it seemed. "I'm sorry, Pen. I'm so sorry. I'm *so sorry.*"

She sniffed and raised her head, looking me in the eyes. "I just can't believe it."

"Me neither. Believe me."

"Dianne, right?"

I nodded.

She shook her head and wiped her eyes. "I should have realized what a risk it was in the first place, back when we—" She caught herself, apparently not wanting to voice what had taken place between us. I silently thanked her for it. "What were we thinking?"

"We weren't, that's the problem. I had tested clean."

"I wasn't even that attracted to you."

I burst out laughing. Thank God for humor. "Well thanks so much. I'll have you know I thought you were hot."

"Oh, whatever. You were too tanked to care."

I grimaced and threw her a sheepish grin. "Touché."

She sighed. "Wow. I don't even know what to do with this."

"Well, forgive me for being clinical, but go get tested; Craig and the kids, too. Don't wait till you start presenting, like I did."

"And how are you?"

I shrugged. "Still here. More synthetic material in my bloodstream than natural by now, I should think, given what all I'm on. But overall I feel all right."

"Going public?"

"Kinda figure I've gotta. After talking to, ah, everyone that needs to know, I figure it'll get leaked eventually. I'd rather be the one to say it first than have the press find out and come to me."

She bit her lip, staring past me for a moment before speaking again. "Don't do it, Jack," she finally said. "Keep it quiet. No one is going to tell, trust me. If they leak it, the press will do their homework and figure out they'd been linked with you at some point, then people will think they've got it too, whether they do or not, and they won't want that. I know I don't. If you tell, you're outing all of us as possible carriers, whoever 'us' is." A momentary look of disgust crossed her face, and though she tried to disguise it with a quick sip of water, I caught it. She set down her glass and reached across the table to take my hand in hers. Her face was kind. "We've both done things we wish we could erase. Let's not let the whole world know."

I could see her point. I thanked her and paid for our meal, barely touched, and walked her to her car. She said she'd pray for me, and I told her the same, relieved that the last of my meetings had gone so well.

There was one more hurdle to jump: I had to retire. Being an actor meant kissing someone at some point in nearly every movie I did. There was no way I was going to kiss anyone without them knowing I had HIV, and once anyone knew, no one would want to kiss me. We both knew the risk of transfer that way was minute, but why would I dare take the gamble with someone else's life—I'd already done that four times, and look at the consequences.

Besides, the last thing I wanted to do was spend my limited time on a set. I wanted to be with my family. Who knew how long I'd be here?

We told Todd and Zoe our plan over dinner one night. Sell the house, move to something smaller and cheaper but still close to Beverly Hills so my involvement with HAP wouldn't be hindered, and we'd still be close to our friends. Most important, we didn't want to pull completely out of the industry; we were too excited about the influence God was allowing us to have there.

"Only one hitch I can see," Todd remarked.

I frowned, thinking we'd covered every imaginable base. "What?"

"Everyone will wonder why the sudden retirement. Granted you haven't been in a film in a while, but you're still a major force in the industry. People will question your motivation when you're at the top of your game."

This stopped conversation for a while; you could practically see the wheels turning as everyone considered the ramifications and how to avoid them.

Eventually I shrugged and said, "I have a family, I have more money than I could spend in a lifetime, and I need a change of pace. It's an excuse few people will understand, but there's nothing dodgy about it. And it's 100 percent true. I've been doing this for sixteen years, and it's old. I'll jump in and do the occasional cameo now and then, just to keep up my profile, but no more leads and no more major works. I'm through with it."

"I'll drink to that!" Todd piped up with a goofy grin.

"As would I, if I could drink. Is it uncouth to toast with lemon water?"

Zoe chuckled. "Better get used to it."

GRACE

WE SOLD THE HOUSE in less than a week and moved to Pasadena just after our anniversary. There was wild speculation as to why we'd downgraded so drastically, but we were old news within days. Jack didn't officially voice his retirement, opting instead to simply stop taking parts. No one seemed to notice, and we were thankful for the chance to finally live a normal life.

Greg became our only other confidante besides Zoe and Todd when he called to ask after our well-being. We'd not mentioned the move to him—everything had happened rather quickly—and we invited him to dinner to tell him what was going on. He was tremendously supportive and offered to do whatever he could to help us, not that there was anything anyone could do besides pray.

In August, Jack announced on behalf of HAP that a new fundraising plan had been created with the help of many corporations and generous donors who would match donations made by the general public over the course of the next year. The goal was to raise ten million dollars for AIDS and HIV research. Only a handful of us knew the real reason why Jack seemed so gripped by this project.

Once settled in our new home, we began to hold our meetings again with the fifteen or so people who still expressed an interest. I felt bad never having explained to them why we had suspended the meetings, but once we started again, it was as if we'd never stopped. We grew like crazy, and after four months Zoe and Todd opened their home to allow the group to split and make more room for newcomers. We were amazed every week at the number of people who showed up; God was obviously up to something.

As time passed, we found ourselves at the middle of a revolution in that small but powerful niche carved out in Southern California. Had people told us the effect our ministry would eventually have, we'd have laughed in their faces. HAP raised its ten million and did it again three years in a row with Jack at the helm. In addition to that organization, Jack and Todd co-led a group the four of us founded called Inside Job, a loose coalition of Bible studies and house churches like ours that existed specifically for the industry—many of which had actually spun off of the weekly meetings at both our house and Todd's.

For two years Jack was able to keep up with the demands of both these groups, but a bout with bronchitis one winter forced him to cut back dramatically. He had been battling HIV for nearly six years, and while his prognosis had always been excellent, the bronchitis seemed to strip him of whatever strength had been keeping the HIV at bay. After that, his health started a slow but steady decline, and by the time Bree started first grade, his doctors were being optimistic at giving him two more years.

Todd took over Inside Job completely, and a successor was chosen to lead HAP after Jack resigned to "pursue other projects." After dinner with Greg one night, when Jack was putting Bree to bed, Greg remarked to me how incredible it was that someone like Jack, with all he had before him in Hollywood, had become such a servant and leader. "It's a bit humbling," he laughed. "I've been a Christian for ten times longer, and he's the one God chooses to lead this movement."

"But if it weren't for you he'd never be here," I reminded him.

He shrugged and grinned. "And if it weren't for Him, none of us would be."

Jack came to me one night and confessed he was bored. "This is ridiculous," he said, slapping a magazine on his knee in an obvious sign of frustration. "How can someone who has so little time left allow himself to be bored?"

"You're living life, babe, and life is sometimes dull. Even for celebrities."

"I *know,* but there's so much we should be doing."

"I'd love to know with what energy you plan on doing all this 'so much stuff.'"

We stared out at the houses across the way. Lights were slowly being extinguished for the night, and we snuggled beneath the quilt we kept on the porch swing for these late-night talks. After a while he said thoughtfully, "How about we write a book?"

EPILOGUE

THE CALL COMES at six one evening. "It's Grace," says the quiet voice on the other end. "You might want to come over." I know this is the call I've been dreading.

We finished the interviews a month ago. I called a couple times a week to check up and ask the follow-up questions I came up with as I wrote the first draft. Just before we finished, Jack took a turn for the worse; Grace told me privately she didn't know if he'd have the energy to finish. But he promised me one afternoon not to go anywhere until I got his side of things. "There's a reason for this book," he said. "I don't know what it is, but I know God wants me to finish before I leave."

During the past six months we've become quite good friends, Grace and Jack and I. They've had me over for dinner many times, and when Jack was sleeping and Grace was tired of talking about herself, she would ask about me, and for a while the tables were turned, and I was the interviewee. I've watched her closely during these last few weeks, after Jack's health took a nosedive; her gentleness and peace have been extraordinary. Seeing her with Jack, hearing her talk with him and pray with him, the simple touches of affection and recognition, are heartbreaking.

We sat one night on their balcony, she wrapped in a quilt on the porch swing, and I on a deck chair across from her—I couldn't bear to take the seat beside her, knowing it was Jack that should be there—and I asked how she could be so calm when her husband was dying. "How can you not spend all your time together," I asked, "when every time with him might be your last?"

She smiled and shrugged wearily. "It won't be the last time. There will be a day when we'll be together again, and Bree, too, without the shroud of sickness to ruin things. He needs his time alone with God, with himself, with Bree. I don't want him to worry about us. I don't want to make him feel guilty. I know he still does, and I'm afraid if I hover he'll feel like a burden, and then he'll feel more guilty. Why cloud his last days and hours with that?"

I shook my head in disbelief. "You're so sure of yourself."

"Oh, no," she said. "I'm not sure of myself at all. I'm only sure of God." And again, for perhaps the thousandth time since I'd met her and her husband, she told me about the God she believed in, and why. It was a liturgy I had come to love, if only because the look of serenity on their faces as they explained it eased the pain of losing a new friend. But tonight it was not enough for me to hear it, and I told her as much.

"Then perhaps," she said with a quiet thoughtfulness, "it's time for you to believe it."

When I pull into their driveway, I park alongside Todd and Zoe's SUV. Through the front window I can see Bree in Zoe's arms, her head on Zoe's shoulder. She is crying. I literally run to the door, slowing myself just enough to enter the house without bursting in. Todd, Zoe, and Grace are there, tears on their cheeks, and I know I'm too late. Grace comes to me and puts her arms around my neck. We hold each other and cry. "Jack wanted me to tell you something," she says as she wipes tears from her eyes and pulls a tissue from a nearby box. "He said to tell you he had to finish the book for you. You were the reason he had to stay. God wanted you to hear our story."

I nod. I know. God told me as much on my way here. How I know it was Him, I can't explain.

Grace leads me to the guest bedroom, Jack's home for the past month. The hospice workers are still there, quietly putting away the materials that have collected over the past four weeks. They move quietly out of the room, sensing the need I have to be here alone with these two friends. Jack looks at peace, simply sleeping, and I fight back tears.

I tell Grace what God told me, that I knew before she even said it. I tell her I understand what she meant about no longer listening, but believing. I tell her their lives, their story, have made me question the things I've always believed. I'm not sure yet I agree with them, but I want to learn more.

Grace puts an arm around my shoulder. "You know," she says, "there's a group of people who meet at Zoe and Todd's on Monday nights..."